AGE OF AZTEC

AGE OF AZTEC

JAMES LOVEGROVE

SOLARIS

First published 2012 by Solaris
an imprint of Rebellion Publishing Ltd,
Riverside House, Osney Mead,
Oxford, OX2 0ES, UK

www.solarisbooks.com

ISBN: 978 1 907992 81 0

10 9 8 7 6 5 4 3 2 1

A CIP catalogue record for this book is available from the
British Library.

Designed & typeset by Rebellion Publishing

Printed in the US

A Note on Pronunciation

Nahuatl, the language of the Aztecs, was transliterated into our alphabet by Spanish missionaries. Hence many of the letter sounds are pronounced as in Spanish. For example, "x" is sounded as "sh," "qu" as "k," "z" as "s," and "hu" as "w." The diphthong "tl," when it appears at the end of a word, should be treated as a single short phoneme rather than a syllable. Quetzalcoatl, therefore, is "kayt-sahl-ko-tluh." The same rules apply to Mayan names.

PART ONE
LONDON

ONE

4 Jaguar 1 Monkey 1 House
(Sunday 25th November 2012)

IT WAS ANOTHER sultry, sweltering winter's day, and the plaza around the City of London ziggurat was packed. Thousands clustered in the palm-fringed square itself, many of them having camped out overnight to be assured of a good view. Thousands more thronged the adjacent streets – Cheapside, Ludgate Hill, Paternoster Row – to watch the action on giant screens, close enough that they would just be able to hear the screams of the dying.

The atmosphere was, as ever, festive. Vendors did a roaring trade in heart-shaped hamburgers, gooey crimson-coloured iced drinks, and skull candy. Soon, when the sun reached its zenith, blood would flow.

The onlookers in the plaza were held back from

its central avenue by a cordon of Jaguar Warrior constables. Resplendent in their golden armour and cat-head helmets, the constables stood with their arms folded, vigilant. Other Jaguar Warriors prowled in pairs, cradling their lightning guns. There were more of them present than was usual for such an occasion.

The avenue, which led to the base of the ziggurat, was reserved for the queue of blood rite participants. Most of these hundred or so souls looked patient, eager, serene as they waited. A few wore the glassy, dreamy expressions of people who'd taken the precaution of anaesthetising themselves beforehand, perhaps by chewing a paste of morning glory seeds or downing a few stiff shots of *pulque* or tequila. Here and there a child shivered and wept and had to be comforted by his parents: *It's an honour to die at the priest's hand. The gods love all sacrifices but they love the sacrifice of the young more than anything. A little pain, and then it will be bliss in Tamoanchan for ever after. Hush, dear, hush. Soon be over.*

Animal din competed with the human hubbub. Parrots chattered amid the palm fronds. Monkeys hooted as they swung among the vines and creepers that coated the surrounding buildings like verdant fur. A quetzal bird screeched as it shot overhead in a sudden, brilliant flash of rainbow plumage. Those who saw it gasped in delight. A good omen. Quetzalcoatl himself watched through the bird's eyes. He was putting his personal stamp of approval on the proceedings.

Once a Christian place of worship had stood on this spot, one of the largest of its kind, and one of the last. A century ago almost to the day, after Britain finally allowed itself to be subsumed into the Aztec Empire, St Paul's Cathedral had been razed to the ground. The demolished stonemasonry, statuary and iconography had been dynamited and used to form the foundations and ballast of the ziggurat. The Empire was nothing if not thrifty. Nor was it averse to cannibalising.

In the steely-hot blue sky, three short-range aerodiscs hovered. Two bore the logo of Sun Broadcasting, the state TV network, and carried film crews, who were shooting live footage of the event. The third, a Jaguar Warrior patrol craft, was keeping a no-less beady eye on the public below.

At noon precisely, the officiating priest emerged from the low temple building that capped the ziggurat. He was accompanied by a flock of acolytes and flanked, too, by a pair of Jaguar Warriors serving as bodyguards. The two men, both sergeants, had been selected for the sacred duty by virtue of their intimidating bulk, skill at arms, and unwavering willingness to die protecting their charge. With eyes like flint, they scanned in all directions as the priest raised his arms and spoke.

"People of Britain," he said, his voice relayed to the plaza's PA system by a radio mike embedded in the ornate feathery folds of his headdress. "On this auspicious day we gather here to show obeisance to the gods, who have blessed us this solar year with fine weather, a bountiful harvest, and continued national wellbeing."

Cheers erupted from the plaza and beyond. What the priest said was true. It had, almost indisputably, been a good year. The *chinampas* fields had yielded plenty of maize. A territorial dispute with Iceland had been resolved in Britain's favour. The summer had blazed long and blissfully hot, the run of sunny days broken by just enough downpours to keep the reservoirs topped up and the crops irrigated.

"We have much to be grateful for," the priest continued. "And as I see before me a long line of volunteers, civilians willing to shed their blood in the name of the gods, I know that the gratitude is felt universally. You, you brave ones, you blessed ones" – he addressed the blood rite participants – "wish to convey how glad we are for all we have been given, by giving your all. You perish today, not just for the gods' benefit, but for the benefit of your fellow countrymen. Your blood will nourish the soil and ensure our future happiness and prosperity."

At these words the onlookers in the plaza started cheering like mad. They showered the blood rite participants with flower petals and praise. The participants lapped it up, beaming around them, some of them punching the air. Truly, there was no greater glory than this. Even the fretful children were placated. All these strangers insisting how fantastic they were – they must be indeed doing something worthwhile.

One of the Sun Broadcasting aerodiscs descended a couple of hundred feet, presumably to get a better view, a tighter camera angle.

"Come, then," the priest said, beckoning. "Ascend the steps, as your souls will shortly be ascending to Tamoanchan."

The first of the sacrificial victims stepped forward. He was a *tlachtli* player, captain of one of the most successful London premier-league teams, a national hero. His celebrity put him at the head of the queue. He, with all his fame and money, not to mention being in the prime of youth and health and recently wedded to a glamour model, stood to lose more than most. It was only right and proper that the enormity of his unselfishness be recognised. Not all martyrs were equal.

The *tlachtli* player sprinted up the 300 steps to the apex of the ziggurat, displaying the fitness and fearlessness that had made him such a star of the ball court. To tumultuous applause from the onlookers, he threw himself flat on his back on the altar, all smiles. Naked save for a loincloth, he had ceremonially anointed himself beforehand with sweet-smelling oils. He offered his bare, glistening chest to the priest, who muttered ritual phrases over him, then took an obsidian-bladed dagger and raised it aloft.

With a practised, powerful stroke, the priest pierced the *tlachtli* player's torso. Blood exploded from the wound, and the young man died with a scream and a shudder that were as much ecstasy as agony. The acolytes then hauled the body off the altar and set about hacking the ribcage open and sawing out the heart.

They placed the still-twitching organ in a large iron basin which sat on a tripod over a bellows-stoked fire. The heart sizzled and sent a wisp of smoke up to heaven. Meanwhile, the acolytes pitched the eviscerated corpse off the rear of the ziggurat. It tumbled into a fenced-off enclosure below, for later disposal.

The cooked heart was handed to the priest on a skewer. He took a bite, then tossed the remainder aside. He would do the same with every victim's heart this afternoon, although the bites would become increasingly small until, by the end, they would be the tiniest nibbles. There was only so much meat one man's stomach could handle in one go, and the human heart was a tough, tasteless morsel.

The next victims climbed the stairs, somewhat more slowly and reluctantly than the *tlachtli* player had, in a group. They were a quartet of high-ranking Icelandic diplomats who had been chosen by their country's High Priest as the official scapegoats in the matter of the recent dispute with Britain over fishing rights around the Faroe Islands. The Great Speaker had decreed that the Faroes should be considered a sovereign British dependency. Iceland had no claim over their territorial waters and the cod stocks therein. Both countries' navies had been on the brink of hostilities at that point, but the Great Speaker's verdict was final and Iceland had wisely conceded.

The diplomats' lives were by way of compensation for trouble caused. All four of them had drunk themselves into a stupor in order to appear calm in the face of death and not let the side down. Intoning slurred prayers to Tlazolteotl, goddess of purification, eater of sins, they presented themselves at the altar. There were moments of almost comic confusion as each, professionally tactful to the end, insisted that the others should go first. Finally they settled the matter by lining up in order of seniority. The priest despatched them with the rapidity and dispassionate efficiency that their status merited.

After that came an aristocratic family, three generations all wishing to die together. The dynasty was not completely extinguishing itself, however. An adult male heir had been singled out to be exempt from martyrdom. He would inherit the family wealth – minus the odd death duty – and carry on the lineage.

The Sun Broadcasting aerodisc dipped even lower until its bulbous underside was mere metres above the temple roof. The bassy throb of its negative-mass drive vibrated through the ziggurat's stonework.

One of the Jaguar Warrior sergeants waved the disc away, but the pilot either didn't notice or chose to ignore the irritable gesture. The sergeant scowled. TV news people. They thought they were hot shit, especially when covering state occasions like this which garnered huge ratings and similarly huge advertising revenues. They thought themselves as important as, if not more important than, the law of the land.

By now the topmost of the ziggurat's steps were slick with spilled blood, making them treacherous for the participants who followed in the wake of the initial wave of the great and good. Several of these people, middle-class professionals mostly, slipped and lost their footing as they neared the summit. They were bloodstained even before they reached the wet red altar and prostrated themselves on it.

The sergeant waved yet again at the TV news disc. The aircraft was literally casting a shadow over the blood rite, and its engine thrum was making the priest's words hard to distinguish. The sergeant flipped down his helmet mike and instructed the patrol disc to intervene. There was an edge in his voice. The Sun Broadcasting disc's antics were making him very nervous. Was this what Chief Superintendent Kellaway had warned them to be on the lookout for? The suspicious activity that might herald a terrorist attack?

Wary, the sergeant unshipped and primed his lightning gun. Meanwhile, the Jaguar Warrior disc drew alongside the Sun Broadcasting aircraft and hailed it over the aviation frequency. "By order of the High Priest of Great Britain, and in the name of the law, please ascend to a safe distance. This is your only warning. Fail to comply and we will open fire."

At that moment, a shrill cry came from within the TV news disc. The sergeant spied movement in one of the hatches from which a camera protruded. He glimpsed a shape, a silvery silhouette, darting.

Next instant, a cameraman came flying out, fell

flailing, and hit the temple roof with a bone-crushing thud. He was followed by an armour-clad figure who leapt nimbly down from the disc, landing on the roof and dropping straight into a crouching, catlike stance.

The sergeant swore softly.

Him.

Bold as brass. Clear as day.

Top of the Jaguar Warriors' Most Wanted list. Public enemy number one.

The Conquistador.

THE LIGHTNING GUN was warm and humming in the sergeant's hands, plasma generator charged. He raised it to fire, but the Conquistador reacted quickly – too quickly. He snatched up the injured cameraman and threw him at the Jaguar Warrior, a kind of moving human shield. A bolt of blue-white brilliance leapt from the l-gun and struck the hapless cameraman full on. He howled and writhed and burned, laced with crackling light.

The cameraman's smouldering corpse tumbled towards the sergeant, who twisted aside to avoid being hit. When he regained his balance, he found himself directly face to face with the Conquistador. Implacable blue eyes stared out from slits in the terrorist's face mask. A rapier flashed. The sergeant looked down to see snakes emerging from a gash in his abdomen. He tried to catch them but they slithered out of his hands, falling at his feet in coils. That was when he realised the snakes were his own intestines. He looked up again at the Conquistador, who opened his throat with a swift transverse stroke of his sword.

The sacrificial victim currently on the altar started screaming – not in pain, but in alarm and horror, as the sergeant slumped to the floor. The priest gaped, dagger hanging uselessly from his fingers. The other Jaguar Warrior sergeant sprang into action. It would cost precious seconds to prime his lightning gun, so he drew his *macuahitl* from its scabbard and lunged at the Conquistador.

The Conquistador countered the first blow with ease, the *macuahitl*'s obsidian blade glancing off the rapier's steel. The sergeant went for the Conquistador's neck on the back swing, but again the blow was deflected, this time rebounding off the rapier's hilt guard. The two men thrust and parried. Metal and volcanic glass chimed as they met and met again. The sergeant managed to get a jab past his opponent's defences, but it glanced off the Conquistador's cuirass, leaving nothing but a scratch.

The Conquistador retaliated with a downward slash that cleaved the sergeant's left arm almost all the way through at the shoulder. The limb dangled, flopping, at the Jaguar Warrior's side. Shock greyed his face and turned his legs to jelly. He tried to lift his *macuahitl* for one last swing, but the sword's weight seemed too much for him and he toppled sideways.

The Conquistador polished the sergeant off matter-of-factly, plunging the rapier deep into his armpit. Then he turned to the priest.

The priest's face was a mask of pure panic. In a quavering voice he shouted at the acolytes, "It's me he's after. Don't let him get me. Stop him! By the Four Who Rule Supreme, that's an order!"

The acolytes obeyed, if a little hesitantly. They ran at the Conquistador, throwing themselves at him singly and in pairs. These were not fighting men; they belonged to a caste accustomed to luxury and soft living. Not one of them knew what it was like to land a blow in anger. The Conquistador cut them down like poppies.

The priest came to the realisation that no one was going to save him. He bounded down the steps, barging aside the blood rite participants who were coming up. Down below, the onlookers milled about uncertainly. Disquiet was growing in the plaza. It wasn't entirely apparent what was going on up there on top of the ziggurat, but the blood rite had been interrupted, that much was plain; people were getting killed who weren't meant to be getting killed.

The Conquistador eyed the fleeing priest and, with something like a shrug, pulled out a pistol. This was no sleek, contoured weapon like a lightning gun but closer in appearance to a flintlock or an blunderbuss, with a flared tip to the barrel. Primitive by modern standards, it fired physical projectiles rather than a bolt of ionised, superheated gas.

The Conquistador took careful aim. The pistol barked in his hand, spitting out a cluster of flechettes. The tiny brass arrows entered the priest's back and exited through his chest in an expanding burst.

His ribs erupted outwards so that, as he crashed to the steps, his body resembled any of the countless hundreds whose deaths he had presided over in the course of his career – hollowed, heartless.

Terror now gripped the people in the plaza. There would have been a stampede, only there was scant room to move and nowhere to go. The streets that fed into the plaza were crammed. All exits were blocked. The onlookers surged and swirled but stayed in one place. The Jaguar Warriors in their midst tried to reach the ziggurat, but couldn't forge a path through.

The Conquistador didn't have long to survey his handiwork. As the priest's corpse came to rest halfway down the steps – although his headdress bounced on all the way to the bottom – the Jaguar Warrior patrol disc loomed overhead. Its forward guns fired, left and right alternately, strafing the top of the ziggurat with coruscating, percussive blasts.

The Conquistador sprang this way and that, dodging the l-gun salvos. Stonework shattered. Sprawled bodies were incinerated. The altar was destroyed. Yet somehow the Conquistador managed to stay alive. He was fast on his feet, and a small target. The patrol disc's guns were designed for bludgeoning, not sniping. Ground vehicles and other aircraft were its principal quarry, not a lone man who kept scurrying about like a cornered mouse.

Then, perhaps inevitably, the patrol disc's gunner scored a hit. The Conquistador had taken refuge in the temple doorway. The gunner let loose with both forward guns at once, and the temple more or less evaporated. Roof collapsed, walls crumbled, and when the smoke and dust cleared there was nothing but a heap of broken granite slabs. No sign of the Conquistador.

Whoops of joy echoed through the disc's interior. Pilot and gunner yelled at each other, grinning from ear to ear.

"We did it!"

"The fucking Conquistador!"

"We'll get medals for this!"

"Promotion!"

"A commendation from the Great Speaker!"

"Fuck yeah!"

In the event, they were to be disappointed. None of the above would happen. But their moment of triumph, while it lasted, was sweet.

JAGUAR WARRIORS TOOK charge in the plaza, restoring calm and arranging an orderly evacuation. The streets emptied. People filed homeward, dazed and disturbed. The plaza was designated an official crime scene. The death toll was totted up. The remains of the ruined temple were combed through.

What the Jaguar Warriors unearthed among the debris was not, as they'd hoped, a mangled corpse in a suit of armour. They found armour all right. Portions of it were strewn across the apex of the ziggurat, here a gauntlet, there the morion helmet with comb crest and cheek guards. But no body. Nor was any of the armour pieces spattered with blood, as might have been expected.

The armour, it was obvious, had been discarded. The Conquistador, under cover of the obscuring haze of smoke and dust, had undressed himself and...

Disappeared.

But where to? Where had he gone?

Into the crowd? But he wouldn't have had time to unbuckle his armour *and* get down to the plaza.

Where, then?

A COUPLE OF hours after the blood rite came to its premature end, a flatbed truck arrived at the plaza to cart away the bodies of the sacrificial victims.

The Jaguar Warriors refused it access, and the workmen in the truck said that that was no problem with them, *but*... A pyre was already alight over at the burning grounds in Leamouth, building up heat. The clock was ticking. In this weather, the corpses would soon start to putrefy. Swift removal and immolation was standard procedure, as mandated by tradition. If the Jaguar Warriors wished that not to happen, then fine. But they would have to explain to the High Priest himself why they had interfered with proper religious observance. Good luck with that.

The Jaguar Warriors saw sense and allowed the truck through. Parking behind the ziggurat, the workmen donned filter masks and rubber gloves and aprons. Then they got busy scooping up the corpses in the enclosure and stacking them onto the back of the truck. They'd been expecting a hundred bodies but, in the event, it was a couple of dozen. Still, never mind. They were on a flat rate. Less work, same pay, and it meant a single trip from Leamouth and back rather than three or four.

The truck trundled out of the plaza with its gory load. The corpses in the back jogged and jiggled with every sharp turn and pothole.

The drivers were blithely oblivious when, while the truck stood stationary at traffic lights, one of the corpses got up, shinned over the tailgate, and sprinted off down a nearby alleyway.

TWO

5 Eagle 1 Monkey 1 House
(Monday 26th November 2012)

THE LAST THING Mal wanted to hear when she reported for work at Scotland Yard that morning was the first thing her DS, Aaronson, said to her.

"Kellaway's looking for you."

The groan inside Mal was so loud it was almost a shout. Outwardly she confined herself to a soft oath.

"Where is he? His office?"

Aaronson glanced down the corridor. "If he was, you'd be able to hear him."

"On the warpath?"

"Seriously. It's been stamping and ranting ever since he got in. I know he usually has a tarantula up his arse but never one this big. He could teach Tezcatlipoca himself a thing or two about anger."

"Well, wherever he is, he can wait a few more minutes. Here." She handed Aaronson one of the two paper cups she was carrying.

Her DS frowned at the logo on the side. "Koka Klub? I thought you hated the big chains. You said they water it down too much."

"I didn't have a choice."

"What about the street stand outside Victoria Station? You usually get your –" Aaronson's expression turned sly. "Ah. We didn't come in that way today, did we? We weren't home last night, were we?"

"You'll make an inspector yet, Aaronson."

"Come on, who was it?"

"No one."

"That means he was young."

"I can't even remember his name, to be honest."

"Bad girl! Bet he was handsome."

"Gorgeous," Mal said with feeling.

"Where did you find him?"

"The pub, lunchtime. We played a few games of *patillo*. I let him win the first. Wiped the floor with him for the rest."

"Would I have liked him?"

"If he swung your way, definitely."

"They all swing my way," said Aaronson. "When persuaded."

The two of them uncapped their cups, blew off the steam, and took a sip. The coca-leaf tea hit the spot simultaneously.

"You hear about the blood rite yesterday?"

Aaronson asked. He was lisping slightly, his tongue coca-numbed.

"Of course. Why shouldn't I have?" .

"I don't know, because you were having rampant monkey sex with a casual pickup maybe?"

"I caught the newspaper headlines on the way here."

"Conquistador made us look like a bunch of fucking idiots."

"Which'll be the reason for the chief super's mood," said Mal. "What I want to know is why's he after me?" She had a hunch she knew the answer. She prayed she was wrong. She took another slug of her tea. "Better go find him, I suppose. Face the music."

"Good luck, boss. I'll bring flowers to your funeral."

"Detective Sergeant Aaronson, sincerely, fuck off."

SHE TRACKED DOWN Kellaway in the central quadrangle.

Normally you could count on there being a scratch game of *tlachtli* under way here, off-duty personnel running around, jostling to put the ball through the wall-mounted hoop with a shoulder nudge or thigh kick. Now, however, the quadrangle was deserted, except for the chief superintendent, two constables, and a man Mal recognised as Chief Inspector Stephen Nyman.

From everyone's body language she could tell exactly what the situation was and what was about to occur. She started to backtrack out of the quadrangle, but too late. Kellaway spotted her.

"Inspector Vaughn. Just in time. Come on over."

The chief superintendent was calm, no longer raging. Punishment was about to be doled out. He had something to assuage his wrath.

Mal crossed to his side, trying not to catch Nyman's eye. The detective looked defeated, exhausted, his face pinched and fraught. He was doing his very best not to tremble. Nyman had always struck her as one of the most phlegmatic, self-effacing Jaguar Warriors on the force, efficient without being flashy, a doer, not a show-off. It was painful watching him struggle to keep his composure now.

"Chief Inspector Nyman, as you're aware, has been the senior investigating officer heading up the Conquistador enquiry," said Kellaway. "He was in charge of security arrangements at yesterday's blood rite. Responsibility for the safety of His Holiness Priest Sanderson lay with him and him alone. He fell short in that duty – dismally. The entire event was a shambles. The Conquistador remains at large, having notched up another eleven murders, including those of Sergeants Gravett and Fielding. I want you to witness this, Vaughn. I want you to see what happens when someone lets the whole division down, and lets the priesthood down, too."

Vaughn already knew the penalty for failure at such a level, and Kellaway knew she knew. This wasn't just a display of Jaguar Warrior internal policy. This was a warning. A threat. And, also, an overture.

"Gentlemen?"

The two constables took hold of Nyman's arms and forced him to his knees. One of them grasped a handful of hair and yanked the detective's head back, exposing his gulping Adam's apple. Nyman's face reddened. The fight-or-flight instinct was powerful in him, and he desperately tried to control it.

Kellaway unsheathed his *macuahitl*, something he had not had to do in years other than for this purpose.

"Inspector Nyman." His voice took on a mollifying tone, stern but kind. "You have, up to this point, been an exemplary Jaguar Warrior, and I regret the solemn duty I must now perform. Make your peace with the gods and beg their forgiveness. May the Four Who Rule Supreme – Quetzalcoatl, Tezcatlipoca, Huitzilopochtli, and dread Xipe Totec – welcome your soul into their arms and absolve you of all wrongdoing, so that you may live eternal in their company, as pure and blessed as they."

Like a final punctuation mark, the sword flickered across Nyman's throat. A crosswise thread of blood appeared, oozing into tiny beads. Nyman gurgled. His eyes rolled back and a deep red fissure suddenly split his neck. Blood gushed in fountains. His severed windpipe frothed. The constables lowered him to the ground, dancing back to avoid their boots getting splashed. Chief Inspector Nyman lay curled in his death throes. In all, from the sword cut to the last shuddering spasm, it took a minute and a half. Mal forced herself to watch the whole time, because she knew Kellaway expected her to and his scorn would be terrible if she didn't. She would have given anything to be permitted to turn away, even just for a second.

"There." Kellaway fastidiously wiped off the flecks of blood from his *macuahitl* with a handkerchief. As a mark of rank, the obsidian from which his sword blade was made was not sheer black but bore a golden sheen. Mal's, similarly, bore a rainbow iridescence and had seemed to her, when she first took possession of it, the most beautiful thing she had ever laid eyes on. It was still beautiful, although she was not sure she felt so proud of it any more. The discolouration, after all, was caused by microscopic bubbles in the mineral – imperfections, impurities.

"Deal with that," Kellaway said to the constables, indicating the body. And to Mal, "Walk with me."

They circled the quadrangle in a silence that Mal found increasingly unnerving. *Come on, out with it, get it over with.* Kellaway just scowled to himself.

Finally he said, "I'm afraid, Vaughn, it's a good news, bad news scenario. The good news is, you're promoted. You're a chief inspector now. The bad news... The Conquistador case is yours."

It was strangely a relief, to hear the worst.

"The bastard has been making a mockery of us for months," Kellaway went on. "He's killed five priests, a few dozen acolytes, several civilians, and eighteen Jaguar Warriors. He's disrupted nine major religious ceremonies and left behind a trail of carnage each time. He's a blasphemer, an insurgent, an affront to the Empire, and the fact that he dresses up like one of the would-be conquerors of Anahuac is the final insult. He's saying that where Cortés, Pizarro and de Alvarado failed, he will succeed. The arrogance of it is quite breathtaking. His campaign of terror cannot be allowed to go on. Do you hear me? He needs to be stopped, as soon as possible, by whatever means necessary."

"Yes, sir." Mal couldn't trust herself to say anything more than that.

"The High Priest is absolutely livid. Commissioner Brockenhurst had to go and see him in person last night. Old chums they may be, but by all accounts it was no fun, and Brockenhurst made his feelings about that known to me in no uncertain terms. His Very Holiness, in turn, has been hauled over the coals by the Great Speaker himself, so we're passing the pissed-off-ness down through the ranks, one to the next. It's the trickle-down effect in all its glory. You understand, then, that you have to get this right, Vaughn? We're clear on that? You can't – mustn't – screw up the way Nyman did."

Just at that moment they were passing the congealing puddle of blood that marked the site of Nyman's execution. His heels had left two parallel smeared lines where the constables had dragged his body away.

"Yes, sir," Mal said again. She wanted to run. She wanted to scream. She wanted to kick Kellaway to the ground and stamp on his balding sunburned head, stamp on it until it was pancake flat.

"Otherwise that'll be your blood there," Kellaway added, unnecessarily. "You'll be the one bringing disgrace on the Jaguar Warriors. And neither of us would wish that, would we?"

The chief superintendent's smile was never convincing. Nor, with the tumbledown, caries-clogged teeth it revealed, was it pretty.

"I think you can do this," he said. "I think you're the woman for the job... chief inspector."

Now he was trying to be consoling, ingratiating.

Both he and Mal knew he had just handed her a poisoned chalice and it was very likely that, sooner or later, she would have to drink from it.

"SHIT," BREATHED AARONSON. "Oh, shit. Oh, fucking shit."

"Yes, marvellous, isn't it?" said Mal.

"I mean, congrats on the bump-up. Richly deserved and all that. And a handsome raise, too."

"I was just thinking I could do with a new pair of curtains in the flat."

"I've got a better idea. Buy us a few rounds at the nearest pub. Because that's what we really need to do – go out and get totally rat-arsed. This minute. Because our lives have just become about ten times harder."

"No. No, we do not need to get rat-arsed. That is exactly the opposite of what we need to do."

"But –"

"Maybe later, another day, but right now we've been given an assignment. We have a crook to catch. We work for the criminal investigation department of the Jaguars, so we're going to do what they pay us to do and investigate. The Conquistador is just a man. He pulls off audacious terrorist outrages and

gets away with it every time, but he's still just a man."
Mal thumped the desk. She wasn't sure why, except
that it made a loud noise and she felt better for it.
"The more we know about him, the easier he'll be
to take down. So we have to figure out how he does
what he does. How he chooses when and where to
strike. How he gets in and out. Above all, who the
fuck he is, behind that mask. Let's get cracking."

She grabbed her jacket.

"Where are we going?" asked Aaronson.

"Where do you think? Where he was last seen.
Scene of the crime."

THEY SIGNED OUT a car and drove east. En route to the
City of London ziggurat, they reviewed what they
knew of yesterday's incident. In his lap, Aaronson
had a copy of Chief Inspector Nyman's case report,
which the detective had been typing up half an hour
before his execution. Aaronson went through it,
reading out salient details.

"The Conquistador stowed away aboard the
Sun Broadcasting aerodisc, hidden in a locker.
He emerged and threatened the pilot at gunpoint,
forcing him to descend to within jumping distance of
the ziggurat. The cameraman decided to play have-
a-go hero and tackled him. He came off worse. The
Conquistador beat the guy senseless, chucked him
out of a hatch, and followed. He also made short
work of those two sergeants, by all accounts. Elite
officers, and he made them look like amateurs."

"I've seen him in news footage, how he fights," said Mal. "I'm not saying I couldn't take him. It wouldn't be easy, though."

"DCI Nyman's theory is that he's had training. Eagle Warrior training. What do you reckon to that?"

"I'd say Nyman is – was – correct. The Conquistador, whoever he really is, is military. Or ex-military. You don't pick up sword skills like those from private tuition."

"Not Jaguar training, then?"

"What, he's one of us? Is that what you're saying?"

"Just airing the possibility."

Mal mimed a shudder. "Fuck me, I hope not. What's Nyman's verdict on the armour retrieved from the scene?"

"New, bespoke, not a genuine antique, a copy. Somebody must have smithed it for the Conquistador, or the Conquistador smithed it himself. He was going to follow that up as a line of enquiry next. Should we?"

"I don't know how far we'd get. The Conquistador's wily. I doubt he'd leave the armour behind if he felt it could be traced. Anything else relevant?"

"Nyman reckoned the Conquistador knew the patrol disc would start shooting. He was counting on it. It was how he planned on making his getaway."

"His mysterious getaway. Vanishing into thin air."

"You sound like you know how he pulled it off."

"I have an inkling." Mal indicated to turn off the Strand onto Fleet Street. A cabbie braked and politely let her through. The traffic was always on its best behaviour around a marked Jaguar Warrior car.

"Can I make a personal comment, boss?" Aaronson asked.

"You will anyway, even if I tell you not to."

"You're taking this remarkably well. You've just been given the job no one on the force wants. You seem pretty cool about it."

"I don't have a choice. What can I do? I can't tell the chief super to go and stick it up his arse. I just have to make the best of things."

"But Nyman's, what, the third inspector in a row who's handled the Conquistador case."

"And the third Kellaway's executed. Way I see it, he can't go on getting rid of us at this rate, otherwise there soon won't be a CID left. That gives me some breathing space."

"Do you honestly think that?"

"No. But also, the Conquistador's had it easy so far."

"How so?"

Mal flashed a grin. "Fucker hasn't had me to deal with yet."

THEY SCOURED EVERY inch of the plaza, which was still closed to the public. Mal paid particular attention to the corpse enclosure. The flagstones there bore spectacular firework-like patterns of dried blood, baked black by the sun.

Then they climbed the ziggurat and picked their way across the shattered remains of the temple. Again, as below, it was the throwing off of the corpses that interested Mal. She squatted at the ziggurat's rear edge and peered over. She probed the stonework below the lip of the apex, feeling with her fingers. Finally she found what she was after.

"Come and see this."

"No thanks." Aaronson felt dizzy just being this far above ground, never mind watching his superior officer leaning out over empty space.

"Don't be such a wuss."

"Still no."

"I'll hold you."

"Oh, all right."

Aaronson shuffled forward and, with Mal gripping his trouser leg, craned his neck. It was a sheer drop of some two hundred feet to the enclosure below.

"What am I looking for?"

"See that there? In the cement between those two blocks?"

"No. Oh. Yes. Is that...?"

"A climber's piton."

The ring-shaped head of the piton protruded out barely half an inch, and was as dark as the stonework around it. Unless you were searching for it, you could easily have never spotted it.

"Are you a climber, Aaronson?"

"Only career and social. Look at me. I'm shaking like a leaf. Do I look like I've got a head for heights?"

"My guess is our friend the Conquistador anchored the piton in with a hammer and abseiled down on a line looped through it. Then he reeled the line in and hid himself among the dead bodies."

"You're kidding."

"I don't think I am."

"But surely eyewitnesses would have spotted him coming down."

"Maybe. But nobody hangs around close to the corpse enclosure, do they? Plus, it's behind the ziggurat, hardly prime viewing position. The temple obscures the altar from here. And if he abseiled quickly enough, and the line was thin, he might look from a distance like just another body falling. In all the confusion it'd be an easy mistake to make. Then the retrieval truck arrives, and to the workmen he's just another partially clothed stiff."

"The truck didn't turn up until two o'clock. You're saying he lay there for two hours in a pile of hacked-up corpses, playing dead?"

"I am."

Aaronson whistled. "He is one determined fucker, that's for sure."

"I'd guess, too, that he smeared himself with blood, and maybe also stuck on some bone fragments and gristle from the bodies, so that at a glance he'd appear like all the rest of them."

"Determined and sick."

"No," said Mal, "he simply doesn't care. He does what he has to, whatever it takes, so that he can survive and attack again another time."

"A madman."

"It can look like madness, to be that focused on your goal." Mal worked out the piton with a pocket knife, bagged it as evidence, then stepped back from the edge, contemplating. "This man – somebody did something to him once, something that changed him. He was hurt or damaged in some way, and he blames the Empire and wants to show everyone how consumed with hate he is. Everything he does, it's showboating, designed for maximum effect. State occasions. Public ceremonies. Priest investitures. If it's holy, he has to desecrate it. Hence the armour and weaponry resembling something an old-world Spanish explorer would have been kitted out with. This is all about making a statement, the same one over and over."

"Not a *fashion* statement, I hope."

"I'm serious," Mal snapped. Sometimes Aaronson was too flippant for his own good. He needed to rein it in if he ever hoped to get ahead. "He's set himself up as the opponent of the Empire, its nemesis. When the Spanish invaded Anahuac, they were expecting to find a primitive culture ripe for the picking, based on their and other Europeans' experiences in North America. They got a hell of a shock when it turned out that the Land Between The Seas had technology and capabilities far beyond their own, and was in fact readying itself to expand its territory. They fought the Aztecs hard and committed countless atrocities, but it was inevitable that they would be defeated. *Conquistadores* – an ironic name, in the event. It's as if this guy, our Conquistador, wants to reclaim the title, turn it back from something vainglorious to something meaningful again."

"All on his own? One man against the entire world – against billions?"

"In his head, those are acceptable odds," Mal said. "He believes all he has to do is keep hitting the Empire where it hurts, time after time, and eventually it'll fold up and crawl away."

Aaronson grimaced. "If I didn't know better, I'd think you admired him."

"Someone that blindly, nakedly stubborn – what's not to admire? Doesn't mean I'm not going to do everything in my power to nail the bugger. And not just because he's an enemy of the state and a mass murderer. Because it's my neck or his."

"So," said Aaronson as they set off down the steps, "any ideas? Are we going to wait until the Conquistador makes his next move and try to nab him then?"

"That was Nyman's tactic, and look how far it got him. No, I think it would be more sensible to force his hand. Lure him out. Let's us make the running for once."

"You have a plan."

She did. A sketch of one. It would require Kellaway's full backing, some string-pulling, and the mobilisation of considerable manpower and resources, but she doubted she would have trouble securing any of those things. The chief super was no less keen than she was to see the Conquistador dead or in custody. A commanding officer could shift the blame onto subordinates only for so long. Mal sensed she was his last throw of the dice. If she didn't come up with the goods, Kellaway would most likely be kneeling beside her in the quadrangle at HQ, waiting for the shimmering whir of obsidian and the farewell to earthly existence.

The galling thing was – and Mal could never share this with anyone, not even Aaronson – she had been on the point of turning in her resignation this very morning. For the past few weeks she had been trying to pluck up the courage to write her letter of notice and hand it in. Today, she'd been convinced, was going to be the day. In fact, back in the quadrangle earlier, with Kellaway, she had been close to blurting out the words "I quit" several times.

Events had taken on their own momentum, however, and almost before she realised it she'd been assigned the Conquistador investigation. It was too late to change that now. In spite of her disenchantment with her job, the Jaguar motto still had some resonance for her: *Never back down, never pull out.*

Besides, just as this case that could break a career, it could also make one.

All the more crucial, then, that her plan got given the green light, and worked.

THREE

6 Vulture 1 Monkey 1 House
(Tuesday 27th November 2012)

THE BRITISH AIRWAYS aerodisc touched down at Palermo at 11am local time. It was a commercial long-haul flight out of Heathrow, and the yellow quadrant on the disc's compass totem was highlighted to indicate its southerly bearing. For the onward journey east to Beijing, with recharge stopovers at Istanbul and Karachi on the way, the red totem quadrant would be highlighted, in accordance with divine precept.

Stuart Reston disembarked with all the other business class passengers. A flight attendant enquired if he'd had a pleasant trip, and he nodded, although in truth the flying time was so brief – a little over an hour – that he felt like he'd scarcely fastened his seatbelt before it was time to unfasten it again.

He was met in the terminal building by a uniformed chauffeur holding up a sign with his name on it.

"*Niltze*," the chauffeur said.

Reston responded to the Nahuatl greeting with the equivalent in Italian: "*Buòn giorno.*"

The chauffeur took one item of his luggage, a sturdy leather briefcase, and shortly Reston was in the back of a limousine, cruising along the A20 on the northern coast of Sicily. Beside him sat Ettore Addario, CEO of the Compagnia Coltivazione delle Minière di Mongibello, a man with something to sell and every hope that Reston would buy.

"A pleasant flight?" Addario enquired. Like everyone else in the world of non-Anahuac origin, he spoke Nahuatl fluently as a second language, but he happened to have near-perfect English as well and hoped to impress Reston with it.

"The usual. Quick. Boring."

"Ah. Like making love to my wife."

"I wouldn't know about that," Reston said.

"I should hope not, signor. Not for my sake but for yours. A miserable experience. My mistress, on the other hand... Then I would have grounds for jealousy!" He chuckled at the joke. Reston looked unamused. *Oh, the English. So uptight.* Addario realised he wasn't going to break any ice with salaciousness, so changed tack. "Your first visit to our beautiful island?"

Reston nodded.

"If there is time, perhaps I can introduce you to our native cuisine. Rabbit in chocolate sauce, for example, and *pasta alla Norma*. I know this wonderful trattoria in Taormina, right by the beach, where they serve the most delicious *pani cà meusa*. Some say a burger made from fried spleen sounds disgusting, but believe me, when you taste it..."

"My return flight departs at four. Just show me your operation, so I can see for myself what I might or might not be purchasing."

"Of course, signor." Not just uptight – businesslike to the point of being rude. Well, that was an admirable trait, Addario supposed, if you ran as large a corporation as Reston did. No one got to earn a seven-figure annual salary by being nice. Still, would a *little* civility go amiss?

The Mediterranean glittered to their left. To the right, pale against the brilliant blue sky, stood Mount Etna, growing ever closer. A plume of smoke drifted from the summit of its snow-streaked cone, a smudge of grey pastel in the air. It seemed a benign thing, that plume, given the seething subterranean turmoil that generated it. The sigh of a man whose passion for life is spent.

Etna could rage, though, if the Great Speaker willed it. Nearly every volcano on the planet could.

The limo wound through low fertile foothills, eventually pulling into the public car park on Etna's eastern flank. A four-wheel drive waited to ferry Reston and Addario onward to the CCMM site. They bumped along a track grooved by truck tyres and caterpillar treads, upwards through a landscape of ash and rough clinkery rock. Here on these barren black slopes it seemed like the world was constantly being rubbed out and restarted, never finished, an eternal first draft.

Addario pointed out the fusion plant that hunkered half a mile away in the huge depression known as the Valley of the Ox. Its domes and cooling towers wobbled like mercury in the heat haze. On the Great Speaker's say-so, the plant could send intense bursts of energy deep into Etna's magma chambers in order to trigger volcanic activity. This might happen at any time, contingent on His Imperial Holiness's whim. It was rare if a volcano was not erupting somewhere on earth, spewing ash and gas into the atmosphere and keeping the thermostat on the planetary greenhouse turned up high.

"As long as we receive the standard twenty-four hours' notice," said Addario, "we can pack up our equipment and be off-site with plenty of time to spare. In fact, our safety record is amazing, if I do say so myself. In the past decade we have lost only thirteen workers, and all those fatalities have been due to sudden catastrophic machinery failure or individual negligence. Not a bad statistic, and well below average for a company this size."

"Nothing worth obtaining comes without loss of life."

"Well put, signor. Indeed."

The four-wheel drive deposited them in the thick of CCMM's current mining site. The obsidian lode was located not far from the Piano Caldera near the base of Etna's summit cone – a deep seam of felsic lava that had been churned up during recent eruptions and cooled under just the right conditions. A high silica content gave it the necessary viscosity to remain solid rather than become crystalline.

Mechanical diggers were busy excavating the area, exposing the layers of volcanic glass for workmen to hew out with pneumatic drills. Addario handed Reston a pair of overboots, a hard hat and an emergency particulate respirator. Then he led the Englishman on a tour of the site.

Conversation was kept to a minimum, as they had to compete with the roar of diesel engines and the staccato hammering of the drills. Addario assumed anyway that Reston already knew what he was looking at. The man's family had been in the obsidian trade for four generations, and Reston Rhyolitic Ltd. was Britain's largest importer and distributor of the mineraloid. It would be odd, to say the least, if the Englishman had had no first-hand experience of the noise, dust, heat and sulphur stench of a volcano-side mine, nor any understanding of the crude, brute-force methods needed to extract obsidian from where it was birthed at these rupture points in the earth's crust.

Work halted as Etna stirred underfoot. The ground heaved, growling louder than the drills whose chatter it had silenced. Everyone waited for the tremor to pass, poised, ready to down tools and run if need be. There hadn't been an unscheduled eruption here in years, but you could never be complacent. The Great Speaker could manipulate volcanoes but they also had minds of their own.

"Tlaltecuhtli is groaning," Addario commented. Reston just gave him a curt smile. Perhaps he didn't believe in dismembered monster goddesses writhing in agony below ground, causing earthquakes and other upheavals. Addario, who had a degree in geology and had written a thesis on plate tectonics, wasn't sure he himself did.

The tremor faded. Work resumed. Addario noted that Reston hadn't blanched or betrayed a flicker of anxiety. The Englishman was a cold fish, but nerveless too. He'd been an Eagle Warrior at one time, hadn't he? Addario had done a fair amount of research into the background of CCMM's potential new majority shareholder. He knew that Reston had taken the unusual step of submitting himself for national service rather than go to university. Unusual in that he'd been offered unconditional places by both Oxford and Cambridge and because his father, grandfather and great-grandfather had all been graduates. By and large it was the less academically-gifted, or those whose families couldn't afford the steep exemption fees, who did the mandatory three-year stint with the Eagles.

Reston, therefore, had clearly felt he had something to prove, or else had a bloody-minded streak a mile wide, because not only had he stuck out the three years, he had gone on to serve for another five in the infantry, rising to major. He might well have continued had his father not died, obliging him to quit the army and assume directorship of the family firm.

No mere pampered rich kid, then. And observing him, Addario could see Eagle Warrior discipline in his bearing still. Reston strode with his fists beside his hips as though on a parade ground, and he remained in good fighting trim, judging by his lean cheeks, broad shoulders and narrow waist. By contrast, Addario's own pot belly and double chin attested to his love of *cannolo siciliano* and Marsala wine and his aversion to physical exertion of any kind that did not take place in the boudoir.

It would be interesting, he thought, to be answerable professionally to this man. Not always easy, or enjoyable, but there would be no bullshit, that was for sure. With CCMM's current Italian owners, it was all bullshit all the time. Addario yearned for a straight-talking employer, as a person lost in the desert yearns for water.

"Seen enough?"

Reston indicated that he had, and they returned to the four-wheel drive. On the way downhill Addario didn't expressly ask for a verdict, but dropped so many hints that only a fool could have missed them. Finally Reston said, "I can't give you a definitive answer right now. I need to go over the figures one more time. Tell me, are kickbacks involved?"

"In the purchase?" Addario shrugged. "This is Sicily. There are always kickbacks. You can't even repaint your front door without bribing some official or other. And there are certain other bodies one must always take into account..." He wasn't going to say the word *mafia* out loud.

"I thought the Empire had put paid to all that."

"The Empire likes to think it has. We Sicilians know better. Some of our traditions go back further than the end of Fortress Europe and the installation of the High Priests. Does that change anything?" Addario asked, a little plaintively.

"It bumps up my initial outlay," Reston replied. "But all said and done, things are looking positive."

AFTER ADDARIO HAD seen Reston off at the airport, he headed straight to his apartment in Palermo's Four Corners district to share the good news with the woman who mattered most to him. Then he went home to his wife.

Signora Addario wasn't surprised to learn that Reston, in person, was a reticent, tightly buttoned individual. "Didn't you tell me he lost his wife and child recently?" she said. "You can't expect a man touched by so profound a tragedy to be overflowing with joy."

"But they sacrificed themselves to the gods," said her husband. "Many would consider that a badge of honour."

Once again Signora Addario was forced to confront the fact that the man she had married was an idiot of the highest order.

"Would you," she said, "not be distraught if I put myself forward to have my heart carved out by the priest?"

Provided he could find it, Addario thought, but

said, "My dear, it would leave me helpless with grief, but I would somehow find the strength to carry on."

To carry on visiting that trollop you keep in the Four Corners, his wife thought, but said, "There, then. Somehow Signor Reston is finding that strength. Clearly it comes harder to some than others."

STUART RESTON'S FLIGHT home was delayed because the disc had to wait for a VIP passenger whose connecting flight from Tangier was running behind schedule. When the VIP finally stepped aboard, he made his way to the first class cabin without tendering regret or apology to anyone. He swanned through business class with his pair of burly minders as if no one had been inconvenienced here but himself. He was a priest – plainclothes, no robes, but the sacred facial tattoos gave the game away – and other people's considerations came second to a priest's. That was just how it was. If you didn't like it, tough. Take the matter up with the gods.

For the entire hour of the journey, as the disc skimmed over sea and France, Stuart wrestled with his better judgement. It lost, he won.

If an opportunity comes, he told himself, *if you think you can get away with it, go for it.*

At Heathrow, the priest was first out of the disc and onto the gangway. For him, there would be no standing in line at customs and passport control. International travel was a breeze for the theocracy.

Wherever they went, they were just waved on through.

Stuart still got the chance he was looking for, however. No sooner had the priest entered the terminal than he had to answer a sudden, rather urgent call of nature. He scuttled off to the nearest public convenience, minders in tow.

After a pause, Stuart followed.

The minders had taken up position just inside the door to the gents, forming a two-man wall. Both were giants – professional security consultants with necks as broad as their heads and wrists as thick as their fists.

"Sorry, sir," said one to Stuart. "You can't use this facility right now."

"Try somewhere else," the other chimed in.

Stuart hopped from foot to foot as though his bladder was past capacity. "But I'm bursting."

"You'll have to hold it, sir."

"I'm sure it won't be long."

"Who are you guarding, anyway?" Stuart demanded, gesturing past the minders. "Why's his need more important than mine?"

"I'd advise you to keep your tone civil, sir. You're in the presence of His Holiness Jasper Marquand, priest of Birmingham."

"Oh." Stuart cringed with feigned contrition. "I had no idea. How stupid of me. Of course I'll wait outside 'til his holiness is finished."

He turned, and turned again, pivoting on the ball of his foot and swinging his briefcase into the face of the nearer of the two minders. As the man sank to his knees, clutching a shattered nose, Stuart delivered a knife-hand jab to the throat of the other minder, crushing his larynx. He whacked the briefcase against the first minder's head, knocking him cold. The second was already close to unconsciousness, struggling to draw breath. Stuart locked an arm around his neck and put pressure on his carotid until he fainted.

In all, it took less than fifteen seconds, and was as quiet as it was swift.

Stuart approached the only cubicle with a closed door. From within came the sounds of someone grappling with an explosive digestive disorder.

"Carling, is that you?" the priest called out. "I heard a bit of a scuffle. What's happened? Has that insolent moron gone?"

"All sorted, Your Holiness," Stuart said in an approximation of the minders' gravelly growl. "Nothing to worry about."

"Bloody Moroccan food," Jasper Marquand muttered. "You go there for a short break, some jollies with the local catamites, and what do you end up with? The worst case of the runs imaginable. Sun, sea, sodomy, salmonella. Never again, I tell you. Never again."

"If you insist, your holiness."

The toilet flushed. The bolt unlatched.

Stuart kicked the door violently inward. It struck the priest on the forehead and he staggered back. Stuart grabbed him, spun him round, and slammed him down face first onto the toilet bowl. He repeated the action twice more, until blood flowed freely and Marquand was gibbering in pain and distress.

"Please," the priest begged, "I can give you money. However much you want. Please stop hurting me."

"I already have money," said Stuart, "and as for hurting you, that's not what I'm here for."

"What, then? Anything. Name it."

"You dead. That's all."

Marquand bucked in sheer terror. Stuart took a firmer grip on him and plunged his head deep into the toilet. He held the priest's face under the water until his struggles ebbed and became death twitches. He kept him there for another minute, just to be sure, before letting go. Remarkably, he had managed to get very little water on himself, just the odd splash here and there on his suit and shirt cuffs.

He exited the cubicle and went to deal with the minders. Unfortunately for them, he couldn't leave them alive. They had seen his face and might be able to identify him to the Jaguars; at the very least, furnish a decent description. He gave each man's head a short, sharp twist, separating skull from Atlas bone. Then he lugged the bodies into two empty cubicles and shut them in.

He washed his hands at the basin and sprinkled cold water on his face. His heart rate was returning to normal. The adrenaline surge that came with murder had begun to abate.

He stared hard at his reflection. A handsome but hollow man stared back. He composed himself.

Hand-combed a stray lock of hair into place. Adjusted his tie.

Businessman Stuart Reston emerged from the gents and sauntered over to rejoin the passport queue. Within twenty minutes, he was out of the building and hailing a taxi.

Not long after that, a janitor wheeled his cleaning cart into the gents to give the place its hourly spruce-up.

His screams of horror could be heard halfway across the terminal.

STUART'S PENTHOUSE FLAT boasted enviable views of the Thames, all the way from Blackfriars Bridge to Limehouse Reach. He stood on the balcony with a glass of whisky and a bowl of pistachios and watched the sun sink into the red fires of the western horizon. One of London's few remaining pigeons alighted on the balustrade with a dainty coo. It was soon seen off its perch by a brash macaw and went flapping mournfully away, merging with the grey dusk. The more colourful bird sidestepped along the handrail, bowing and scraping, begging for a nut. Stuart showed it what he thought of that by swiping a fist at it. The macaw got the message.

Stuart was aware he had taken a ridiculous risk, slaying the priest like that at the airport. He had gone off-mission. The chances of being caught *in flagrante* had been huge.

He'd not been able to help himself, though. Once Marquand went into the gents, his fate had been sealed. Had Stuart believed in the gods, he would have said it was a gift from them. He had felt the familiar tingle of cold certainty in his gut: *what you are about to do is right, and righteous.* After that, there'd been no turning back.

Indoors, he flicked on the TV, and there on the news they were talking about Priest Marquand. "A vicious assassination," said the reporter on the spot. "Murdered in cold blood at Heathrow Airport by an unknown assailant as he returned from a *trecena*-long cultural exchange trip to north Africa."

"Cultural exchange trip," Stuart echoed dryly.

Then the inevitable. "Is this the work of the Conquistador? The Jaguar Warriors have refused to speculate. Certainly nobody at the scene reports seeing an armoured figure matching the Conquistador's description, but it has all the hallmarks, from the choice of victim to the sheer wanton brutality of the execution. The alternative theory is a copycat killing. Someone inspired by the Conquistador's example is targeting the hieratic caste, mimicking his methods. If so, could this be the first of many such attacks? Are we seeing the beginning of a widespread civil uprising?"

Stuart raised an eyebrow. "Now that would be interesting."

Leaving the television to jabber to itself, he went to the walk-in wardrobe that adjoined his bedroom. Suits and shirts hung in neat rows. Dozens of pairs of shoes sat, polished to a gleam, on racks. Stuart passed them by and halted at the far end. He felt for the hidden spring catch that released a secret sliding panel. The rear of the wardrobe opened up, and there in an alcove stood several suits of steel armour, perched on mannequins. Rapiers and flechette guns were mounted on the walls. Black masks dangled slackly from pegs.

Stuart could not suppress a smile. It was like some glorious treasure trove – a museum exhibit crossed with a functioning arsenal.

He reached out and stroked the nearest suit of armour.

"Soon," he said, as though soothing a baby to sleep. "Soon."

FOUR

7 Movement 1 Monkey 1 House
(Wednesday 28th November 2012)

THE SPOTLIGHTS AROUND the Regent's Park amphitheatre dimmed, and the audience hushed. The stage lights came up. The performance began.

A woman entered from the wings, dressed as the hermaphroditic god/goddess Ometeotl, half male, half female. She performed an elaborate, graceful dance set to a score that fused traditional instruments – clay flutes and ocarinas, mainly – with a contemporary pop rhythm. As she darted from one side of the stage to the other, her stance and style changed. On the left, she was all stomping, square-shouldered machismo. On the right, she was lighter-footed, more feminine.

She was Oneness In Duality, the coming together of opposites. She was the primordial flux that existed before the first great age. She was neither one thing nor the other, and both at once.

Her dance culminated in a symbolic birth. As the music crescendoed, from between Ometeotl's legs (and up through a trapdoor) the Four Who Rule Supreme emerged.

First came Quetzalcoatl, resplendent in feathers and scales.

Next, Tezcatlipoca in a dark mirror-bedecked costume, amid swirls of smoke.

Then Huitzilopochtli, the wings on his back blurring like a hummingbird's.

Finally hideous Xipe Totec, the Flayed One.

They were followed by Tlaloc, lord of rain and lightning, and a rapid procession of lesser deities, including the thirteen Lords of the Day and the nine Lords of the Night.

As Ometeotl faded into the background, his/her work done, the Four Who Rule Supreme danced around Tlaloc in a circle, each at his respective cardinal compass point. Then began a series of individual dances, accompanied by corps members representing the beings who lived during each of the first four great ages.

Primitive earth dwellers, giants who could uproot whole trees with their bare hands, thundered about in the first age, whose ruler was Tezcatlipoca.

Tezcatlipoca was supplanted violently by Quetzalcoatl. The two gods were born rivals, dark versus light, uncertainty versus stability, cunning versus integrity. Quetzalcoatl's age was an age of air and wind, and his subjects were monkey men who flew among the treetops like leaves on the breeze.

Tezcatlipoca returned and struck Quetzalcoatl to the ground, usurping him. The third great age was a time of rain, and Tlaloc was set in place as its lord and master by Tezcatlipoca. Quetzalcoatl brought it to a close with a downpour of fire from the sky, which wiped out the global population of winged, turkey-like folk.

The fourth age belonged to Chalchiuhtlicue, jade-skirted goddess of streams and still water. Amphibious fish men thrived in this time, which ended in a massive, all-erasing flood.

The next age began with Quetzalcoatl and Tezcatlipoca setting aside their differences and suing for peace, since up until now their strife had inflicted so much carnage and devastation. The two moved in beautiful balletic unison, mirroring each other's posture and gestures, to an elegant, waltz-like tune.

To mark their truce they collaborated in the slaughter of the she-beast Tlaltecuhtli. Transforming themselves into giant serpents, they seized the many-mouthed monster and tore her to bits. From her mutilated body a fresh world was formed. Her hair became vegetation. Her eye sockets became caves. Hills and valleys were her nose, mountains her shoulders.

This miraculous if messy metamorphosis was rendered through a variety of forms of stagecraft: props, puppetry, mime, and shifts in the lighting that revealed backdrop images painted on successive layers of scrim. The audience appreciated it immensely, cheering and applauding as the fifth great age – the current age – took shape before their eyes.

But where were the people? Who would inhabit the earth now? Quetzalcoatl descended into the underworld, Mictlan, to retrieve bones of the ancestor races, from which he intended to create a brand new race. Mictlantecuhtli, the Dark One, the god who presided over Mictlan, tried to trick and entrap him, but Quetzalcoatl outsmarted him at every turn. He evaded the Dark One's devious snares and surfaced victorious with an armful of broken bones. These he handed to the snake goddess Cihuacoatl, who ground them to powder in a bowl. Then every god donated drops of blood, Cihuacoatl mixed it all together, and hey presto, humans appeared.

Again, the audience loved it, including the twenty-strong group of priests who occupied the best seats in the house. While everyone else had to make do with hard, bleacher-like benches, the priests sat in cushioned comfort on a specially erected platform at the centre of the amphitheatre's arc. Bowls of fresh fruit and maize snacks had been laid on for them, and they were regularly doused with a mist of insect repellent to keep the mosquitoes at bay.

The platform blocked the view of the stage for dozens of people in the rows behind, but nothing could be done about it and nobody complained. The presence of priests at the performance was indisputably an honour and, thanks to the theatre's publicity department, had been heavily touted in the press and on TV. The show ran nightly, weather permitting, but never until this evening had any of their holinesses attended, and in such numbers too. The dancers and actors were, as a consequence, giving it their all, and the audience members were doing their bit by showing more than usual enthusiasm for the action onstage – even those who couldn't see much more than the backs of the priests' heads.

AFTER THE INTERVAL, the performance switched from dance to drama, in order to tell how the non-aggression pact between Quetzalcoatl and Tezcatlipoca foundered and the god of smoke and mirrors played a vile trick on his brother.

The original text of this play was said to date back to Shakespeare, who composed it towards the end of his life after becoming a secret convert to the Aztec faith. Of course it was never staged in his lifetime, nor during the many calendar rounds that followed, at least not in public. With the Aztec Empire busy storming the gates of Europe and threatening to lay siege to Britain, that would have been tantamount to treason. Only after Britain finally fell to the Empire, just over a hundred solar years ago, did the play emerge into the light of day.

By then, Shakespeare would have been hard pushed to recognise it. His draft – assuming it ever existed – had been handed down through the generations orally. A process of continual revision and updating had taken place with each clandestine rendition. Lines had been added and removed. New scenes had been improvised, old ones discarded.

The basic narrative, however, which every schoolchild learned almost as soon as he or she could talk, stayed the same. The story beats were as familiar to people as the beats of their own hearts.

One day, Tezcatlipoca held up his scrying mirror to Quetzalcoatl, promising to reveal to him his true face.

The mirror falsely showed, not a magnificent god in the prime of his life, but a withered, decayed old man with a long white beard.

"This," said Tezcatlipoca, "is the truth of what you are – the truth of all flesh."

Quetzalcoatl was appalled; repelled.

To calm him in his agitation, Tezcatlipoca gave him a goblet of *pulque* laced with magic mushrooms.

Quetzalcoatl took a sip. Liked it. Drank deep.

He fetched his younger sister, Quetzalpetlatl, and made her drink too.

They lay together, the siblings, inebriated beyond all sense and propriety. They copulated. They slept.

The following morning, Quetzalcoatl, utterly ashamed, took his leave of the world. He could rule it no longer, not after committing the sin of incest. He was not worthy.

The other gods elected to go with him, even deceitful Tezcatlipoca, who was likewise ashamed by his own behaviour.

They left behind them the sum of their knowledge and wisdom – their arts, their crafts, their technology – for humans to use as they saw fit.

And they bestowed the gift of eternal life on one man, the Aztec emperor Moctezuma II, who would forever after be known as the Great Speaker and would rule in the gods' stead, their voice on earth.

The Great Speaker's word was law. All who lived in Anahuac obeyed him, and in time all who lived in the rest of the world would too.

His destiny was to extend the realm of the Aztecs beyond the Land Between The Seas until it covered every land and every sea.

It was a destiny he gladly embraced.

THE APPOINTMENT OF Moctezuma II as the Great Speaker provided the play's climax and was the moment everyone looked forward to. Traditionally it had to be a spectacular theatrical coup, as the old, mortal Moctezuma vanished and was replaced by a masked, robed figure who appeared as if from nowhere, conjured into being by the Four Who Rule Supreme. Sometimes there would be thunderflashes, sometimes wreaths of dry ice. Sometimes the Great Speaker would rise from below, sometimes descend from above. It didn't really matter how he came on, as long he did so in a majestic and magical fashion.

In this particular production, the actor lucky enough to have been given the role of His Imperial Holiness was lowered from the flies on a harness. Stroboscopic lights flickered all around him. Sound cues mimicked a tropical storm. Huge electric fans stirred up a kind of onstage cyclone. Everything was designed to give the impression of power and might, the crackle of primal energy, the churn of vast creative forces.

The audience was so dazzled and deafened that, at first, no one noticed that the figure who was supposed to be the Great Speaker didn't actually resemble the Great Speaker at all.

Slowly it dawned on them. Where was the extravagant, floor-sweeping robe? Where was the full-head mask – that near-featureless slab of gold?

Confusion turned to consternation, and then to fear.

Centre stage, surrounded by a very perplexed-looking quartet of actors portraying Quetzalcoatl, Tezcatlipoca, Huitzilopochtli and Xipe Totec, stood...

...the Conquistador.

Who fixed the audience with a gimlet stare and shouted, "Bullshit!"

The barrage of effects stopped abruptly, some backstage technician realising that the show had just been hijacked and leaping to hit the off button.

"This is a fiction," the Conquistador went on, addressing the rows of slack-jawed faces in front of him. "A complete fabrication. Revisionist garbage. Don't believe a word of it. Shakespeare never wrote any such play, no matter what they tell you, and it never became some kind of underground mystery cult kept alive by pro-Aztec secret societies, because there were no such things. Britain stood solidly against the Empire to the last. Anyone who says otherwise is simply being the Empire's parrot. Our rulers would have us think we wanted to be conquered all along, and only the pigheadedness of our monarchy and parliament kept that from happening. The truth is, we defied the Empire's encroachment to the bitter end, all of us, the entire British people, and it cost us dear. It brought our country to its knees. It starved us, bankrupted us, nearly destroyed us. But we clung on, with the enemy coming at us on every shore, until it became clear that to continue would be suicide. We were the last nation to fall, the bravest. This play – this travesty – this farce – came into life *after* the Aztec hordes overran us, not before."

Some in the audience dared to boo. Others frowned, wondering whether there might not be something in what the Conquistador said.

From the priests, there was only stony silence.

The Conquistador peered imperiously around the amphitheatre. He had the stage, and an audience that was too startled and intimidated to move. He was going to make the most of it while he could.

"As for the Great Speaker," he said, "he's no more Moctezuma than I am. He isn't immortal. Beneath that ridiculous mask there has been a succession of men – ordinary mortal men – who have played the role just as these actors here play theirs. One after another they assume the mantle of Great Speaker and give out orders and edicts from the Lake Palace at Tenochtitlan, and when each dies the next in line replaces him, and it is all done behind closed doors, amid a conspiracy of silence, and we are none the wiser. You know in your heart of hearts that I'm right. Nothing you've seen here tonight is real. What you've been watching is a lie. Artful propaganda.

Stage managed in every sense. A myth masquerading as legend. And it's all to help keep that lot" – he jabbed a finger at the priests – "in power. Reinforce their tyranny. Tighten their stranglehold still further."

He unsheathed his rapier, to gasps and squeals.

"Well, you're looking at a man who will not be strangled. A man who's sick and tired of living under this regime and wants rid of it. They call me a terrorist. Maybe I am. But the only people who should be terrified of me are the hieratic caste and anyone who supports them."

With that, he bounded over the footlights and off the front of the stage, making for the priests' platform. Panicking audience members leapt from their seats and ran shrieking. Their Holinesses themselves seemed rooted to the spot, paralysed by fear. They exchanged looks, as if to ask how this could have happened, how it could be that so many of them at once were about to become the Conquistador's next victims.

The Conquistador sprang up onto the platform.

"Should've thought this through a bit better, shouldn't you?" he crowed. "You arrogant bastards. Not one Jaguar Warrior bodyguard? Talk about sitting ducks."

"Actually," said one of the priests, the tallest of them, "I think you'll find *you're* the sitting duck."

The Conquistador cocked his head. "Oh, yes? And how do you work that out?"

"Well..." The priest reached beneath his chair and snatched out the *macuahitl* concealed there.

All the others did exactly the same thing.

Behind his mask, the Conquistador's face fell. His eyes gave it away. A moment of pure, uncomprehending shock.

The priests, as one, rose.

"No Jaguar Warriors, mate?" sneered the tall one. "Try twenty of them!"

In HER SEAT, five rows back from the platform, Chief Inspector Mal Vaughn watched with satisfaction as her trap was sprung.

Really, it was a surprise the Conquistador had fallen for it. Mal had had her doubts he would. Surely he'd be too smart. Surely he'd think that it was just too blatant. Twenty priests unexpectedly attending a show at an open-air theatre in the middle of a park? A venue where watertight security was virtually impossible? It must have been screaming *STAY AWAY!* to him.

But no, he hadn't stayed away. He'd come charging in, unable to resist the bait.

That fitted with the psychological impression Mal had built up of him. He was a narcissist. He enjoyed the big gesture, the grandstanding performance. He liked to make an impact.

All the same, she was vaguely disappointed. Somehow she'd felt he was cannier than this.

The bogus priests moved in on the Conquistador, swords aloft. He backed away a couple of steps.

Mal's masterstroke was that there was no way the

Conquistador could have suspected the priests were not what they appeared to be. To impersonate a priest – hieratic fraud – was one of the most heinous offences on the statute books. The punishment was a litany of hideous tortures. You would have skewers driven through your most sensitive parts. You would be flayed alive. Your skinned body would be roasted over hot coals. You would then, if not already dead, be disembowelled and, for good measure, beheaded. And the same treatment would be visited on every single member of your immediate family. Even your cousins, even your pets, would not be immune. It was something only a lunatic would consider doing.

Chief Superintendent Kellaway had laughed at Mal when she'd suggested disguising a squad of Jaguars as priests. Then he'd realised she was deadly serious, and he'd laughed again, this time scornfully. It would never happen, he'd said. The High Priest would never allow it.

But he might, Mal had insisted. He might make a special dispensation, in this one instance, if he could be convinced that it was the best, the *only* way of drawing out the Conquistador and catching him unawares. Could the chief super just try? Ask him? Plead?

In the event, the High Priest had gone for the idea and granted permission. Twenty Jaguar Warriors had had their heads shaved and their skin adorned with non-permanent tattoo designs, the customary assortment of iguanas and quetzals and hieroglyphs. They had spent hours practising how to sit, stand and behave in a priestly manner. Few of them had been able to resist the temptation to walk with a mincing gait and make lisping demands for peeled grapes and depilated virgins, and Mal had let them have their fun, even though by rights she should have reported them for gross impertinence. Mocking a priest was nearly as bad as impersonating one, and the penalty might not be as severe but you and your kin would still regret it – at least a dozen of your relatives would have a hand lopped off, and you yourself would lose both hands and a foot as well. Like the old joke went: *I called a priest an idiot then hopped it.*

And it had paid off. The Conquistador was now surrounded and heavily outnumbered by some of the best swordsmen on the force.

He managed to recover from his dumbstruck stupor in time. As the first of the Jaguars attacked, up came his rapier. Blades clashed. The fight was on.

Mal turned to Aaronson, seated beside her.

"Come on. Let's get in there."

"What?" said her DS. "Have you gone mad? Twenty of them, one of him. They don't need our help."

"Maybe not, but he's my fucking collar. I'm not letting someone else hog the glory. Whoever kills him, the body is still mine and I'll gut the man who tries to take it off me."

"You know, boss," Aaronson said, getting to his feet, "you scare me sometimes."

"Good."

* * *

THE ONE ADVANTAGE the Conquistador had over his opponents was that he was fully armoured and they were not. Their garb was the standard plainclothes wear for a priest, a light alpaca wool suit over a multicoloured brocade waistcoat which echoed the much fancier garment used for ceremonies. Underneath their shirts, many of the Jaguar Warriors had taken the precaution of donning stab-proof vests, but that still left their heads and limbs unprotected. It was a vulnerability the Conquistador was quick to exploit.

The tall Jaguar, Constable Carey, died first. The Conquistador ducked inside his guard and ran him through the groin. He yanked the rapier out just in time to counter a *macuahitl* slash from the left. Grabbing the Jaguar's sword arm, he opened his neck from ear to ear. As the man went down, he twisted the *macuahitl* out of his grasp.

Now, armed on both sides, he met the onslaught of the next two Jaguars, matching them blow for blow. The two of them flanked him at the platform's edge. The Conquistador feinted forwards, then leapt backwards, off the platform. Both Jaguars lunged at him at the same time and were wrongfooted. They stared down in astonishment to find each other's swords embedded in their thighs, and collapsed against each other like a pair of broken bookends.

Down in the area between the seating and the stage front, the Conquistador discarded the borrowed *macuahitl* and drew his pistol. With three shots he eviscerated the nearest three Jaguar Warriors. Even a stab-proof vest was no protection against a high-velocity cluster of flechettes.

Another Jaguar, however, got close enough to knock the pistol out of his hand before he could inflict any more damage with it. In retaliation, the Conquistador sliced through the man's arm with his rapier, severing the limb at the elbow.

At that point it became clear that the Conquistador was cornered. His back was against the stage. Several very angry and determined Jaguars were closing in on him.

All at once they rushed him. Obsidian blades hammered at his armour from all directions, seeking chinks. Someone with a sense of irony might have seen the very image of what he had described onstage a moment ago, Britain embattled on all sides, a lonely island beleaguered by the might of the Empire.

He fought back gamely, but the Jaguar Warriors were giving him no quarter. Mal, at the rear of the pack, was convinced it would be only moments before a crippling sword stroke got through, maybe a fatal one. She allowed herself a quick gloat. She had done it. She had succeeded where all the previous investigating officers had not. She had pulled off a feat most would have thought impossible. The Conquistador was about to become an ugly footnote in modern British history, not to mention a significant feather in her cap. Nobody would forget tonight. This was the kind of achievement that future chief superintendents were made of.

And to think that a week ago she had been contemplating quitting the force.

A week was a long time in policing. Maybe all she'd needed was this – the opportunity to do something worthwhile with the job, the chance to feel like she was helping society rather than simply serving the state.

The pommel of a *macuahitl* pounded down on the Conquistador's helmet. He fell.

Yes!

It was then, as Mal was enjoying a surge of triumph, that everything turned to shit.

ONE OF THE Jaguar Warriors masquerading as priests suddenly grabbed his neck. His eyes rolled up, his knees buckled, and he crumpled to the ground.

A hoarse shout came from the trees surrounding the amphitheatre, giving an order in a language Mal didn't recognise. Then men came leaping down from the branches onto the topmost seats.

They hurtled down the raked rows, uttering battle cries as they ran. They were small and dark-haired, and their faces were daubed with white warpaint so as to resemble, more than anything, skulls. Their clothing mixed combat fatigues with chunky jewellery, and some of them whirled bolases above their heads while others brandished blowpipes. Everyone was startled by their unexpected appearance, and none more so than Mal.

The Jaguar Warriors turned as a volley of blowpipe

darts came whipping towards them. Wherever a dart scored a hit, the man fell immediately and lay prostrate on the ground, motionless as a waxwork. The remaining, unscathed Jaguars threw themselves at the new arrivals. Linked trios of bolas balls helicoptered through the air, catching them around their necks and legs. They toppled, and as they sprawled flat out, yet more blowpipe darts rendered them inert and insensible.

They're hunting us, Mal thought. *Bringing us down like animals on the pampas plains.*

One of the skull-faced attackers ran at her, bolas spinning. Before he could launch it, she narrowed the distance between them and spiked her *macuahitl* at him. His momentum drove him straight onto the blade, impaling him up to the hilt.

As Mal heaved the sword out, another of the skull-faces sprang. This one wasn't taking any chances. His blowpipe was already at his lips. The range was point blank. Mal swung her sword anyway, hoping against hope that she could get him before he sent the dart on its way.

His cheeks inflated, and at the very same instant Aaronson jumped at him with a frantic cry of "No!" There was a *phooooft!* and Aaronson yelped. He and the skull-face tumbled to the ground together in a heap.

Mal pounced on the two tangled bodies, thrusting the point of her *macuahitl* down into the skull-face's eye and piercing him to the brain.

"Aaronson! Talk to me. Are you okay?"

She turned him over. He moaned. His eyes rolled in their sockets. His limbs were floppy, rubbery. Was he dying or simply lapsing into unconsciousness? Was the poison on the dart's tip fatal or just a powerful paralytic?

Either way, there was nothing she could do for him right now. She rose, scanning around. The attackers had cleared a path through to the Conquistador. They were after *her* villain. Well, they weren't bloody well having him.

She sprinted towards him, leaping over the bodies of downed comrades. The Conquistador looked stunned and exhausted. The skull-faces were helping him to his feet. He didn't seem to know who they were, but was plainly relieved that they had intervened.

Mal was just yards from him when a rotund individual stepped into her way. His warpaint was the most detailed of all of them, savage and snarly. Yet his eyes were weirdly compassionate. He looked almost sorry as he loosed off his bolas at her.

She tried to duck, but wasn't fast enough. The bolas cords twined around her head, tightening in an instant. There was a triple impact, a triple burst of lightning and thunder.

Then darkness.

FIVE

8 Flint Knife 1 Monkey 1 House
(Thursday 29th November 2012)

STUART WOKE UP in his own bed, in his own bedroom. Not where he expected to be at all, but he was very glad he was there.

As he heaved himself to a sitting position, a tsunami of aches and pains crashed over him. His arms and legs felt stiff as cardboard. Examining himself, he found bruises almost everywhere, as though someone had planted a garden of purple and yellow orchids under his skin. His head rang like a gong.

He tottered to the bathroom in his underpants. There, amid the marble fixtures, he almost passed out. The world greyed, wavered, dimmed. A glass of cold water helped bring him back to his senses, and a second glass washed down a fistful of aspirin.

As he shuffled along the corridor to the kitchen, Stuart felt a sudden, instinctive certainty.

He wasn't alone in the flat.

It was too early for the maid, Grace. Besides, in spite of her name, Grace moved with all the elegance of a rhino. You always knew which room she was cleaning, by the thudding footfalls and the clunk of ornaments not quite being broken.

Someone was here and doing their best to keep quiet.

Razor-alert, Stuart slid a carving knife out of the block on the kitchen counter. The intruder was in the living room. Stuart padded to the connecting door, which stood slightly ajar. He peeked through the crack. He had a view of half the room and there was nobody in sight, but the certainty remained. It was something in the air, in the sounds of the flat; something almost unconscious.

He eased the door open just enough to slip through sideways. He held the carving knife at his hip in a backhand grip, the blunt edge of the blade resting against his forearm. It wasn't the most precise of weapons but, in experienced hands, it would serve.

There was a short, portly man standing in the far corner with his back to the doorway. He wore a neat tropical suit and appeared to be admiring Stuart's bookshelves, which were laden with first editions of pre-Empire British fiction. His hands were laced together behind him as he keenly ran his gaze over the books' spines, the cloth and leather bindings, the gold stencilled lettering.

Stuart crept towards him using all the stealthcraft at his disposal. His bare feet made not a sound on the floor tiles. His breathing was slow and measured, drifting silently in through the nostrils, out through the mouth. He skirted the sofa. He was almost within striking distance.

"H.G. Wells," said the man abruptly, without turning round.

Stuart halted mid-step.

The man gestured at a blue-bound volume. "He foresaw the eventual fall of Britain to the Empire. What are the Martians in *The War Of The Worlds* if not a thinly disguised allegorical warning of an Aztec invasion? Whereas Kipling" – he pointed to a green book on the shelf above, a Collected Poetical Works adorned with beautiful blind-tooled patterns – "insisted your country would remain independent, an empire unto itself, for all time. Two authors, contemporaries, both equally brilliant, yet one got it so right and the other so wrong. Funny, that."

Now, finally, he turned. He was round-faced, twinkly-eyed, with an impish cast to his features.

"Kindly put the knife down, Mr Reston. Were you to attack me, I would be forced to disarm you, possibly hurt you. Neither of us would want that."

Stuart did not do as asked. Looking at the man, he doubted he could make good on the threat. Soft and chubby. Slow reflexes. Then again, he'd somehow been aware Stuart was sneaking up on him. There could be more to him than met the eye.

"Who are you?" Stuart demanded in English.

The intruder had addressed him in Nahuatl, which Stuart refused to use if he didn't have to.

"I'm sorry, my knowledge of your native tongue extends to basic reading, that's all. What did you say?"

Stuart switched to the other language, reluctantly. "I asked who you are."

"You don't remember me from last night? No surprise, I suppose. Like you, I am in my civvies." A grin doubled the number of plump folds in the man's face. "My name is Ah Balam Chel, and I helped save your life at the theatre. Ringing any bells yet?"

"I have no idea what you're talking about," Stuart replied. He brandished the knife. "You have five seconds to get out of here, or else."

Ah Balam Chel gently pushed the blade aside. "No need to keep waving that thing around. I mean you no harm. I am not your enemy. Believe me, if I wanted you dead, you would be. I had ample opportunity to kill you last night. That I did not must tell you something. The fact is, I want you alive. Very much so."

"And why would that be?"

"Because you are the Conquistador."

"Oh, come on!" Stuart scoffed.

Chel just smiled knowingly. "When I removed your mask and armour in the back of the getaway van last night, it surprised me to see such a well-known face beneath. I'd had the Conquistador pegged as a nobody, some disgruntled member of the lower orders – not an obsidian magnate whose fortune is based on a product so beloved of the Empire. Far from being an outsider or a social outcast, you're part of the establishment. You're the last person I'd ever think would go running around London playing the radical revolutionary."

"Seriously, you're mistaken," Stuart insisted. "You've got the wrong man."

"Who helped you back into this building, when you were so dazed you could barely walk? Who cleaned you up and put you to bed? Me. And all the while, I couldn't quite get my head round the fact that this pillar of the community is also the man who would tear down the Empire. The final confirmation came when I inspected the premises while you slept, and found the stash of equipment and spare suits of armour at the back of your wardrobe."

"All right," Stuart said, relenting. There was no point trying to brazen it out any more. Chel knew what he knew. "I am the Conquistador. What are you going to do about it?"

"Nothing. Why would I? You think I'm going to turn you over to the Jaguar Warriors?"

"There's a substantial reward on offer."

"But I'm an outlaw too," said Chel. "Remember at the theatre? When you were surrounded by those priests who weren't priests?"

Stuart recalled the men with the death's head faces. From the moment a Jaguar Warrior clobbered him on the head, events had taken on a hazy, surreal glow. The death's heads had dragged him out of the theatre. There'd been a mad dash through the jungle of Regent's Park, and then...? Chel had mentioned a getaway van, and Stuart had a dim recollection of a tumbling, swerving journey and the tang of diesel fumes. By that point he'd become half convinced the death's heads were supernatural beings, the souls of the dead come to escort him to Mictlan. It seemed absurd now, especially as he didn't believe in Mictlan, or Tamoanchan, or any form of afterlife. At the time, though, he'd felt it was a distinct possibility – at the very least, part of a dying man's fever dream.

And yes, yes. Ah Balam Chel had been one of the death's heads. Not just one of them, their leader. He'd been barking out orders from the passenger seat, even as he busily scrubbed his makeup off.

"Now, I imagine you're hungry after your ordeal," Chel said. "Why not put on some clothes, eat some breakfast? And then we shall talk, you and I. I have things I'd like to tell you, and a proposal to put."

Stuart studied Chel's face. He saw neither deceit nor fear there. Stuart trusted no one, but he didn't sense any danger coming from this man.

Almost without meaning to, he lowered the knife. "All right."

"How long's this going to take?" Stuart had just wolfed down a bowl of porridge and two rounds of hot buttered toast. He'd also drunk a pot of proper tea, not coca infusion, which like most of the Empire's cultural impositions he spurned. He was starting to feel himself again.

"Why, do you have somewhere you'd rather be?"

replied Chel amiably. "A holding cell at Scotland Yard, perhaps?"

"Is that a threat?"

"Merely a joke. Perhaps not a funny one."

"As it happens, I have a business meeting at nine o'clock sharp."

"Ah yes, your other life. The man you are when you're not in your Conquistador costume."

"It's not a costume," Stuart said. "It's a pretence, a necessary disguise. I wouldn't have been getting away with doing what I've been doing for half as long as I have, if I did it as plain old me. Plus, it gives me protection."

"The image the armour projects, though, that's important."

"I don't deny there's some theatrics involved. I want the Conquistador's deeds to stick in people's minds. I want to be memorable – unignorable. I want TV coverage and newspaper headlines. I'd get none of that if I was just some bloke running about in street clothes and a balaclava." Stuart pointed an accusing finger at Chel. "All this is pretty rich coming from you. You and your friends with the death's head faces, the ethnic weaponry. And that jewellery you were wearing. The jade frogs and carved circle pendants. Mayan, right?"

Chel nodded.

"Which explains why you speak Nahuatl without an accent, and you look Anahuac. So why are you over here?"

"To meet you, of course."

"No, really."

"Really. Well, it is a little more complicated than that. Have you got time?"

Stuart glanced at his wristwatch. "The meeting's in half an hour, and it's twenty minutes from here to Reston Rhyolitic if the traffic's good."

"Then we should perhaps do this on some other occasion, when you're not so busy." Chel stood up as if to leave. "Mustn't interfere with the wheels of industry, must we?"

"Or," said Stuart, "I could phone my PA and have her postpone the meeting. It's not *urgent* urgent. Just going over the half-yearly figures with the accounts team."

"That would be your decision. If you're interested in listening to what I have to say..."

"I don't know." Stuart genuinely didn't know. He was intrigued by Chel, that was for sure, and there was no getting around the fact that this man and his band of bolas-wielding paramilitaries had pulled the Conquistador's fat out of the fire last night. Stuart owed him for his continued liberty – his life, indeed. Hearing him out seemed the least he could do.

"It shouldn't take too long," Chel said.

"I'll make the call."

"THERE IS, OF course, no such thing as the Mayan nation," Ah Balam Chel said. "Everyone knows that. The Maya are no more. We were the last of the Aztecs' conquests in Anahuac, before the Empire's expansion out into the rest of the world began. The Olmec, the Zapotec, the Inca and the Mixtec had been enslaved and become tributary states. The Aztecs then swarmed across the Isthmus of Tehuantepec and up into the Yucatan Peninsula. Urged on by the Great Speaker, they slaughtered and pillaged, committing atrocities on a scale you wouldn't believe. Mayan men were killed in their thousands, children too, and women raped in their tens of thousands. That, the mass rape, was a vital plank in the Aztecs' plan. Their footsoldiers took a particular, vindictive pleasure in carrying out that particular duty. Within months, countless mixed-race infants were born. The bloodline of the Maya was thinned and sullied and would never be pure again."

"Yes, yes, a history lesson," said Stuart. "I already know all this. Everybody does."

"You should not be so dismissive. It may have happened a long time ago, but it is as fresh in my people's memory as if it were last week. We make sure to keep it that way. It is our duty as Mayans never to forget how we were treated. Other early Aztec conquests were mild by comparison. For us, they reserved a special contempt, perhaps because we were so civilised and they were not. Where they knew only aggression, we knew peace. Where they had their god-given technology, we had astronomy, sciences, art, all of which we had devised on our own. Where they had a single supreme ruler, we had a system of sovereign city states that worked collectively for the good of the nation as a whole.

They loathed us for being all they could never be, and we paid for their envy by being abused like dogs and butchered like cattle."

"Conquest is never pretty. You want to compare sob stories? How about Southampton, eh?"

"One city destroyed is hardly the equivalent of an entire race nearly wiped out."

"The Aztecs flattened the place with fusion warheads. Well, the French navy did, on their behalf. I visited there once, sort of a pilgrimage. It's marshland now, all the way to the sea. A few bits of building left standing, covered in moss. The spire of an old church. And no graves. Thousands upon thousands killed, all in a single day, and not a single headstone to mark it, because there were no bodies to be buried. They'd all been incinerated."

"I see the outrage in your eyes, hear it in your voice. Southampton happened long before you were born, yet you feel considerable anger about it. You must understand it's the same for us. The injury on the Maya was inflicted longer ago, but it was terrible, and we have not recovered."

"We both hate the Empire, then. We have that in common."

"We do. And we, my men and I, have been doing our bit to let the Aztecs at home know that their act of near-genocide has been neither forgotten nor forgiven."

"So you're, what, a local guerrilla faction?" said Stuart.

"Precisely."

"I've heard the rumours. Rebels in the rainforest, carrying out hit-and-run raids on Empire targets. That's you?"

"We're one of several loosely affiliated Mayan groups who've made it their mission to harry the Aztecs in Anahuac – sabotaging installations, killing dignitaries, and so forth. It's a thankless task. There are very few real Maya left. Most of the inhabitants of the Yucatan are so homogenised, so downtrodden, so under the yoke, that they regard us as traitors. Everybody around us scorns us and would rather we were dead. Yet we fight on, in the name of our distant ancestors, exacting revenge for their deaths and seeking to re-establish an independent Mayan state."

"And of course the Empire reciprocates."

"Violently, which doesn't aid our cause one bit. The retaliation for our attacks is always wildly disproportionate. Ten civilians are killed for every one Aztec official we execute. Whole villages are razed to the ground on suspicion of harbouring rebels. People are tortured horribly if it's believed they're withholding information that could lead to our capture." Chel raised his hands and let them drop into his lap. His eyes had lost some of their amiable twinkle. "It's awful. I feel guilt for the deaths of these innocents as if I personally have slain each and every one of them. Yet we must soldier on, because our motives are good, our goal a noble one."

"This is all very fascinating," Stuart said, "but..."

"But how does it relate to you? We in Xibalba

have been following the Conquistador's activities for a while, Mr Reston. Following them closely."

"Xibalba?"

"My group's name. Taken from the Mayan word for the underworld, the land of the dead. We consider ourselves as belonging there. Our skull makeup is disguise, like your mask and armour, and is intended to unnerve and intimidate our enemies. But it also symbolises our creed. We are, we believe, as good as dead. Every raid we embark on could be our last. Each of us isn't simply prepared to lay down his life, he has in effect done so in advance. 'Only by dying do you leave leave Xibalba.' That is our motto. We are committed to the hilt. We fight, liberated from fear by the knowledge that nobody can kill the man who is, in his mind, deceased already."

"Kind of fatalistic. Didn't the Japanese have a similar philosophy during the Pacific Takeover years? And look at them now. Among the Empire's most ardent supporters. The hub of Aztechnological development."

"What are you implying? That resistance is futile? Doomed to failure? Ironic, coming from a man who so nearly got brought down by Jaguar Warriors last night. If we hadn't rescued you..."

"I was doing fine," Stuart snapped.

"Bah!" Chel snorted. "Delusion. The Jaguars had you at bay. You were incredibly lucky that Xibalba chose to stake out that show, expecting the Conquistador would put in an appearance. We at least had foreseen what you had not: the possibility that the whole thing was a setup, those priests imposters."

"I realised there was a chance of that. It seemed remote, though, and the opportunity was too good, too juicy, to pass up. Twenty priests in one fell swoop."

"Admit it, you got overconfident. You saw a big fat prize you couldn't resist, and you didn't think twice."

Stuart kept his expression impassive, but inwardly he couldn't deny the truth of Chel's statement. He *had* got overconfident. Zeal had overcome prudence, and he had blundered straight into a trap. If not for Xibalba, right now he would be dead, the Conquistador's campaign at an end.

"I'm not looking for gratitude," Chel said. "I'm glad we were there and able to help out in your hour of need. But it does seem to me, as an observer, that you've been taking ever wilder risks. Your stunts are becoming more extreme by the day, as if you're trying to outdo yourself. Sooner or later you'll slip up, as you did last night – sorry, *nearly* did. You'll be caught and killed, and I for one would hate to see that happen. You see, we've been admiring your handiwork greatly, Mr Reston. Inspiring stuff. In just a few short months you, on your own, have caused the Empire as much grief as Xibalba's many members have in years. That's why we're here in Britain."

"To congratulate me? Give me a medal?"

"Don't be obtuse. To recruit you. We have need of your skills and expertise. Xibalba could truly do with a man like you in its ranks."

"I'm a solo operator," Stuart said immediately.

"I know, but –"

"It's worked okay for me so far. I don't think I could be part of a unit. I wouldn't mesh well."

"I would debate that. With your Eagle Warrior background, you know about giving and taking orders, chain of command, watching a comrade's back, teamwork, all of that."

"That was a long time ago. I've been my own boss ever since."

"You'd still be an invaluable asset to us," said Chel. "And, really, don't you yearn for a chance to hit the Empire right at its very heart? Destroy it once and for all?" The Mayan paused, then smiled. "I saw it – that telltale flash of curiosity on your face, just before you concealed it. You were thinking, Is it possible? Is this funny little round man really saying he can bring down the Empire?"

"I'd like to think it can be done," said Stuart. "Of course I would."

"But you'd settle for simply liberating your own country from oppression? Free Britain and leave the rest of the world to sort itself out?"

"Why not?"

"Do you honestly, in your heart of hearts, think that's going to happen? How?"

"The Conquistador's example will spark an uprising. People have seen me kill priests. I've shown our government to be vulnerable. In time, there'll be a groundswell, a mounting tide of anti-imperial sentiment that'll become a full-fledged revolt."

"Shouldn't it have begun by now? Where are the

protestors on the streets, Mr Reston? Where are the hordes of Conquistador-alikes emulating you?"

"Turning a large ship around takes a long time. If I keep at it, the public mood will shift eventually."

"Well, perhaps. Or perhaps, if you're really fortunate, a microbial infection will come along and wipe out all Aztecs, as it did the Martians in Wells's novel. A somewhat unconvincing conclusion, I've always thought. It suggests the author was dredging up hope where he himself felt none. Nevertheless, my proposal to you is this. Come with us to Anahuac. Work alongside us. We have a plan of action that will finish the Empire, and we'd like your assistance is implementing it."

"Go on, then," said Stuart. "What is it? What's the big idea?"

"Simple. Kill the Great Speaker."

STUART WAS SILENT for a full minute.

Then, shaking his head, he whistled softly and said, "You're crazy."

"Am I?"

"It's not possible. Can't be done. Tenochtitlan, the guards, the levels of security around him, not to mention his palace is stuck in the middle of a fucking great lake... Out of the question."

"But if it *could* be done, would you join us?"

"No."

"You're not even tempted? You've been a gadfly to the Empire, and that's all well and good, but what if you could help be its executioner? Kill the Great Speaker, cut off the Empire's head, and the Empire itself will surely wither and collapse."

"Still no. It sounds like a recipe for suicide. Pointless suicide. You'd never get anywhere near the Great Speaker. Certainly never get within striking range."

Chel sighed with heavy emphasis. "Then, alas, it seems I've had a wasted journey. Well, not entirely wasted. I've met the Conquistador in person, and managed to ensure that he can continue his dissidence a little while longer. That's something."

He rose and held out his hand.

"It's been a pleasure, Mr Reston," he said as they shook. "I can't say I'm not disappointed by the outcome of our chat, but" – he shrugged – "win some, lose some. Oh, we still have your armour, don't we? I know you have those other suits, but would you like it back?"

"Yes. They don't come cheap."

"Let us arrange its return. We'll be discreet, I assure you. In the meantime, please give further consideration to what I'm suggesting. Perhaps you'll change your mind."

"I won't," said Stuart.

"You might just," said Chel. "I'll see myself out."

SIX

Same Day

MAL AWOKE WITH a clanging hangover, her head throbbing as though there was a chainmailed fist inside trying to punch its way out. She made it to the bathroom just in time. Bent double over the toilet, she vomited until there seemed to be nothing left to come up but stomach lining.

A whole bottle of *pulque* would do that to you.

Trembling, her entire skeleton feeling as brittle as chalk, she fixed herself a mug of coca tea. She sat at the kitchen table, staring out of the window at the glow of yet another furnace-hot day. When the phone rang, she refused to answer it. It would be work calling. Probably Kellaway himself, full of spite and spittle. *Where the hell are you, chief inspector? Drag your sorry arse down to the Yard immediately!*

Twice more in the next half hour the phone rang. The sound bored into her ears like an electric drill. She nearly picked up the receiver just to stop the pain.

She was tempted to go back to bed, haul the covers over her head, and sleep for as long as she could. But her troubles weren't going to magically disappear, however hard she ignored them. The fiasco at Regent's Park had happened, and wishing it hadn't couldn't *un*happen it.

She showered, turning the water as cold as it would go. By means of this chilly dousing and more coca tea, she wrestled the hangover into submission. By the time she was dressed, Mal had regained some semblance of normality.

The phone rang yet again, and now she picked up. Bracing herself for the chief super at full blast, she was relieved to hear Aaronson's voice instead.

"Boss? Finally. It's gone ten. Why aren't you at work yet?"

"Why are you? You're supposed to be in hospital recovering."

"Aah, I discharged myself. It was fucking boring. Not a decent-looking doctor in sight, not like on the TV shows."

"But they said something about running more tests. On all of you who got poison-darted."

"For what? It was heavily-diluted curare. Enough of a dose to turn your muscles to noodles, but that's all, nothing worse. It wasn't much fun lying there unable to move, and I feel like shit now, but hey, I'm not dead. How about you?"

"Aftereffects of mild concussion. I've got a couple of goose-egg bruises on my skull, but I spent most of the night self-medicating. I'll be fine."

"Paying your respects to Mayahuel?"

"The goddess of the fermented agave plant did get a good deal of worshipping, yes," said Mal. "What's the mood like over there? Dare I show my face?"

"Everyone's still a bit staggered. Can't quite figure out how it all went so wrong, just when it looked like we were about to pull it off. Nobody's blaming you, but... Permission to speak freely?"

"Granted," Mal sighed.

"You need to be here. You need to put on a brave face and bluff it out. Better that than skulking at home, hiding. It'll look bad if you don't show, however much you'd like not to."

"Okay, Aaronson. Thanks for that. And thanks again for what you did at the theatre. Taking the dart for me. I... I really appreciate it."

"Too bad the Conquistador still got away. Who were those people, boss? Why did they save him?"

"Not the foggiest. But I aim to find out, and when I do, the bastards are dead meat."

"That's the spirit, boss. That's the Mal Vaughn I know and fear."

MAL COULDN'T REMEMBER a time when she hadn't dreamed of becoming a Jaguar Warrior. As a child, she had loved the formal uniform, especially the cat-head helmet that gleamed and snarled, with jade-like eyes that flashed in the sun.

Her brother Ix used to laugh at her whenever she admitted her ambition to join the force. At first, when they were little, he laughed because she was a girl, and a puny one at that, and he couldn't believe she would ever grow tall enough or brawny enough to look like the Jaguars they saw out patrolling the streets.

Later, when they were in their teens, Ix's laughter became more cynical. "Yeah, sis, great idea," he would say. "Be a paid thug. Carry a *macuahitl* and an l-gun. Beat up innocents and enforce the status quo. You go right ahead." By then Ix was running with a gang, petty crooks committing petty crimes, and his anti-establishment posturing was a self-justifying rationale for his delinquent behaviour. The Empire, the hieratic caste, the Jaguars, they were all parts of a machine designed to suppress the freedom of the individual – by which Ix meant the freedom of the individual to shoplift, vandalise, drink underage, and mug pensioners. He believed, although perhaps not as wholeheartedly as he might have liked, that by hanging out with his cronies and causing trouble he was somehow striking a blow against the system.

Whereas to Mal, and other right-thinking types, he was simply being a mindless twat.

They stopped talking, the two of them, the day Mal sent in her Jaguar Warrior application form. She had just turned eighteen, the minimum required age. She had filled out, too, no longer the stick insect she had been when little, now a sturdy young woman who had captained the school's senior girls *tlachtli* team and gained a reputation as the toughest player in the south London education authority leagues, with a string of broken opponents' noses and ankles to her credit.

"You disgust me," were Ix's last words to her before he turned his back on her for good. "Go be the Empire's whore. See if I care. You're fucking scum, that's what you are."

Brother and sister weren't to see each other again until a year after Mal finished her training and made constable. She knew from her parents that Ix had gone completely off the rails. He would turn up at their house now and then, usually after dark, looking wretched and demanding cash. He would become abusive if they didn't cough up, and there was that time he threatened their father with a knife. The old man was whisked to hospital the next day with a suspected heart attack. He recovered, but from then on was never the same. Weakened and sad. A shell of himself.

Eventually Ix's and Mal's paths crossed again, as she had somehow known they would. Ix had started working for a mob boss, Davey Furman, whose gang, the Battersea Batterers, ran most of the rackets south of the Thames, from Putney to Camberwell. Ix made himself useful shaking down shopkeepers for protection money, intimidating would-be grasses, and defending Batterers turf against incursions from rival gangs. At least he was earning a decent wage now, so that he didn't have to go terrorising their parents for handouts any more.

Furman had several people high up in the Jaguar Warrior ranks in his back pocket, and it was informal policy to turn a blind eye to his gangster activities unless they were unusually egregious. Then the incumbent High Priest died and a new man was elevated to that position, the current holder of the office, His Very Holiness Seldon Whitaker. Whitaker fancied himself a hardliner, with zero tolerance for criminality of any description. One of his first edicts, issued with new-broom zeal, was that organised racketeering in Britain's cities must come to an end.

Even corrupt police officials could not soft-pedal a direct and unequivocal order like that, so a clampdown got under way. In London that meant Battersea Batterer haunts were raided and ransacked. Known associates of Furman were brought in for interrogation, which many of them did not survive. Underlings were snatched off the streets, never to be seen again, except for those who ended up doing hard time in one of the Empire's notorious subterranean jails, and they were broken ghosts of themselves when they finally returned home. The gang was dismantled piecemeal, and its worst, most notorious felons were convicted of offences ranging from GBH to first degree murder, all of which carried the death penalty. The months after Whitaker took charge were not good ones for the urban mob fraternity, and the Batterers bore the brunt.

Which was why Mal was less than shocked when

her brother appeared on her doorstep in the small hours one night. She had been expecting it. That or finding his name on the list of death row inmates, awaiting execution.

"Help me," Ix begged. "Please. Only you can."

He looked a mess, grubby and unshaven, his expensive suit wrinkled and creased. He had been on the run for several days, he told Mal, sleeping rough or on friends' floors. The net was closing in around him. He'd gone to visit Furman but the Batterers' leader was nowhere to be found; word on the street was that he'd fled the country. The whole enterprise was falling down around the gang's ears. It had all turned to shit. There were Jaguars on every corner, hunting. Nowhere to hide.

"But you'll do right for me, won't you, Mal? I mean, I know we've had our differences in the past, but we're still brother and sister, still blood, beneath it all. And blood helps blood, yeah? If I'm caught, I'm dead, simple as that. But you can see that that doesn't happen, can't you?"

"How, Ix? What am I supposed to do? Put in a good word for you somewhere? Ask my colleagues to just sort of step around you? How exactly can I help? You got yourself up shit creek. I don't have the paddle."

He looked so crestfallen then that it nearly broke her heart. He became the little boy she remembered, two years older than her and often cruelly dismissive of her, but sensitive, too, at times, easily hurt if *she* rejected *him*. She recalled how he could be her mortal enemy at home but was ever ready to leap to her defence at school if she got bullied or was in trouble. She hated to see him crushed in this way. He regarded her as his last and only hope.

"Look," she said, "come in. I'll put you up for the night. I'll do right for you."

"Oh, thank you, Mal! By all the Four, thank you! I don't know what to say. You're the best," and he hugged her, hard, as he had never hugged her before. Mal made up a bed for him on the sofa, and Ix dropped straight off, snoring soundly in what was probably the deepest, sweetest sleep he had had in ages. She stayed up watching him for a long while, and then she did what was right for him. And for her.

Jaguar Warriors came at dawn. Mal let them in. Ix awoke to find himself surrounded by drawn *macuahitl*s. The Jaguars handcuffed him. He went quietly, too overwhelmed by her betrayal to resist or even to speak. At the last moment, as he was being manhandled out through the door to the waiting squad car, he turned and shot his sister a fulminous look. His eyes seethed with rage and outrage and, beneath that, sheer despairing agony.

Mal was invited to attend his beheading. She chose not to. Likewise their parents. Ix Vaughn was consigned to Mictlan alone, unwitnessed, sobbing his eyes out.

In return for having done her duty, Mal was promoted to acting sergeant, transferred to the CID and put on the fast track to an inspectorship. Loyalty to the Jaguars had outweighed loyalty to family, and that was truly laudable and deserving of reward.

Mal of course had not shopped her brother for personal gain. Her motive had simply been a desire not to see bad deeds go unpunished. That, to her, mattered more, far more than kinship.

She would never again feel the same way about being a Jaguar Warrior, however. Like her father after the heart attack, she had lost something vital. There was a taint on her life. Where before she'd had the courage of her convictions and an ability to keep the shadows of doubt at bay, now all that was gone. A single decision – a taking of sides – had changed her utterly and irrevocably.

In the years that followed, Mal advanced professionally in leaps and bounds, fully repaying the force's faith in her abilities. She was not quite the youngest person ever to be appointed detective, but close. She set about racking up an enviable tally of arrests and commendations. She earned a reputation as a harsh but fair taskmaster. She had the kind of career that parents would boast about, especially parents who were staunch Empire loyalists and showed it by giving their children Nahuatl forenames such as Ixtli and Malinalli, and even more especially parents whose other child had proved such a disappointment.

Where Mal's private life was concerned, things were less rosy. A lot of alcohol abuse went on, and the closest she got to a committed relationship was a short run of assignations with the same person, although that was rare. Usually she preferred the anonymous, no-strings drunken fuck, at the other participant's place not hers, followed by a bad-breathed but guiltless departure before breakfast. One-night stands with men, ideally much younger men, whom she would never have to meet again. Those and the booze stopped her thinking too hard about anything much. Her conscience was quietened. The shadows shrank.

Shrank but returned. Constantly returned, denser and darker. For almost a full solar year, Mal had felt she was losing the battle with her misgivings. Ix's words from all that time ago kept recurring to her. *Be a paid thug. Enforce the status quo. Empire's whore.* Was that all she was? Was that all any Jaguar Warrior was?

She wanted to do good. She wanted to help those who needed helping. And if somebody broke the law, they needed to be caught and made to face the consequences, however drastic. Morally, it was that straightforward.

Wasn't it?

Why, then, had it become so difficult to face going into work each morning? Why had she written that letter of resignation in her head, and refined and rewritten it, over and over until she had it by heart? Why did almost every punishment the Jaguars meted out, in the Empire's name, sicken her these days?

While a bus ferried her to Scotland Yard, Mal ran over these questions in her mind, as she often did. By journey's end she was no nearer answers than before.

The only positive she could glean from the previous night's spectacular cock-up was that if she carried on handling the Conquistador case as badly as this, the future wouldn't hold much more worrying for her. A *macuahitl* would soon be putting her out of her misery, and that would be that.

It was always good to look on the bright side.

KELLAWAY HARANGUED HER publicly, in front of the whole department, and she took it on the chin, drawing solace from two thoughts. One: the chief super needed to be seen to be yelling at someone, otherwise people might assume he was going soft. Two: as long as he was tearing a strip off her, he wasn't going to execute her. The latter was the more significant. It meant she still had breathing space. She was in the last chance saloon but the bartender hadn't called time yet.

An hour later Kellaway summoned her to his office. He was a whole lot more sanguine, and less red-faced, now, in private.

"Last night was a damn good shot, Vaughn," he said. "Best anyone's made to date. The shittest of luck that it didn't come off. Anything on those fellows with the blowpipes?"

"My guess is Anahuac, sir. Mayan separatists."

"That would make sense. Recruited by the Conquistador, or maybe employed. Hired muscle."

"Or possibly sympathisers to his cause. Fellow travellers. He seemed to have no idea who they were when they first appeared. Could be they're over here and on his side because they're... well, fans."

Kellaway rolled his eyes. "That's just what we need – more of the buggers. Think we can root this lot out somehow? Check the immigration records, for instance?"

"I can have Aaronson look to see if a bunch of Anahuac nationals have passed through customs lately, but we get people arriving from there all the time, and if our guys are on tourist visas, as is likely, they won't have to have specified a place of residence in Britain."

"How about shaking a few cheap hotels, see what falls out?"

"Could do."

"You don't sound too enthusiastic."

"With respect, sir, I think the Mayans are a red herring. A sideshow, not the main event. I should really be focusing on the Conquistador."

"If you say so," said Kellaway.

"I'm not against exploring other avenues, but it's the Conquistador who's at the centre of all this, and catching him might just lead us to the Mayans, too. If I could only figure out who he really is... I mean, he's a civilian when he's not playing sociopath dress-up. He has another, discrete existence. It shouldn't be impossible, based on what we know about him, to narrow down a shortlist of suspects and interview all of them."

"Interview as in 'interview'?" The emphasis Kellaway placed on the word was unmistakable. What went on in the basement of Scotland Yard wasn't pleasant, but it had been proven to work.

"It needn't be that drastic," said Mal. "Under duress or not, whichever one's the Conquistador is bound to give himself away. There's a vanity about the man. Up on that stage yesterday, he wouldn't bloody shut up. We prey on that, goad him, prompt him, he'll reveal his true colours soon enough. Plus, I'll recognise his voice."

"How? The mask distorts it."

"Not so much the voice itself – the speech patterns, the syntax, the choice of words. Some one-on-one time with him, that's all it'll take. Me and him in a room together. I'll know."

"How many would there be on this shortlist?"

"I don't know, sir. A dozen. Two dozen. A hundred. Depends on what my researches turn up. Why?"

"Why do you think?" Kellaway smoothed a hand compulsively through his thinning hair. So few strands left, all the more important to keep them in line. "The commissioner's leaning even more heavily on me. Wants results, and now. The news people have been asked to go easy on reporting the Conquistador's exploits, play it down, not sensationalise, and mostly they're falling into line. But you can't avoid the bare facts getting out there. Skew them how you will, they spread, the public takes note, and the Conquistador gets the attention he craves. My theory is that's what's behind the murder of Priest Marquand. Someone's been reading the headlines and decided to get in on the action. And we can't have that, Vaughn. We can't have Conquistador wannabes. One's bad enough. And now these Mayans... If this should turn into some kind of contagion, which is what the commissioner's afraid of, then where will we be?"

"How about instituting a blanket ban on all media coverage of the Conquistador? High Priest Whitaker could issue a formal decree. That might help limit the, as you put it, contagion."

"The commissioner and I discussed the possibility. Partly the trouble is, we're too late. The cat is well out of the bag. If the Conquistador suddenly vanished from the airwaves and the front pages, it would smack of government interference. And above all else the freedom of the press is sacrosanct."

"The illusion of the freedom of the press, don't you mean?"

"Yes, well." Kellaway waved airily: *same difference.* "His Very Holiness would have no problem with the idea of depriving the Conquistador of the oxygen of publicity, but all said and done, he'd rather deprive him of oxygen full stop. In fact, as I understand it from the commissioner, the only thing that'll make the High Priest truly happy is the Conquistador's head on a railing spike outside Westminster. Which brings us back to you."

Mal nodded sombrely. "Yes, it does."

"The one surefire means of undoing everything the Conquistador's done, rectifying the damage he's caused, is capturing him and making an example of him. All the very worst punishments available have to be visited on him, and his suffering has to be photographed and written about and filmed and broadcast, every minute of it, every single excruciating second. So that people know. So that they won't forget. So that they'll be discouraged from trying anything like it, ever again. I like this shortlist idea of yours, chief inspector. It shows I was right to give you the job. You've got flair and imagination, something all your predecessors lacked, including that plodder Nyman."

"Thank you, sir."

"You have *carte blanche* to carry on the investigation in whatever way you see fit. You have an unlimited budget at your disposal. What you don't have is time. Get cracking. We need resolution on this. We need a result. For the good of the nation, find the fucking Conquistador!"

"You. You. And you. You as well. And you, the one trying to hide – yes, you."

Mal swept through the department, pulling junior officers from their desks.

"Drop what you're doing. Whatever it is, it's not important right now. As of this moment, you're on my detail. You answer to me. And if you want to whinge about it, take it up with the chief super. Then watch him wrench off some vital part of your anatomy along with your badge."

She commandeered a situation room, and addressed her small task force of new recruits.

"Here's how it is," she said. "By tonight I want you to have compiled a list of potential Conquistadors.

We don't have a lot to go on, but we do know this about him. He's male. About six one, solidly built, thirteen, fourteen stone, something like that. In his late twenties, early thirties. Military background. I know, I know, that could describe thousands of people, but we can whittle it down further. He's local, that's almost certain. Almost all of his attacks have occurred in and around the capital. It'd be reasonable to assume he's a Londoner. Also, he has a fair bit of dosh. Not rich, necessarily, but he abandoned a suit of armour the other day and turned up in another one yesterday evening. Those things must cost a bob or two, so we can assume he's not penniless. Finally, he's nursing some sort of deep-felt grudge against the Empire. Don't know what, don't know why, but it'll flag itself up when combined with all the other criteria. Questions?"

There was a way of asking "Questions?" that indicated you weren't actually interested in hearing any. Mal used it.

"Then what are you waiting for, ladies and gentlemen? Quetzalcoatl to return? Move your arses."

IT WAS A long day, and it stretched well into the evening. Mal coaxed, chivvied and cajoled throughout, fuelled by the cups of coca Aaronson fetched for her, every hour, on the hour. Her team went through criminal records, military records, financial records, sifting, sorting, cross-referencing. When she saw their energy levels begin to wane, she pushed them to redouble their efforts. She led by example, refusing to show an ounce of the bone-deep tiredness she was feeling. The bruises left by the bolas balls ached. Just to hold her head up required superhuman stamina. But she could not flag, could not fail. There was so much at stake here, not least her own life. She was thirty-two. Not ready for Tamoanchan yet, or even the other place. And the chief super was depending on her, the commissioner too, the High Priest himself. She wasn't going to let anyone down.

Finally, verging on midnight, she sent everyone home, Aaronson included. They'd all put in a good day's work, and plenty of overtime, and between them they'd managed to rustle up a list of thirty-odd candidates each of whom fit the profile for the Conquistador.

Mal herself would gladly have gone home too. She was so exhausted she could barely see straight. Her coca buzz was fading and she knew that if she drank any more of the stuff she could pass out and maybe even end up in hospital with cardiac arrhythmia. It was down to just her now, her and her own inner resources.

She arranged the candidate dossiers on a table. Some had mugshots clipped to them, others not. She read through each one carefully. In many instances, the sum total of knowledge about the man amounted to no more than a few lines of text. With others, particularly those who had spent time being detained at His Very Holiness's pleasure, there was a great deal of information, none of it painting them in a flattering light. Her gut instinct told her that the Conquistador wasn't likely to be part of this parade of model citizens – stalkers, pub brawlers, wife beaters, flashers, kiddie fiddlers. They all of them used to be lower-ranked Eagle Warriors, non-coms, cannon fodder. Given his cunning and his articulacy, the Conquistador would have been higher up the pecking order, officer class.

By this process of elimination she was able to cut the number of suspects by half. That still left nigh-on twenty possibles, however, and no amount of filtering or compare-and-contrasting could seem to get that total any lower. Each man was as much Conquistador material as the next. The business executive? The blueblood? The publishing tycoon? The *tlachtli* team manager? Which?

There was nothing else for it. Mal jotted down the remaining candidates' names on a sheet of paper, then left the building. She went out into Campbell-Bannerman Street, the broad thoroughfare formerly known as Victoria Street, renamed after the prime minister who signed the peace accord with the Empire, embraced the faith and became Britain's first ever High Priest – all on the same day. A few blocks down from the Yard, there was a twenty-four-hour pharmacy. Mal approached the counter and asked for a vision quest package. The pharmacist demanded to be shown ID. The sight of Mal's Jaguar Warrior badge knocked some of the snootiness out of him.

"That seems to be in order, madam," he said. "One has to be careful. One doesn't sell vision quest packages to just anybody. The law prohibits... but then you already know what the law prohibits." He was flustered.

"Don't panic, I'm not here to bust you. Unless you've been selling drug tinctures to people who aren't certified sane enough to use, which I'm sure you haven't."

"Indeed not! Never!"

"Then we're fine. I really am here to buy a package, that's all."

"Then let me be of service. Any particular preference? What sort of vision are you hoping to achieve? Prognostication? Communion with the gods? Self-realisation? Recreation? We have tinctures to suit all sorts, all of them naturally sourced and prepared according to time-honoured recipes."

"I'm looking for answers. I need to make a choice."

"Any specific choice?"

"Between men."

The pharmacist interpreted this in a certain way and raised an eyebrow. "You're after a husband?"

"No, I'm not. And I hope you're not volunteering."

He wanted to snipe back at her, but couldn't. It didn't pay to get lippy with a Jaguar. "I misunderstood. I beg your pardon."

"I'm just after... clarity, I suppose. Insight into a dilemma."

"Ah. Might I recommend, then, a draught of psilocybin mixed with honey? It's traditional, highly palatable, goes down a treat, and the effects are gentle but potent. I prepare it specially myself, from mushrooms grown by reputable wholesalers, and my customers report back that the results are always satisfactory and that – ahem – 'bad trips' are rare."

"Okay. If that fits the bill. I'll take one dose."

"Might I enquire whether you've had experience with hallucinogens before, madam?"

"A little. I used to dabble. Nowadays, not so much."

"Are you on any medication?"

"No."

"Do you have any underlying chronic health problems?"

"No."

"Any ailments or diseases you're presently suffering from?"

"Only premature mortality syndrome," Mal muttered under her breath.

"Excuse me?"

"Nothing. No diseases."

"Splendid. I've just mixed up a fresh batch of 'magic honey,' as it happens. It's in the cold store. Back in a jiffy."

MAL TOOK THE psilocybin-honey draught home. The pharmacist recommended using it in a familiar, comfortable environment. That would help anchor her, in the event of "problems" occurring. He also suggested she void bladder and bowels beforehand, wear a loose-fitting garment, keep the telephone to hand just in case, and light a single candle but place it well out of reach where it couldn't be accidentally knocked over. He wished her luck on her vision quest and handed her a receipt so that she could claim back the cost of the trip on expenses.

Mal set everything up as suggested. She sat herself cross-legged on the floor in a cotton kimono. The candle flickered on the mantelshelf. She held up the little phial of amber-yellow liquid, studying it by the dim flame light. At last she unstoppered it, raised it to her lips, took a deep breath, then swigged the tincture down in one gulp.

This was it. No going back now.

She placed the sheet of paper with the suspects' names on it in front of her, propping it up against a cushion. She ran her gaze over the list countless times until she had memorised them all. Then she closed her eyes.

The sickly-sweet taste of the tincture clogged the back of her throat. She listened to the sounds in the flat – the whir of the air conditioning in the bedroom, the churn of the refrigerator in the kitchen, the occasional moth's wingbeat of the candle as it guttered. She listened to the city noises outside too, and the floorboard-creaking footfalls of the young couple in the flat above as they prepared for bed. She hoped they weren't about to indulge in one of their marathon sex sessions. That could definitely mess with her trip, hearing the accelerating thudding of bedstead against wall and the rising moans and groans that seemed to last forever.

The names, Mal told herself. *Fix your focus on the names, nothing else.*

She felt odd. She felt light-headed. It passed. Then it returned, and her consciousness seemed to narrow inside her brain, becoming attenuated, like a wisp of smoke. There was herself and another self. She was Mal Vaughn, the physical entity, and a separate Mal Vaughn, a traveller in her body, a driver, a woman at the wheel who was gradually taking her hands off the controls. The car was coasting to a halt. It was on a night road somewhere, at a clifftop, far above a crashing sea. The cliff was extraordinarily tall, so high she couldn't hear the sea any more. There were only stars. She was up among constellations, where the gods flew. The stars were points of ice, not suns. They had no heat. If you touched them they could cut like diamonds. You could pluck them out of the earth, if you wished to, like a miner in a mine. With your rock hammer and chisel you could dig pure raw starstuff out of the ground, the elements of creation, brilliant glints in the darkness. Mal was down below and up above at once, at the same time, in a confined space and surrounded by infinite space. Two things simultaneously. Opposites. Oneness in duality.

Almost as if on instinct, she latched on to that. Oneness in duality. A basic tenet of faith. One of the fundamentals of the Aztec religion. But also the Conquistador. What was he but two people in one, one person acting as two? He was contradiction. He had his real face and his public face. He had the face he saw in the mirror every day and his other face, his masked face, his not-face, the one he was famed for. He was a known unknown. He was a presence who was an absence. He was a celebrity whose identity was a secret. His truth was a falsehood. His pretence was a fact. His existence was nonexistent.

Who are you?

The names cycled through Mal's mind. The names had colours. No, the names *were* colours. Each came with its own particular shade, its own suite of emotions and resonances. Some were brighter, brasher than others. They flared and swirled. Some came to the fore, others retreated into the background. They were like a painting she could walk through. Some were hot to the touch, others cool. They formed arches, corridors, labyrinthine crystalline structures.

Who are you? Tell me.

The names blurred and sharpened as though a camera was pulling focus, trying to zoom in on distant objects, fathoming depth of field. They echoed, speaking themselves. They became a jumble of syllables, overlapping, fusing together in new and unintelligible amalgamations. She was losing hold. Her grip on the vision was slipping. The names were melting, growing meaningless, the blabbering idiolect of a pre-speech infant.

Come on!

One of them must be her man. One of them, she was sure, had to be the key to the Conquistador.

Remember them. Remember the names.

There was Charles Wooding. There was Christopher Martin. There was Christopher Wooding. No. Martin Christopher. Christin Martopher. Inopher Chrismart.

No. Try again. Try harder.

Will Wood. No. Will Wilson. No. Wilson Willing.
Concentrate.

There was Mick Land. No, no such person. She was thinking of Mictlan. There was Stuart Land. No, not Land. But Stuart someone, definitely. There was Chal Wooding. Yes. Chal. Full forename Chalchiuhtotolin, after an aspect of Quetzalcoatl.

Him?

No. Cold blue. Hazy. Like a far-off view of mountains. Not him.

Keep trying. Go on.

She fought to keep the names orderly, in shape. She forced herself to pay attention only to the hot ones, the clear ones, that ones that proclaimed themselves more loudly than the rest. She beckoned them towards her like cats, charmed them like snakes, banana-bribed them like monkeys.

One of you. It's one of you.

And now she could feel the honeyed psilocybin wearing off. The magic mushrooms were losing their abracadabra. Gross physicality was setting in, the blood rush and lung heave and wet digestiveness of the body. Her kimono's cotton grated coarsely on her skin. The sounds around her – and yes, the couple upstairs were in the throes of full-throttle nookie – were deafening. Could a humble candle really shine as brilliantly as the sun?

One of you.

It hovered close. The name. Oh, that name. She must make a grab for it, snatch it now, otherwise it would recede, fade, be gone for good.

One of...

A desperate mental lunge. A clawing at a thing that was almost vanished. A grasping at vapour.

...you.

She had it. She had it!

The name in her mind's hand.

Mal snapped back into the world, fully awake.

Gotcha.

SEVEN

9 Rain 1 Monkey 1 House
(Friday 30th November 2012)

"MR RESTON? THERE'S someone in the lobby for you. A Miss Malinalli Vaughn."

"I don't know any Malinalli Vaughn. Does she have an appointment?"

"Nothing down in the diary, sir, but she says you'll want to see her. A matter of some urgency, she says."

"I've a lot on my plate. Book her in for another time, Helen, whoever she is."

"Of course, sir."

Stuart resumed his perusal of the papers relating to the CCMM buyout. The owners of the Mount Etna lode were pushing for some kind of share swap deal with Reston Rhyolitic. This would materially advantage them but not him, and he was loath to accept it. He was already offering a decent price, well above market value, and what with that and the bribes for local officials he didn't feel obliged to throw in any more sweeteners. If Signor Addario's employers weren't happy with the terms of the contract as it stood, all Stuart had to do was tear it up and walk away. Let them find another buyer with the financial leverage and pre-existing infrastructure he had. Good luck with that.

The intercom on his desk buzzed again.

"Sir. Sorry to trouble you."

"What, Helen?"

The receptionist coughed and lowered her voice. "This Miss Vaughn. She's very insistent. She's, erm, she's a Jaguar Warrior. Plainclothes. Says she'll make a fuss, rather loudly, if she doesn't see you immediately."

"Jaguar? You're sure?"

"She has a badge."

"Did she mention what this is in connection with?"

"No, sir. Should I ask?"

"No. No, don't. Just send her up."

"Very good, sir."

Stuart shunted the CCMM papers aside. He straightened his tie and smoothed down the lapels of his jacket. He clenched and unclenched his fists, then flexed all his fingers, like a concert pianist warming up to play some complex étude.

It could be nothing. Routine Jaguar business. They liked to poke their noses into other people's affairs every now and then, just because they could.

Rummage about. Throw their weight around. Remind everyone who was boss.

But if it wasn't that...

He could front it out. Easily. They had nothing on him. He'd left no tracks.

At worst, this was a fishing expedition. And the Vaughn woman could dangle her line all she liked, she wouldn't be getting so much as a nibble.

His PA, Tara, escorted the Jaguar Warrior from the lift, through her own antechamber office and into her boss's much larger and plusher office. She enquired if she could fetch anyone anything. Drink? Snack? Stuart dismissed her.

"Mal Vaughn. Detective chief inspector, Metropolitan Jaguar CID."

"Mind if I see credentials?"

"Of course not." She showed him a gold badge in a wallet – the yowling cat's head – with her photograph and warrant number on a card next to it. "Satisfied?"

"Looks authentic enough."

"Believe me, Mr Reston, the person who carries a forged one of these is living on borrowed time."

Chief Inspector Vaughn was broad-shouldered, short-necked, perhaps running to fat a little, but with a bosom and bum like hers that was no sin. She had fulsome lips and a close-cropped bob with a severe fringe. Her eyes were large and round, the irises steel grey. From first impressions she was, Stuart thought, his type. Intelligent without being cerebral, slightly dissolute, physically assured, in control of herself and well able to keep her neuroses in check. She was the polar opposite of Sofia, whom he had loved dearly and should never have married.

As he sized her up, he could see her doing the same to him. Her job demanded she look unimpressed, but she didn't quite manage to pull it off.

"Nice place," she said, glancing around. "Triple aspect. Amazing views. You're a lucky man, Mr Reston."

"I had a good start in life, but it's my own acumen that's kept me and my company on top. Luck's had nothing to do with it."

"Good thing obsidian is so popular with the regime. Where would we all be without it?"

"You wouldn't have a sword, for starters."

"True. Not that I carry one in the normal course of duty."

"You leave that to the uniforms."

"Right. I only wear mine on special occasions. Like, for instance, when I'm hot on the trail of a felon."

"Pleasing to note you're swordless right now."

"Why would you assume I think you're a felon, Mr Reston? Guilty conscience?"

"On the contrary. I'm merely pointing out that, by your logic, your lack of armament indicates that you don't suspect me of anything."

"Why am I here, then?"

"Aren't you meant to tell me that? Or have you come just to admire the decor and the view?"

Chief Inspector Vaughn approached one of the massive tinted plate-glass windows and looked out.

"Might as well, while I can. How the other half lives and all that. Don't see anything like this when I'm stuck in my little cubbyhole at the Yard."

London simmered. The ziggurat-shaped tower blocks of Canary Wharf, the apex of one of which was home to Reston Rhyolitic, seemed to pulse beneath the hard-beating sun. The palm-lined streets and avenues were strips of scintillating green. A storm was brewing to the east, purple-black thunderheads boiling up on the horizon, out over the North Sea. When the rain came, it would be a welcome antidote to the heat.

"You had a wife and son," she said.

"That's correct."

"Sofia and Jack."

"*Jake.*" *But you knew that already. You're not the sort to slip up on details.*

"They're not with us any more."

"Yes. So?"

"Would you mind telling me how they died?"

"I would. I don't see that it's any business of yours."

"Jaguar Warrior. Everything's my business."

"Perhaps if I knew why you want to know..."

"Perhaps if you could just answer the fucking question."

They held each other's gazes. Seconds stretched.

"Well," said Stuart, "as it happens, they volunteered for sacrifice. I say 'they.' Sofia did."

"Your son had no choice?"

"How could he? He was two."

"And why did Mrs Reston put herself and your son forward for sacrifice?"

"You'd have to ask her."

"You don't know?"

"Sofia was... not always a well-balanced individual. There were psychological issues. She was prone to mental disturbance, depression."

"So to opt for sacrifice one must be mentally disturbed, is that what you're saying?"

"No, chief inspector. I never said anything of the sort. Don't put words in my mouth."

"Most regard giving your life to the gods as the sanest, most rational act imaginable. Patriotic, what's more."

"Most do."

"But you're not one of them," the policewoman said archly.

"I wouldn't go in for it myself." Stuart gestured around him. "Why, when I have such a good life?"

"Your wife, presumably, had a good life too. Being Mrs Stuart Reston, she couldn't have wanted for much. A lovely home, I'd imagine. Plenty of disposable income. A respected, successful husband. A son."

"Materially she had all she could wish for. But – perhaps you've heard this, Miss Vaughn – money can't buy happiness."

"Were you cruel to her?"

"Of course not. I resent you even suggesting it."

"Why did you marry her?"

"What do you mean?"

"If she was unstable. Didn't you sense that? Didn't alarm bells start ringing before the wedding bells did?"

Stuart drew a deep breath. She was not going to rattle him, this lackey of the state. She was trying to, with her probing, her impertinence. She would not succeed.

"Sofia was a vibrant human being," he said. "She was beautiful. When she was comfortable within her skin, when she was herself, she was a dream. She lit up a room. She had a way of drawing everyone around her to her and making them feel at home and at ease. She was also a woman of high standing, accomplished, eminently marriageable. She'd had a hundred proposals and turned them all down."

"But then you came along, number one hundred and one, and she said yes."

"It wasn't easy. It was a long, drawn-out campaign. But I was persistent, and in the end she succumbed."

"Campaign," said Chief Inspector Vaughn. "Interesting use of military terminology."

Stuart gave a light shrug. "A stint with the Eagles. You pick up a phrase or two along the way."

The detective moved away from the window, closer to him. "You achieved your objective, then. Set your sights on a high-society lady and bagged her. Made a good match. And you had no reason to suspect there was anything wrong with her?"

"There *was* nothing wrong with Sofia," Stuart stated adamantly. "She had her flaws, she wasn't perfect, but then who of us is, chief inspector? You could say she was a bit tightly wound at times. At other times, perhaps not tightly wound enough. But it wasn't until after Jake was born that the trouble really began. He was a difficult birth and an awkward baby. Sofia had a wretched time with him. He wouldn't sleep, wouldn't feed properly. Colicky. Sick a lot. She had help, of course. Nannies, nurses, domestic staff, the best available, the costliest. But she insisted on doing the bulk of the work herself. She felt such a depth of maternal responsibility. She loved Jake as hard as any mother loved a child."

"Could you have done more?"

The needling was persistent, he had to give her that. And accurate.

"Maybe I could have," he admitted. "But I couldn't neglect my job. I had responsibilities too. I blame myself for not spotting the cracks sooner. The changes in Sofia's behaviour. The mood swings. The long periods when she was withdrawn and uncommunicative. I just thought she was exhausted, wrung out to the last drop. Had I been a little less preoccupied with Reston Rhyolitic, maybe I could have leapt in and saved her. Saved them both."

"Was there any warning?"

"What of?"

"That she was going to do what she did."

"No. None. Had Sofia discussed it with me, I'd have done my damnedest to talk her out of it."

"Why?"

"What do you mean, why?"

"Why would you try to talk her out of answering the call of the gods? If she felt a compulsion to be part of a blood rite, why would you not approve?"

"Because she was my wife and I loved her and I didn't want to lose her. Or my son."

"But children are especially blessed if they die under the priest's knife. Their souls go straight to Tamoanchan, where they frolic at the feet of Quetzalcoatl all day and sleep in a dormitory next to his throne room all night. Jake could not be happier on earth than he is now, in the gods' company."

"Jake," said Stuart, "belongs at my side. He would be four now, just starting school, and I would be with him every step of the way, teaching him what I know, giving him all he needs to become a man. Sofia took him from me, and herself as well, and the gods received what the gods did not deserve to have."

Those grey eyes glinted like gunmetal. "Must make you pretty cross, that, huh? I bet you're pissed off with your wife, but because she's not around to be pissed off with, you resent the Empire instead."

"That would be absurd. To transfer one's emotions onto an abstract, unfeeling entity? What would be the point?"

"The blame's got to go somewhere."

"I told you, if I blame anyone, it's myself. I could have been more on the ball. I could have been more sensitive to Sofia's needs. A better husband."

"Self-hatred has a way of turning outward."

"I still don't see what all this is about, Inspector Vaughn. What are you driving at? Why all these questions about my wife and son? Their deaths are a matter of public record. There's no secret involved. I've nothing to hide. It happened while I was abroad on a business trip. Sofia chose her moment well. She was cunning, in the way that the mentally ill sometimes are. She knew if I'd got a sniff of what she was up to, I'd have moved heaven and earth to prevent it."

"Business trip," said the chief inspector. "Funny you should mention that."

"Funny why?"

"Actually, you know what? I'm parched. Long day yesterday, late night last night. Could your PA whip me up a coca tea?"

"I'm sure it could be arranged." Stuart pressed a button on the intercom and placed the drink order with Tara. Five minutes of smouldering silence later, in she came with a tray.

Vaughn noted the single cup. "Nothing for you?"

"I don't partake," said Stuart. "That'll be all, Tara, thanks. Hold my calls for the time being. The chief inspector here seems to have a lot she wants to chat about."

"Yes, sir."

"You were saying?" he prompted, after Tara had gone. "Something about a business trip?"

"Yes. Ooh, good coca. Classy stuff. Straight from the slopes of the Andes, if I don't miss my guess."

"They have the best plantations there. I'm told the home-grown strains don't compare."

"I speak as someone with a lifelong habit – this is seriously good shit."

She meant it, too. Stuart could see this wasn't some devious tactic of hers, designed to disarm.

Chief Inspector Vaughn was genuinely taken with the quality of the coca on offer at Reston Rhyolitic.

He didn't believe for one moment, however, that he had won the duel.

"Anyway, business trip, yes," she continued. "Would I be right in thinking that you travelled to Italy recently, on business?"

"You would be wrong."

"Really?"

"It was Sicily. Don't ever confuse the two places, certainly not in the presence of a Sicilian."

"But the date of the excursion was Six Vulture One Monkey, yes? I'm not wrong about that?"

"I believe it was."

"I know it was. I checked. What's curious is, that very same day His Holiness Priest Marquand was killed – nastily – at Heathrow, along with his bodyguards. In fact, I understand His Holiness happened to be on the very same inbound flight that you were on."

"I don't recall. In all likelihood he was."

"I'm telling you he was, because the records back me up."

"How do you know? Priests don't have to log their comings and goings. They don't have to register at customs."

"True, but airlines are obliged by law to make a special note of every commercial flight that carries a priest. Should the aerodisc crash or go missing, the hieratic caste need to know if one of their own is aboard, so that steps can be taken as soon as possible to replace him. It's not public knowledge that this happens, but it's been official protocol for many years."

Shit, thought Stuart.

He said, "So what if we were on the same disc? There were three hundred other passengers on the flight. Any one of them could have murdered His Holiness. As could any one of the hundreds of people who were airside at the time."

"It's an intriguing coincidence, though," said Chief Inspector Vaughn. "You being there. A man with Eagle training, what's more."

"My Eagle days were long ago."

"But the army taught you how to kill with your bare hands."

"And the police taught you the same. Maybe one of your lot did it. Ever thought of that?"

"No motive," she replied flatly. "The Jaguars exist to serve and protect the state, not murder its representatives."

"But it is, after all, as you say, a coincidence. Just chance. That's not enough to pin the guilt for it on me."

"True. As a matter of fact, it's probably the one crime for which nobody could lay a finger on you."

"Implying there are others you can."

"Where were you, Mr Reston, on the night of Seven Movement One Monkey?"

"Look, when the fuck *was* that?" said Stuart. "The *tonalpohualli* calendar is so damn confusing. Day-signs, *trecena*s, two different lengths of year...

Why couldn't we have kept the Gregorian? So much more bloody logical and easy to follow."

"Let me simplify it for you, then," said the detective. "The evening before last. Where were you?"

"Home."

"That's it? Home?"

"Home."

"Is there anybody who can confirm that?"

"No."

"You were just... home."

"Yes. Alone. Catching up on a spot of paperwork."

"You weren't, by any chance, at the Regent's Park outdoor theatre?"

"No. Should I have been? What was on?"

"A hell of a show, actually."

"Really? Well, I'm sorry to have missed it."

"So you can't account for your whereabouts that night."

"Yes, I can. I told you. I was home."

"If you start getting obstructive with me, Mr Reston, we can always carry on this conversation down at the Yard. It's a whole lot less congenial there than here, and the tone will be a whole lot less civil."

"How am I being obstructive?" Stuart protested. "I'm giving you straight answers to your questions. What more do you want?"

"So you're telling me that no one else can confirm that you were at your house all evening?"

"My flat. I'm a widower, a single man. I don't need a house any more. And no, no one can corroborate my claim. What part of 'alone' are you finding so hard to comprehend, chief inspector?"

"It's really not much of an alibi, is it?"

"Agreed, it's not. Had I known in advance that I'd need to come up with an alibi for myself on the night in question, then I'd have made sure I had one. I simply didn't realise it would be required. Sorry."

The detective looked at him askance. "You are one conceited son of a bitch, you know that?"

Stuart gave her a blank stare in return. "Let's get down to brass tacks, inspector. Are you or are you not here to accuse me of something? And if so, what?"

"You know full well what."

"Clearly I don't."

"Am I going to have to come right out and say it?"

"I think you are."

"All right." She set her jaw. "Mr Reston, I have good reason to believe that you are the mass-murdering terrorist known as the Conquistador."

Stuart hesitated. Then he burst out laughing. "Preposterous! What proof do you have? Give me a single shred of evidence that says I am."

"Priest Marquand's murder."

"Was the Conquistador seen there? Are there any eyewitnesses who can place him at the scene?"

"No, but –"

"There you go."

"But it has all the hallmarks of a Conquistador attack. The only difference was, it was unplanned. You just didn't happen to have your armour handy.

You seized the moment, thinking you'd rack up another dead priest to add to your total."

"Pure supposition. Assuming I was the Conquistador, would I really do something so rash? Why?"

"Because you're cocky. You're out of control. You're so far into this, you just can't help yourself any more."

"And I'm killing priests for what reason, precisely?"

"Because priests killed your wife and son."

"*Sacrificed* them. Crucial distinction."

"Same end result, though. They wound up dead."

"My wife put herself on the altar voluntarily. It was her decision. Nobody forced her to do it."

"Except the voices inside her head."

"Crudely put, but yes. You could, perhaps, call it suicide by theocracy. But then to hate the entire hieratic caste for it, to want to seek revenge on them – it's not logical."

"Is it not?" said Chief Inspector Vaughn. "Grief *isn't* logical, though. It takes all sorts of strange forms. Grievance is one of them."

"You sound like someone who knows whereof she speaks."

Bullseye. A tiny flinch of the policewoman's eyes. Stuart had at last scored a hit against her.

"You think grief would compel a man to dress up in armour," he continued, "and visit vigilante justice on his nation's ruling elite?"

"I wouldn't put it past him. Past you. You fit all the criteria. You have the resources, the training, the capability, above all the motivation."

"Ultimately a self-defeating course of action,

though, wouldn't you agree?" said Stuart. "Suppose I, as the Conquistador, manage to foment a revolution, as he intends to. The people rise up, stage a coup, throw off the shackles of imperial rule, declare an independent Britain. What then? I'm out of a job, for starters. What use is the obsidian trade in a country no longer run along Empire lines?"

"In answer to that, I'd say that you haven't thought that far ahead. You want to satisfy your thirst for vengeance here and now. The rest – the further ramifications – can all take care of itself. You're not bothered, so long as priests and acolytes and anyone else directly associated with the Empire die in their droves. Besides," she added, "rich man like you, I reckon you've got enough money salted away in assets and savings that you could manage pretty well for yourself even without income from your company."

"What this comes down to, Miss Vaughn, is that you've made your mind up about me. I'm the Conquistador, that's decided, and you won't be swayed from your opinion. Trouble is, other than the happenstance of me sharing a flight with His Holiness Marquand, there's nothing to connect me to any of the Conquistador's killings – and we're not even sure Marquand was one of those. Therefore, unless you have actual concrete proof to back up these wild allegations of yours, I would ask you kindly to go away now and stop harassing me."

The detective bridled. "You do not talk to a Jaguar Warrior in that way."

"Oh, I think I do," Stuart shot back.

"I could have you down the nick in three seconds flat. I could have a dozen of the burliest men on the force working you over, just on my say-so."

"Then why don't you?"

"Don't tempt me."

"You won't, can't, because you know it won't fly. The Jaguars can get away with pretty much anything, but hauling in Stuart Reston for questioning? *The* Stuart Reston? On the flimsiest of hunches that he might be the Conquistador? I think not. I'm a public figure. I'm regarded as part of the state apparatus, much as you yourself are. Without something cast-iron against me, you'd risk making yourself and the force as a whole look pretty foolish. You'd be doing the Conquistador's work for him. And once I got out of custody – and I would, you can be sure of that – I'd make sure the world knew all about it. A misstep like that, I doubt you'd ever recover from."

"I have nothing to lose."

"I think you do. Otherwise you'd have arrested me already."

"All right. Granted. But..." Chief Inspector Vaughn leaned in close and lowered her voice to a lion-like growl. "You'd better pray I never get to the point where I do have nothing to lose. Because then, matey, you are well and truly buggered."

Stuart stood his ground. The skirmish was over. He didn't think he'd won but he had at least forced a stalemate.

"Perhaps you should leave now, chief inspector," he said.

"Oh, I'm going," she replied. "But this isn't the last you'll be hearing from me. Definitely not the last."

She looked as though she was about to turn away. Stuart saw the punch coming. Her upper body tensed. She began to pivot on the ball of one foot.

He could have blocked it. He knew how. Every instinct told him to.

But a flash-thought said, *It's a test. She wants confirmation. You have to fail it.*

So the punch landed, smack dab on his jaw, undeflected, and it was a cracker of a blow, carrying all her weight behind it, expertly swung. Stuart's head exploded, and his legs crumpled. He had thought he would have to fake pain as he lay there on the floor of his office, so as to discourage her from giving him another wallop, but the pain was genuine and raw. His jaw fucking well hurt. Hurt like flames.

He looked up at her, wincing, smarting. "What the – what the hell was *that* for?"

"Just because. Think of it as a downpayment, Mr Tycoon. A promise of more to come."

So saying, Chief Inspector Vaughn waltzed out. The door slammed behind her.

Stuart slowly picked himself up. He braved a smile, even though his jawbone was throbbing and it felt like there were splinters of glass embedded in it and smiling did nothing to alleviate the pain.

Being the Conquistador had just got rather more interesting.

EIGHT

Same Day

WELL, THAT COULD *have gone more smoothly*, Mal thought as she drove across town.

She hadn't intended to tip her hand to Reston that he was a person of interest in an ongoing investigation. She had let her temper get the better of her. If only he hadn't been so arrogant, so infuriatingly, insufferably smug...

On the other hand, now he knew he was under suspicion. That could work to Mal's advantage. He might just become a whole lot more reckless. He might, like a fox with the hounds on its tail, do something wild and impulsive which would leave him dangerously exposed.

He also might take fright and give up being the Conquistador altogether. Mal didn't think this likely, but if she had managed to bring a halt to the Conquistador atrocities, in spite of there being no arrest and conviction, that would be something.

At least she'd got that punch in. Her knuckles ached agreeably. Never underestimate the cathartic power of a solid roundhouse right.

Back at the Yard, she went looking for Kellaway. She wanted to report her findings – her certainty that Stuart Reston was their man. Having filled the chief superintendent in on her progress with the case and lowered his blood pressure somewhat, she could then start digging into Reston's recent past and trying to correlate his known movements with the timings of the Conquistador's attacks. At present she had only her drug vision and Reston's lofty, egotistical attitude to tell her she was right, and neither was irrefutable proof. She needed more. She needed hard facts to substantiate her gut conviction. Her pride demanded it.

Aaronson intercepted her en route to Kellaway's office.

"I wouldn't go see him now if I were you, boss," he warned.

"Why ever not?"

"He's... he's just had some bad news."

"How bad?"

"The worst. The commissioner called him upstairs a couple of hours ago. Since then, the word's spread like wildfire. Chief super's going to be striped."

Mal reeled. "No. Fucking. Way."

Her DS gave a sombre nod. "This afternoon, at

five. He's on the phone right now to friends and family, making his peace."

"But... *why*?"

"The Conquistador, why else? It's all getting too much for everyone, too embarrassing. A head has to roll – a bigwig's head. As I understand it, this comes all the way from the Great Speaker himself. His Imperial Holiness is not best pleased with how we've been dealing with the Conquistador. Enough's enough."

"Striped. The poor bastard."

"It's a noble death." Aaronson sounded more hopeful than reassuring.

"It's a fucking horrible death," Mal said.

"Well, yes, can't argue with that. But we know what to do, don't we?"

"Too damn right we do."

GETTING ONTO THE striping detail was not easy. Only four could be chosen, and just about everyone in the building was putting their own name forward. Not only was it an honour to take part, it was a valuable addition to your CV. The officer appointed to make the selection, Sergeant Pembroke, was swamped with volunteers.

Mal, however, reckoned she had leverage on Pembroke, and now was the time to apply it. Drawing the sergeant aside for a quiet word, she reminded him about a case they had both worked on a couple of years ago, busting a conclave of anti-Empire radical extremists who had been publishing pamphlets that mocked and derided the Great Speaker, calling him as the "Great Squeaker" and painting him as a frantic, ranting despot in dire need of being deposed.

At the extremists' hideout in a West End backstreet basement, along with reams of paper and a printing press, a wad of cash had been found, hadn't it? A tidy little sum hidden beneath a loose floorboard, no doubt earmarked to fund further subversion. Equivalent to a good three months' salary, if Mal remembered rightly. And, mysteriously, the money had just sort of disappeared on its way to the evidence lockers. There one minute, gone the next. She hadn't mentioned anything about it to anyone, but it had been pretty curious, hadn't it? So much cash going astray.

Pembroke whitened just a little. He said he had no idea what the DCI was talking about. He didn't recall any money.

"Why should you?" Mal replied sweetly. "If we're all doing our duty and acting like professionals, we don't even notice such things. And clerical errors do happen. Someone in Evidence probably mislaid the money, put it in the wrong locker, stuck the wrong label on. It's sitting downstairs in a box gathering dust, and nobody has a clue it's there."

"Yeah, exactly."

"No point raking any of that up. No point bringing it to the attention of Internal Affairs. It's such a small thing, I don't even know why we're discussing it now."

Pembroke nodded avidly. There was a film of perspiration on his upper lip. "Me either," he said.

"And if I was to get onto the striping detail, I'm sure I would forget about it completely."

"Really? That's all it would take?"

"That's all."

He looked at her as if he could scarcely believe it. For what she was selling him, she was charging a remarkably low price.

"Then you're on it," he said. "And the money, nobody's ever going to hear about it again?"

"Not from me. You have my absolute word on that."

"Thank you, chief inspector. Thank you so much."

"Not at all, sergeant. Thank *you*."

IN THE OLD days, during the Empire's infancy, striping was a practice routinely carried out on captured enemy combatants. Only those who had shown notable prowess and bravery on the battlefield were singled out to be put to death in this way; the rest of the captive warriors would be mass-slaughtered like cattle. It was considered a mark of respect and a fitting tribute to their valour, although the victims themselves might not see it that way.

In modern times, striping was the fate of anyone in authority who failed to live up to expectations or disgraced the Empire somehow. It was a chance to redeem oneself before gods and men, make reparation through pain, and depart the world with dignity restored. A "flowery" death, as it was known. A good death.

At five o'clock, punctually, Chief Superintendent Kellaway left Scotland Yard for the Westminster ziggurat, a walk of a few hundred metres. Commissioner Brockenhurst was at his side every step of the way. Both men were in full ceremonial garb, their uniforms sporting the plethora of medals and decorations they had earned in the course of their careers.

Behind them, in square formation, strode the four members of the striping detail, Mal among them. They, too, were dressed up for the occasion. Then came a procession of other ranks, nearly a thousand strong, the entire Yard turning out to see the chief super off. Civilian onlookers lined the route, craning their necks. Tourists and commuters, curious, stopped and stared. The inevitable Sun Broadcasting cameras were there, recording the moment for posterity.

During his final walk, Kellaway loudly sang the praises of the Jaguar Warriors, the High Priest, the Empire, the Great Speaker. It was an integral part of the ritual, and to neglect to do so was shameful. At the top of his voice he proclaimed his loyalty to the force and his regret that he had not discharged his role to the very best of his abilities. He wished his successor, whosoever that might be, all success in the job and confessed how sad he was that he would not be around to see the new chief super prevail where he himself had blundered.

He continued with the protestations of faith and hope as he mounted the ziggurat steps. At the summit, the commissioner relieved him of his helmet and most of his regalia and presented him with the weapons he could use to defend himself. These comprised four pine cudgels for throwing and a war club adorned with quetzal feathers. An acolyte stood nearby, the official pastor to the Metropolitan Jaguars. He had a knife ready, along with a jaguar-shaped iron vessel just large enough to hold a human heart.

To the west, the sun was setting in a gory rage of twilight. To the east, the thunderheads loomed higher than ever, massive as a mountain range. It wouldn't be long now before the storm broke. The air carried a static crackle. Growls echoed over the Thames estuary.

Commissioner Brockenhurst retreated, bowing to Kellaway. The acolyte tethered Kellaway by the waist to a large circular stone mounted on a platform. There was enough slack in the rope to give the chief super the run of the ziggurat's summit, but no further. The acolyte incanted, commending Kellaway's soul to the Four Who Rule Supreme. Then he invited the striping detail to step forward and take their positions around the victim.

"In the name of Xipe Totec," he said to them, "the Flayed One, the Mighty Skinless, I beseech you. Be merciful with slowness. Cut with delicacy. Prolong the suffering, for only in blood and agony may this man's sins be atoned. Begin!"

Mal held back, allowing the other three Jaguars,

all men, to get their licks in first. Unlike Kellaway, the members of the striping detail each carried a decent weapon: a war club edged with shards of flint. The chief super straight away squandered the meagre advantage he had by tossing all four of his pine cudgels at them. Only one found its mark, and bounced all but harmlessly off its target's chest. The cudgels rolled off the top of the ziggurat, putting them forever out of Kellaway's reach.

The three Jaguars closed in and began delivering swift, deft slices to Kellaway's arms and legs. They were careful only to nick the skin, going no deeper into his flesh. Blood was soon pouring down his limbs in ribbons and rivulets.

Kellaway retaliated gamely, lashing out with his feather-fringed club, and managed to get in a few solid connections. He was not going down without a fight. He was not supposed to. However, the odd bruise here and there could hardly compare with the damage that was so insistently being inflicted on him. Moreover, he was an old man, long past his prime, and his opponents were all of them younger, quicker and nimbler.

As the minutes passed, he began to sag. There were wounds all over him now, on torso, neck, buttocks, chest, head. His uniform hung off him in tatters. He was breathing stertorously, his eyes bulging. The three Jaguars did not let up. Kellaway staggered this way and that, flailing with his club, and they continued to dart around him, slashing him as finely and neatly as they could. His body was soon crosshatched all over with shallow gashes and incisions. He was quite literally striped with his own blood.

Mal knew she couldn't loiter on the sidelines any longer. Her three colleagues were casting puzzled looks at her. Why wasn't she joining in? Why the sudden squeamishness? She was letting them down. She was letting the chief super down. She needed to go in and do what she was here to do.

"My turn," she said, and motioned to the others to stand back. She outranked them all, so they did as instructed. Clearly she'd been leaving the preliminary work to them. Now she was going to show what finesse and élan a DCI could bring to the process. Senior officer's prerogative.

She approached Kellaway. He stood hunched over, teetering, bent double. His club dangled from his fingertips, almost too heavy for him to lift any more. He peered up at her. One eye was closed, the upper lid hanging in slivers like a broken Venetian blind. The tip of his nose was absent, revealing a strawberry of cartilage. An ear had been split in two. There was no faulting her colleagues' craftsmanship.

"Sir," she said softly so that only he could hear, "I can finish this for you right now. One blow and it's all over. Just give the word."

Blood bubbled at his lips. "No," he managed to say. "It wouldn't be right. I must go on."

"You've suffered enough. No one would blame you if you wanted it ended. Please let me."

Kellaway tried to hoist his club to strike at her. He brushed her shin feebly with its tip.

Sorrowfully, Mal raked her club across his collarbone, opening up a long thin streak of red. The chief super moaned.

"Then listen," she said. "I have him. I have the Conquistador. I know who he is."

"How?" Kellaway gasped.

"Vision quest."

"Not... Not admissible as grounds for an arrest."

"I know, but still. It means the search is over and it's just a question of time now. Either the Conquistador slips up or I get what I need to haul him in, it doesn't matter which. He's done. I have him by the balls. He's going down."

Kellaway attempted a smile – a skewed, hangdog thing. His one visible eye regained some of its old lustre.

"Not lying about this? To make a doomed man feel better?"

"Not at all, sir. Gospel truth. And when I do get him, it'll be for you, in your name."

The chief super feinted with his club, or at least offered the vague appearance of doing so. Mal duly nicked him on the shoulder.

"Good Jaguar, you are, Vaughn," he said. "Good copper. Glad I never had to execute you. You'll go far."

She gave him a few further little cuts, to show willing. Then she retreated and let the other three have their way with him once more. She could barely bring herself to watch as they reduced the rest of Kellaway's skin to shreds. How he was able to stay on his feet, she had no idea, but some inhuman determination kept him upright long past the stage where most men would have collapsed. It was love, she though. Kellaway loved being a Jaguar. Loved it even unto death.

The sky darkened, thunder rumbled, rain fell. It was a warm rain, but hard, drops so powerful and heavy they could have been hail. Many of the civilians scurried off to find shelter, but all of the Jaguar Warriors in attendance stayed put, while up on the ziggurat the striping continued unabated. Kellaway had sunk to his knees, but refused to lie down. There seemed to be not one square inch of his body that wasn't marked, lacerated, ragged. He was a living effigy of Xipe Totec. It was as though the Flayed One had been brought to earth, reincarnated. A god in all his exposed raw flesh.

The rain puddled around Kellaway's knees, mingling with his blood. Lightning and thunder splintered overhead. Mal raised her face to the pummelling force of the storm, letting it pound her head, her brain, her mind, until she felt empty within, battered into submission, numb.

When, finally, she looked down again, Kellaway was dead and the acolyte was stepping forward to hack out his heart.

THAT NIGHT, NO surprise, Mal went out and got steaming drunk. She wound up in some man's bedroom – she had no clear recollection how she got there – on all fours, letting herself be fucked soundly up the arse and relishing every brutal, piercing thrust of it. At the crucial moment the man withdrew and showered her back with semen. Mal then shat herself and passed out.

She came to in an alleyway some time later, filthy, rain-sodden, no knickers. She hobbled home and sat in a tepid bath while the water slowly turned pink around her. Then she crawled into bed. Hugging her knees to her chest, she waited for sleep to come. Her last thought before she drifted away from herself was: *Fuck procedure. Fuck protocol. Nab him anyway.*

And in the dark, in pain, she smiled.

NINE

11 Crocodile 1 Monkey 1 House
(Sunday 2nd December 2012)

STUART WAS TEN miles into a twelve-mile run when he became aware of someone keeping pace with him a few yards behind.

He glanced over his shoulder and saw that it was a woman. A second glance confirmed her identity: the Jaguar Warrior detective, Vaughn.

He wasn't surprised. For the past twenty-four hours he'd had a feeling he was being watched. Someone was always lurking just at the limits of his vision, a presence more sensed than seen. He would have put it down to imagination, if not for his bruising encounter with Vaughn at the office. It was possible she had been tailing him ever since, and now she was making her move, coming out of the shadows into the light.

Stuart upped his speed, tapping his reserves of energy. He'd done a twelve-miler yesterday as well, along this very same route, and his lungs were aching and his legs were leaden with tiredness, but he could grit his teeth and bludgeon through the discomfort. Only another ten or so minutes to home.

Vaughn matched his acceleration and added a further turn of speed, gradually narrowing the gap between them. Stuart lengthened his stride, but Vaughn was fresher than him. She'd been going for minutes, not an hour plus. Soon she pulled alongside him.

Stuart offered her an ironic salute and focused on his running. There were hundreds of promenaders meandering about on the south bank today, few of them looking where they were going. To steer a safe course through them demanded concentration.

To these passers-by, Stuart and Vaughn looked like a fitness-fanatic couple jogging side by side, enjoying a spot of aerobic exercise together. No one could have guessed, by their appearance, that they were enemies on opposite sides of a moral divide – upholder of the law and flouter of it. Just a man and woman in sportswear, husband and wife maybe, keeping in trim.

They thudded eastbound along the embankment, passing under Waterloo Bridge, then Blackfriars. The stonework on both structures was wreathed with lianas and vines. Cracks and crevices played host to colonies of bats which, come twilight, would emerge from their roosts in black swarms.

Stuart waited for the chief inspector to breach the silence. As they neared Southwark Bridge, she did.

"There's two ways we can do this, Mr Reston."

"Don't tell me. Easy or hard."

"I was going to go with clean or messy, but whatever. You can come in quietly and anonymously with me, or publicly, noisily, melodramatically, surrounded by a bunch of Jaguars in full uniform. It's up to you."

"Why would I do either?" Stuart asked.

"Why isn't open to debate, only how."

"But where's the proof? What grounds do you have for arrest?"

"I've decided I don't need any. I know you're the Conquistador. That's all I need. The rest is academic."

"Even in a police state – and let's face it, this is one – due process of law has to be observed. *Seen* to be observed, at any rate. I'd like to see an arrest warrant, please."

"That can be arranged," said Vaughn. "I can't promise when one will appear, but it will. Probably after I've had a good nose round your flat and unearthed a suit of reproduction Spanish armour hidden somewhere there."

"I'll claim it was planted. Or rather, my hideously expensive lawyer will."

"Lawyers aren't much help to people who are being held downstairs at the Yard. Often they can't get in to see you because they haven't filed the proper paperwork, or else you happen to be asleep each time they visit."

"Sleep and unconsciousness can look alike, can't they?"

"You have a very clear grasp of our methods, Mr Reston."

Stuart thumbed sweat out of his eyes. The Thames, to his left, rolled along thick and brown, dotted with barges and bright little pleasure boats. He was running faster than the river was.

"You won't be able to make any charges stick, you know," he said.

"We'll see."

"The person you answer to, your chief supcrintendent or whoever, he's going to have a very rough time of it."

"How so?"

"Well, at this point I would say, 'Don't you know who I am?' but you already do."

"Wealth and status won't impress him, Mr Reston."

"They should."

"But won't, because he's dead."

"Ah," said Stuart. "Him. The poor sod who was striped the day before yesterday. I thought they'd have replaced him by now."

"Not yet."

"I'm surprised."

"I'm not. His are hard shoes to fill."

"I bet, thanks to the Conquistador, candidates aren't exactly queuing up."

"No, they're not. But what that means for me is, I have a window of opportunity, and I'm going to make the most of it."

"Directly answerable to no one," said Stuart. "Rogue Jaguar."

"Let's just say I'm motivated and I'm unsupervised."

"How did you know where I'd be this morning?"

"I watched you head out for a run yesterday. Apparently you do this on both days of the weekend, the exact same route every time. You're a creature of habit, Mr Reston."

"And you, Chief Inspector Vaughn, have been doing your homework."

"I chatted to a few of your neighbours, and with your PA, Tara. I've been busy charting your comings and goings. She was unusually cooperative, was Tara. I popped round her house yesterday and she supplied me with a list of all your recent business trips."

"There's employee loyalty for you." Stuart tried to sound phlegmatic, not bitter. He couldn't hold it against Tara. She would have felt she was doing her civic duty, and to refuse to assist the Jaguars in their enquiries was not the wisest course of action a person could take. Nonetheless...

"Unlike you, Tara respects the badge." Vaughn was starting to get out of breath, but she ploughed doggedly on. "Now, it seems the Conquistador has never struck while you've been out of town. I find that interesting."

"*I* find it circumstantial."

"But it's something to go on. And if – no, *when* – I find Conquistador armour at your flat... Put all that together and we're looking at a watertight conviction. No lawyer, however much he charges per hour, is going to be able to winkle you free. It'll be a quick trial. Can't say the same about the execution."

Tower Bridge loomed, Stuart's crossing point, the start of the last leg of the journey.

"Miss Vaughn?" he said.

"Yes?"

"Has it ever occurred to you that you're on the wrong side in all this?"

Her hesitation was brief, but the fact that she hesitated at all was telling. "I'm a Jaguar Warrior. I represent law and order. This is all I've ever wanted to do, all I've ever wanted to be."

"You prop up a ruthless dictatorship. You wield authority without accountability. You're the puppet of a theocracy that dominates its subjects through fear and oppression."

"Someone has to administer justice. Someone has to keep crime in check."

"While working for the biggest criminals of all, the unelected rulers?"

"Perhaps I'm just a realist."

"Or perhaps you're so institutionalised, so conditioned by the regime, you no longer have any conception what reality is."

"You're saying I'm brainwashed?"

"That might be putting it strongly, but then how else would one describe a woman who shopped her own brother, her own flesh and blood, knowing the end result would be him being put to death?"

Vaughn's face, already coloured from the exertion of running, reddened further.

"Oh yes," Stuart said. "I've been doing my homework too."

"Well, aren't you just the clever bastard?"

"It can't have been an easy thing, grassing him up. Ixtli, was that his name? I don't suppose you were close, you and Ixtli. What with him being a gang member and you being police, it'd put a strain on any sibling relationship. Nevertheless, what you did was pretty cold, chief inspector."

He sprinted up the flight of stone steps that brought him to the roadway, level with the bridge. Inspector Vaughn remained beside him, and she was fuming now, her face contorted in a scowl of resentment.

"I did what any good citizen would and should," she said. "And I don't have to justify it to you, or myself, or anyone."

"Still, I imagine it gave you the odd sleepless night. Maybe still does."

"Right," she said with finality, as they set foot on the bridge. "I gave you a choice, Reston, remember that. It was entirely your call how we play this. This is all on you now."

"What do you mean?" Stuart replied. "I'm nearly home. Look, I can see my building from here. What are you going to do?"

The chief inspector signalled behind her, and ahead.

All at once the rear doors of the unmarked paddy wagons parked at either end of the bridge opened, and uniformed Jaguars emerged. There were a couple of dozen of them, all told, and they swiftly fanned out across both lanes of the road, halting the traffic. They had lightning guns, and they levelled them at Stuart.

Stuart slowed to a jog, then a walk. He and Vaughn were almost halfway across, near the seam where the bridge divided when raised.

"Ah," he said. "Ambush. Should've seen that coming."

"Isn't that the whole point of an ambush? That you don't?" said Vaughn. "We've got you pincered. No way off. You might as well surrender. It's that or get zapped with enough voltage to remove your eyebrows."

"But not to kill?"

"The High Priest would like to make a lesson of you. You have to have the longest, slowest, vilest death imaginable, and everyone has to see it and know why."

"So you need to take me alive," said Stuart.

"Yes."

"That's a shame."

No sooner had these words left his lips than Stuart sprang up onto the parapet of the bridge and hurled himself over the side.

FOR ONE ASTONISHED second Mal stared at the space where Reston had been standing. She could not believe her eyes. Motherfucker. *Motherfucker.*

Then, "No," she said, and "No!" again, this time yelling, and she scrambled onto the parapet herself and dived after him.

She had just enough time, between leaping off the bridge and landing in the water, to wonder what the hell she thought she was doing. When she hit the river surface the impact smacked the breath out of her lungs. She went under amid a welter of bubbles and flailed her way desperately back up to air.

Dazed, treading water, she searched around for sight of Reston. The tide was running out, the current torpid. She couldn't see him anywhere. There were cries from up on the bridge, Jaguars calling to her, asking if she was all right. She ignored them. Reston. Where was he? Had he drowned?

Damn him if he had. Damn him to Mictlan. She wanted to march him into Scotland Yard for all to see. She didn't want him to have taken the coward's way out.

Downstream, beyond the bridge, a head broke the surface. Reston came up with a mighty heaving gasp and almost immediately began toiling through the water, heading diagonally for shore. Mal set off after him. As she swam between two of the bridge pilings, the channelled current gave her extra impetus. She thrashed along, spitting warm, foul water out of her mouth. Reston was nearly fifty yards ahead, and whether he did or didn't know she was hot on his heels, he powered hard. Mal dug deep and powered hard too.

A small wooden dinghy with an outboard motor hove to beside Reston. The three young men on board extended hands to him over the gunwales. Concerned citizens trying to help, but Mal knew if

Reston got onto the boat he would commandeer it and be off at a rate of knots.

"No!" she spluttered. "Jaguar Warrior in pursuit. Do not touch that man."

Above the idling motor and their own shouts, the young men didn't hear. They grabbed Reston's wrists and started to haul him out.

Up on the bridge a voice echoed Mal's cry. It was Aaronson. Again the demand went unheard, but Aaronson backed it up with a well-aimed shot from his l-gun, which was set at antipersonnel level and so would not to do too much damage to property. The bolt of plasma hit the dinghy's prow, charring and splintering. The three boaters got the message. Reston was dropped back in the river, and the dinghy reversed away with some haste.

Reston resumed his bid for dry land. Mal was now much closer to him, just a few strokes behind, cutting through the swirls of surf left by his kicks. Reston reached the shallows and rose to his feet. The riverbed was thick, sticky mud. He waded laboriously towards a rusting, weed-draped ladder that would take him to street level. Mal, with a final frantic burst of effort, lunged out of the water after him.

For once, being less heavily built than her quarry served her well. She didn't sink as deeply into the mud as Reston did, and was able to traverse it more quickly. At the same time that Reston latched a hand onto a rung of the ladder, she latched a hand onto the back of his running singlet. She yanked hard, catching him off-balance, pulling him down into the mud.

"You had to make a run for it, didn't you?" she panted. "Had to make life as difficult as possible."

Reston reared up from the mud, but Mal whacked him back down with an elbow jab to the crown.

"I was trying to appeal to the gentleman in you," she said. "I thought you'd appreciate decency."

Reston struggled to rise again, while also aiming a punch at Mal's knee. She foiled him with another vicious, stunning strike to the head.

"Just stay put, will you? You're under fucking arrest."

Reston grabbed for her ankle but she kicked his hand away with one muck-caked trainer.

"I said stop resisting. You're only going to get hurt."

He was weakening, exhausted. Mal was exhausted too, but charged up with adrenaline and righteousness. She stamped on Reston's chest, forcing him so far down into the slimy shoreline ooze that his face almost went under. The mud sucked at him and held him fast, resisting his best efforts to writhe out of it. He scrabbled and clawed, but couldn't free himself.

Helmeted heads appeared above, peering over the embankment's barrier railings. Mal looked up, still with one foot on Reston's sternum like a safari hunter posing with a fresh kill.

"Got him," she said. "I want three of you down here now, with handcuffs and leg manacles. We're bringing him in."

Cold, wet, trembling, steeped in mud up to her thighs, Mal had never felt better.

TEN

Same Day

WITHIN MINUTES, A bedraggled, mud-encrusted Stuart found himself being prodded at gunpoint into the back of a paddy wagon.

He liked to think he had given the Jaguar Warriors a run for their money. He'd known, though, from the moment they sprung their little surprise for him on Tower Bridge, that there was a strong possibility the outcome would be this. When that boat had come by he thought his luck had turned, but it was not to be. He was in the authorities' clutches now. At the mercy of Jaguar Warriors. Things could have looked less bleak, but Stuart refused to be discouraged. As long as he was alive there was always a chance of turning the situation around. Something could be done.

He was made to sit on one of the narrow benches lining the interior walls of the paddy wagon. A chain was clamped onto his handcuffs, the other end secured to an eye-bolt in the floor. Jaguars crowded in on either side of him. Chief Inspector Vaughn planted herself directly opposite, so near that her knees were almost touching his. She looked extraordinarily pleased with herself, and frankly Stuart didn't blame her.

The rear doors slammed and the paddy wagon revved and pulled away.

Stuart noticed noses wrinkling around him.

"Yes, I know, I stink," he said. "Phew! Sorry about that, everyone. The Thames isn't the most pleasant of rivers to take a dip in. And all this mud too. Ninety per cent human waste, probably, and the rest fish shit."

The Jaguar to his right chuckled. Vaughn shot the man a look and he instantly fell silent.

"Confined space," Stuart continued. "Can't be much fun for you people. At least the chief inspector here's as guilty of reeking as I am. Although of course in every other respect she's come up smelling of roses."

"Do you ever shut up, Reston?" Vaughn snapped.

"I just felt I should apologise."

"Well, don't. Don't feel you should do anything."

The paddy wagon rumbled on for a little while. The rear section was windowless, partitioned off from the driving cab. A dim overhead bulb was the only illumination, and for Stuart there was nothing to see but policemen and l-guns.

"Nice takedown, by the way," he said to Vaughn. "You are one persistent little bloodhound, and no mistake."

"Why, thank you," she replied in a sarcastic drawl. "Coming from you, that's such a compliment."

"I like to pay beautiful women compliments."

"Ye gods, what a charmer. I'm getting moist between the legs."

Several of the Jaguars chuckled at this, and Vaughn was happy to let them.

"I mean it, though," Stuart said. "You are beautiful – as beautiful as you are formidable. I'm sure I'm not the only man here who fancies you. And I know for a fact that you have something of a reputation. Homework, remember? Word is, your morals are loose and your knicker elastic even looser."

Vaughn's expression soured and hardened. "I'd advise you to stop talking right now."

"Queen of the quickie. Just ask anyone at the Yard."

Stuart hadn't in fact spoken to anyone at the Yard. He'd found out about Vaughn's background by ringing a journalist famed for his Jaguar contacts and offering him a hefty sum of money in return for a spot of private freelance research. The journalist, after a little delving, had come back with the story about Vaughn and her brother and also with rumours, unconfirmed, that the woman liked to put it about a bit and went on the occasional bender. "In every other respect," the hack had told him, "she's a model cop. They've all got bad habits, and hers, such as they are, are far from being the worst."

Vaughn was looking daggers at him across the van. "Are you trying to piss me off, Reston? Does it amuse you? Because believe me, down in the holding cells you're not going to find life nearly so amusing."

"I'm just making light conversation. Trying to get us better acquainted. You can't feel this thing between us?" Stuart gestured as expansively as his restraints would permit. "The sexual tension?"

A Jaguar sniggered, then stopped sniggering when he realised no one else was.

Vaughn's grey eyes had turned to iron.

"I do," Stuart went on. "I'm looking forward to spending some time being interrogated by you. We can put that reputation of yours to the test. You don't even have to untie me. I don't mind a bit of the kinky stuff, and neither, I suspect, do you. We'll just –"

Vaughn jack-knifed out of her seat and struck him across the face, backhand. It was as good a shot as the one she'd got off in his office, and it hit almost exactly the same spot. Stuart tasted blood. Probing with his tongue, he found that a molar had been loosened.

"Ugh," he said. "Not nice. Police brutality."

"That's just a taster of things to come. Given how many of us you've killed, there'll be no shortage of candidates wanting to come see you downstairs and get a little payback."

"Allegedly killed, chief inspector."

"How long are you going to keep up this 'innocent man' routine?"

"I don't know. How long are you going to keep up the pretence that you're happy being a Jaguar?"

She flinched. "Bollocks. I love my job."

"So the drinking, the over-reliance on coca, the cheap sordid assignations with strangers – these are all signs of someone content in herself, with a healthy relationship to her work? And not, say, someone whose conscience plagues her constantly and who knows she's a good person doing bad things and who tries to numb herself so she doesn't have to think about any of it too hard."

"Like I told you, solving crimes, keeping the peace, collaring undesirables, where's the harm in that?"

"You Jaguars are no better than the crooks you round up. The only difference is you have badges and they don't."

"The law –"

"The law is meaningless," Stuart scoffed. "The law is whatever the Great Speaker wishes it to be. It's there to keep him in power and quash anyone who disagrees with him or would like to see him dethroned."

"The Conquistador himself couldn't have put it better."

"He's obviously as much of an advocate of free speech as I am."

"Freedom of speech doesn't extend to insulting the Great Speaker."

"I wasn't insulting His Imperious Stupendousness, merely criticising. And if that's not allowed, then my case is proven. QE-fucking-D."

"I'm not having this argument with you," Vaughn said brusquely. "It's pointless. If you'd like to live in a world of anarchy..."

"Not anarchy, Miss Vaughn. Just democracy. A world where we choose who rules us and how we're ruled. We had a world like that, Britain did, up until a hundred years ago, before the Empire finally ground us down. I can see a time when we might have it again."

"Well, I can't, and neither can anyone else in this van. You're in a minority of one, Reston."

"Maybe if you stopped boozing and spreading your legs like a bitch in heat, you'd have a clearer head and clearer vision too."

Vaughn leapt to her feet and drew back her fist to sock him as hard as she could.

WHAAAMMMM!!!

The entire paddy wagon took to the air. It rolled and rolled, and everyone inside rolled with it. Bodies tumbled. Limbs tangled. Heads collided. Only Stuart, thanks to his bonds, stayed more or less in one place. The Jaguar Warriors were thrown about helplessly while he swung, hung, crash back against his seat; swung, hung, crashed. There were resounding, thunderous thumps as the paddy wagon somersaulted, striking the ground repeatedly. There were also screams, shouts and grunts from its occupants, and once or twice the deep *snap* of a bone breaking.

The paddy wagon came to a rest on its side. In the back, Jaguar was piled on Jaguar in a jumbled heap. Low groans filled the air. Someone whimpered in pain.

Then, with a wrenching squeal, the rear doors were crowbarred open. Men rushed into the stricken vehicle. They had skull-face makeup and paramilitary jumpsuits. One wielded a pair of heavy-duty bolt cutters.

The Xibalba guerrillas dug through the tangled mass of semiconscious Jaguar Warriors to find Stuart buried beneath. The one with the bolt cutters made short work of the chains securing Stuart, and in no time Stuart was being helped out into the daylight.

Blinking around him, he realised he was at the large intersection north of Whitehall, Tenochtitlan Square. Traffic had come to a complete standstill in all directions. Horns honked. Drivers yelled from their windows, and some leaned out to gesticulate.

The guerrillas hustled Stuart across to their van, which stood nearby with a severely dented front bumper and radiator grille. The engine was turning over, rattling somewhat. Stuart was shoved into the back and the van howled off, tyres screeching.

In the passenger seat, Ah Balam Chel swivelled round.

"Hello again, Mr Reston," he said, grinning. "So Xibalba plucks you from the clutches of the Jaguar Warriors a second time. This is becoming a habit."

PART TWO

ANAHUAC

ELEVEN

2 Snake 1 Lizard 1 House
(Thursday 6th December 2012)

STUART SET DOWN the binoculars in order to slap at something biting his wrist. Inspecting the palm of his hand, he found the mushed remnants of a mosquito the size of a bumblebee, along with what seemed like several fluid ounces of his blood, the insect's last meal.

The rainforest. There was nothing here that wasn't trying to sting you, eat you, poison you, suck your blood, or keep you awake half the night with hundred-decibel screeching. Anahuac, the holy land, cradle and hearth of the Empire. Well, you could fucking keep it.

He raised the binoculars and zeroed in again on the object of his scrutiny. It lay at a distance of two miles from his vantage point, across the placid blue waters of Lake Texcoco, on an island approximately a mile long. It covered the whole of the island, its walls rising sheer above the lake to a height of around a hundred metres, Stuart estimated.

Tenochtitlan, home of the Great Speaker. More citadel than city and more fortress than either.

Ziggurat rubbed shoulders with ziggurat. Some of them were topped with roof gardens, others with glassed-in solariums, a couple with aerodisc landing pads. There was one waterfront entry point only, a harbour with a road that led up to a large gate at the city's southern tip. The gate was built as an inverted trapezoid, in true Aztec fashion, and was well defended. There was no other mooring place around the island perimeter as far as Stuart could see, but there were watchtowers at regular intervals along the walls and any number of armed patrol launches circling in the vicinity. Tenochtitlan had been designed to be unbreachable. The Great Speaker's personal army, the Serpent Warriors, added a further layer of security.

Beside Stuart, Zotz shifted impatiently. "Seen enough?" he asked.

"Not yet."

Ah Balam Chel's second-in-command grunted and popped a flake of jatoba bark into his mouth to chew on; it settled his stomach.

As Stuart scanned Tenochtitlan's roofline he caught sight of a private aerodisc making its descent towards the city. The moment the disc touched down, it was surrounded by a dozen Serpent Warriors. Some dignitary or other – an ambassador, a delegate here to crave a boon, a priest, perhaps even a High Priest – came down the gangplank. He waved warily at all the lightning guns that were pointed at him. Only after he had presented identifying documents and a seal of office were he and his entourage permitted off the rooftop, into the city. Several Serpents were posted to stand guard around the disc and would remain there until it was the dignitary's time to leave.

Stuart turned his attention to the outer walls. They were impossible to climb. The battlements were too high to be reached by any kind of grappling device, and the stonework was pure traditional Aztec – slabs of basalt cut so precisely and wedged together so tightly that you couldn't insert even a sheet of paper between them, never mind a piton or a fingertip. You'd have to be some kind of human spider to have any hope of scaling the walls successfully, and all the while you'd be inviting the Serpents in the watchtowers to take potshots at you. They were elite troops, the best of the best, cherry-picked from the ranks of Eagles and Jaguars all over the world. You could be sure that whatever they aimed at, they would not miss.

"Come on," said Zotz. "We can't stay here much longer. Serpent discs make regular sweeps along the lakeshore. Besides, we're losing the light."

"Sun's still well above the horizon," Stuart commented.

"You forget, Englishman, this is the tropics. When the sun goes down, it goes down fast."

Stuart took one last look at Tenochtitlan, hoping against hope that he would find some gap in its defences, some chink in its armour of stonework and sentry. Perched in the middle of an inland sea, it was like a castle with an immense moat. Its army of protectors were disciplined and dedicated, and had the highest wage packet known in professional soldiering, with substantial bonuses awarded for exceptional initiative or diligence in the line of duty. The Great Speaker was ensconced in a remote, impenetrable bastion. He ventured out from it only on rare occasions, and outsiders could not get in unless they were invited, expected, and fully accredited.

So how on earth did Chel think Xibalba could pull off an assassination?

The question rattled around in Stuart's brain as he followed Zotz back through the forest to their canoe. Chel claimed to have the basic ingredients of a plan, but Stuart had wanted to reconnoitre Tenochtitlan to assess the parameters of the situation first-hand before making any sort of commitment. If he was going to throw in his lot with Xibalba, he had to be satisfied that it would be a worthwhile exercise. No point jumping off the fence if there was nowhere to land.

On present evidence, Xibalba stood a cat's chance in hell of killing the Great Speaker. Assuming they managed to get inside Tenochtitlan somehow, in terms of numbers, matériel and strategic capability they were no match for the Serpent Warriors. It wouldn't even be a suicide mission, because that would imply the desired outcome could be achieved through sacrifice of lives. It would just be plain suicide.

Stuart and Zotz reached the edge of one of the tributary rivers that fed into Lake Texcoco. Their kapok-wood canoe was where they'd left it – hauled ashore and secreted among undergrowth. They slid it out onto the water and unshipped the paddles. There was an outboard, but they wouldn't use that until later. A sudden burst of engine noise might attract attention.

The thin, flat-bottomed boat glided along against the sluggish current, propelled by its two oarsmen with slow, easy strokes. The sky purpled quickly and dusk fell, and the forest animals set up their usual nocturnal hullabaloo, as if this was the cue they had been waiting for. As the stars came out, everything with lungs and a throat started to shriek, gibber or howl, while everything that had chitinous body parts to scrape together started to chirp, all at deafening volume.

Zotz switched on a powerful lamp affixed to the canoe's bows to light their way. Instantly a pair of eyes shone from the darkness of the riverbank. They disappeared from sight as the creature that owned them padded its way into the water and slithered under the surface with a just audible splash.

"Caiman," said Zotz. "Didn't look too big. Nine, maybe ten feet long."

"Ten feet sounds big enough to me," Stuart said. "Any danger to us?"

"Not unless it attacks."

"But it won't attack a boat."

"Not unless it thinks the boat is a rival caiman coming to take over its territory or steal its mate."

"How do we know it won't think that?"

"We don't. Just paddle."

Zotz might have been joking. It was impossible to tell. The Mayan was a man of few words, with a set to his chin that suggested he didn't suffer fools gladly and thought most people *were* fools. Stuart quite liked him. He wasn't sure whether Zotz liked him back, but was proceeding on the assumption that he didn't. Possibly Zotz regarded him as a rival, someone who might usurp his position as Chel's right-hand man. Stuart could have assured him he needn't worry on that front. He wasn't sure he wanted to have anything to do with Xibalba at all. He owed the Mayan guerrillas a debt of gratitude, but beyond that, nothing.

As he and Zotz continued to plough their way upriver, Stuart recalled another night-time journey over water, made just four days earlier.

THE XIBALBA VAN, damaged by ramming the paddy wagon side-on, just made it to Woolwich before the engine let out a wheezing groan and expired. The guerrillas dashed through the docklands, Stuart with them, until they arrived at a jetty where a small fishing vessel was waiting. The boat's French captain, Beaudreau, cast off straight away, and they were soon chugging along Barking Reach, past the bleak tufted wastes of Hornchurch Marshes, out towards open sea.

Dry clothes were found for Stuart – a set of fisherman's overalls – and as he stood at the taffrail and watched London recede in the boat's wake he wondered when, if ever, he would return to the city. Perhaps never. How could he go back? He was a marked man now. There could be no more doubt who the Conquistador was. His life as a masked vigilante was over, and likewise his life as an obsidian importer. At a stroke, he had become an exile. From here on, Stuart Reston was a fugitive, a perpetual expatriate, forever on the run.

Chel joined him at the stern as the fishing vessel entered the chop and surf of the North Sea and began rounding the coastline of Kent.

"We were keeping an eye on you," he said. "I thought you might be needing us at some point, once the Jaguars started taking an interest. It was careless, letting that detective woman outmanoeuvre you the way she did."

"Maybe I knew all along I had Mayan guardian angels. Maybe I was relying on you coming to my rescue."

"Maybe. Still, she got past your defences. You underestimated her."

"Implying I was seduced."

"Beguiled."

"By the person who gave me this?" Stuart pointed to the fresh bruise that was swelling on his cheek, overlaying the bruise Vaughn had put there the previous day. "I don't think so."

"You should put her out of your mind anyway. That's all over for you now. For better or worse, you're with us."

"For the time being."

Chel made a dismissive gesture.

Overnight they crossed the Channel, reaching the port of Saint-Malo at dawn the next day. Captain Beaudreau was part of a French resistance network that had been conducting a campaign of passive, surly dissent for a couple of hundred years, ever since imperial annexation. They called themselves the Louisiens, after the monarch who chose to abdicate rather than rule a country that had just capitulated to the Empire. King Louis XVI was arrested at Marseilles attempting to steal away on a schooner bound for Malta. He was guillotined in the Place de l'Entente at the end of the Champs-Élysées before a throng of Parisian well-wishers who showered him with rose petals as he stepped from the tumbrel onto the scaffold. In revenge for this act of mass insubordination, a contingent of Jaguar Warriors, at the behest of newly anointed High Priest Napoleon Bonaparte, rounded up everyone in the square and put them to the guillotine as well.

The massacre had embedded itself in the French consciousness, festering there like an infected splinter. A certain element in the country refused to forget it. The Louisiens made sure that the hieratic caste didn't have an easy time. They achieved this mostly by obstructing theocracy with bureaucracy. Edicts from the Palais Bourbon were seldom implemented in full and never with any haste. Sometimes the wheels of power turned so slowly they seemed to be standing still. Systematically and unobtrusively, a whole sector of the populace made it their role in life to collaborate as little as they could with their leaders while still staying the right side of outright noncompliance. Probably in no other country could this nuanced state of affairs have been achievable, and certainly nowhere but France could it have been carried out with the same sense of sangfroid.

From time to time the Louisiens took a more direct hand in frustrating the will of the powers-that-be, as now, by smuggling the Xibalba guerrillas, and the Conquistador too, out of Britain. At Saint-Malo the harbourmaster turned a blind eye to the fact that Captain Beaudreau claimed to have brought in a catch of one and a half tons of mackerel, dace and skate when his hold was in fact devoid of fish and his nets not even damp. The same harbourmaster then directed Beaudreau's "crew," who hardly looked like native Bretons, to a cargo truck standing at the quayside. Stuart and the Mayans got in the back. A lengthy, suffocating ride later, they were disgorged at the international airport at Nantes, along with the various items of luggage that had come over with them from London.

At the airport, tickets awaited them. Chel bought Stuart a set of new clothes at one of the concession shops and handed him a French passport with a photo of Stuart inserted. "We plan ahead," he said.

For the foreseeable future, Stuart was René

Jolicoeur, a botanist of dual French/Anahuac nationality who preferred to speak to the customs officers and airline staff solely in Nahuatl. "To show where one's true loyalties should lie," he explained, and not, of course, to cover up the fact that he barely knew any French beyond the few loan words that had been incorporated into Nahuatl.

The flight to Mayapan was the first time Stuart had ever travelled coach class, and he noted that neg-mass flight was considerably less slick and smooth when your seat was at the outer edge of the aerodisc, as opposed to being in the central cabin. Airsickness was a novel experience for him, but one, he supposed, he might have to get used to, now that he no longer had access to his many millions.

It wasn't until that evening, however, as he lay in bed in a grimy hotel room in downtown Mayapan, that he grasped the momentousness of what had happened to him. Mosquitoes buzz-bombed his head. Ocarina-led disco music thumped from an open-fronted bar outside. Neon flashed through the threadbare curtains. The bedsheets reeked of other people's sweat. The heat was atrocious, with only a clattery electric fan to alleviate it.

This was another world.

No, it was *the* world. Stuart just hadn't had to experience it quite so intimately before. His entire life, he'd known wealth. It had insulated him from everything, like a wadding of cotton wool.

That was gone now, and he missed it.

Didn't he?

What he did miss, suddenly, gut-wrenchingly, were his wife and son. Grief hit him with the force of a charging rhino, and he realised he'd not felt this way – so hopelessly hollow, so utterly bereft – since the day he first donned the armour of the Conquistador. Everything he'd done as the Conquistador, the manic stunts, the priest slayings, had helped prevent him from dwelling too hard on Sofia and Jake. His head had become perfectly clear, free from conflicting thoughts. He'd no longer felt the yearning, aching need to hug the son who wasn't there any more. He'd no longer switchbacked between adoring and loathing the woman who had ripped the heart out of his existence.

The Conquistador had been a crutch, a way of coping with his bereavement. Without it, he was forced to face all the emotions he'd locked away and tried to deny were there. They flooded upwards, consuming him. Stuart sobbed on the creaking, thin-mattressed bed. In part, he was mourning the loss of his cushioned, moneyed lifestyle, but what he really was mourning was the loss of the two people who had made that lifestyle worthwhile, who had justified it for him.

Prosperity was nothing without family. Only now, when he was deprived of both, did that truly make sense.

THE FOLLOWING MORNING came the news that there had been a spate of volcanic activity in Europe. It was on the tiny TV set jabbering away in a corner of the café where Stuart and the men of Xibalba ate their breakfast. Three major volcanoes had begun erupting yesterday – Vesuvius, Hekla and Etna – and two of them had since calmed down but the third, Etna, continued to spew out ash and lava, so much so that towns in the vicinity had been evacuated.

Naturally this led talking-head commentators to speculate on whether the Great Speaker was sending some kind of message. Rarely did a cluster of eruptions occur unless it was at the Great Speaker's command, and if he had given the order for the fusion plant at each site to stoke the earthly fires, why? It wasn't just to push a few million tons more of sulphur dioxide into the atmosphere and keep the planet nice and toasty. What point was he making?

The fact that one of the volcanoes was in Iceland suggested that the Faroe Islands fishing dispute was still an unresolved issue. Could it be that yet more sacrifices of Icelandic worthies would have to be made? The four diplomats had not sufficed?

European High Priests would have to consult with the Great Speaker to learn why he was angered and how he could be appeased.

In the meantime, Ah Balam Chel had his own interpretation of the matter.

"You," he said, pointing across the table at Stuart. "It's you. You got away. Slipped the noose. And that's made him very unhappy."

Stuart could see the logic in this. "They're the three volcanoes closest to Britain," he said, nodding, "and Reston Rhyolitic was in negotiations to take over the mining of an obsidian lode on Etna. That'd be why Etna's the worst affected, the one still blowing its top. The Speaker's telling me he knows all about me. This is a targeted fuck-you."

"Which, I imagine, irks you."

"I don't know. It seems more petty than anything. An impotent gesture. Like flicking someone a V after they've left the room."

They spoke openly; there was nobody else in the café apart from the proprietor, and he was, Chel had said earlier, "a good man," meaning aligned with the Xibalba cause. He also knew how to lay on a hearty breakfast: quinoa porridge, fried eggs, sourdough toast, boiled corn, fresh guava juice, plenty of everything.

"So you don't feel personally affronted?" Chel said.

"If you're trying to turn this into a feud between me and him..." Stuart finished off the sentence with a shrug.

The Xibalba leader frowned, concerned. "Tell me you still wish to see the Speaker dead. Surely you do."

"I wouldn't mind."

"That's hardly the ringing declaration of intent I was hoping for. Need I remind you, Mr Reston, that without Xibalba you would right now be languishing in a cell at Scotland Yard? Were it not for us, the best you'd have to look forward to from this point on would be the final plunge of a priest's knife into your chest, bringing to an end what would be days of torture."

"All right. I get it. You saved me from a fate worse

than death. You think you should get something in return."

"Not just something. We want *you*. We want the Conquistador. We want all that he's done, all that he embodies, all that he *can* do. We travelled a long way to meet you. We risked our necks for you. I think that deserves recognition." Chel was aggrieved. All signs of his usual good nature were gone. He wore the scowl of a man who did not like to be denied what he felt was his due.

Stuart was aware that he was in a room with a dozen hardened paramilitaries who would do whatever their leader asked of them. He was also in a foreign land where someone with his looks and complexion stood out like a sore thumb. Vaguely at the back of his mind there was the notion that Chel might, if so inclined, sell him out to the Jaguars. *Psst. Listen. I know where that English troublemaker, the Conquistador, is. I'll take you to where you can find him.* He didn't know Chel well enough to know if he was the vindictive type. He felt, however, that he shouldn't cross the Mayan, just in case.

"I'm not saying I'm not onside. Just saying we need to think about this. *I* need to think about this. There's no point going off half-cocked. I have to have more intel. A clearer idea of what you have in mind."

"Ah well," said Chel, looking and sounding placated. "For that, you'll just have to stick with us."

By which Stuart understood him to mean, *Your wagon is hitched to Xibalba. You're one of us, whether you like it or not. One of the good-as-dead.*

*   *   *

CHEL HAD INFLUENCE and supporters within the Mayapan area. To those in the know, he was a local hero. What he desired, he got. He put the word about that he was looking for transportation. In no time at all he was in possession of a canvas-topped truck, military surplus. He also received donations of diesel from Xibalba sympathisers, enough jerry-cans of it to travel several hundred miles.

It was a long, jolting journey out of the Yucatan Peninsula, through lush agricultural lowlands, round the rim of the Gulf of Anahuac, north through what had once been Olmec country, on towards the mountainous heart of the Land Between The Seas. They drove through dark and daylight, stopping only to top up the fuel tank, relieve themselves, and refill their bellies.

A day and a half later they were in rainforested high ground. The roads were twisting and treacherous here. The main highways had hairpin bends that teetered above sheer, plummeting drops with often not even a crash barrier to give the illusion of safety. The back roads were worse still, their poor asphalting and the leftover debris from mudslides adding to the general hazardousness, but Chel insisted on using them as much as possible. Less chance of running into a random Jaguar stop-and-search patrol. Less likelihood of someone spying a Caucasian among a group of Anahuac nationals and reporting this suspicious incongruity to the authorities.

Evening was falling as the truck pulled into a hill village perched at high altitude, just below the cloud line. Chel had cousins here, or cousins of cousins. He was vague on the true nature of the connection, perhaps not even sure himself. Distant relatives, at any rate, and they knew Xibalba's goal and were broadly in favour. The guerrillas and Stuart were put up in the village longhouse, where bedrolls were laid out for them in rows.

"From here to Tenochtitlan, it's not far," Chel said that night, as the villagers prepared to roast a wild pig in honour of their guests. "Forty miles in a straight line. We are near the Empire's beating heart. The Great Speaker doesn't know it yet, but his days are numbered."

"If he's truly a god, then maybe he does know it," Stuart said. "Divine omniscience and all that."

"But you don't believe he is."

"Of course not. If he's anything, he's a man who dreams he's a god, but more likely he's a man who knows he's just pretending. There's a fiction to be maintained, and he maintains it. The entire Empire is predicated on a lie."

"And if we can spear that lie and kill it, then the whole structure surrounding it will die too." The light of the cooking fire danced in Chel's eyes. The smoke carried delicious smells.

"I'd like to think so. But a ship without its captain will still float."

"But it won't sail anywhere, will it?" Chel gave an impatient shake of the head. "You are, if I may say,

Mr Reston, proving to be a lot more circumspect than I thought you would be. The Conquistador never struck me as a doubter. His actions carried the weight of absolute conviction. What has happened to that man?"

"Maybe I need my armour," came the sardonic reply. "Can't function without it."

"Ah well, I can help you there. Come with me."

Chel led him across the village to a hut belonging to one of his relatives. He himself was lodged there. Some of the Xibalba luggage was stacked in a corner, and Chel unzipped a couple of large rucksacks and produced, bit by bit, Stuart's Conquistador armour. The individual pieces were wrapped in items of clothing so that they wouldn't clank against one another. The rapier was there, even the flechette gun.

"It's the one you wore at the theatre," he said. "The one we removed from you."

"You've had it all along?" Stuart picked up the morion helmet and examined it by the light of the hut's solitary battery-powered lantern. He turned it this way and that, as if seeing it for the first time in years. That was how unfamiliar it seemed, here in this remote rainforest village, thousands of miles from home. Utterly out of context, and oddly nostalgic.

"I told you I'd get the armour back to you. Now I have. Does it change your mind at all? Persuade you in any way?"

Funnily enough, being reunited with his Conquistador outfit did restore some of Stuart's sense of mission. He was reminded how invincible he felt while wearing it, how shot through with purpose. It was like some bizarre form of addiction. He was nothing – adrift, rudderless, at the mercy of the elements – without this steel carapace around him and these weapons in his hands. He was an empty shell, and the armour, a shell around shell, somehow made him whole.

"I'll need to see," he said slowly. "Tenochtitlan, I mean. See it for myself. Because that's where we're going to have to go, isn't it? And photographs are one thing – everyone knows what Tenochtitlan looks like – but there's nothing like an eyeball recce to give you a true idea of the nature of a place, its strengths, its weaknesses."

Chel was encouraged by these words. "I think you should go. Definitely. Zotz can take you. He knows these parts well. Used to live at Tula, to the north."

Stuart could put a face to the name and knew Zotz was Chel's lieutenant, but beyond that he'd had little to do with the man. "He seems trustworthy."

"Trustworthy!" Chel exclaimed. "Zotz would die for me, and I for him. I count him among my closest friends. I'm sure, once you and he have spent some time together, you'll be able to say the same."

DURING THE JOURNEY to Lake Texcoco, Stuart didn't feel that he and Zotz were becoming bosom buddies. Zotz seemed to have formed an opinion of him as an effete urbanite unused to hardship. And while there might be some truth in that, Stuart was determined to prove him wrong. As they trekked through the forest, Zotz hacking a path with a machete, he kept pace with him, didn't lag behind. When it came to paddling the canoe, he gave it his all, tirelessly. He didn't complain once or query Zotz's lead. He rested only when Zotz decided to rest, never himself suggesting they take a break.

It wasn't clear if any of this raised him in the Mayan's estimation, but gradually Zotz began to treat him with less overt contempt. That had to be counted as positive progress.

Why did he want to get in this man's good books, if he had no intention of accompanying Xibalba on their fool's errand?

Stuart couldn't answer that.

But he reckoned the Conquistador could.

TWELVE

3 Skull 1 Lizard 1 House
(Friday 7th December 2012)

THEY HALTED AT midnight, mid-river. Zotz roped the canoe to a branch of a teak tree that had toppled into the water. The trunk reached almost all the way across to the opposite bank, like an unfinished bridge. They slept under blankets on the bare boards of the hull while the boat swung gently side to side in the current.

At first light they carried on, using the outboard now. The sound of the two-stroke motor putt-putting, as the boat cut through the tendrils of mist that drifted up from the river, was like someone lazily slapping congas. They passed hamlets where two or three families lived in cramped stilt-dwellings and eked an existence from fishing. Children waved as they went by – skinny, half-naked urchins, splashing barefoot in the shallows. "Hey, white man!" they yelled at Stuart. "Don't melt in the sun!" It was a hilarious joke, worth repeating over and over until the butt of it was out of earshot. "Don't melt like ice cream!"

Isolated communities of this kind could be found all over Anahuac, tribal folk living at subsistence level. It was one of the great ironies of the Empire that, while it had the wealth of the world at its disposal, its homeland was littered with pockets of extreme poverty. The Empire looked outward, and consequently paid little attention to what was on its doorstep. Outside the major metropolises – thriving industrial conurbations like Oaxaca, Palenque and Yaxchilan – the people of Anahuac benefited little from Imperial bounty. It was as though the Great Speaker took his own country for granted. Aztec hegemony had existed here for so long, it scarcely merited his interest any more. The newer conquests were more exciting, riper, worthier of cultivation.

No wonder, then, that anti-Empire sentiment was as rife in Anahuac as anywhere, fermenting in the wilds, in the darker, more distant reaches of the land. No wonder Xibalba could find a warm reception in so many places. The Empire wasn't tending to its roots. That kind of neglect could lead to terminal rot.

STUART AND ZOTZ arrived back at the point they had set out from, a village that was little more than a landing stage with a handful of huts attached. Even as they approached, rounding a bend in the river, Stuart sensed there was something wrong. Yesterday there'd been noise and bustle, dogs scampering about, the inevitable pack of semi-feral children. Today, silence.

Nobody came out to greet them as they tied up the canoe at the jetty. Stuart's ears detected furtive activity within the huts – muffled footfalls, hushed voices.

"What's up?" he murmured to Zotz.

"No idea," came the reply. "But I don't like it."

"Me either. We should move on upriver."

"We hired the canoe here, we return it here. Besides, not much further on, the river becomes impassable. Rapids, rocks, waterfalls."

As Zotz stepped out of the boat, he swore softly.

Jaguar Warriors had emerged from the largest of the buildings, which belonged to the canoe's owner. There were four of them in all. Two had lightning guns, and Stuart could hear a faint whine. The weapons were charging.

"How should we handle this?" he said to Zotz out of the corner of his mouth as he, too, stepped onto the jetty.

"Play it by ear. It could be nothing, a routine visit."

"If it isn't? Those l-guns say they're ready for trouble."

"Anahuac Jaguars are always ready for trouble. Let me do the talking." Zotz raised a hand in greeting. "Gentlemen! Good day to you. How are you this fine morning?"

The Jaguar group's leader made a hand-slash gesture: *cut the chitchat*. "Who are you? Names."

"Hunab Ku Zotz. And this is René Jolicoeur, a botanist from France. I'm his guide. I've been taking him into the forest to study plants."

"Botanist, huh?" The Jaguar eyed Stuart sceptically. "What particular plants in our country interest you?"

"Well, all of them, I suppose," said Stuart. "The diversity of flora in the region is remarkable."

We're not going to pull this off, he thought. *I know bugger-all about any of this stuff if he tries to cross-examine me.* He calculated which of the Jaguars to attack first. One of the pair with guns stood close by. A few quick steps, a well-aimed jab to the throat, he could have the weapon out of the man's hands, shoot the other gun holder before the element of surprise was lost.

"But especially," said Zotz, "medicinal herbs. Monsieur Jolicoeur works for a pharmaceutical company based in... Rennes, is it?"

He looked to Stuart, who nodded.

"They're constantly on the lookout for new drugs to develop from traditional natural remedies. Like jatoba bark." Zotz took out a handful of his own supply from his pocket, to show the policemen. "It's a huge market, and Anahuac is at the centre of it. As ever, the Land Between The Seas leads the way, and the rest of the world follows. What we have, everyone else desires."

The Jaguars nodded to one another as though Zotz had uttered pearls of great wisdom.

"And Anahuac has provided the cure to all ills," said Zotz, still pursuing his not-so-subtle subtext.

"True," said the Jaguars' leader. Abruptly he turned back to Stuart. "I'd like to see some ID, if I may." He held out a hand. Stuart fished out his bogus passport.

He'll see that it's been doctored. He'll ask me to show him plant samples I've collected. The whole charade was about to crumble to pieces. Stuart tensed, preparing himself for a quick, dirty fight.

"Seems to be in order." The Jaguar handed the passport back. "I wish you luck, Mr Jolicoeur." He turned and motioned to the other three with a circular sweep of his arm. "Let's move out, men. We've wasted enough time here. We've another half-dozen of these hick-towns to cover today."

They tramped out of the village along the path that led to a nearby dirt track. Shortly, there was the sound of two-stroke engines spluttering into life. Motorbikes. The waspish drone faded into the forest.

"Whew," said Stuart to Zotz. "Nicely done. I thought they were here looking for me."

"Don't flatter yourself, Englishman. Like I said, routine. Jaguar patrols come through every so often. They shake down the villages. Kick in a few doors, prise up a few floorboards. Not sure what they hope to find. Some sort of contraband. There isn't any. What do these people have? Nothing. Mainly it's a show of power, to remind everybody, even in the boondocks, who's carrying the biggest stick. A bit of swaggering. The locals know to keep their heads down and wait until they pass."

Sure enough, with the Jaguar Warriors gone, the villagers emerged from indoors. In just a few minutes the air was filled with shouting and hurly-burly again. Normal village life had been resumed.

"Still," said Zotz, as he and Stuart began the arduous four-hour hike uphill to the village where Xibalba were billeted, "we'd better tell Chel. There's a chance one of them might not be as lazy and complacent as the Jaguars round these parts usually are. He might check with his counterparts in France to see if there really is a botanist called René Jolicoeur."

"And is there?"

"Yes, there is. That's his stolen passport you're carrying. Trouble is, he doesn't look a bit like you."

AH BALAM CHEL agreed that they had a problem. The encounter with the patrol was unfortunate. He'd known having Stuart among them would be a risk. A tall white man in the company of a group of short, brown-skinned Anahuac nationals was always going to attract attention.

"You are, at least as far as physical appearance goes, a liability, Reston. And it means, I'm afraid, that we must abandon this cosy little perch sooner than planned."

"And go where?"

"Where we have to go," Chel replied cryptically. "To the place the military would call our forward operating base. The bad news is, we won't be travelling by truck. We can't. We'll be too visible on the roads – *you* will be. We'll have to go cross-country instead, on foot. But we have enough time, that's the main thing. Still enough time. We're ahead of schedule."

"Schedule? What schedule? This is the first I've heard of it."

"The countdown, Reston. The cosmic clock is ticking."

"You what?"

"Come now, don't look like that."

"No, you're really going to have that explain that remark."

"I will, I swear. But tomorrow, after we head out. Go get some sleep. You look done in. In the morning, we march."

THIRTEEN

4 Deer – 6 Water 1 Lizard 1 House
(Saturday 8th – Monday 10th December 2012)

THE RAIN WAS like no rain Stuart had ever known. Britain had its downpours – torrential cloudbursts that could soak you to the skin in seconds. They seldom lasted long, though. They came, they went.

This rain was relentless, merciless, endless.

The deluge started shortly after dawn, and Stuart expected that Chel would postpone departure. But instead, Chel claimed the rain was a great opportunity. "It'll keep the Jaguar Warriors off our backs. If we wait for it to stop, we could be hanging around for days."

So, heads bent, packs on backs, they set out. Within minutes they were drenched. The trees were no protection. The forest canopy didn't act as an umbrella; instead, the foliage served to channel and focus the rain, turning it into thick rods and shimmering, sluicing sheets. It was like taking a tepid shower, fully clothed. You couldn't see much further than a dozen yards ahead. Everything beyond dissolved into a haze of falling water.

The Mayans didn't appear to mind. They marched along in a line, singing a song in a language unfamiliar to Stuart but not dissimilar to Nahuatl. The melody was dirge-like, but peculiarly haunting, as it vied with the rapid staccato drumming of the rain.

"Old Mayan lullaby," Chel explained, "learned at one's mother's knee. A tradition the Aztecs haven't managed to eradicate, not for want of trying. Most of these men don't understand the actual words. Mayan is a dead language, its use forbidden. But they know what the song is about."

"Which is?"

"The twin brothers Hunahpu and Xbalanque and how they played the ball game against the Lords of Death in the underworld. The Lords of Death cheated, trying to injure the twins both on and off the court. They still couldn't beat them, so they killed them."

"Cheery."

"It has a happy ending. Happy-ish. The brothers were resurrected and turned the tables. They tricked the Lords of Death into letting themselves be slain with a knife, making them believe that they would be resurrected too. From that day on Death no longer had quite such a hold over humankind. Its power was not completely broken, but it had to play fair forever after. No more luring the innocent and unwary into its domain, as it had done."

"So then, inspirational."

"Very much so. Afterwards, Hunahpu and Xbalanque rose into the sky to become the sun and moon, eternally alternating but interconnected." Chel chuckled, casting an upward glance. "Not that we're seeing much of Hunahpu today."

"You said something last night about a schedule. A cosmic clock."

"I did. You'd like me to explain?"

"Anything to take my mind off this pissing rain."

"Well now, first off, I don't want you getting the impression that I'm some kind of fruitcake who puts his faith in prophecies and the like."

Stuart shot him a wry sidelong look. "From the sound of it, that's exactly what I'm going to end up thinking."

"The truth is, I do sincerely believe that the Empire's dominance is coming to an end. Things can't go on like this. The Empire has become decadent and corrupt at every level. It's had its time; its comeuppance is due. You feel that too, don't you? That the Age of Aztec has run its course?"

"All empires collapse eventually," Stuart said. "Although this one does seem to have lasted longer than most. Alexander the Great didn't manage to conquer the entire world. Neither did the Romans. But has the decline begun? I don't know. Perhaps."

"It just so happens that we're in a time of endings. Have you heard of the long count calendar?"

"Vaguely. It's the Mayan equivalent of the *tonalpohualli*."

"Equivalent!" Chel snorted. "It was the forerunner. The Aztecs copied their calendar from us. Mayan astronomers devised it, the Aztecs took it and modified it and claimed it as their own, much as they do everything. The *tonalpohualli* is based on our dual calendar, which consists of the *haab* and the *tzolk'in*. The *haab* is the solar calendar, and the *tzolk'in* the base-twenty calendar, with a two-hundred-and-sixty-day cycle. The two calendars turn and turn, one inside the other, a wheel within a wheel, meeting again at zero every fifty-two years. However, there is a further, larger unit of time called a *b'ak'tun*, roughly four centuries. Thirteen *b'ak'tun*s constitute a 'world age,' the time it's reckoned it takes for Creation to commence, evolve, and be complete. That's approximately five thousand, one hundred and twenty-five solar years. With me so far?"

"My head's starting to swim," said Stuart, "but that could just be rainwater."

"According to a Mayan sacred text, the *Popul Vuh*, the current world age – the fourth – began in 3114 BC Gregorian."

Stuart did a swift bit of mental arithmetic. "Five thousand years ago, give or take."

"It's nearing its climax," said Chel. "Another Creation is due to begin."

"When, precisely? Soon?"

"Four Flower One Movement One House."

"Very soon. That's just over a *trecena* from now."

"Fourteen days on the nose. Of course, none of this is widely known. When they invaded, the Aztecs suppressed all Mayan culture, including the *Popul Vuh* and the concept of world ages. They stole what they liked the look of and stamped out the rest. But we know. A few of us, true Maya, have kept our folklore and beliefs alive. We've passed our culture on down through the generations orally: the legends, the myths – like the story of Hunahpu and Xbalanque – the learning, the lore, all of it. We remember what we used to know, even if no one else does."

Stuart thought of the books in his library. He'd done much the same thing as the Maya, in his own small way. He'd sought out and bought novels and works of nonfiction that pre-dated Britain's fall. Extraordinarily expensive, some of them, and only available from a handful of very greedy and jealous collectors. Not illegal to own, but no self-respecting subject of the Empire would dream of having them in the home, let alone displaying them openly on shelves. Precious artefacts from the time when Britain was Great and a slave to none.

"So if the fourth world age is nearly over," he said, "will there be a fifth? Or is now the time to find a remote cave and start stocking up on provisions?"

"Some believe the end of the fourth age heralds apocalypse," said Chel. "Not me. I think there'll be a fifth, and a sixth, and many more. Why not? The long count calendar is a cycle, not a straight line. Everything comes round again. What's inarguable is that the completion of thirteen *b'ak'tun*s is a significant date. It's a period of transition as one world age pivots around and becomes the next. Creation begins anew. Life is transformed."

"The Empire falls."

"If it's to happen, when better? We can look on this as an auspicious time to be undertaking our mission. The stars are aligned in our favour. The universe is smiling on us. A state of flux approaches, and in flux anything is possible."

IT WOULD HAVE been easy to dismiss outright Chel's talk of world ages and periods of transition – to treat it as meaningless mumbo-jumbo number wrangling.

Stuart, however, was in a state of flux himself. So was the forest he was trudging through, literal flux, as the clouds continued to dump water onto it in epic quantities, turning the ground to an ankle-deep mush of dirt and leaf mould. Nothing seemed stable, as the rain beat down on Stuart's skull and made the world around him a smeary green blur. Time itself became elastic. So did distance. He lost all sense of the hours passing and couldn't even guess how far he and the guerrillas had been walking. They climbed and descended ridges, pushing through thick stands of fern and bromeliad, ducking beneath vines, straddling over rotten deadfall trunks, wading through the slurry the soil had become. Only when the greyness of the daylight darkened did Stuart realise that nightfall was on its way.

They bivouacked beneath an enormous cedar that

provided some shelter from the continuing rain. No one could get a cooking fire started, so they ate their tinned rations cold.

When they woke the next morning, it was still raining. They squelched on through the rain on a westward course. The Mayans were no longer singing to counteract the rain. Zotz cursed the rain. All Stuart could think about was the rain. The rain had soaked into his brain. He felt like a sponge filled with rain. His clothes hung heavy with rain. There was only rain. There had only ever been rain. There would only ever be rain. Rain reigned.

They spent another night shivering beneath the tarpaulins they were using as tents. Sometime during the small hours the rain stopped. Everyone snapped out of sleep, startled by the sudden hush. Nobody could quite believe the watery onslaught was over. Even the forest fauna took a while getting used to the idea, but once one animal let out a first tentative hoot, the others pitched in. The nocturnal chorus was back with a vengeance, louder than ever as if to make up for its silence the previous night. The frogs in particular were overjoyed, creaking and booming.

When dawn arrived, the air turned to steam. The guerrillas resumed their journey in better spirits than before, strolling along, chatty and cheery. Stuart himself felt his mood lighten with every step, and his clothes lighten too as they gradually dried out. When Chel paused to take a compass bearing, Stuart asked how much further they had to go and was pleased to learn that it was only another day's walk. Tomorrow morning at the latest they would reach their destination. If it had still been raining, he wouldn't have dared ask. Any answer would have been too depressing.

By the middle of the day, the heat had become ferocious, accompanied by a humidity that sapped the life out of you. Even the Mayans, who had struck Stuart as indefatigable, began to drag their feet. The air was a thick, unbreathable broth. Zotz collected some berries from a guarana vine and passed them round for all to munch on. The caffeine in the bitter-tasting fruit helped, giving an energy surge, but tiredness soon set in again. After a while every step was an effort. Clothing became wringing wet again, now with sweat.

Chel sensibly decided they should make camp early. A fire was lit – a minor miracle – and hot stew was consumed. For Stuart it was a pleasure beyond all reckoning just to sit on the forest floor, not moving, with his bare blistered feet stretched towards the flames, soles gently warming. None of the forced marches he'd undergone during his Eagle Warrior training could compare to the yomp he was on right now. He couldn't find a part of his body that didn't ache. It took all his remaining strength just to crawl under canvas and lay himself out on a blanket; he was asleep before he knew it.

And awake again, in the darkest part of the night. Someone was yelling frantically. Stuart scrambled out into the open. All the guerrillas were up, milling about. It took a while for the cause of the commotion to become clear.

One man, Tohil, had got up and gone to the edge of the campsite to relieve himself. Mid-flow, he'd spotted something between the trees. A shape. A person. Watching him.

Tohil had let out a cry of surprise and the watcher had fled.

No, not fled.

Kind of vanished.

Definitely vanished.

Melted into the darkness as though being swallowed up by ink.

And Tohil was sure – not absolutely sure, but pretty sure – that it had been a woman. The watcher had had a female silhouette. Not too tall. He'd glimpsed the contours of hips and breasts.

The other guerrillas scoffed. "A woman? You don't think you just imagined it? You were maybe asleep and dreamed her?" Snide allusions were made to Tohil's manliness and how long it had been since he'd last had a girlfriend.

Tohil became indignant, insisting he had seen something. But the more he protested, the louder the mockery grew. Eventually he stomped off to his tent, muttering under his breath.

Only Stuart considered his claims with any seriousness.

Was it possible? Could DCI Vaughn have followed him to Anahuac? Be on his trail now?

No. Absurd. How could he even think it? Vaughn was still in London. Had to be. There was, in fact, every chance that she was dead. If she hadn't been killed when the Xibalba van hit the paddy wagon, the Jaguar Warrior code of honour would have swiftly remedied that situation. A high-profile murder suspect had been snatched from right under her nose. You couldn't cock up an arrest that badly and expect to be allowed to live.

If Tohil was right and a woman had been spying on the guerrillas' camp, it wasn't Chief Inspector Malinalli Vaughn.

Which, Stuart was bemused to find himself thinking, was a pity.

FOURTEEN

7 Dog 1 Lizard 1 House
(Tuesday 11th December 2012)

THE FOURTH AND final day of the journey began innocuously enough. After a breakfast of maize cake and dried broad beans, Stuart and the guerrillas tramped off, reassured by Chel that there were ten miles remaining, perhaps less. Stuart's inner compass told him they weren't far from Lake Texcoco. They had more or less retraced his and Zotz's river recce trip, overland.

The mood was genial.

That changed when one of the guerrillas spotted something overhead. Among the leaves. Too large to be a monkey.

It was there one moment, gone the next. Nobody else saw it.

"A jaguar?" Chel suggested.

It could have been. The big cats did sometimes lurk in trees, balancing on a thick branch, poised to pounce on prey below.

But whatever the guerrilla had seen was larger, he said, than a jaguar. And he could have sworn it had *flown* upwards as it disappeared from view. On wings that shimmered like a hummingbird's. A hummingbird the size of a human.

Tohil was gleeful. "Hey, so I wasn't imagining things last night, was I? There *was* someone watching us."

"Something's going on, that's for certain," growled Chel.

"We're close to enemy territory," said Stuart. "Your men are getting jumpy."

"My men don't get jumpy," Chel snapped. "I've been feeling it since we struck camp. Haven't you?"

"Feeling what?"

"That we're being followed. Stalked."

"By something up in the trees?"

"Not just there. Behind us as well."

"You're kidding."

"He's not," said Zotz. "I've noticed it too. I didn't want to say anything, so as not to spark alarm, but I'm convinced we're not alone."

"But who? A forest tribe?"

"Not round here."

"Jaguar Warriors?"

"I don't think so. They're not nearly this subtle."

"Serpents, then."

"Again, I don't think so. They're good, but this

isn't their style. Why follow us when they could just as easily ambush us?"

"Maybe there's only one or two of them. They're waiting for reinforcements."

"No," said Zotz. "It's something else. Something I can't figure out. Whoever they are, it isn't natural, what they can do. They're as stealthy as spiders."

"We have to keep going," said Chel. "But we should break out the weapons."

The guerrillas armed themselves from their backpacks. In addition to bolas and blowpipe, they had brought along more contemporary items, including a stolen lightning gun and several conventional rifles and pistols. Stuart was glad to strap his rapier on again and have his flechette gun holstered at his hip.

They carried on in silence, bunched together, aiming wary looks in all directions. The forest seemed denser and more oppressive. Every shadow held something. The moss on the tree trunks took on humanoid shapes. Leaves made faces.

One of the Mayans suddenly opened fire. A couple of the others joined in. They raked a thicket of rattan palm with bullets, scything the stems and spiky fronds. Chel ordered them to stop. As the echoes rumbled away across the hills he demanded to know why they were shooting.

"I heard a sound," said the man who had started it off. "A rustling."

"And I fired because he did," said one of the others, and the third nodded in agreement.

Chel approached the demolished thicket and peered in. He gave a sour smile.

"Unless we're being hunted by agoutis, I think we're all right."

Everyone took a look at the bullet-riddled remains of the agouti. There wasn't much of it left, but it was still just identifiable as a harmless rodent.

Nervous laughter was accompanied by quips at the expense of the men who'd let rip with their guns. "Fancied some lunch, did you?" "What's next, a big scary guinea pig?" and so on.

"Onward, men," said Chel. "And less of the itchy trigger fingers, if you don't mind. Those reports will have carried for miles, and who knows who might have heard them."

An hour later, they took a break beside a stream. Cigars were smoked, water boiled for tea.

Over the next ridge, Chel promised, lay their final destination. The trip was nearly over. There'd be food and beds, a roof over one's head. All the comforts of home.

Still, no one could quite relax. Even Stuart, who had little in the way of jungle instinct, was convinced they were not alone. There was someone out there lurking, observing him and the band of guerrillas. He felt this not just because the Mayans were thoroughly spooked: he could actually sense eyes on him. That primitive, ingrained intuition. You knew when you were being watched. You just knew. He'd experienced it in London and had assumed it was the Jaguars keeping tabs on him – although it had in fact been Xibalba as well – and he was feeling it again, now, strongly.

The guerrillas were preparing to move out again when Zotz noticed the ants.

He drew everyone's attention to the insects quietly, calmly. Remaining unflappable whatever the circumstances was one of Zotz's defining characteristics.

"They're big ones," he said. "Everybody keep still. Let's see where they're going."

The ants marched in a column, a dozen abreast, trickling out from the undergrowth like a leaking liquid. They *were* big, each the size of an infant's finger, and they were red-brown, the colour of dried blood. They were coming straight towards the cluster of men, thousands of antennae and legs bristling.

"*Sauba* ants," Chel murmured. "Don't let any get on you. They're leaf cutters. Very sharp mandibles, very powerful too. They'll give you a nasty bite and won't let go."

Then another of the Mayans let out a hiss of dismay.

"There's more," he said. "Coming the other way. Look."

A second column of *sauba* ants appeared from the opposite direction. They headed towards the first as if on a collision course. The guerrillas were sandwiched in between.

"This is ridiculous," said Chel. "This doesn't happen. Ants go outwards from the central nest. They send out foraging parties in a radial pattern. You don't get two lots at once like this."

"No one told that to these ants," Stuart remarked. "Maybe they're from different nests."

"Who cares?" said Tohil. "I'm not hanging around. I'm going that way." He pointed to the side, away from both ant columns. Then his face fell. "Oh, fucking balls. There's even more of them."

A third contingent of ants had appeared, approaching perpendicular to the other two. The guerrillas backed away, gathering in a huddle at the stream's edge, clutching their weapons. All at once blowpipes, even guns, seemed wholly inadequate. You couldn't deter ants with a bullet or a dart.

The three columns of ants met and merged in the middle of the clearing. They became a single, almost perfectly circular carpet which expanded outwards as more of them fed into it. The perimeter of the carpet crept towards the guerrillas' feet.

"Cross the stream," said Chel.

His men didn't need to be told twice. They splashed through the knee-deep water, retreating to the far side. There they waited to see what the ants would do next.

Watching the insects, Stuart felt a horrified fascination, which he saw reflected in the expressions of the Mayans. Whether or not what the *sauba* ants were doing was standard practice for their species, there was something uncanny in the organisation they showed, the precision with which they coordinated themselves. It could of course be pure coincidence that they'd flowed in and overrun the space where a group of humans had happened to be sitting. But there seemed an element of deliberateness, even vindictiveness, in their actions. They'd not simply taken over, they'd ousted and occupied.

And that wasn't the end of it.

Out of the scurrying ground-swirl of ants a pillar began to rise. It grew upwards, ant clambering over ant to add to it. Moments later a second pillar sprang up alongside. Each was several inches in diameter, and they climbed in parallel to a height of a metre or more.

Then ants at the summits of both formed horizontal chains which reached out towards each other. The two chains joined, locking into position, and hundreds more ants charged up the pillars and got busy constructing a central pillar on top, this one oval in cross-section and as thick as a watermelon.

"I don't fucking believe it," Stuart said in English. The Mayans didn't understand the words, but they recognised the tone well enough and echoed the sentiment in Nahuatl.

The central pillar mounted and swelled before branching out on either side. The ants were now building downwards as well as up. Two new long extrusions descended while a third, a sphere, formed in the middle at the top. It was obvious – eerily obvious – that the ants were working according to a specific plan. This was no random agglomeration. It had purpose and design.

Chel was the one who identified it first – saw the pattern, the overall aim.

"A figure. Fuck my mother, a human figure."

And it was. It could be nothing else. Thousand upon thousand of the *sauba* ants had come together to create a life-size mannequin, a shifting thing composed of hard little bodies whose exoskeletons glittered dully in the sun. The head was bulbous, the limbs stocky and featureless, but it was unmistakably a representation of a person.

All of a sudden the ten-foot span of the stream didn't seem wide enough. Stuart wanted to be as far away as was humanly possible from this... this *thing*.

Then the ant mannequin raised an arm towards the guerrillas.

As one, the Xibalba men responded with an involuntary communal groan of horror. Stuart joined in.

That was when Ah Balam Chel, who had the lightning gun and more presence of mind than most, decided enough was enough. He slapped down the l-gun's charge lever. He rotated the setting dial to maximum. The men beside him were still giving voice to their dread, and the ant mannequin still lifting its arm with appalling, zombie-like slowness, the *sauba* ants clambering over each other. A light winked blue on the side of the lightning gun, signalling readiness. Chel took aim and pulled the trigger.

The plasma bolt blasted the ant mannequin, dead centre in its body mass. One moment there was a rust-coloured figure on the other side of the stream. The next, it had disintegrated into several thousand individual components. Ants and bits of ant sprayed everywhere like confetti.

The parts of the mannequin not directly hit by the l-gun collapsed. The carpet of ants in which the figure had stood recoiled, a shockwave passing through it in concentric ripples. Order became chaos. The *sauba* ants dashed in all directions in a mad panic. They disappeared into the undergrowth they had emerged from, a marauding army put to rout. In less than a minute all that remained of them was a scattering of body parts on the ground – charred abdomens, frazzled thoraxes, tiny exploded heads, legs fried to a crisp.

It was a while before anybody could speak.

"We imagined that, right?" said one of the Mayans. "Please tell me we did. Too damn long in the forest. A mass hallucination."

"I wish it was," said Zotz.

"What the hell is going on?" said Tohil. "I mean, that wasn't just ants. That was... ants gone crazy."

Stuart looked at Chel.

"I don't think," the Xibalba leader began, "that that was anything. Ants can arrange themselves into structures. It's been recorded. Bridges across crevices, between trees, to reach food or prey. Huge ball-shaped bivouacs that serve as temporary nests while they're migrating. This was just that."

"But it looked like –"

Chel chopped Tohil off, his voice an axe. "It didn't look like *anything*. We thought it did, but it didn't. Our minds made us think what we were seeing was a particular shape, but that was an accident of vision. The tendency people have to – what's the word? – anthropomorphise things."

"But you yourself said –"

"I was wrong," Chel snapped, shouldering the l-gun. "I was wrong and that's an end of it. Nothing just happened. We saw some ants, that is all, nothing more. Am I making myself clear?"

There were hesitant nods all round.

"Good. Then gather up your belongings and let's get on with it."

He set off at a fast lick. Everyone else exchanged glances and the odd shrug, and followed.

Stuart reckoned he wasn't alone in thinking that Ah Balam Chel had been too quick to debunk the bizarre phenomenon they had all just witnessed.

The man's eyes had given it away.

He was profoundly unnerved and did not like feeling that way. Did not like it at all.

FIFTEEN

Same Day

COME NOON, THEY emerged into a large clearing in the forest. The first thing Stuart noticed was a medium-range aerodisc parked on the grass. It was hard to miss, as it filled a good two thirds of the available space. A huge square of camouflage netting was stretched over it, with a garnish of vines, moss and other plant matter to make the disguise complete. The disc would be impossible to spot from the air, even to a vessel passing just a couple of hundred feet above.

Near the aerodisc was a small plank-built cabin, its roof so overgrown with foliage that it too was effectively camouflaged. Beside the cabin sat a row of tents, military issue, made of green jungle-pattern canvas. A small waterfall gurgled nearby, cascading into a deep, limpid pool. The surrounding trees formed a sturdy stockade.

This was the forward operating base Chel had spoken of.

A pretty, petite woman stepped out from behind one of the legs of the aerodisc's landing gear. She was dressed in dungarees and wiping her hands on an oily rag. Seeing Chel, she let out a cry of delight and made a beeline for him. She leapt on him, scissoring her legs around his waist, and they kissed passionately for several minutes, or at least so it seemed to those watching.

"That's Chimalmat," Zotz informed Stuart.

"Mrs Chel?"

"They're not married, though they might as well be, the way they argue sometimes. Chimalmat's our resident mechanic, in case you couldn't guess. She's been out here for weeks maintaining that disc, keeping the damp and the bugs from getting into the works. She and the boss don't like being apart for that long, so I doubt we'll be seeing either of them for the next few hours, if you catch my drift."

Sure enough, Chel and Chimalmat disappeared into the aerodisc. She said she had something to show him, some technical problem she needed to discuss with him. He replied that he would give the matter his full attention and do all he could to help out. If either of them thought this coded talk was fooling anyone, they were sorely mistaken. Probably neither cared. They were like a pair of horny teenagers.

The guerrillas chose tents for themselves, dumping

their backpacks in front as claim markers. The tents were two-man, but there were enough of them that not everyone had to share. Stuart, for instance, had one to himself. The cabin was for Chel and Chimalmat's exclusive use, their little love nest.

Some of the guerrillas clambered into the relative coolness of their tents for a nap. Others went out to bathe in the pool and wash their clothes. Everyone was careful not to mention the events of the past twelve hours, the strange visitations in the forest. Chel had made it clear that topic of conversation was embargoed. There had been no weirdness. *Nothing just happened.* End of story.

Zotz broke out a *patillo* board and found two of his fellow Mayans to play with. Stuart was invited to make up a four. He refused at first; *Patillo* was an Empire game, and for that reason alone, he scorned it. It was also far too dependent on the roll of the dice for his liking. Little skill involved. Zotz insisted, however, and in the end Stuart relented.

They played several games, betting with matchsticks. The dice fell in Stuart's favour often enough that he won twice, getting all his four pieces home first. In general, however, Zotz was the victor. He had a knack for throwing just the right number he needed to capture an opponent's piece or occupy one square with two of his own pieces and form a blockade.

"Luck, that's all it is," he told Stuart as he packed up the board afterwards. "I've always been lucky."

"That would account for your permanently sunny disposition."

"Don't push it, Englishman," came the reply. "Just because Chel thinks you're hot shit, doesn't mean we all have to. Frankly, nothing I've seen from you yet has impressed me. The Conquistador's supposed to be this big action hero, but the evidence says otherwise. Big pussy more like. Always getting himself into difficulties. Screwing up at the crucial moment. If you ask me, we can manage without you, and we should. You'll be nothing but a millstone round our necks."

For punctuation, Zotz hawked up a wad of phlegm and spat it at Stuart's feet.

The other two *patillo* players waited to see how Stuart would respond. The spitting was out-and-out provocation. Nobody could let an insult like that pass unchallenged.

Stuart had no alternative. Zotz had set things up well and selected his moment with care. Ah Balam Chel wasn't around to intervene and defuse the situation. This was where something got settled. Zotz didn't hate Stuart; he just wanted the Englishman to prove his mettle, with other Xibalba men present to see it happen.

"Pussy, huh?" Stuart said. "Well, that's better than being a big fat cheat."

"What did you just call me?"

"You heard. I saw you spinning the dice rather than throwing them. Pathetic, really. I mean, if there'd been money on the table, then I could understand. But in a friendly game? For matchsticks? That's just sad."

"Say that again." Zotz bellied up to Stuart. He

was shorter by several inches, but that didn't seem to bother him.

"Which part? The part about being a cheat, or the part about being pathetic?"

"You want pathetic? I'll tell you what pathetic is. It's getting your butt kicked by a woman. We all saw that Jaguar detective taking you down, shoving you into the river mud. No self-respecting man should let himself be bested like that – by a girl half his size."

"Speaking of half my size, what's the weather like down there, shrimp?"

"I prefer 'piranha.' I eat big sluggish catfish like you for breakfast."

This wasn't going to stop at putdowns, and both of them knew it. Blows would have to be traded too. *Might as well get it over with.*

Stuart threw the first punch. Zotz was quick and ducked, then retaliated with a jab to Stuart's midriff.

What followed was vicious and inelegant. Stuart couldn't decide if the fight was a genuine grudge match or just for show. Both, he thought. Zotz certainly didn't hesitate to play dirty, trying head-butts and ball grabs and even going for an eye gouge. Stuart blocked, warding off all of the Mayan's attacks, and in return he employed every close-combat technique the Eagles had taught him, aiming for nerve clusters and vulnerable spots such as the floating rib and the Adam's apple. He had no wish to injure Zotz seriously, and he sensed the feeling was mutual. At the same time, it had to look authentic. They both had to acquit themselves well. Otherwise honour would not be served and Zotz would have nothing to show for picking the fight in the first place.

The other guerrillas gathered round to egg on the fighters. The noise roused the ones indoors and brought them out. Soon everyone was cheering Stuart and Zotz on with gusto. Nobody was taking sides. They were simply relishing watching a good scrap.

The two combatants ended up on the ground, scuffling like junkyard dogs. They rolled and hammered and elbowed and kneed, eventually falling into the pool. They reared up from the water and went at each other. They crashed under the surface sideways and staggered upright again.

Stuart was tiring; the Mayan, too. They lumbered together in a bear hug, scrabbling below the water with their feet to kick each other's legs from under them. They toppled simultaneously and rose to their knees, panting furiously. They grabbed each other's shirtfronts, holding each other up now rather than brawling. One of Zotz's eyes was swelling shut. Stuart could feel blood pouring from his nose.

"Enough!"

It was Chel, striding across the clearing, doing up his belt as he went. Chimalmat was close behind, fastening one strap of her dungarees back into place.

"What is this?" the Xibalba leader bellowed. "I leave you alone for two minutes and a brawl breaks out? Explain yourselves!"

Stuart looked at Zotz, Zotz at Stuart. In the Mayan's eyes Stuart glimpsed what he took to be approval. Stuart nodded to him, an almost imperceptible tipping of the head. They had both performed as required. There was respect now, and the guerrillas knew Stuart was not to be trifled with.

"It was nothing," said Zotz to Chel. "A misunderstanding. I think Reston's grasp of Nahuatl may be faulty."

"Yes, that's it," Stuart said. "I used the wrong verb tense. Got my syntax muddled up. What sounded like a rude remark wasn't meant to be. I'll be more careful in future."

Chel appraised them both. His expression said he understood what was going on but couldn't be seen to condone it. "Get out of the water, the pair of you. Don't let this happen again."

As Stuart and Zotz waded exhaustedly out of the pool, Chel turned to Chimalmat. "Now, where were we? You said the neg-mass drive has been playing up."

"Yes," said Chimalmat with a sly smile. "But I'm sure we can have it lifting off again in no time."

CHEL REAPPEARED AT dinnertime, looking deeply satisfied with his lot in life. He ate a hearty meal, and when the table talk strayed in the direction of what had been seen in the forest, as it couldn't help but doing, he steered it back to more mundane subjects.

That night, however, he posted men on guard round the edge of the clearing, on four-hour shifts. He said it was just a basic precaution, in case a Serpent patrol should happen by.

If anyone believed that, they were a fool.

SIXTEEN

8 Monkey 1 Lizard 1 House
(Wednesday 12th December 2012)

"YOU'RE STILL WITH US," Ah Balam Chel said to Stuart. "You haven't fled for the hills. That must mean you're still interested."

"Where am I going to go round here? There's a lot of rainforest to get lost in."

"You'd find your way back to civilisation if you had to. I think it's now time I clued you in on the master plan. You've earned it. Follow me."

He led Stuart across the clearing. It was midmorning, after an uneventful night, and the men of Xibalba were taking the opportunity to laze around and do as little as possible. Some cleaned their rifles in a desultory fashion. Others flirted with Chimalmat, who enjoyed the attention and had fun parrying their innuendo with even cruder remarks of her own.

"Hold on, we're going inside the disc?" Stuart gave a droll smile. "Does Chimalmat know?"

Chel gave Stuart a blank look. The man had a remarkable capacity for ignoring the things it suited him to ignore.

Inside, the aerodisc revealed itself to be a cargo transport model. There were few seats. Most of the interior was hold space, stripped of all adornment, bare down to the ribs of the airframe. The fittings showed their age, even a few specks of rust visible. Stuart reckoned the disc was at least forty years old, close to the end of its lifespan.

"This'll fly?"

"It got here, didn't it? And Chimalmat's taken it up a couple of times since, to test it out."

"But it looks ready for the knackers' yard."

"It is of some vintage, I admit. In fact, its destination before we got hold of it was the Mojave Desert."

Where it was going to be scrapped. There were aerodisc decommissioning plants all over the American southwest. Dismantling neg-mass drives was hazardous work, best carried out in remote uninhabited locations in case of accident. Antigrav particles, if not handled correctly, were deadly stuff.

"But Xibalba has contacts in that region," Chel continued.

"Xibalba has contacts everywhere, it seems."

"Fellow travellers. Some of the native Americans in the southwest, especially the Anasazi and the Mogollon, haven't forgotten how the Aztecs swept up across the border and subjugated them. Nor will they forgive the Empire for the way it treated all Americans, natives and settlers alike, during the War of Independence."

Every schoolchild was taught that the American War of Independence, more properly called the Act of Necessary Suppression, was a vainglorious failure. George Washington and his cronies foolishly attempted to sever all ties between their portion of the country and the Aztec-controlled areas. As well as battling on various fronts with their militiamen, they roped in the indigenous peoples in the southwest, using them to attack the Imperial territories from within, hoping to undermine through sabotage.

It was all in vain, and the Empire's retribution was swift and absolute. The punishments they meted out afterwards were terrible even by their own standards, and although the settlers suffered – Washington himself being hacked to death with an axe – it was the native Americans who bore the brunt. All members of the Hohokam nation, for instance, were forced at gunpoint to kill and eat one another. Most refused, and were repaid for their obstinacy by being staked out under the sun and skinned alive, then having fire ants poured on their flensed bodies. Many, though, did as bidden. Parents murdered and consumed their children, husbands their wives, in the belief that they would be allowed to live as a reward for their compliance. They weren't.

The history books were unequivocal: they had it coming. But even as a boy, Stuart had been appalled as he read the eyewitness accounts and studied the sometimes very graphic illustrations. In quelling the native Americans and ending the American uprising, the Empire had come very close to committing absolute genocide. They had also snuffed out whatever small spark of selfhood America had been kindling in its breast, leaving it what it was now – a spacious, largely undeveloped land full of natural resources which the Empire plundered freely and at will.

America had had the potential to be the Empire's greatest rival in the world. The Aztecs had turned it into a ghost country.

"My friends in America got wind that I was looking for an aerodisc," Chel said. "This one belonged to a German freight airline. Not the most elegant of vessels, but beggars can't be choosers. It was diverted on its way to the breakers in Mojave and brought here. The official records have it lost at sea. A malfunction in the antigrav over the Atlantic. No great surprise, given its age and state of repair."

He showed Stuart to the cockpit. The controls were marked in German. Someone – Chimalmat was the likeliest candidate – had stuck pieces of tape on several of the instruments, with the Nahuatl words for their functions written on in marker pen.

"You know," Stuart said, "if I was a pro-Empire kind of guy and someone asked me 'What have the Aztecs ever done for us?' I'd have to say that the power of flight is certainly a point in their favour."

"Ah, but did they? Weren't they just passing on a gift from the gods?"

"True. If you believe that sort of bollocks." Stuart slapped the cracked leather headrest of the pilot's chair. "So, what are we intending to do with this particular fine specimen of Aztechnology?"

"We" – Chel approved of Stuart's use of the plural pronoun – "are going to fly it to Tenochtitlan and land there."

Stuart gave a hollow laugh. "And get blasted to buggery the moment we step out."

"Not if we don't step out."

"Just sit there on the landing pad, then, and wait for Serpent Warriors to board. The slightest hint of something dodgy going on, and they'll storm the disc all guns blazing. In a confined space, against dozens of them, I don't rate our chances."

"Neither would I," said Chel. "What you're not seeing, Reston – and it's not your fault, because you're not in possession of the full facts – is that the Great Speaker himself will walk voluntarily up the gangplank, straight into our waiting arms."

"Yeah, right. Because he does that, climbs aboard random aircraft that touch down on his roof."

"He will if he's under the impression that this is the disc that's been chartered to fly him to China for a High Priestly conference due to take place on Two Flint Knife." Chel grinned. He'd just played the card he'd been keeping up his sleeve all this time, and he was convinced it trumped all.

"Conference?" said Stuart. "I didn't know there was one happening."

"It's not been widely advertised. These hieratic

synods rarely are, for security reasons. Only much closer to the date does the information get released, a day or so, and then it's touted all over the news networks, the biggest thing since, well, the last one. I happen to have heard about it well in advance thanks to an insider in Beijing. Preparations at the Forbidden City have been going on for months. It's supposed to have been kept under wraps, but you can't hide that much construction work or that level of heightened security around the venue. The more hush-hush the activity is, the more obvious it becomes that something big is in train."

"And your man in China knows for a fact that it's a conference? All the High Priests are going to attend?"

"He does. He's an Anahuac, a cousin of a cousin of mine. Works in the building trade over there. He's been supplying labour to the site. They're putting up a convention hall right where one of the main palaces in the Forbidden City used to stand. They're also raising a brand new temple ziggurat. There's going to be some serious sacrificing once the Great Speaker blows into town."

"How do you know he's on the level, your cousin's cousin? Mightn't the Empire have turned him? Could he be feeding you deliberate misinformation? Couldn't this all be some Imperial plot to smoke Xibalba out?"

"Ah, so suspicious," said Chel. "And you are wise to be. However, I'm in absolutely no doubt that he's telling the truth. He's sympathetic to our aims, and what with that and our shared blood, I trust him implicitly. That's why I've obtained this aerodisc. That's why I've cooked up this kidnap plan."

"Kidnap? It isn't going to stop at that, though, is it?"

"No." Chel looked grave. "It can't. The Great Speaker has to die. And he has to die publicly, screaming, begging for his life. As a man, not a god. In mortal terror."

"In Beijing."

"That would be the ideal location. The world's press are going to be there. It'll be the focus of international media attention. Before hundreds of cameras, before millions of watching eyes, Xibalba will unmask the Speaker and show him to be a human being, as frail as any of us and as capable of dying. We will cut him down just as his priests have cut down so many countless others, and the Empire's reign of terror will be over."

Off the top of his head Stuart could think of a dozen objections to this plan. The ways it could go wrong were many and obvious. For one thing, they had to make sure the Serpent Warriors at Tenochtitlan were fooled into believing this disc was the one that had come to fetch their master. For another, it was a distance of several thousand miles from Anahuac to Beijing. Could such a rusty old rattletrap make it that far? And assuming they got there in one piece and were able to stage a public execution for the Great Speaker, wasn't there a chance people might be made to think it was faked? The Empire could claim the whole thing was a setup, with some hapless impostor duped into wearing a replica set of robes and golden mask. A replacement Great Speaker could be wheeled out at short notice and declare that a vicious prank had been played by enemies of the Empire and the world should pay it no attention.

Chel studied his face and saw all the doubts there. But he saw something else as well.

"It's not without its potential drawbacks," he admitted. "I'm well aware of that. Some might even call it harebrained. But imagine if we manage to pull it off. Just imagine. The Empire is predicated on the fact that its Emperor is Moctezuma the Second, ancient and everlasting. If we were to prove convincingly otherwise, it would have nothing to stand on. It would fall heavily and hard. And..."

He moved a step closer to Stuart.

"What a grand gesture it would be. What a spectacular coup. I know your love of the bold, flashy statement, your flair for the dramatic. You understand that that's what's needed to get one's point across. A slumbering public has to be woken up. It has to be shocked out of its complacency. People are numb, docile – sheep. What else was the Conquistador about if not throwing a metaphorical grenade in their laps? *This* would be the biggest grenade of all. The effects of its explosion would be felt for all time. It could change everything!"

Chel looked deep into his eyes.

"Let's set it off. Let's at least try."

SEVENTEEN

Same Day

STUART WAS ON first watch that night. He and a man called Auilix patrolled the perimeter of the clearing separately, Stuart at one end, Auilix at the other. Every now and then they met in the middle to exchange nods and maybe a word or two.

Since his conversation with Chel, Stuart had oscillated between feeling the Xibalba leader was hopelessly deluded and wondering if he might not be on to something. If the plan could be carried out without a hitch, it would make everything Stuart had done as the Conquistador look small-time indeed. It might even, as Chel insisted, cause the Empire to crumble. At the very least, shake it to its foundations and leave significant cracks in its façade.

But...

The odds against success were inordinately, almost ridiculously high.

But...

If there was even a tiny percentage chance it would work, wasn't it worth attempting?

One Flint Knife was half a *trecena* away. Stuart had seven days to make up his mind.

The rainforest was unusually loud this evening. The animals seemed to have recruited several new members to their nightly glee club. The racket made it hard to think. Stuart, as he did his semicircular circuits of the clearing, could scarcely hear his own footfalls.

Then, all of a sudden, it stopped.

A hush descended.

The hush stretched on, as eerie as it was absolute.

Stuart strode over to Auilix. The Mayan had the lightning gun, while Stuart had a semiautomatic rifle. Stuart could see he was perturbed.

"What's up?" he whispered. "Why's it gone so quiet?"

Auilix shook his head uncertainly, and both men stared into the darkness of the trees. The only sounds were the burble of the waterfall, the faint ripple of a breeze through high branches, and their own breathing.

"Sometimes, if there's an apex predator around, the other animals are subdued," Auilix said. "But not like this. Not this silent."

Stuart felt the hairs prickle on the backs of his hands.

"Someone..." said the Mayan, so softly it was almost inaudible. "Someone is moving around out there."

Immediately Stuart racked the bolt handle on the rifle. The sound seemed astonishingly loud, but he was happy with that. Whoever was in the forest, he wanted them to know he and Auilix were aware of their presence and ready to deal with them.

His eyes searched for movement. With the Eagles he had learned to use peripheral vision at night. The blind spot at your focal point, his training sergeant had said, could hide an elephant.

There.

Black amidst the blackness. Something shining. A glint.

Stuart raised the rifle and sighted along the barrel.

But the glint had gone. It could just have been moonlight reflected off a leaf.

But Auilix beside him had glimpsed something too. The l-gun began to whine.

Stuart moved closer to the trees, leading with the rifle. He was expecting to come under enemy fire at any moment. In his gut, he was terrified. In his head, he was calm. The real danger here was losing his nerve. Keep that and he might just keep living.

"Come on, you bastard," he murmured under his breath. "Where are you? Show yourself."

He reached the tree line. Behind him, Auilix grunted, urging caution, but Stuart didn't pause. The best tactic, when facing the possibility of ambush, was to take the fight to the ambushers. Your opponents' one advantage was their hidden position, and that could be negated by a direct, full-frontal approach, flushing them out from cover.

He entered the forest, and the tree canopy closed overhead, blotting out the moon. Everything was a play of silver and black, patterns of pale filigree light. He trod toe-to-heel, feeling for each step with his feet, never dropping his gaze once to look where he was treading.

The whole of the forest held its breath.

Then there was a yelp of surprise, and the percussive *snap!* of a lightning gun being fired.

Stuart whirled round in time to see Auilix disappearing.

Upwards.

The Mayan was whisked into the air above the clearing, suspended beneath something large, black and insectlike. Stuart glimpsed shiny curved contours, giant outspread wings – then the thing and its squirming human burden were gone, soaring out of sight. It had happened so swiftly that Auilix had managed to get off that single, reflexive shot with his l-gun, and that was all.

Stuart had time to wonder what the winged creature was. Then he heard voices. They were coming from nearby in the forest. Two of them. Conversing urgently and low. He couldn't make out what was being said... but there was something weirdly familiar about both of the voices. The cadences, the timbres.

He couldn't help Auilix. The Mayan was a captive now, possibly dead already. He could, he supposed, alert the rest of Xibalba. Chances were the l-gun discharge had done that anyway.

But the voices...

Who was talking? He had to find out.

Stuart turned and headed in the direction of the sound. He wasn't so unwary as to think this might not be a trap; he was most likely being lured. But he had a weapon, didn't he? That evened the odds somewhat.

He ventured away from the clearing, further into the forest. Everything had suddenly become strange. That thing, that flying creature – it didn't make sense. Far bigger than any airborne animal he knew of. Encased in a hard armour like a beetle's. What with that and those ants the day before yesterday... The world was topsy-turvy. This place, this sector of rainforest, harboured anomalies, phenomena that shouldn't by all the laws of nature exist. He felt as though he was in some alien zone where the usual rules no longer applied.

Steady, he told himself. *Focus*.

He concentrated on regulating his breathing. Pinning his mind on the task at hand.

The voices grew louder, clearer, as he homed in on their source.

One of them, now, he was certain he could identify. It was Ah Balam Chel's.

Damn it, what was Chel doing out here, chatting away in the forest? Why wasn't he back there at his and Chimalmat's cabin where he ought to be?

A thought occurred. Was the Xibalba leader behind all these shenanigans? Was this some sort of exercise? A test of his men's preparedness? No, it didn't seem reasonable. Or possible.

Now Stuart was within a few yards of the two people who were talking so intently, Chel and another man. He still couldn't see them, but he could hear every word. They were speaking in Nahuatl, and the tone was distinctly conspiratorial.

"We," said Chel, "are going to fly it to Tenochtitlan and land there."

Chel was sharing his plan with someone else. But who?

The other person laughed. "And get blasted to buggery the moment we step out."

Stuart couldn't have put it better himself.

"Not if we don't step out," the Xibalba leader replied.

"Just sit there on the landing pad, then, and wait for Serpent Warriors to board."

Hold on a sec, Stuart thought.

"The slightest hint of something dodgy going on," Chel's interlocutor continued, "and they'll storm the disc all guns blazing."

What the fuck...?

"In a confined space, against dozens of them, I don't rate our chances."

Stuart reeled. That was him. That was *his* voice. Those were his exact words from that very morning.

This wasn't any old conversation. It was a playback of the talk he and Chel had had in the aerodisc.

Chel's next statement confirmed it. "Neither would I. What you're not seeing, Reston – and it's not your fault, because you're not in possession of the full facts – is..."

Stuart charged the last few paces towards where the playback was coming from. He expected to find a loudspeaker attached to some kind of recording device. Somebody had bugged the aerodisc, eavesdropping on Chel's revelation of his intentions for the Great Speaker. Somebody was taunting Stuart with the knowledge that they, too, knew what Xibalba was up to. If this was the Serpent Warriors' doing, then it was unusually sneaky behaviour. Stuart felt almost indignant.

There was no loudspeaker, no recording device. Stuart rounded a tree trunk and found himself confronted by a man.

A tall man, dressed in smooth, sleek armour.

And crouching at the man's side, a dog. Or something that resembled a dog, at any rate. In the dim light it was hard to make out its features, or those of its master. It had fur, certainly, and sharp pointed ears. But it was big, too, almost apelike. And the way it sat on its haunches was very un-canine. More human, if anything.

What Stuart could see quite clearly was that it was the dog that was doing the talking. All the talking. Its jaws moved and speech came out – speech that mimicked precisely his and Chel's voices.

"What conference?" the dog said, in Stuart's own tones. "I didn't know there was one happening."

Then, as Chel, it said, "It's not been widely advertised. These hieratic synods rarely are, for security reasons."

Stuart suddenly felt small and unreal, his soul

shrivelling inside him. He was witnessing an impossibility, to add to the other impossibilities of the past day and a half. It wasn't just the latest in the list, it was the one that capped the previous ones, the final straw.

A dog that spoke. That could replay conversations like a parrot.

Everything had gone stark staring mad.

But he still had the rifle in his hands. A loaded weapon.

Bullets were hard and reassuringly real. They could change things – end madness.

He took aim at the dog's head. He curled his finger round the trigger, braced for recoil, and squeezed.

The gun bucked. The muzzle flashed.

Stuart almost didn't see the armoured man move. Move he did, though. So fast it was more like a flicker of light, a quicksilver ripple in the darkness. His hand darted out in front of the dog's face and darted back again.

Stuart's aim had been good. At this range, virtually point blank, he couldn't have missed.

But the dog was alive, and intact. And the armoured man was holding up his hand, and a small object was pinched between his thumb and forefinger.

A bullet.

The round that was meant to have blown the dog's brains out.

Stuart gaped. Stuart gasped.

Then the tall man stiffened, straightened. From the back of his armour, objects began to unfurl. Pointed extrusions fanned out behind his head, forming a semicircle of comb-like teeth.

The dog, which had stopped talking the moment Stuart shot at it, looked up at its master with admiration and approval.

The armour started to glow. All at once, brilliant light shot out from it. Stuart was blinded. He threw a hand in front of his eyes. The light was dazzling, shimmering, iridescent. Even through eyelids squeezed shut, Stuart could see multicoloured patterns, a pulsing full-spectrum radiance. The light had power. He could feel it all over him, bathing him, putting pressure on his skin, driving itself into him. The rifle dropped from his hands. He could no longer hold it. He could barely stand. He reeled before the light as though before a strong wind. It was a physical force pummelling him. He staggered backwards, hoping to escape, yet there was no escape. The light was suffusing him. Its rainbow intensity was within him, crawling through his muscles, sinking into his bones. Nothing could withstand it. The light was all-consuming. It was taking him over completely, leaving nothing left, just a shell in the shape of Stuart Reston. He was vaguely aware of himself screaming, but his scream seemed to have no substance. It was weightless and meaningless, as light as light.

Unconsciousness, when it came, was a blessing. Stuart blacked out, and the blackness extinguished the light.

EIGHTEEN

9 Grass 1 Lizard 1 House
(Thursday 13th December 2012)

"Did you really have to hit him so hard, Kay?"

"He shot Xolotl. What else was I supposed to do?"

"But he's just a human."

"Again – he shot Xolotl."

"Shot *at* him. Not the same thing."

"He had no idea I'd be able to catch the bullet. He meant to kill him."

"Still, you didn't have to razzle-dazzle the poor fool to quite the extent you did. Look at the state of him. You could have destroyed him inside and out. We'll be lucky if you haven't completely burned out his mind."

"I'm sorry, Toci, all right? I overreacted."

"Negating a threat is one thing. But this?"

"Work your magic. Bring him back to health."

"Oh, I will. Just be more careful in future. He isn't your enemy."

"Yes, Toci."

All this Stuart heard as though from a distance, from behind a thick screen of pain. He smelled a strange smell – neutral, antiseptic, like nothing he could name or knew. He felt remote, lost. Who was talking? He knew those names.

The blackness returned.

HIS EYELIDS FLUTTERED open. Light spiked his retinas. Everything hurt. He could just make out a figure bending over him. A woman. Long blonde hair.

Sofia?

Sofia.

He reached for her, even though every muscle in his body begged him not to. He wanted to touch her. He had so much to say. He wanted to forgive her, and rage at her, and hug her, and plead with her.

What it all came down to was a single question.

Why?

Why had she done it?

Couldn't she have talked to him first? Discussed it with him? Given him the chance to put a counterargument, talk her out of it?

Why go off so selfishly like that? And why drag Jake along?

If only she'd given him some forewarning, even come right out and said that she was thinking about putting herself forward for sacrifice, then he would have been able to do something about it.

But she had hidden the truth from him, keeping it buried in her mad, secret heart.

For fuck's sake, if she'd told him, he might even have gone with her.

That was how much he loved Sofia: he'd have been willing to die with her rather than live without her.

And Jake.

Just a kid. Barely out of nappies.

His world.

His future.

Stuart's hand clamped around Sofia's wrist. His vision swam into focus.

It wasn't Sofia. Some other woman. As beautiful, if not more so.

She flashed him a businesslike, doctorly smile. In her hand was a device like a syringe and a pistol. In a clear capsule, a cloudy pink lymph-like liquid swilled.

"You need to rest," she said. "This'll make you better."

She pressed the hypodermic gun to Stuart's arm.

"Repairs. You'll soon be good as new."

A moment's pain.

A numb warmth spreading outwards.

Blackness again.

JAKE IN ALL his chubby glory. Gurgling with delight as his father tossed him into the air and caught him. Tossed him and caught him. Tossed and caught.

Never doubting for one second that he was safe. Knowing Daddy's strong hands would not drop him. Sublimely fearless.

This was all Stuart wanted. All he could have asked for.

To have Jake for the rest of his life, and always catch him, never drop him.

IN THE FACES of the priests the Conquistador killed there was often the same expression. As the sword went in, as life oozed out, a kind of outraged incomprehension. The look of someone who'd been made the victim of a practical joke, an undeserving stooge. *I don't understand. Why me? What did I do?*

With each death Stuart had been hoping to claw back some of himself. Murders as milestones on a road to recovery. A metaphysical transaction, the lives of those he hated helping him to regain his own life.

The emptiness inside him never seemed to fill up, though, and this was baffling. The Conquistador's deeds were supposed to be some kind of cure, a medicine for grief. Why wasn't it working? How come he never felt any better?

He kept at it, convinced a change would come, a corner would be turned, the longed-for satisfaction would finally arrive. He pushed himself to new heights of daring, wilder and more inflammatory feats of bravado. Putting on the armour became more than an act of provocation and transgression. He began to live for it. He missed it badly during the lulls between. To be Stuart Reston was to be ordinary, boring, a dweller in a world of routine and falsehood, where deals and smiles and handshakes were everything and meant nothing.

He found he was starting to play at being Stuart Reston. The Conquistador was his true self. Both were hollow vessels, but of the two, the Conquistador was by far the more pleasing.

THEN CAME THE cop. Detective Inspector Malinalli Vaughn. The only Jaguar Warrior to take the jigsaw of the Conquistador case and fit the pieces together in exactly the right way. She was on to him so quickly. She figured out what nobody else had. In that first meeting between them, she saw past the mask of Stuart Reston, respectable citizen. Peered into his eyes and glimpsed the firebrand within. Nearly caught the Conquistador once. *Did* catch him, the second time.

He admired her for that. He'd almost welcomed it when she ensnared him on Tower Bridge. Cunning. If he were to be arrested – and he'd known he would be eventually, there had to be an end to it all – then at least he had been arrested cleverly, by someone with the wherewithal to outwit him. Mal Vaughn had proved to be his equal. It had been a short contest, but he knew almost from the start that he'd met his match. Maybe even – whisper it – his better.

And yes, Chel was right, he was ever so slightly infatuated with her, too. She was extraordinarily sexy. She didn't seem to realise it, which helped.

Made her even sexier, in fact. Many good-looking women swaggered through life all too aware of their attractiveness, expecting men to fall at their feet, disappointed if they did, offended if they didn't. Mal Vaughn was not that banal. She didn't put on airs, didn't live by illusions. She was who she was, take it or leave it.

Stuart would have liked to take it. All of it.

THE ANTISEPTIC SMELL wafted in on him again. Stuart came to, feeling weird, quite unlike himself. All the pain was gone, but that wasn't the difference. He felt... *refreshed*. Yes, refreshed, although that didn't quite cover the whole of it. As though his mind had been transplanted into a new-minted body.

He pulled himself off the narrow bed he was lying on. He got to his feet. He bounced springily on the balls of his toes.

Invigorated. That sort of described it, too.

He stretched from head to toe. Nothing creaked or cracked. His tongue went to the molar Mal Vaughn had loosened with one of her punches. The tooth was firmly rooted in place again, not giving him gyp any more. The lumps and abrasions left by his scuffle with Zotz were gone. Even his many mosquito bites were no longer bothering him. All the little bumps of inflammation had subsided, and with them the aggravating itching.

The blonde woman's words returned to him. *Repairs. Good as new.*

Yes. He hadn't felt this spry in ages.

This hungry, either. He was famished.

He took stock of his surroundings. It was a small, plain room without windows. Almost everything was made of a dull platinum-grey metal. There were no ornaments of any type and no furniture other than the bed, not even a chair or a cupboard. It could have been a single-occupancy hospital ward. Or, equally, a prison cell.

The smell was strong now, and Stuart realised why he couldn't place it. It was actually no smell at all. The room was entirely odourless, as though nothing that carried any kind of scent was permitted here. Even bacteria were forbidden. He bent and put his nose to the bed mattress, which was made of a grey, form-fitting foam. Nothing came up from it, not even a whiff of his own body, although he had been lying on it for several hours at least.

The room was beyond antiseptic; it was sanitised to the nth degree.

His stomach growled. The hunger was getting bad, but he could see nothing to eat.

He went to the door, only to find it lacked a handle. No opening device of any sort was evident, nor any keyhole.

A cell, then.

He thumped on the door. "Hey! Anyone out there? What's going on?"

Nothing from the other side.

He thumped harder.

"Hey! Somebody must be able to hear me. I don't

know who the hell you are but you have no right to be keeping me here."

If his captors were Serpent Warriors, they did in fact have every right. But Stuart wasn't going to let a small detail like the rule of law bother him.

"Come on! Let me out. You're making a big mistake. I'm really not the sort of person you want to be holding against his will."

An impotent threat, but it was all he had.

Still no one came.

He stepped back, took a run-up and barged the door. It didn't so much as shudder within its frame. He tried again, launching himself as hard as he could across the meagre breadth of the room, rebounding uselessly off the door. A couple more times, but he was left with nothing to show for his efforts except an aching shoulder. The door would not budge.

"Shit," he hissed. "All right," he called out. "At least bring me something to eat. I'm bloody starving. You can't deny a captive a meal. You're going to torture me later, fair enough, but in the meantime you could show a bit of common decen–"

At that instant, the door vanished. It was as if the metal had turned to thin air.

And standing the other side was a skinless man.

Stuart recoiled in revulsion.

The man was over six feet tall, and every fibre of sinew and muscle could be seen, clear as day, except at his nether regions which were swathed in a loincloth. Eyeballs stared from skull sockets. Flesh flexed wetly. Veins pulsed with blood. Here and there were pallid glimpses of bone.

Stuart wanted to believe this was some ghastly life-imitating statue, an anatomical effigy designed to give prisoners a heart-stopping fright.

Then it spoke.

"Who said anything about torture?"

Stuart may have said something in reply, he wasn't sure. Right then, his thoughts were skittering in all directions, like panicked rats.

"Oh, wait a moment," said the skinless man. His voice was a low, sibilant rasp. "I've done it again. I'm see-through, aren't I? Everything on display. Let me opaque myself."

In the space of a few seconds, skin formed all over his body. It appeared in patches, which spread and merged, until the man was fully covered in his proper sheath of epidermis. The skin hadn't grown from scratch, Stuart thought. It was more a case of the invisible becoming visible.

"That's better, eh?" Though the man looked markedly less horrifying now, there was still something disconcerting about his appearance. Possibly it was because he lacked hair of any kind. Right down to the eyebrows, he was baby-smooth and follicle-free. "Don't know what was going through my head," he continued. "I usually save that look for when I'm in combat. Scares the living daylights out of the opposition."

He said it deadpan, but with a hint of disingenuousness. Stuart was in no doubt he had done it on purpose, this "glass skin" trick of his or whatever it was. He liked the effect it had on people. Relished the disgust and helpless horror it evoked.

"So, you could do with a bite to eat, could you? Always the way after one of Toci's treatments. They take it out of you. You need to replenish the system. Why don't you come with me to the refectory? I believe everyone's having lunch."

He made an ushering gesture. Stuart hesitated, then stepped out through the now doorless doorway. He gave the frame a quick inspection as he exited. The jamb was solid all round and he could see no slot that a door could have retracted into. There'd been a sheet of metal firmly in place, and then not. How was that possible?

He had a different question, however, for his escort. "You said Toci. As in the goddess, yes? The patroness of midwives?"

"None other."

"But people aren't named after the gods. It's not allowed. It's considered blasphemy."

"Then it's a good thing Toci isn't named after Toci," said the hairless man. "Just as it's a good thing I'm not named after Xipe Totec. Mustn't have blasphemy, must we?"

Stuart couldn't fully fathom the meaning of the remark. He was, however, beginning to glimpse the shape of something here. Something he couldn't quite wrap his head around yet, mainly because he was loath to. It was too huge, too extreme. Too insane.

A short corridor led to a terrace that ran round the rim of a vast open area. The terrace made four right-angle turns, describing a square, and there were more such terraces above and below, linked to one another by staircases. Stuart seemed to be inside an inverted ziggurat, its hollow interior forming an immense atrium. The whole was capped with a ceiling which glowed with light, enough to turn the interior into day. You could have stuffed the largest ziggurat on earth, upended, into this space and still had room to spare.

"Where are we?" he asked the hairless man.

"Halfway there." Stuart's query had been misconstrued deliberately. "Just a little further along."

They arrived at a door larger than the one to the room Stuart had been in, but just as devoid of obvious unlocking system. The hairless man simply rested a palm on it and the door was gone in a blink.

"So that's what you do," Stuart said, bemused. "Touch it and it's gone. Why didn't that happen when I hit the other one?"

"It wasn't keyed to your bio-data, that's why. You're not one of us."

They entered a dining area complete with tables and chairs that were all wrought from the same dull metal as everything else. There was decoration here, at least. The walls carried designs that were similar to the carved murals on display in any temple or hieratic building: pictograms, hieroglyphs, symbols, all pertaining to the gods, or to sacred animals such as lizards or hummingbirds. The difference was that these were drawn in patterns of bright light, and weren't static. Colours and imagery shifted constantly, a series of tableaux that flowed one to the next. It was mesmerising to watch and Stuart could have gazed at it for hours were it not for the fact that, seated at one of the tables, was the oddest assortment of human beings he had ever laid eyes on.

They were all tall, like the formerly skinless man. They had that in common, but little else. A couple of them were extraordinarily old, withered to the point of desiccation. Others were young and almost impossibly healthy-looking, vibrant with life. One man was so dark-complexioned he seemed to have been hewn from black marble. Another man was clearly quite physically incapacitated, his twisted frame showing deformities of all sorts, from a club foot to tumorous growths. Next to him was a person who could have been male or female, with sensuous lips and swept-back hair. Loose clothing draped his or her physique, making gender even harder to determine.

Seated at the head of the table was a very handsome, olive-skinned man with eyes that were both kindly and grave – the eyes of someone who knew the worst but tried to see the best. He rose, pushing back his chair, and nodded to Stuart.

"Nice to see you up and about. Glad you're feeling better. Take a seat."

This was the man Stuart had overheard earlier talking to Toci, the one who'd incapacitated him in the forest with an explosion of light. The one Toci had addressed as Kay.

The androgynous man-or-woman drew out an empty chair next to him or her in invitation. Stuart sat down. One of the other people at the table, the dark man, grumbled: "Shouldn't be here. No right." His neighbour, an elderly woman with a regal bearing and a spectacularly sumptuous bosom, hushed him.

Food lay heaped on dishes in the centre of the table. A plate was set in front of Stuart. He helped himself. It was good fare, simple, classically Aztec, centred on the twin staples of maize and agave. He stuffed his belly, aware of everyone's eyes on him, not caring. They seemed, most of them, to regard him as an interloper. Well, so what? He never asked to be here.

"So," said the one called Kay, as Stuart cleared a second plateful of food. "I expect you have questions, Mr Reston."

"Are you going to answer them honestly?"

"Yes."

"Then I do. First off, what is this place? It feels like we're underground. Partly that's an instinct, but also an inverted pyramid makes no sense otherwise, in practical architectural terms. Am I right?"

"Very good. We are underground. As to our location, we're not far from what your friend Mr Chel described as his forward operating base. A few miles to the west, within spitting distance of Lake Texcoco."

"Should you be telling him this much?" griped the dark man. His body was massively muscled, of bodybuilder proportions, while his voice was like gravel grinding on granite. "Should you be telling him anything?"

"I don't see why not, Mic," Kay replied. "Mr Reston is our guest. We brought him to our lair. So why hide the truth from him?"

"*You* brought him here."

"He was hurt. He needed our help. I had no choice."

"But we're not ready to make our presence known. This could ruin everything."

"I'm sure we can rely on Mr Reston, a.k.a. the Conquistador, to be discreet. He, perhaps more than anyone else on earth, understands the value of keeping secrets."

"Oh, yes," said the person who was either a feminine man or a masculine woman. His or her voice was pitched mid-range, indeterminately husky. "He has led a double life. He has balanced on the tightrope between what is and what seems to be. He knows how to appear one thing and be the other." The androgyne placed a slender hand on Stuart's arm and caressed it approvingly.

"Of course we could always kill him," said the hairless man matter-of-factly. "I can do it right now if you like. Fork, table knife, bare hands, whatever you prefer."

"Enough, Xipe," Kay rebuked him. "Save the resident-psycho act for when it's really needed."

"Just saying."

"No one is killing Mr Reston. He is under my protection. I've been keen to meet him. I was hoping he and I might have a quiet chat in the forest last night, but that was not to be. I blame myself for that.

I should have anticipated his reaction to the sight of Xolotl reiterating his own words, in his own voice. Anyway, he's here now, among us, and that's just how it is. All of you accept that and move on."

"Why me?" Stuart asked. "That's my next question. You've singled me out for some reason, some purpose. What?"

"Because you're mixed up in this Xibalba business, this plot to assassinate the Great Speaker. But unlike the ringleader, Chel, you strike me as someone who's open to debating matters – someone who's less committed to a certain course of action than the rest of them are – someone I can deal with on a polite, diplomatic level."

"I'm not as hell-bent on suicide as the others, if that's what you mean."

"That's the impression I get from our surveillance."

"Okay, so I'm beginning to get a handle on what's been happening this past couple of days," said Stuart. "You people have been trying to warn Xibalba off, haven't you? We're in your neck of the woods, on your turf. We've strayed into the middle of something that's already in progress. We're treading on your toes and you don't appreciate that. Hence stalking us through the forest. Hence, also, that business with the ants. That was something you lot arranged, wasn't it? Hoping to frighten us away."

One man at the table, sporting a shock of red hair, held up a hand in acknowledgement. "Guilty as charged. Did you like my composite-colony figure? I thought it an impressive piece of ant wrangling.

Great deal of finesse required to get it to wave its arm like that. You didn't have to go and blow it to bits, though. My lads weren't going to do you any harm. The colony's pretty upset so many of them got vaporised. I spent the whole of yesterday having to soothe them and get them to calm down."

"Your 'lads.' You talk to ants. And they have feelings."

"Yes, I do," said the redhead. "Not *talk* talk, of course. That would be absurd. Ants lack ears. It's more... pheromonal and vibrational. And yes, they do have feelings. They may look all hard and military on the outside but they're sensitive, too, underneath it all."

"All right," Stuart said sternly, slapping the tabletop, startling several of the people around him. "That's enough. Let's drop the charade. I get what this is now. I know who you're pretending to be. It's a clever act. The props are good, too. Doors that disappear, someone whose skin goes transparent, a dog that can talk... I've no idea how you're doing any of it, although I suspect the dog was some sort of high-class ventriloquism act. But bravo, well done. Spectacular work. Round of applause."

"Pretending to be?" said Kay, eyes crinkling. The rest seemed offended by their guest's sudden outburst, but he was amused.

"Yes, Kay. Or should I call you Quetzalcoatl? And you." Stuart pointed to the redhead. "Azcatl. The 'red ant.' The messenger. And you." He turned to the androgyne next to him. "Ometeotl, the dual divinity, opposites reconciled. Not forgetting Xipe Totec over there, the Flayed One. And Mictlantecuhtli, if I'm not mistaken."

The dark man just blinked slowly, otherwise impassive.

"The pantheon," Stuart declared. "Pardon me if I can't put a name to every face, but that's who you're all supposed to be, right? The gods and goddesses. It's blindingly obvious, really. I was a bit slow on the uptake but I was disorientated and my blood sugar was low. Penny's finally dropped."

"Go on," said the regal-looking woman.

"Coatlicue, I presume?" The matriarch, the earth mother, giver and devourer of life, mother of Huitzilopochtli.

A necklace of jewelled hands, hearts and skulls bounced on the woman's deep cleavage as she nodded. Two bulky metal snake earrings clinked slightly.

"Well, I'm surrounded by some sort of religious re-enactment group, aren't I? A society of role-players holed up in the Anahuac rainforest, fancying themselves the Aztecs' long-gone deities, dressing the part, acting the part, even throwing in a few parlour tricks to add to the illusion. All very entertaining. I'm sure you all have super fun doing this in this splendid clubhouse of yours. You've spent some money on the place, too, so I imagine you're pretty well off, or maybe just one of you is. But if you're after me to join, the answer's thanks, but no thanks. It's a neat piece of performance art you've cooked up, and I'm grateful for the grub and everything, but you're barking up the wrong tree."

Just plain barking, he nearly added.

"And now, I really should be going." Stuart stood. "If someone could point me in the direction of the nearest exit...?"

"He speaks like that?" snapped the oldest person in the room, a wizened white-haired crone with a peevish cast to her features. "To *us*?"

"Well put, Tzitzi," said Xipe Totec. "Told you we should kill him. Who's in favour? Show of hands."

There were loud murmurs around the table, a rumble of disgruntled agreement. Hands rose.

"Now, now," said Quetzalcoatl firmly. "None of that. Everybody, settle. Mr Reston, sit back down."

Stuart considered disobeying; weighed the options; sat.

"It's interesting that you take this view," Quetzalcoatl went on, "that we must be impostors."

Stuart shrugged. "What else can you be? There are no gods. Never have been. And even if there were, I can't imagine them being anything like you."

"How so? In what way are we not what you imagine?"

"Gods aren't physical. Touchable. Human."

"Human we'll set aside for now, but physical, touchable? Why not?"

"Where's the otherworldliness? The mystery?"

"Is that what you want from gods? Distance? Ineffability?"

"Isn't that what we're supposed to get?"

"Tell me, Mr Reston, how much exactly do you know about the pantheon?"

"You mean apart from all the mythology I had shoved down my throat during religious instruction lessons at school? The mystery plays I kept getting dragged to by my parents? The references that priests constantly insert into their public speeches? Oh, not much."

"You must be aware, then, that the gods bicker, the gods try to outdo one another, the gods eat, shit, fart, fornicate, just like people do. The gods aren't paragons. They can die, too. Take what happened to Mayahuel, for instance."

"That wanton slut," muttered the crone known as Tzitzi. This, Stuart assumed, was Tzitzimitl, queen of demons. Or rather, meant to be her.

"Fine way to speak about your own granddaughter," said Quetzalcoatl.

"Girl was no better than she ought to be. She deserved what I did to her."

"Yes, yes," Stuart said. "A charming story. A lesson in family values. Mayahuel wanted to bring humans happiness, and so she decided to share with them the recipe for *pulque*. Tzitzimitl wasn't too pleased about this."

"Why should we have given humans *pulque*?" Tzitzimitl grumbled. "If they couldn't figure out how to make it for themselves, why should they have any help? It doesn't always bring them happiness, anyway. Just makes them maudlin and sick most of the time."

This was turning into the most surreal conversation Stuart had ever had. These people, nutjobs all, were adamant that they were gods. They were immersed in their various divine personas, playing them to the hilt. There was little point in him trying to persuade them otherwise. They wouldn't listen. All he could do was play along, humour them, and hope he could get out of this place before any harm came to him. He didn't think any of them could outfight him, but with nutjobs you never knew.

"So Tzitzimitl sent some of her demons to stop Mayahuel," he said, "which seems a bit petty to me, but there you go. Quetzalcoatl was on Mayahuel's side and hid her in a tree."

"Disguised her *as* a tree, I think you'll find," Quetzalcoatl said. "Camouflaged her."

"But the demons, the Tzitzimime, found her anyway and tore her to bits. Quetzalcoatl buried her bones."

"With great sadness. She was a lovely creature, Mayahuel. Naïve, but sweet."

"And from her bones, so it's said, a spiny plant grew – agave – and Quetzalcoatl taught the Aztecs how to milk it for its sap, ferment the sap to 'honey water,' distil that further for greater potency, and hey presto, *pulque*."

"An accomplishment of which I am justly proud."

"Not that any of it actually happened," said Stuart. "It's just an explanatory myth. If it's of any interest, it's because it informs us that even gods aren't above killing one another."

"True enough, Mr Reston," said Quetzalcoatl.

"Nevertheless, being familiar with this tale of vindictiveness and murderous jealousy, and knowing it to be typical of divine behaviour, do you really still feel gods are ineffable? Perfect? Shouldn't they in fact behave more like, well, the way you're seeing *us* behave?" He touched a finger to his own chest, then indicated his companions.

"I'm not saying you people aren't accurate representations of the pantheon. I've already told you I think you're making a nice job of that. I just think I'd prefer gods, if we must have gods at all, who are a bit more, well, godly. A god is something one should look up to, isn't it? By definition. Not something that's just a human with a few extra bells and whistles."

"Death," Mictlantecuhtli intoned. "This little thing, this crawling bug, this *worm*, he insults us at every turn. Every word that comes out of his mouth is another drip of disrespectful venom. He is as contemptuous and discourteous as any of his kind. Death, I say. Swift and sudden. He must pay for his temerity."

"I agree, Dark One." This from Xipe Totec, who was half out of his seat, with an item of cutlery glinting in his hand. Stuart got up too and backed away from the table in order to give himself room to manoeuvre. Xipe Totec – the man who was claiming to be Xipe Totec – took a menacing step towards him. Stuart ran through all the permutations for disarming and crippling an opponent. For all that Xipe Totec was fit-looking and young, for all that he had a mad gleam in his eye and a reasonably sharp knife in his hand, Stuart was confident about being able to beat him. If all the other so-called gods piled in as well, that would be a different matter, but if Stuart made his treatment of Xipe Totec sufficiently brutal and devastating, perhaps he could scare them off and buy himself time to make a getaway.

Quetzalcoatl placed himself between the two of them. "Flayed One," he warned Xipe Totec. "What did I say? This man is under my protection. You do not lay a finger on him."

"Try and stop me, Plumed Serpent."

"Don't make me have to. Mr Reston's problem is not a lack of deference. It's that he's labouring under a misapprehension. He still hasn't perceived the full import of what's in front of him, and he's not to blame for that. He has somewhat been thrown in at the deep end. Would any of you, I wonder, on meeting gods for the first time, meekly accept they were what they said they were?"

"Maybe not," said Azcatl, "if I had a human's limitations and a human's frailties. I wouldn't want to believe they were gods, because that would drive home my own weakness and insignificance."

"I'm just not one of the faithful," Stuart said. "Sorry, folks. If you'd tried this stunt on almost anybody else, it might well have worked. You've really thought it through, all the little details, the interrelationships, everything. But I've had the belief trait, whatever little of it I was born with, burned out of me by life. You couldn't have picked a worse test subject."

People at the table were still bristling. Nothing he was saying pleased them.

"Mr Reston." Quetzalcoatl laid an arm round his shoulders. "May I call you Stuart? Perhaps you'd like to walk with me, Stuart. Staying in this room and continuing to speak as you do might not be good for your health. My protection extends only so far. Xipe Totec ranks as high as I do. We are two of the Four. I can't order him to keep his hands off you, I can only recommend and, perhaps, plead."

"You're telling me if I value my life, go with you."

"That," said Quetzalcoatl, "is exactly what I'm telling you."

"Fine. Works for me."

NINETEEN

Same Day

THEY EXITED THE refectory, leaving behind a baleful silence.

"I didn't make myself any friends back there, did I?" said Stuart.

"Don't judge them too harshly," said Quetzalcoatl. "They're not in the most forgiving of moods at present. They're not sure why we're back here after all this time, even though I've convinced them it's essential. They felt this particular exercise was long over and done with. They don't like treading over old ground."

"Whereas you...?"

"Whereas I feel we have unfinished business, and so do they, really, although they don't want to admit it. We haven't served the people of Earth as well as we ought and what's being done in our name now isn't right. There's amends to be made. And so some of us, a handful of the pantheon, have returned."

"Okay," said Stuart as they climbed a flight of stairs to a higher tier of the upside-down, inside-out ziggurat. "From now on I'm going to take you, and everything you say, at face value. Frankly I don't know why, as I think you're bonkers, all of you. But you yourself seem decent enough, underneath it all. I don't get the 'oh-so-superior' vibe off you that I get off the others. Or not as much of it."

Quetzalcoatl smiled. "What would it take to make you believe?"

"A lot more than you've got. So: 'unfinished business.' Elucidate. You gods took off some five hundred solar years ago, allegedly. You're back now. Why?"

"Why did we go, or why have we returned?"

"Either. Both."

"If you know anything about us, you know why we went. My spat with Tezcatlipoca. The Smoking Mirror and I fought after he practised his foul deceit on me, when he got me intoxicated and gulled me into... Well, I don't have to tell you what I did."

"Shagged Quetzalpetlatl. Little sis."

Quetzalcoatl winced. "Please. I don't care to be reminded. I confronted Tezcatlipoca the morning after and we ended up brawling like tomcats. I was in a towering rage, though mainly at myself, not him. He's a born trickster; he couldn't help his own nature. I, who hold myself to a higher standard of behaviour, should have known better."

"And when the dust settled, you were so embarrassed you felt it was time to go."

"I'm still embarrassed, even after all this time. We had so much left to do, so much more to show the people of earth, so much more to give you. The Aztecs were meant to be just the beginning. They at the time were the most interesting nation on the planet, which is why we chose them. Not the most technologically astute – that would be the Chinese – nor the most culturally sophisticated – that would be the Italians – but they had a self-confidence that was remarkable, and a knack for adaptability, not to mention a ferocious drive. They were to be our starting point, whence a wave of advancement and progress would ripple outwards until it encompassed the globe. That was the plan, and Tezcatlipoca's mischief and my own lack of self-restraint ruined it. We left with the project still running, partway done but nowhere near complete. It was an egregious mistake, as we've since learned."

They mounted the next staircase.

"And now you've come to fix it," Stuart said.

"If we can. What the Aztecs have done since we departed, what they've become, is not what we envisaged. The growth of this vast, sprawling, cruel Empire of theirs is the last thing we expected to happen, or wanted to. Rather than the Aztecs helping others with the gifts we gave them – what you call Aztechnology – they took it and used it to conquer and enslave, fashioning the world in their own image. But we still hope the situation can be remedied. The damage isn't irreversible."

"It really didn't cross your minds that, left to their own devices, a bloodthirsty race like the Aztecs would run rampant? I thought gods had foresight."

"You're thinking of the infallible, omniscient model of god. That's not us."

Another tier up. They were one level below the ceiling, the surface.

"So what are you proposing?" said Stuart. "How are you going to undo what's been done?"

"We have an idea."

"Is it a better idea than Xibalba's?"

"Perhaps. It certainly has a greater likelihood of success."

"That wouldn't be hard."

"We have knowledge, Stuart," said the man purporting to be divine. "We have capabilities far in excess of those of humans. You've seen that for yourself. With luck, though, we won't have to resort to drastic measures. We're looking for a peaceful, nonviolent resolution."

"Which you're going to try for, but Xibalba has to step aside first."

"Step aside, or face the consequences." Quetzalcoatl said this genially enough, but the words themselves were undeniably a threat. A sugar-coated cyanide pill was still cyanide.

"My guess is you want me to act as a go-between," said Stuart. "That's the reason I'm here. You'd like me to talk Chel out of going ahead with his plan, so you'll be free to implement yours."

"That's exactly what I'm after. Call it a courtesy.

We could simply eradicate Xibalba and have done with it, but we're giving Chel a chance. Just the one chance. Back off and let us do it our way."

"I'm not sure I have that much sway with him." They were now ascending the staircase that led to the topmost tier. "Even if I was willing to do as you ask, I'm the new kid on the block, still an outsider. You'd be better off talking directly to him yourself."

"Chel respects you. He knows you. I am a complete stranger to him. Also there's his religious persuasion to consider. I would be repugnant to him – a heathen deity, anathema to all that he believes in. He wouldn't listen. His faith would give him no choice but to spurn me."

"I honestly have no idea how I'd broach the subject with him," Stuart insisted. "I can't imagine what sort of angle would work."

"Try. That's all I'm asking."

"He's dead set on killing the Speaker. It's a point of honour, almost, with him."

"Impress upon him that, for his own sake and the sake of his men, it would be wiser not to."

"But if Chel won't back down..."

"Then, Stuart, my advice to you would be get as far away from this place as you can before the trouble starts." Again, Quetzalcoatl's smile did little to mitigate the bald menace of what he was saying. "But I'm confident it won't come to that," he added, patting Stuart on the shoulder. "You're a smart man. You have a way with words. You'll manage. And here we are: the way back to the world."

They had reached a final staircase, which rose to a rectangular hatch in the ceiling.

"Now where's Xolotl got to?" said Quetzalcoatl. "He can guide you back to your encampment, to save you having to search for it yourself. Xolotl!"

There was a thumping of paws as Quetzalcoatl's doglike companion, summoned by the sound of his name, came bounding out from a nearby corridor. In proper light, Stuart could see that Xolotl was truly ugly as dogs went. He was lumpenly muscular and sparsely furred, with long gangling limbs and a head that was far too round and big. Worst of all, one of his eyes was missing, the socket a puckered mess of scar tissue. He pulled up beside Quetzalcoatl, tongue lolling fatly from his mouth, dripping strings of drool onto the floor.

"Take Stuart back," Quetzalcoatl said.

"Take Stuart back," Xolotl echoed in reply, exactly simulating his master's voice. He turned and looked at Stuart, and Stuart was convinced he saw depths of resentment and contempt smouldering in that single yellow eye.

"I can find my own way –" Stuart began, but Xolotl lunged past him and up the stairs.

"Take Stuart back," Xolotl repeated as he climbed. It was remarkable. Reston didn't see Quetzalcoatl's lips move. The words actually seemed to be coming from the dog's throat.

Xolotl touched the hatch with a forepaw. Suddenly there was a rectangular space in the ceiling. The sounds and damp odours of the rainforest drifted in. Trees reared above like cathedral columns, green sunbeams piercing down through their lush leaves like light through stained glass.

"Go on," Quetzalcoatl said to Stuart. "You'll be quite safe. Xolotl's my other half. He won't lead you astray."

"All right," Stuart said, not reassured.

"Best of luck, my friend." Quetzalcoatl offered a warm, sincere handshake. "We'll be monitoring your progress, so we'll know how you get on. I'm sure you won't let us down."

No sooner was Stuart out of the hatch than it disappeared. Or rather, a section of forest floor *re*appeared where the hatch had been. There was undergrowth, ferns, leaf mould. Nothing indicated the presence of a doorway or, for that matter, a massive building buried beneath the soil. Stuart trod on the spot where the hatch was, probing with his foot. Through a layer of mossy, spongy earth he could just detect the hardness of metal, but if he hadn't known it was there he would never have thought to look for it. Whatever else these bogus gods might be, they were bloody ingenious, he had to give them that.

Xolotl let out an impatient growl.

"Yeah, yeah. 'Take Stuart back.' Coming."

Stuart followed the lolloping one-eyed dog through the forest. Xolotl had a powerful but ungainly stride. He moved as though going on all fours was as unnatural to him as walking on its hindlegs was to an ordinary canine. Holy lore stated that Xolotl was Quetzalcoatl's deformed twin, a constant reminder to the god that his own brilliant perfection should not be taken for granted. The absent eye, which had burst out of Xolotl's head of its own accord, was the most obvious manifestation of this, a disfigurement that literally stared you in the face.

Soon Stuart began to hear distant voices – the sounds of the Xibalba camp. He was still no nearer a decision as to what to say to Chel. What could he tell him? That he'd just met a bunch of delusional individuals who had got it into their heads that they were gods? That they were evidently powerful, these madmen, and it might be as well to abort the assassination attempt?

Xolotl halted while he and Stuart were still just out of sight of the camp. He gestured with a forepaw.

"Stuart back," he said, then about-turned and loped off in the direction they had just come.

Okay, Stuart thought. *Not ventriloquism. Something else. Maybe some kind of radio transceiver implant? One that was linked to a device which galvanised the dog's jaw and made it move in synchronisation with the words?*

Stuart had to concede that the people in the inverted ziggurat had access to some highly advanced technology.

But gods?

No. Never.

TWENTY

Same Day

AS STUART ENTERED the camp he found the guerrillas busy around a portable gas stove. Two of them were pouring a viscous brown liquid out of a cooking pot into small jars, and the others then took a jar each and ran the contents through a sieve, mashing out excess water with a spoon until all that was left was a resin-like paste. Stuart's best guess was that they were preparing curare for their blowpipe darts. The original brown liquid was a stewed mulch of leaves and bark fragments from the curare plant.

They were so intent on their work that they didn't even notice Stuart was there watching them. He had to clear his throat to get their attention. Immediately they leapt to their feet. Guns and knives appeared. The guerrillas moved in on Stuart, Zotz to the fore.

"Where have you been?" Zotz demanded.

"'Welcome back, Englishman,'" Stuart said sardonically. "'We missed you. We were worried.'"

"Don't piss about. What happened last night? We heard an l-gun discharge, and then you'd vanished and Auilix too."

"Where is Auilix? Is he all right?"

"Asleep in his tent. He's shaken up but fine. At first we assumed you must have killed him and run off. Then we heard him calling. He was stuck halfway up a tree, terrified out of his wits. He was gibbering, saying something about hurtling up into the air – something about a big black insect with wings. We thought he'd been at the tequila but he swears not. What's going on?"

"I'm not sure you'd believe me if I told you. I need to speak to Chel. He around?"

"I'm around," said Chel, emerging from the cabin. "Zotz poses a very good question. What *is* going on? We were under the impression you'd deserted us. Maybe even run off with a view to betraying our whereabouts to the Serpent Warriors. Hence the curare." He indicated the gas stove. "We're making a fresh batch in anticipation of a Serpent attack. Now that you're back, is it safe to assume that no such attack is coming?"

"No attack to the best of my knowledge, no."

"Can I believe that answer?" said Chel, taking a few steps closer to Stuart.

"I'm here, aren't I? If I'd sold you out to the Serpents, why would I return?"

"To lull us into a false sense of security. Then, when they arrive, they make sure to kill everyone else but spare you."

"But it would still be a foolish risk," said Stuart. "And judging by the way you're all acting now, I'd have been justified in not taking it."

"Forgive me, but it's going to take a bit more than that to convince me. Men?"

Chel nodded to Stuart's left and right, and Stuart glanced around him and cursed himself. While he'd been talking to Chel, guerrillas had sneaked round and taken up position on either side of him. He'd been so focused on protesting his innocence that he hadn't noticed he was being flanked. He made to turn, to defend himself, but too late. The guerrillas pounced, and within seconds he was being gripped tightly and painfully by several sets of strong hands. One man had a chokehold around his neck, and two others were twisting Stuart's arms backwards. He struggled, but he was helpless.

"Listen to me," he said, having to force the words out through his constricted larynx. "You're not alone in this forest. There's somebody else here and they want you out."

"Of course we're not alone in this forest," said Chel. "It's a big damn forest. But as for somebody wanting us out – I sincerely doubt that. Xibalba is popular. You've seen it for yourself."

"But these people –"

"Reston," Chel interrupted. "Do you know what a lethal dose of curare does to a person?"

Stuart tried to let nothing show in his eyes. "I've a pretty good idea."

"Do you?" Chel gestured to one of his men, and in no time he had a blowpipe dart in his hand. The tip had been dipped in the paste. He approached Stuart. "Then I'm sure you're aware that it's not a pleasant death. Curare is a muscle relaxant. In weak doses, it merely incapacitates. Remember when we rescued you at the theatre in London; we'd decided we would not kill Jaguar Warriors if it could be avoided. Shame they didn't return the courtesy, but there you go. Each one we hit with a dart went down in an instant, paralysed, without use of their limbs for an hour or so. Well, in more concentrated form, as has just been brewed here, curare causes every muscle in the body to stop functioning. Ultimately death comes in the form of asphyxiation. Your diaphragm fails and your lungs cease to work. But it can take up to twenty minutes, and the horror of it is, you're conscious the whole time, fully aware of what's happening to you but powerless to do a thing about it. You lie there unable to move, unable even to scream, feeling yourself gradually, inexorably shutting down. It is, I imagine, a truly terrifying experience."

He held the dart up in front of Stuart's cheek.

"You wouldn't dare," Stuart said.

"Wouldn't I? One prick, and a long, lingering death awaits you. So tell us the truth. Where have you been these past eighteen hours? Are there Serpent Warriors on their way?"

He brought the dart closer. Stuart strained away from it. The guerrilla who had him in a chokehold pressed his head towards it again.

"No, no Serpents, I swear."

"Or Jaguars?"

"No, no bloody Jaguars either. But these others I'm talking about, they definitely don't like having you around. They're who I've been with all this time, and they've asked me to ask you to leave. They have plans for the Great Speaker and you're standing in the way."

"Plans? What plans?"

"I – I don't know. They didn't say."

Chel gave a scoffing laugh.

"But you'd be wise to do as they ask," Stuart went on. "They have weaponry, skills... abilities. They outclass you in every department. Auilix's 'big black insect,' that was one of them. And those mystery figures stalking us through the trees the other morning – them again. And the ants. Remember the ants?"

"Ants!" Chel boomed. "I'm supposed to be intimidated by a bunch of *ants*?"

"Someone controlled them, made them act as they did. You can deny it, but we all saw it, how they built a human figure. I'm not saying it's ants themselves you should worry about. But someone who has the technological knowhow to get insects to obey commands – you've got to at least wonder what else they might be capable of."

The dart hovered at Stuart's cheek, a hairsbreadth from his skin. The point loomed as large as a javelin in his vision, the curare a thick dark smear. He felt a bead of sweat roll from his hairline, down his forehead, out along his eyebrow.

"Who are they, then, this unseen enemy of ours?" Chel wanted to know. "And why should what they want take precedence over what we want?"

"They're your enemy only if you make them your enemy by not conceding to them. This isn't about who's got first dibs or who has more of a claim on the Great Speaker or any of that. It's about who's carrying the bigger stick, simple as that, and from what I've seen, the answer isn't Xibalba. You're up against a superior force, Chel, a bunch of very determined and well-equipped people. A couple of them could even be genuine psychopaths."

"And our own fighting prowess can't compare?" Chel sounded offended. "Now you're belittling us?"

"I'm being as honest as anyone would be with a poison-tipped dart being waved at them."

"Fear of death will make a man say anything to save his skin."

"So what's the point in threatening to kill me? Eh? If you're not even going to believe what I tell you. Look at it this way. Would I have come up with a story as preposterous as this if it wasn't true? I could just have given you some bollocks about wandering off and getting lost for a day. I didn't. Fact is, I'm trying to help you. I'm delivering an ultimatum from some very serious people, and I urge you – beg you – to listen up and act accordingly. You may not survive if you don't."

Chel gave this some thought. Behind those warm eyes and that chubby, easygoing face lurked an iron resolve, a will that was like a torrential river, carving its own channel, meeting resistance with force.

The dart dipped away from Stuart's cheek, just fractionally.

"You need to choose, my friend," Chel said softly, grimly. "You need to commit yourself one way or the other. You did that as the Conquistador, but it seems you've lost your bearings since you last put on your armour. You've weakened. And I can't have weakness on my team. It's a liability. So decide, once and for all. Are you with us or against us? Look inside your heart and make that call. It doesn't have to be right now, but it must be soon, because time is marching on, the *b'ak'tun* is drawing to an end, the hieratic synod is imminent, and our hour of reckoning is approaching. Are you going to carry through your mission as the Conquistador to its logical conclusion? Or are you going to be a coward?"

Well, when you put it like that, it's no choice at all. "If you're trying to win me over, Chel, you've got a damn funny way of going about it. But I will tell you that, threats notwithstanding, basically I'm still onside. In spite of everything" – Stuart lowered his eyes to the deadly dart – "you can count on me."

"Can I?"

"Yes. Now, please put that bloody thing away and tell your men to let me go."

Chel pondered, then with some finality jerked the dart back and passed it, flighted end first, to the man who had fetched it for him. A flick of Chel's fingers, and Stuart was released.

"Be careful," the Xibalba leader said to him. "Watch your step. Every move you make from now on is going to be scrutinised. More than ever you will have to prove you are worth the huge trouble we went to, the lives it cost us, to find you and bring you here. Don't give us the slightest excuse to doubt you again. You will not live to regret it."

"And about what I've been saying?" Stuart said. "These people I've told you about?"

Chel was striding away. He didn't look back, just flapped a hand dismissively in the air. "If they're coming, let them come. They won't find us easy prey. Xibalba knows how to fight. We don't give up on our goals, no matter what the obstacles. We're dead already, remember? So we fear nothing."

The guerrillas around Stuart echoed the sentiment with a low cheer.

"Well, I gave it my best shot," Stuart said, mostly to himself, but also for the benefit of anybody who might be observing, eavesdropping by means of some sensitive listening device. "I really did."

TWENTY-ONE

10 Reed – 12 Eagle 1 Lizard 1 House
(Thursday 14th – Saturday 16th December 2012)

TWO DAYS PASSED, and no move from Quetzalcoatl and his cohorts, no sign of an attack.

Preparations in the camp stepped up several notches. Chel began drilling the guerrillas, demonstrating what they would do in the moments immediately after the aerodisc touched down at Tenochtitlan. He ran through several possible permutations of the event: what if the Serpent Warriors insisted on coming aboard to perform a security check, what if one of them smelled a rat and they stormed the disc, what if the Great Speaker wouldn't come quietly and had to be coerced...

According to Chel's informant in China, the Speaker was due to arrive in Beijing at seven o'clock the evening before the conference. Extrapolating backwards from that, and allowing for changes of time zone, the aerodisc which would be transporting the Great Speaker across the Pacific would be departing at twelve noon on that same day, 1 Movement 1 Movement. The Xibalba disc should therefore turn up a few minutes in advance of that other disc.

The landing point for private flights in and out of Tenochtitlan was always the roof of the city's main building, the Speaker's palatial private residence. On the way in, the Xibalba disc would almost certainly receive a radio challenge asking its pilots for identification and clearance codes. Chel's intention was to prevaricate and bluster until they were so close to the residence that it didn't matter. If his assumptions were correct, and if providence was on their side, the Speaker would be waiting at the apex of the building, accompanied by a travelling retinue of personal servants and a bodyguard of no more than four Serpent Warriors.

It was the boldness of his scheme that was its strongest suit, he maintained. Nobody – nobody in the world – would expect enemies of the Empire to have the effrontery to swoop in on the capital itself and snatch the Speaker away in broad daylight, from under the very noses of his elite bodyguard. Xibalba would succeed through sheer balls alone.

Several times they rehearsed the kidnap, with Stuart dragooned into the role of stand-in Great Speaker. The guerrillas raced down the gangplank, dispatched imaginary Serpent Warriors, grabbed Stuart and hustled him aboard. They were as gentle with him as they would doubtless be with the Speaker himself, which is to say, not at all. They yanked him along like some recalcitrant donkey, oblivious if he tripped and fell, or barked a shin, or was accidentally winded by a flailing elbow.

Stuart endured the mistreatment with great forbearance. Partly he wanted to show willing – *I can be a team player, see?* – but also he was convinced Xibalba's days were numbered, meaning nothing they did to him mattered. The longer the "gods" held off from attacking, the more certain he became that an attack was inevitable.

He could imagine Quetzalcoatl and friends debating the issue hotly amongst themselves in their underground lair. Xipe Totec and Mictantecuhtli would be the ones urging a pre-emptive strike the most vociferously. Quetzalcoatl himself would counsel caution, saying that Chel should be given every last chance to reconsider and withdraw. Coatlicue, for all her airs and graces, was a belligerent old witch and would be in favour of hostilities. Quetzalcoatl's sister Quetzalpetlatl would side with her brother, thanks to their more-than-merely-sibling bond. Ometeotl, parent of all, would typically be unable to make up his/her mind either way.

In the end, though, the pro-aggression faction would win. The pantheon had a tendency to go for destructive solutions. The divine myths were a gory litany of bloodshed, vindictiveness and murder. There was no reason to think these would-be gods would behave any differently.

It was ludicrous, Stuart knew, to picture the people he'd met as though they really were what they claimed to be. But it was also unavoidable. They, by their own lights, *were* the gods. They behaved according to the character traits enshrined in holy lore. They had the gods' known mannerisms down to a T. Though he had spent only a short time in their company, he could see that they had established an exact replica of the taut, contrary network of relationships which gave the pantheon its unique piquancy. Their common artifice had become a kind of reality, in as much as it was utterly real to them themselves, and he couldn't help but treat it that way too, albeit with considerable irony.

By dawn of the third day, Stuart knew they were coming. The gods were coming. He sensed it the moment he woke up, could almost taste it. Danger like a scent in the air, a tang on the breeze. A dam ready to burst.

Quetzalcoatl's words came back to him: *My advice to you would be get as far away from this place as you can before the trouble starts.*

Easier said than done. The guerrillas were keeping a weather eye on him all the time. They were also patrolling the clearing's perimeter and the adjacent patch of rainforest more diligently than ever before. Skulking off without getting spotted and challenged would be next to impossible.

Instead he opted for making one final go of it with Chel. He clambered out of his tent and went to the cabin. A dishevelled, bleary-looking Chimalmat responded to his knock.

"Yes?"

"Is he up?"

Chimalmat grimaced. "Hear that?" Heavy snoring buzzsawed from within. "There's your answer."

"Give him a kick. Get him out of bed. He and I really need to talk."

"He hates having his sleep interrupted."

"He'll hate it even more if what I think is about to happen happens and he's not awake to face it."

"And what is about to happen?"

"Nothing, if I can just get Chel to see reason."

"You're being very cryptic, Englishman," said Chimalmat. "It would make everyone's life simpler if you just –"

A scream from the forest cut her off.

A raw-edged, keening wail.

The sound of a man in pain and abject terror.

Stuart was too late.

It had begun.

FIRST TO ENTER the clearing was Mictlantecuhtli.

The Dark One sauntered out from the trees as calmly as though taking a summer stroll. His great black head was split by a fierce smile. With one hand he dragged a body behind him – Tohil, part of the pre-dawn sentry shift – pulling it along by the ankle as a child might pull along a toy wagon. The Mayan had been slashed open from pubic region to sternum. A knot of intestines trailed in his wake, gradually uncoiling into a single long ribbon as it bumped over the grass.

Stuart's immediate assumption was that Tohil was dead. Then he realised, to his horror, that this was not the case. Tohil's eyes were wide open and rolling. His jaw worked, shaping soundless cries. One hand kept pawing the slit in his belly, vainly trying to scoop his entrails back into place.

"Humans!" Mictlantecuhtli bellowed. "You were given due notice of our wishes. You failed to heed them. We have been more than patient and more than fair. You've brought this on yourselves."

He upended Tohil, grasped his other ankle as well, then slowly, massive muscles bunching, tore him in two. He split him like some giant wishbone, longitudinally and downwards. First the crotch. Then the hips. The spine, which unfastened like a zip. Finally the ribcage. Tohil hung limp, a ghastly V of carcass, parts of him spilling out and spattering down around Mictlantecuhtli's feet.

Chel emerged from the cabin just in time to catch the tail end of this horrendous spectacle. His expression flashed from disgust to fury. He shoved Chimalmat inside the cabin, telling her to barricade the door and not come out under any circumstances. Then he snatched up a rifle leaning beside the door and barked out an order at the top of his lungs.

"Xibalba! Enemy action! Move!"

No sooner had the words left his lips than he began firing at Mictlantecuhtli, who retreated at speed, using Tohil's remains as a bullet shield, smiling all the way. Several of the guerrillas had already scrambled out of their tents, clutching blowpipes and guns.

Now the rest emerged too. Under Chel's supervision, they fanned out and divided into groups, adopting defensive positions all round the clearing. They knelt or crouched, fearful but alert, rifles cocked and loaded, ready.

"My stuff," Stuart said to Chel. "Armour, sword, flechette gun. Where?"

"In there, where we've been keeping it for you." Chel jerked a thumb at the cabin doorway. "So you'll stand shoulder to shoulder with us after all?"

"We're going to get massacred. Might as well die with my boots on."

"Good man. Christ bless you."

Chel jogged off to join his men while Stuart hurried indoors. Chimalmat was already opening the backpack that contained his Conquistador gear.

"Here." She tugged out the cuirass and helped him strap it on. "They're going to slaughter us, aren't they? We're all going to end up like poor Tohil."

"If only Chel had listened."

"Such a stubborn man. Once he fixes on something..."

"You should try to get away, Chimalmat. This isn't your fight."

"I disagree."

"But you don't have a weapon."

"So chivalrous. Don't worry about me. I'll think of something." Chimalmat handed Stuart his rapier and helmet. He put them on.

From outside came panicked shouts and a rippling fusillade of gunfire.

Chimalmat started pulling more pieces of armour from the backpack, but Stuart stopped her. "No time. I'm needed out there. I'll have to make do with what I've got."

She dug out his flechette gun. "At least take this."

Stuart didn't think it would be much use. He didn't think anything would be much use against the opponents they were facing. Mictlantecuhtli had already as good as proved that. Still, he strapped the gun holster to his hip anyway.

It felt good to be the Conquistador again, even with an incomplete suit of armour on. At once, doubt was banished. There was only certainty. The cuirass and helm pressed coldly but comfortably on him. The weight of the armour was the weight of purpose, of vengeance. Stuart hefted the rapier, eyeing the blade's keen edge. He had become, once again, a being who existed for a single reason: to fight and kill. Life was exhilaratingly simplified.

He stepped out of the cabin. Chimalmat followed, and they both took stock of the situation.

The guerrillas were blasting away with their rifles, their fire concentrated on a solitary figure striding towards them. Clad in night-black metallic armour, the person was unmistakably a woman. The armour hugged her contours, its segmented sections sheathing her snugly and completely. An ovoid helmet encased her head, sleek and featureless other than two dark hemispheres that bulged at the front like an insect's eyes. The fingers of the gauntlets on each hand narrowed to ferocious long talons.

To judge by the ease with which the woman walked, the armour was made of some exceptionally light material. It was also impervious to bullets and somehow could disperse their kinetic force. Rounds whined and ricocheted off, leaving not a mark on the armour's glossy surfaces, and its wearer didn't so much as flinch at the impacts.

Within a stone's throw of the frontmost Xibalba line, she halted. Domed casings on her back opened and a pair of wings unfurled. They were black too, and they spread out on either side of her. Flexible planes expanded and rigidified, until the wings settled into a shape that was more than a little like the wings of a butterfly.

"Itzpapalotl," Stuart said under his breath. The goddess also known as the Obsidian Butterfly.

One downthrust of those stiff black wings, and she was in the air. Another beat, and she was hurtling towards the guerrillas. She grabbed one of them, digging her talons into the man's armpits, and veered perpendicular. The wings propelled both of them into the sky at such speed that within seconds they were almost lost from view, just a tiny dark speck amid the blue. The guerrilla's desperate screams faded to almost nothing. Then they grew louder again as he came plummeting down, alone now. Itzpapalotl had dropped him as casually as she had plucked him up. His arms were whirling and flailing as if he hoped somehow to counteract gravity and fly himself. He hit the ground head first with a tremendous meaty thump, his body bursting like a sack of jelly. Blood showered around him in all directions, along with gobbets of organs, partially liquefied by the impact.

Out of the corner of his eye Stuart saw Chimalmat dart off, heading purposefully towards the aerodisc. Meanwhile Chel and his men scanned trees and sky, fingers on triggers, searching for the next source of assault.

In the event, it came from right in their midst. A knot of three guerrillas found their number unexpectedly reduced to two; one of them had had his neck brutally broken. By whom and how, was unclear. One moment the man was kneeling beside them, rifle stock pressed to shoulder. The next, the rifle was gone and his head was canted at such an angle that his ear was resting on his shoulder. His tongue stuck out from his mouth like a lump of gristly veal he was trying to get rid of.

Something shimmered. It was like a silhouette in heat haze, a glassy wavering outline of a man. Before their astonished eyes, it gained solidity and colour. There stood Xipe Totec in his "flayed" form, a grotesque living anatomy of muscle and bone.

His death's head grin glinted whitely as Xipe Totec took hold of another of the three guerrillas and snapped his neck too. He twisted the Mayan's head through almost one hundred and eighty degrees. Vertebrae popped with a sound like pebbles crunching underfoot.

The third guerrilla was briefly frozen with shock, but managed to recover his wits. He raised his rifle. Xipe Totec yanked the gun out his hands and tossed it aside. The man lunged for the only other weapon within reach, his blowpipe. He clenched a dart between his teeth and put the pipe to his lips. Xipe Totec leaned back, his exposed facial muscles contorting into what could only be a sneer. The guerrilla puffed out his cheeks and blew. At this range he could scarcely miss, but somehow Xipe Totec was able to duck aside so that the dart whisked past him.

A faction of a second later Xipe Totec was grasping the tip of the blowpipe and ramming it into the guerrilla's mouth before the man could do anything to prevent him. He thrust the wooden tube so hard that the other end smashed out through the back of the Mayan's skull, carrying bone shards and bits of brain with it.

The other guerrillas trained their weapons on Xipe Totec. Zotz had the lightning gun and took careful aim. Xipe Totec, however, faded from view as soon as he had dealt with the last of his trio of victims. There was that shimmering heat-haze effect again, and he was gone. A few bullets zinged in his direction, but there was nothing to see to hit. Invisible or absent, either way he had evaded retaliation.

Xibalba was getting picked apart bit by bit. Stuart was appalled by the methodicality of it, the relentlessness of it. He had known that something like this might happen, but foreseeing an event was very different from actually watching it unfold in front of you. There seemed to be nothing any of them could do, except wait for the next attack, the next cold-blooded, merciless infliction of death.

A guerrilla came tottering out of the forest. He had been one of Tohil's companions on the pre-dawn sentry shift, and he was lucky not to get shot as he stumbled into view. His nerve-rattled fellow guerrillas mistook him for an enemy, and would have planted bullets in him if Chel hadn't shouted at them to hold their fire. He sent two of them forward to help the man, who looked dull-eyed and bewildered, as though unsure of where he was and why he was there.

The two approached him with caution, softly calling his name. "Mulac. Mulac. This way. Quick. Get to cover, Mulac."

Mulac seemed barely to hear a word. He came to a standstill, his mouth slack, his gaze unfocused. Then he began feeling his chest and abdomen with his hands. The touching turned to scratching, some terrible itch needing attention. He ripped open his shirt and started clawing at his bare skin with his nails.

"In me..." he murmured. "He put them... in me..."

"Who do you mean, Mulac?" asked one of his confederates.

"Put what in you?" asked the other.

"Eggs. Made me swallow. And now they're growing. Too fast. Hundreds of them. They want out."

All of a sudden Mulac shuddered. A moan escaped his lips, rising in pitch and intensity as convulsions ran through his body. He was tearing at himself now, desperately trying to get at something under his skin. Stuart could see movement where his fingers were, small lumps pulsing and wriggling, dozens of them, like sentient cysts. The other two guerrillas exchanged looks of alarm. They didn't know whether to go to Mulac's aid or back away and leave him to whatever fate he was about to suffer.

A scarlet dot appeared at the centre of one of the lumps, just above Mulac's right nipple. There was a splitting sound like a blister bursting, and from the Mayan a sharp gasp that was almost a sigh of relief, as if the worst was over.

The worst was not over. Far from it.

The scarlet dot grew. A droplet of blood trickled down from it. Something was pushing its way out from Mulac's pectoral muscle.

No, not pushing.

Gnawing.

A tiny black and yellow head forced itself through a gap it had created in Mulac's skin. It chewed rapidly round in a circle, widening the hole. All over Mulac other similar apertures opened up and more tiny heads poked out. He looked down and watched as countless little creatures birthed themselves bloodily from his body. His expression was that of someone who had passed beyond pain and reason. His face showed nothing but a kind of sickly wonderment, a look that said, *This is me. I'm doing this. This vileness is coming out of* me.

The creatures were hornets, and the first thing they did after vacating their host was wipe his blood off their wings with their rear legs and take to the air. They hovered around Mulac in a darkening cloud, their communal buzz mounting in volume as more and yet more of them broke free from him. Mulac sank to his knees, his body a glistening moonscape of deep raw gouges.

Some of the hornets had burrowed upward rather than outward, through Mulac's throat. They flew out of his mouth in ones and twos as nonchalantly as commuters filing out of a subway tunnel. Others exited the other end and crawled out from his trouser cuffs.

At some point during the whole terrible ordeal, while he was slumped in a kneeling position, Mulac died. It wasn't easy to pinpoint the exact moment, as his body continued to twitch and spasm. The activity of the hornets still within him gave him a semblance of life long after his heart gave out.

Above Mulac's drooping head, the hornets gathered into a swarm, forming a single rough sphere that started to split into two smaller spheres.

Loud as he could, Stuart yelled at the two guerrillas near Mulac, telling them to move, run, *now*. Chel added his voice to Stuart's. He had no way of knowing that the hornets were under the control of Azcatl, but he'd seen the ants in the forest, as they all had. All he knew was that the swarms spelled obvious danger and his two men were closer to them than they ought to be.

Too late, the guerrillas roused themselves from their ecstasy of horror and stirred their numb limbs into action. The swarms launched themselves separately at them, in arrowhead formations. A dense whirring cluster of hornets overtook and engulfed each of the fleeing Mayans.

The winged insects set to work stinging every inch of skin they could find. Their victims screamed and slapped frantically, but the hornets were legion in number and remorseless. For each that got swatted or crushed there were another dozen to take its place. In no time the two men were festooned in red welts. Their eyelids puffed shut, blinding them. Hornets crawled into their ears and stung, into their noses and stung, into their mouths and stung. The build-up of venom in the men's systems reached fatal levels in less than a minute. They fell. They writhed on the ground. Their windpipes swelled and sealed up. Their hearts failed. They lay still.

The hornets took off and coalesced into a single swarm once more. Zotz levelled the l-gun at it, but the swarm didn't go on the offensive again. Instead it moved off, meandering out of the clearing. The noise it made as it departed was a satisfied, contented drone, a noise that spoke of orders discharged, a job well done.

Silence fell. It was broken by sobbing – one of the Mayans weeping as helplessly as child.

Then the aerodisc's neg-mass drive started up.

Chimalmat was in the cockpit, and through the disc's windshield she could be seen gesticulating urgently to the guerrillas and mouthing the words, "Come on!"

It spoke well of Xibalba's bravery that the notion of retreat hadn't even occurred to any of them until then. Chel had been confident they could ride out the attack, and his men had shared that confidence. Events having proved otherwise, it now seemed eminently reasonable to think in terms of a tactical withdrawal. Chimalmat had been well ahead of everyone else in this respect; her forethought was going to be the salvation of them all.

The aerodisc thrummed loudly, like a bass note on an organ pipe. The grass and shrubs beneath it stood on end, vibrating like a rat's whiskers as electromagnets excited the antigravity particles inside the drive chamber and the disc started to lose mass and resist the earth's pull. At Chel's command the guerrillas fell back from their positions, ducking under the camouflage netting and making for the gangplank. The netting itself began to strain at the pegs tethering it.

Stuart took a step forward to join the exodus. Then a hand fell on his shoulder.

Quetzalcoatl, in full armour, stood behind him, pinning him to the spot with a powerful gauntleted grip.

Quick as a flash Stuart lashed out with his rapier, but Quetzalcoatl deflected the blade easily with his free hand.

"No," he said.

"Let me go," Stuart hissed.

Again, "No," this time accompanied by a resolute shake of the head.

"Then kill me. Get on with it. Just make it quick."

A third "No."

Quetzalcoatl's eyes were sombre, and Stuart grasped his meaning.

He wasn't going to die.

The guerrillas were.

The aerodisc lifted off, and several of the netting pegs were wrenched out of the ground. The gangplank was still extended, like a beckoning arm. Chimalmat was gazing down at Stuart as she manipulated the controls, her face a mask of pity. Stuart was in the enemy's clutches. As far as she was concerned, he was doomed.

"Hey! Englishman!"

Stuart turned to see Zotz crouched in the doorway at the top of the gangplank, sighting down the barrel of the lightning gun. Chel was beside him, brow furrowed with concern.

"I can zap him," Zotz called out. "Buy you time to get over here. Just break free from him if you can."

"Reston!" Chel yelled. "You can do it!"

Neither man fully believed what he was saying. They, like Chimalmat, reckoned Stuart was a goner, the next in line to be eliminated by these implacable and seemingly unstoppable aggressors.

Little did they realise who was really next.

"Don't do this," Stuart said to Quetzalcoatl. "Please. Let them live."

More of the pegs pinged loose, and the camouflage netting slithered off the aerodisc. The disc bobbed upwards, free.

"Too late. Can't be stopped." Quetzalcoatl cast a glance skyward. "Huitzilopochtli is here."

Stuart's gaze met Chel's. Each, in his way, said a silent, solemn farewell to the other.

Directly above the aerodisc, unseen by Chimalmat or any of the guerrillas, a man in iridescent armour hovered. Shimmering translucent wings kept him aloft. In his hands was a large tubular device like a cross between a harpoon gun and a bazooka. Some kind of conical-tipped missile sat snug inside.

Huitzilopochtli, the Hummingbird God, thrower of flame spears.

The aerodisc gained more height, rising in a smooth vertical. The gangplank began to close, hydraulic rams hauling it up to slot into the hull. The undercarriage retracted.

From on high, Huitzilopochtli took aim with his spear launcher. The weapon was pointed at the dead centre of the disc.

"He'll hit the neg-mass drive," Stuart breathed. "He can't do that. It'll kill us all."

"Not necessarily. Not all," said Quetzalcoatl, and the metal plumage sprouted from his shoulders and all at once he and Stuart were enclosed in a bubble of light. It was bright but not dazzlingly so, and it appeared to have substance, a sort of just-tangible jelly-like texture that put faint pressure on the skin. Stuart couldn't help but think of egg albumen, or a cocoon.

"We're protected now," Quetzalcoatl said. "Nothing can get through."

The aerodisc lifted level with the treetops. Everyone aboard was under the impression that they had escaped; they were safe.

Huitzilopochtli's launcher bucked in his grasp and the spear lanced down.

The disc recoiled, then detonated. As the drive chamber was breached, the sudden escape of antigravity particles caused a complete localised disintegration. Everything within a hundred-metre radius lost cohesion. Subatomic binding forces were negated. There was a temporary, catastrophic disruption of the laws of physics.

Organic matter broke down at a cellular level.

Metal turned to dust.

Water vaporised.

The very air came apart, molecules hissing asunder.

It all took place in a microsecond and was followed by a gargantuan implosion, a violent reassertion of the proper order of things. The fragments of the aerodisc and the nebulised remains of the people in it were collapsed back together into a tight ball some three metres in diameter. The vacuum thus created sucked up debris from all around: dirt, leaves, blades of grass, bits of shredded tent, splinters of the cabin. A hurricane-holocaust of particles filled the air.

Through this the ball that had been the aerodisc plummeted, hitting the ground with an almighty *whump* and shattering into a million pieces on impact. Granules of wreckage were strewn across the entire floor of the clearing and into the muddy wallow that had been the pool.

It took minutes for the fog of debris to clear, and when it finally did, a scene of utter devastation stood revealed. A rainforest glade was now, almost literally, scorched earth. Nothing was left that lived or grew. The surrounding trees were scarred and battered; some had toppled, their roots yawning like giant mouths. The waterfall oozed grey sludge.

Within Quetzalcoatl's protective bubble of light Stuart had seen everything and felt nothing. He'd not been buffeted even slightly by the colossal destructive power being unleashed around him. Not so much as a hair on his head had been disturbed. It was an eerie experience, like being in a car crash, that same sense of disembodiment, as though the disaster were happening to someone else, somewhere else.

The bubble vanished as it had appeared, abruptly and without a sound. Dazed, Stuart watched the snow-like settling of the last few floating flakes of detritus. He breathed in smells of ash and ozone.

He looked behind him. He looked up.

Both Quetzalcoatl and Huitzilopochtli were gone. He was alone.

Silent, the wounded rainforest swayed and grieved.

PART THREE
TENOCHTITLAN

TWENTY-TWO

3 Rain 1 Movement 1 House
(Thursday 20th December 2012)

MAL VAUGHN GOT the call at 4am. The phone next to her hotel bed rang shrilly and insistently. In the adjacent bed, fast asleep, Aaronson moaned and swore. Mal herself had been only drowsing. She groped for the phone in the dark and pressed the receiver to her ear.

"Vaughn."

As the voice on the other end of the line spoke, Mal slowly sat up. Then she lunged for the bedside lamp switch.

"Really? You're absolutely certain?"

"Whassat?" said Aaronson.

She shushed him. "Hold on," she said into the phone. "Wait just a second." She rummaged in the bedside table drawer for a pad of hotel stationery and a pen. "Give me the name of the town again." She jotted it down. "And your name?" She jotted that down too. "You're the arresting officer? The duty officer. Okay. Well, if he is who you say he is, Mr Necalli, then I reckon you and your whole station are in line for some kind of citation. I'll be there as soon as I can. How far are you from Teotihuacan? What's that in miles, about seventy? Give me an hour and a half, then. And don't, whatever you do, let the slippery bastard out of your sight."

She planted the receiver back down in its cradle. There was a look of something like elation on her face.

Aaronson propped himself up on his elbows. Beneath the bedcovers he was sporting a prominent morning glory that he did little to hide. Aaronson being who and what he was, an erection on him meant nothing to Mal, just a biological function. Besides, she'd already seen every bit of him, in every conceivable state, during the fortnight he and she had been travelling together to and fro across Anahuac. He was a remarkably immodest hotel room sharer.

"Look at you, boss. The cat that got the cream."

"Ten fucking bowls of cream, with a mouse on top."

"Another person's seen him?"

"Better yet, he's only gone and got himself arrested."

"You're shitting me."

"In a town called Mixquiahuala. It's north of here. Local Jaguars have him in the nick. Picked him up yesterday. Charge of vagrancy."

"How are they sure it's him?"

"Armour. Smug idiot had his armour on. Came wandering out of the rainforest, dressed as the Conquistador. Even carrying his sword."

"I don't believe it."

"Well, I do, so let's get dressed and on the road."

"What, no breakfast?"

"It's four in the ruddy morning. Nowhere'll be open."

Grumbling, and now beginning to wilt, Aaronson climbed out of bed and grabbed his clothes.

AS SHE DROVE the hire car out of Teotihuacan, through prosperous adobe-built suburbs slumbering beneath a pearly grey pre-dawn sky, Mal reflected on the two and a half weeks gone by and the fragile trail of clues that had brought her and her sergeant all the way from London to the Land Between The Seas.

After the unmitigated farce that was her second attempt to bring Stuart Reston to book, Mal had been certain that summary execution lay just around the corner. No way was she going to be allowed to live, not after she'd had Reston in her grasp – chained up in the back of a paddy wagon, no less – and still managed to lose him. Never mind that it hadn't been her fault. Never mind that she had been blindsided by Reston's Mayan cronies. She'd had the man, *had* him, and he'd got away. No self-respecting Jaguar could screw up on so grand a scale and not expect to pay the penalty for it.

The two days she spent in hospital recuperating from

a mild concussion were, she was sure, destined to be the last two days of her life. As soon as she was discharged and she reported back in for work, she would get the word from on high. *Be in the quadrangle at midday sharp. Full dress uniform not compulsory but preferable.* Serve her right, too. She had masterminded what she'd thought would be a textbook takedown, and it had degenerated into a total shambles, first with Reston leaping into the Thames, then with the Mayans ramming the paddy wagon side-on with their van. Net result for all her efforts? Eight Jaguars injured, including herself, most with cuts and contusions but a couple with broken bones. One paddy wagon written off. No villain in custody.

Oh, and she'd picked up a gruesome eye infection from the river water as well, which was going to take a while to fix with antibiotics.

All in all, execution was going to come as a relief. She wouldn't have to live with her shame for long, or for that matter her sore, pus-gummed eyes.

When she tipped up at Scotland Yard on the morning of 13 House 1 Monkey, everyone shunned her. It was predictable, only to be expected. She was a pariah. Dead woman walking. Aaronson alone met her gaze and spoke to her more or less as normal. Even with him, though, there was awkwardness. He was too cheery, making too many forced jokes and studiously sidestepping any mention of the events of the previous Sunday.

But then, as the hours passed, a curious thing happened.

And the curious thing was that nothing happened.

No execution order. No summons from her superiors. Not even a message requesting Mal to deliver a full account of the arrest and the reasons why it went awry.

She wrote a report anyway, because protocol demanded it, and she filed it with the secretary of the commissioner, and she waited for the fury and derision to rain down from above.

It didn't that day, and it didn't the next.

And gradually it dawned on Mal that nobody knew what to do, nobody was sure how matters stood, because there was no new chief superintendent in place yet. The chain of command had a gap in it, and communication channels between upstairs and downstairs were open but for the time being in hiatus. As in any state of interregnum, caution was the watchword. Until the position left vacant by Kellaway was filled and the status quo was restored, it was better not to make any firm decisions or put forward any radical plans of action. Better simply to coast along, keep your head down, and wait for the situation to settle.

For Mal, this was something akin to a reprieve. It was at least a stay of execution, and she resolved to make the most of it.

First thing she did was go with Aaronson to the imposing Thames-side apartment complex Reston called home, with a view to searching his penthouse flat for a suit of Conquistador armour. A rabble of reporters was camped outside the building. At the sight of two Jaguar Warriors, a flurry of questions and camera flashes began. Mal's response was to swan past, offering no comment beyond a through-the-teeth "Fuck off."

Ordinarily a Jaguar was obliged to bring along a locksmith to effect non-destructive ingress to a property, and of course obtaining a warrant to search private premises beforehand was considered good manners. Mal wasn't in the mood for such procedural niceties. In her view, Reston had forfeited his citizen's rights, such as they were, long, long ago. So she kicked down the rather smart mahogany door – strong wood, weak hinges – and got busy ransacking.

In the event, it was Aaronson who discovered the secret panel at the back of the walk-in wardrobe. He had excellent spatial awareness, and something about the layout of the master bedroom bothered him: unless the flat was a very odd shape, it should have been four or five yards longer. A full-length wardrobe ran alongside the en suite bathroom, and the wall at the rear seemed unusually thin: more a partition than a wall.

His probing fingers triggered the hidden spring catch more by accident than design. When the panel slid open, he was so startled he squealed.

"Not the most manly sound I've ever heard," Mal called out from the kitchen.

"Boss," Aaronson said, in as gruff a voice as he could manage, "you should take a look at this."

* * *

MAL WENT STRAIGHT to the commissioner with her findings. She all but barged into his office, oblivious to the protestations of his secretary. She had come to settle things once and for all. The cloud of execution hung over her, shadowing her every step, and she was fed up. She wanted it gone. Failing that, she wanted it confirmed. She needed to know her fate either way.

Commissioner Brockenhurst was a distinguished-looking man with white hair, grey eyes, and a way of talking that some found kindly and others patronising. He had been a friend of His Very Holiness Seldon Whitaker since boyhood, pursuing parallel paths from Eton and Harrow to Oxford and Cambridge and from there into the priesthood and policing. They maintained a close working relationship and often weekended at each other's country retreat with their families. To be in the same room as Brockenhurst was to be a heartbeat away from the very highest power in the land.

Brockenhurst, though irritated by Mal's intrusion, heard her out. He told her he was impressed by her discovery of the armour and weapons cache at Reston's, and also by her persistence. Most officers, having let a prominent felon slip through their fingers not once but twice, would retreat to a dark corner and await the inevitable disciplining. Her pluck and grit were to be commended.

However...

And it was a deep-breath, long-drawn-out, sighing "however."

"His Very Holiness," Brockenhurst said, "has

asked for a line to be drawn under the whole Conquistador affair."

"I'm sorry, sir, what did you just say?"

"You heard, chief inspector. The case goes on the back burner, with a lid on."

Mal was stunned. "May I ask why?"

"I'm under no compunction to explain to you if I don't want to, but I think you deserve it. The Conquistador has fled, who knows where to. I very much doubt he'll be coming back. How can he? His identity has been compromised. His face is all over the newspapers and TV. As Stuart Reston, he can't go anywhere, be seen anywhere, for fear of being recognised. He can never show himself in public again. His life as a British citizen is over. Therefore the danger from him as a masked vigilante is also over, at least to us. If he's abroad, then he's someone else's problem."

"But... but..." Mal stammered. "With all due respect, sir, how do we know that? How do we know he and his Mayan friends aren't planning some new atrocity even as we speak, here, on British soil? While Reston is at large he remains a threat. You can't expect him to give up this crusade of his. He's an obsessive. He has an axe to grind with the Empire, and he won't rest until it's ground completely, or whatever it is people are supposed to do with axes."

"Are you trying to be funny, Vaughn?"

"No, sir. I'm flabbergasted, that's all. You're telling me we're just going to forget about the whole thing? All those priests and Jaguars dead, civilians too, and we're going to carry on as if nothing happened?"

"The High Priest believes it would be easiest that way, and I'm minded to agree with him. If we keep harping on about Reston, keep worrying at the man and his actions, we run the risk of perpetuating what he did. His deeds will dominate the headlines long after they ought to. Whereas if we quietly let the matter drop, the Conquistador will soon be history. All anyone will remember about him is his ignominious, cowardly departure. His final act wasn't to go down in a blaze of glory but to skulk away like a whipped dog, helped by others. We feed his reputation, and diminish ours, if we make a big show of continuing to chase him. This way the Conquistador slips quickly and quietly from the limelight, and life can carry on as before."

"I'm having real trouble with this," Mal said. "What about the Jaguar oath? 'Never back down, never pull out.' That means nothing?"

"I'd advise you not to take that tone with me, chief inspector. Your life already hangs by a very thin thread. What you must consider here, above all, is your own position, precarious as it is. The only reason you're still breathing at this moment is because you were right about Reston. You fingered him as the Conquistador's alter ego and you acted on your suspicions and you were damned unfortunate he got away from you. In the event, you achieved the next best result after catching him, and that's scaring him off and making it impossible for him to return. Which is a win in my book. Don't now jeopardise it all by pushing any further. Accept what you're being handed, which amounts to a complete, unconditional pardon and the opportunity to start over with a clean slate. Few get a chance like this, especially after making such a godawful hash of things."

"In other words, shut up and be grateful."

"I wouldn't put it so crudely myself, but yes. Perhaps you should also bear in mind that a senior position lies vacant and in dire need of being filled. The appointment of a new chief superintendent is entirely in my gift, and I would look favourably on a candidate who not only excels as a Jaguar but understands, too, how there are certain unavoidable compromises that must be made on the road to promotion."

It was quite clear what the commissioner was offering, and just as clear that he was confident his words would mollify and appease.

Instead, Mal's festering indignation simply grew. She knew she should keep it in check, but she just couldn't. In a way she'd have preferred punishment – a good, honest death – to the prize that was being dangled in front of her, with its faint polluting whiff of bribery.

"So this has nothing to do with the fact that Reston's one of your own?" she said in a steely hiss.

Brockenhurst's eyes widened. "I beg your pardon? Just what are you implying?"

"Posh boy. Society type. Right background. But for a twist of fate, could have been you, or even the High Priest."

"Vaughn, I would strongly suggest you stop right there."

"I bet you ran into him from time to time. At those

fancy functions your lot go to. Maybe had a nice polite chat about the weather or the stock market while knocking back the champagne and canapés."

"I'll have you know I've never met Stuart Reston socially even once."

"Still, he's like you. Top of the heap. Cream of the crop. One of the cosy, gilded elite. Only, he went wrong, didn't he? Snapped. Flipped out. And it scares you how easily he did. It makes you fear for your own loyalty to the Empire. His Very Holiness's too."

"Another word and I'll have you on report."

She should have heeded the warning, but she couldn't, just couldn't. Brockenhurst had asked her to do the one thing she was unable to: be less than the perfect Jaguar Warrior. It had cost her so much, in personal terms, to buy into the Jaguar ethos. The life of her own brother, indeed. If she doubted even for one second that the price had not been worth paying, then everything was lost. Ix's death had been in vain.

"So let's just sweep it under the carpet. Pretend it doesn't matter. So what if Reston's a mass murderer? If he'd been part of the hoi polloi, like me, then we'd stop at nothing to exterminate him like the scum he is. But because he's establishment, he deserves special treatment."

"How dare you –"

"He deserves leniency, like all prodigals."

"Out!" Brockenhurst roared. "Get out!"

"Don't worry, I'm going," Mal said.

"You are suspended," the commissioner said, bent across his desk, finger jabbing as though he was trying to poke a hole in the fabric of space. "Effective immediately. And that is me being lenient on *you*, chief inspector. Very lenient. By every right, a subordinate who spoke to me like you just have ought at least to be sacked, if not worse. Go home, stay there, and come back only when I say so. Your pay will be suspended, of course. And the chief superintendent's job? I think we can safely say you've kissed that goodbye."

Downstairs, Aaronson enquired how the meeting had gone.

"Better than anticipated," Mal replied, and what was odd was that she meant it. She felt an incredible sense of release. Brockenhurst had cut her loose. She was at liberty to do as she wished.

And what she wished, more than anything, was to hunt Reston down.

Aaronson consented to act as her man on the inside at the Yard, and it was he who informed her, two days later, that the Mayans' van had been located in Woolwich, near the docks. The vehicle had been rolled into a side alley and abandoned. Scavengers had relieved it of everything of resale value, tyres and engine parts mostly, but it was still unmistakably the van used in the Reston rescue. The radiator grille was stove in and the front bumper bore scrapings of paint that matched paint from a paddy wagon.

So Reston had been smuggled out of the country by boat. That was the only conclusion Mal could draw.

And where would he go? France was the logical answer. Not only was it closest to hand but it had a longstanding tradition of resistance and subversion. The Louisiens would have clasped someone like the Conquistador to their bosom. He was one of them, as overt in his actions as they were covert in theirs, but no less opposed to Imperial rule.

Mal had neither the jurisdiction nor the resources to go haring round all of France looking for Reston. But she didn't believe she needed to. He wouldn't be there for long. It was the Mayans. The Mayans were key to all this. She had Aaronson do some digging, and made a few transatlantic calls herself, and soon she knew everything there was to know about a group of Mayan nationalists who painted skulls on their faces and whose preferred weapons were blowpipes and bolases.

Reston was in Anahuac. Had to be. In the company of the separatist guerrilla faction known as Xibalba.

Aaronson claimed he had a backlog of paid leave due which he would lose if he didn't use, and he'd always had a hankering to visit the birthplace of the Empire. Call it a pilgrimage, if you will. Mal pointed out that she was currently persona non grata at work. It might hurt Aaronson's career prospects if he continued to be associated with her, not least when she was busy doing that which Commissioner Brockenhurst had expressly forbidden.

In answer, all Aaronson said was, "What can I tell you, boss? I'm your bitch, and I always have been."

Mal owned a few gilt-edged Empire bonds, a nest

egg for her retirement, which she cashed in. That, along with money in a savings account amounted to just enough to secure two return flights to the Land Between The Seas and cover two or three weeks' worth of travel and accommodation expenses.

They flew to Teotihuacan and made that city their base of operations. Then next few days all followed the same pattern. They drove out in their hire car to some other city or major town and introduced themselves at the Jaguar Warrior HQ there. They showed pictures of Reston, both in and out of armour, and explained who he was and what he'd done. A few of the Anahuac Jaguars had heard of the Conquistador's exploits. The majority hadn't. As far as they were concerned it had been a domestic matter in a small, far-flung outpost of the Empire, no business of theirs. However, they promised to keep an eye out for Reston, in the event that he really was over here and consorting with local rebels.

Mal could tell she wasn't being taken seriously; she was being patronised. It peeved her but she didn't let it get to her. She stayed polite. They'd take her even less seriously if she lost her cool. She had to be the consummate professional. Were she to give them the slightest reason to doubt or distrust her they might be seized by the desire to check up on her back home.

Evening after evening, she and Aaronson returned to their hotel in the centre of Teotihuacan. Mal would be despondent, Aaronson would do his best to keep her spirits up. Then she would find some bar and would drown her sorrows in *pulque* while her sergeant cruised the neighbourhood, looking for some action. There wasn't a thriving gay scene in Teotihuacan, but through instinct and a little bit of luck Aaronson could usually find someone to hook up with. Mal herself got propositioned a few times and was often drunk enough to be tempted but not so drunk as to succumb. It didn't help that almost every adult male in Anahuac was shorter than her, sometimes by as much as a head. She had a problem with smaller men. Try as she might, she could never bring herself to fancy one. They made her feel gangly and uncomfortable. She preferred a lover she could literally look up to. Someone around Stuart Reston's height, a shade over six feet, was just right. Although not Reston himself, obviously. Sleep with *him*? Hideous thought. She'd rather stick a *macuahitl* up her snatch.

Two weeks in, just as Mal's funds were beginning to run out, came some good news. Good-ish. There'd been a sighting of a man matching Reston's description in the general vicinity of Lake Texcoco. A few days earlier a Jaguar patrol, visiting rainforest villages on a routine stop-and-search expedition, had come across a Caucasian male in a canoe. He was a botanist apparently, hailing from France. Name of René Jolicoeur. He'd shown a valid passport, and there had been someone with him, an Anahuac national acting as his guide, who had vouched for him.

The patrol leader had thought nothing of it at the time. Later, however, having learned that a British Jaguar was over here trying to track down an absconded criminal, he decided to consult the Jaguars in France about Monsieur *le Professeur*. It didn't take him long to establish that the person he'd met was an impostor. The impostor and René Jolicoeur were roughly the same age, but there the similarities ended. The real René Jolicoeur had a receding hairline, wore thick bifocals to counteract profound myopia, and was about thirty pounds overweight. In addition, he suffered from chronic-progressive multiple sclerosis, which was not disabling but which discouraged him from overseas travel and fieldwork, and meant he was largely restricted to the laboratory and the library. In short, the fine physical specimen of a man who'd pitched up in that canoe that day was not – emphatically not – René Jolicoeur.

The sighting of Reston was too old to be of any immediate practical use to Mal. He wouldn't be anywhere near that river now, not if he had any sense. The trail there would be stone cold.

It was, all the same, encouraging. It confirmed that Reston was in Anahuac and also that he had, as she suspected, come there via France – hence the passport, furnished by Louisiens no doubt. It suggested, too, that he was up to something. Why else would he be hiding under an alias and venturing along the rivers?

That the river in question fed into Lake Texcoco was also suggestive. After all, what lay at the middle of said lake but Tenochtitlan itself?

Could that be Reston's objective? Could he really have something so audacious in mind? An attempt on the life of the Great Speaker himself?

It beggared belief. Mal knew the man was arrogant but this took arrogance to a whole new level. This was hubris in the extreme. Almost a kind of insanity.

She didn't share her suspicions with the local Jaguars, but then she didn't need to. They were quite capable of drawing the same inferences themselves. Rogue British terrorist spotted at large in Anahuac, not a million miles from the capital? It was cause for concern, at least. So the search for Reston was escalated to a higher priority status. His picture was more widely circulated among the various regional HQs. His name was added to the national Most Wanted list. The word went out. A small reward was being offered for information leading to the capture of this known fugitive from justice. By the same token, anyone found to have been harbouring Stuart Reston or giving him succour or assistance of any kind would be subject to the harshest of penalties. Apprehending him became a matter of relative urgency.

For the first time since arriving in Anahuac, Mal felt able to relax a little. Underlying tension remained. Reston was not in the bag yet, far from it. But her judgement had been proved right. She had taken a terrific gamble and it looked as though it might pay off.

As a reward, she treated herself and Aaronson to courtside seats at a *tlachtli* game. It was a Teotihuacan derby between the Quails and the Wild Boars. Each team had its mob of fanatical supporters, many of whom came dressed in appropriate animal garb. Each team was also solely and exclusively made up of, in the case of the Quails, men with Olmec ancestry and, in the case of the Wild Boars, men with Zapotec ancestry. *Tlachtli* was one of the last bastions of tribalism in Anahuac. In no other walk of life was ethnic derivation allowed to be a distinguishing factor. Officially every inhabitant of the Land Between The Seas was an Aztec, end of story. But an exception was made for the ball game. Here, origins mattered. A player's bloodline had to be traced and verified before he could join his chosen side. If nothing else, this made for a better contest, especially when rival ethnicities clashed. Those matches were grudge matches, bloodier and more brutal than any other fixture. The animosities were ancient and bone-marrow deep, and the ball court was the only place where parading and venting them was tolerated. Severe injuries were guaranteed, fatalities not unheard of.

Mal and Aaronson, being foreigners and unaligned, opted to root for the Quails. The choice was made on no other grounds than that Aaronson took a shine to one of the Quails' hoop defenders, a beautiful slender creature whose kilt, as he and his teammates went through their warm-up exercises before the start of the match, rode up to expose a pair of buttocks to die for. "Unless you can think of a better reason, boss," Aaronson said, and Mal could not.

The game was tooth-and-nail almost from the outset. For the first few minutes both teams did genuinely seem to be vying to win by notching up a greater number of points than the opposition, and there were displays of considerable *tlachtli* artistry. Players bounced the solid rubber ball off their bodies using every part of themselves except heads, hands and feet. With expert precision they passed it amongst their own teams and nudged it up along the angled side wall towards the hoop. Goals were scored. The crowd roared.

Gradually, though, the fouling crept in, and then worsened. Leather hip pads and shoulder guards stopped became more offensive weapons than protection. Elbows jabbed. Heads butted. Fists flew. Several times, play degenerated into out-and-out brawling. The referee stepped in and dispensed stern cautions, and for a while good sportsmanship would resume, but never for long. Eventually there was open combat on the court, with no pretence of chasing the ball, and the referee gave up trying to umpire the proceedings and devoted himself to preventing any of the players coming to serious harm. He wasn't very successful in that endeavour, as on several occasions a stray blow landed on him and he pitched into the fray himself.

The crowd lapped it up. They bayed for blood. They could hardly contain their glee as fistfight followed fistfight. By the time the final whistle blew, the scoreboard showed 9-4 to the Quails, a convincing victory. In every other respect, however, the team got trounced. The Wild Boars left five of them in need of medical attention, compared with the Quails' own tally of just two opponents hospitalised.

Among the Quail injured was Aaronson's beloved hoop defender, who'd gone down with a gouged-out eye. All the way back to the hotel Aaronson lamented the fact that a potential love affair had been so cruelly nipped in the bud, over before it could even begin. He also bemoaned the ruination of such sublime physical beauty.

"I think he could really have been The One," he said.

"With you they're always The One," Mal replied, "right up until they turn out to be The One Night Only. Besides, you didn't even talk to him. You didn't even *meet* him. He's just someone you leered at from a distance."

"It was true love."

"True lust, more like."

"You don't have a romantic bone in your body, do you, boss? You wouldn't know love if it came up and slapped you in the face. No. Correction. With you, love *is* a slap in the face."

"Easy there, sergeant," Mal warned.

"I'm just saying, from what I've seen you don't have relationships – you have mutual abuse. You go for men you either feel nothing for or who feel nothing for you, and the more sordid and seamy your trysts are, the better. You know what? I think you don't like yourself very much. You punish yourself all the time. You don't believe you're worthy of love or of anything good. It's like you're doing penance, who knows for what."

"Here's the mark, Aaronson." Mal held out a hand in front of her, like a meat cleaver. She moved it a couple of feet to the right. "Here's how far you're overstepping it."

"Look, let's forget we're DCI and sergeant for a moment," Aaronson said. "Let's just be what we are, which is friends. Good friends, I like to think. That means I can be frank with you if I want, and I do want. You're a good-looking woman, Malinalli. If I was straight, I'd take a crack at you, definitely. You're a success in a tough, unforgiving profession. You're intimidatingly smart and sharp. You've got it all. But you're also a fool to yourself. You're never happy. Whatever it is that drives you inside so hard, it won't let you rest, it won't let you find contentment, it leads you to sabotage everything you achieve. Why can't you tell that voice inside your head just to shut up every once in a while? I don't mean deaden it with drink or drugs so you can't hear it. I mean get it to pipe down and stop nagging so you can actually enjoy life for a change."

"That's rich, coming from you. When I need a lecture in self-restraint and sobriety from the world's greatest hedonist..."

"At least I know how to kick back and have fun."

"I have fun!" Mal said indignantly.

"When? When was the last time? Recently? This year? Last year?"

Mal was all set to answer, but she stalled. She couldn't do it. She couldn't recall a single occasion, as an adult, when she'd done something for the sheer pleasure of it. Sex with strangers didn't qualify. There was physical satisfaction to be had, but that was about all. Beyond that, the encounters were brief and meaningless and usually conducted through an alcoholic haze.

"Tonight," she said at last. "The game. That was fun, wasn't it?"

"It was a bloodbath."

"Still, I heard you cheering."

"Granted, but did you? Cheer, I mean."

"Yes," said Mal. "I think so. Didn't I?"

"Not so's anyone would notice. You sat there stony-faced throughout."

"Inside, I was cheering."

"Doesn't count."

They'd reached the hotel. After checking at the reception desk for messages, they crossed the lobby and rode the rickety lift to the sixth floor.

"Fun's overrated, anyway," Mal said as she unlocked the door to their room. "Fun's for idiots."

"Which is unquestionably the most idiotic thing you've ever said," Aaronson replied.

They got ready for bed in frigid silence, like an old married couple after a tiff.

It was in the small hours of that night that the call came about Reston's arrest.

THE TOWN OF Mixquiahuala sat perched on a ridge of high ground above a plain. At its feet, *chinampas* fields stretched as far as the eye could see. Behind it, dark green rainforested slopes glowered.

The main approach road ran along a causeway,

raised between deep irrigation canals in the *chinampas*. Farmhands were already out amid the maize crop, wrenching out weeds and relieving the vermin traps of their overnight haul of cavy and capybara corpses.

Past the fields the road snaked upslope to the town and, once inside its environs, branched off a dozen different ways. Mal pulled up alongside a pastry seller who was setting out his wares in front of his shop. He gave her directions to the town's Jaguar HQ, and she purchased a couple of meringue-topped sponge cakes from him to placate Aaronson, who'd not stopped whingeing about how hungry he was the entire journey.

Necalli, the duty officer at the Jaguar HQ, had an amazing shovel-shaped nose, so large that it left little room on his face for his other features. After a few preliminaries he escorted the two British Jaguars downstairs to the holding cells. He told them that the prisoner had been in a disorientated state when he was brought in yesterday evening. He appeared underfed and showed all the signs of someone who'd been in the rainforest for several days: covered in bites, stings and scratches, not properly bathed, hair and clothing unkempt.

"Also, he's been babbling, on and off. In English. No one round here speaks it, so we haven't been able to make head or tail of what he's saying. We haven't even been able to process him properly. We're hoping you'll be able to help with that, now you're here."

"You took his armour off him, I suppose."

Necalli gave her a look: *This is Anahuac. You breeze in from a piddling little island colony like*

Britain and speak to us like we don't know how to do our jobs?

"Just asking," she said.

"As it happened, he surrendered the armour quietly. The arresting officers thought he was going to put up a fight, but he just handed everything over when invited to – sword, gun, the works – and went with them meek as a lamb. The funny thing was, he was wearing only a few items of armour, not a whole set. Like he'd dressed in a hurry and not been able to finish. All in all, he's a queer fish. If it hadn't been for you distributing round that intel about him, we'd have had a hell of a time figuring out who and what he was. We'd probably have assumed he was some kind of mental case and handed him over to a psychiatric care unit. I doubt any of us would have identified him as a terrorist. More likely a victim of bewilderness."

"Bewilderness?" said Aaronson.

"You know. Civilian heads off for a jaunt into the forest, underprepared, thinks it'll be just like a meander through the woods, a nice daytrip. He gets hopelessly lost, walks in circles for days or even weeks, and finally finds his way out, but by that time he's been driven half mad by thirst, hunger and fever. Bewilderness. It happens more often than you'd think. And it's almost always white foreigners. Some urge they have to conquer nature, challenge themselves, find themselves, maybe have a kind of ascetic spiritual experience, like religious hermits in the olden days. Anahuac natives are far too sensible for that. We know how fucking dangerous the rainforest is. We prefer our towns, most of us, with our air-conditioned buildings and our clean running water."

"But the armour," said Mal. "Wouldn't that have been a big clue that he was something out of the ordinary?"

Necalli shrugged. "I've seen stranger. This one guy, a few years back, he turned up on the outskirts of Mixquiahuala naked apart from an anaconda skin. He'd killed the snake and cut the skin off and draped it around himself like a sort of cloak. There was plenty of it, too, so the snake itself must have been a monster. He was under the delusion that by wearing it he had become an anaconda himself. He died in custody."

"Oh, one of those. Resisting arrest."

"No, a genuine accident. There was a rat in his cell – crawled in via the toilet. He caught it and tried to swallow it whole. Choked to death." Necalli chuckled ghoulishly at the memory. It seemed there wasn't a Jaguar in the world who didn't have a streak of gallows humour. It went with the territory. "The forest can do things to a man's mind. Make him lose it completely, sometimes. I think that's what may have happened to your Mr Reston."

"He's not 'my' Mr Reston," Mal said, but in a way he was. She felt about him much as a lioness must feel about the carcass of her prey – proprietorial, covetous.

"Visitors, Reston," Necalli called out, peering through the spy hole in one of the cell doors. "Up and at 'em." To Mal and Aaronson he said, "He's not very lively. All he's done since he got here is wallow on the bunk. I doubt he'll give us any trouble, but let's keep our *macuahitl*s at the ready just in case."

He patted his sword and nodded at Mal's. She was reminded that she hadn't yet got round to upgrading to a DCI's *macuahitl* yet, the version with the crystal snowflake patterns embedded in its obsidian. She'd been, to say the least, preoccupied.

The cell reeked of unwashed body. Reston lay on his back on the narrow, mattress-less bunk. He stirred as they entered, blinking groggily and rolling onto his side. His hair was lank and matted and several days' growth of stubble coarsened his chin. Scabs and swellings stippled his forearms and neck, constellations of infection, and he'd shed several pounds. His clothes were torn and caked in dirt. All in all, he was a far cry from the sleek, groomed businessman Mal had met at Reston Rhyolitic or for that matter the fit, muscular jogger she had run alongside the Thames with. His eyes were red-rimmed and he looked fragile. No, *cracked*, that was the word. Like a dropped cup.

"Stuart Reston," Mal said. "Fancy meeting you here. You should have realised you could never get away. Long arm of the law and all that."

At the sound of his native tongue, Reston become more animated. He propped himself up into a sitting position. He peered up at the faces of his three visitors, his gaze alighting last on Mal's.

"Fuck me, it's you," he croaked. "My supercop nemesis." He forced a smile. "Well, welcome to my new abode, Inspector Vaughn. Slightly more humble than I'm accustomed to, but make yourself at home anyway. I'd offer you and your friends seats, except..."

There was barely floorspace in the cell for the three Jaguars to stand.

"You've been having a hell of a time of it, by the looks of you," Mal said. "Hard, isn't it, living rough and on the run? And ending up in this grotty little cell – it must make you regret all the choices you've made."

"I never had you pegged as the gloating type, but you're just loving this, aren't you?"

"I am feeling a warm rosy glow inside, I can't deny. You've put me through several tons of shit, Reston. It would take a better person than I am to not get some satisfaction out of seeing you in the state you're in now. The phrase 'how are the mighty fallen' springs to mind. That and 'serves you bloody well right.'"

"So what now? I'm getting dragged back to England, presumably."

"That's the general idea. A few arrangements have to be made first, but basically you're coming back with us to face the music."

"Any chance we can use Nahuatl?" Necalli interjected. "I don't like being excluded from a conversation in my own station."

"Fine by me," said Mal, in Nahuatl.

"If we must," said Reston, likewise.

"Ah, bilingual after all," said Necalli. "I was starting to wonder."

"I wasn't in the frame of mind to co-operate before. Wasn't in the frame of mind to do much at all, as a matter of fact. But now that the delightful Inspector Vaughn has appeared..."

Reston accompanied the remark with a gesture in

Mal's direction. Instantly, all three Jaguars' hands flashed to their sword hilts.

"Hey," Reston said. "Easy does it. I'd be crazy to try and take on three of law enforcement's finest. Especially at such close quarters. I wouldn't stand a chance."

"But you *are* crazy," Mal said, "that's just it. Haven't you realised? Nutty as squirrel shit."

"In your opinion. Although I must say, there are things I've seen recently that have made even me begin to doubt my own sanity." Reston's voice trailed off. He became lost in some deep inner musing, grappling with bafflement and despair. "Men as gods," he said, mostly to himself. "Gods as men. Demigods? Who knows? Where do you draw the line? How do you distinguish?"

"Nahuatl," Necalli growled. Reston had reverted to English. "If you please."

Mal shook her head in an exaggerated show of pity. "Maybe you *aren't* mad, Reston. Maybe for the first time in a long while you're lucid and the consequences of your actions are hitting home. The guilt's catching up. In which case, now is the time to ask if you've given any thought to what's going to become of your company now that its CEO has been unmasked as an anti-Imperial seditionary? Did you even think that far ahead? All those people on your payroll – however many hundreds it is – suddenly their jobs are up in the air, their livelihoods on the line, thanks to you and your psychopathic dog-and-pony show. Do you have any idea how far Reston

Rhyolitic stock has fallen since word got out who the Conquistador really is?"

"I imagine the shares hit rock bottom but bounced back. Some other company has launched a takeover bid and now owns a controlling stake. Am I right?"

"Well, yes actually, but –"

"Who is it? CCMM in Italy? One of the Indian consortiums?"

"I have no idea, and I care even less. I only know that someone has."

"No surprise. Reston Rhyolitic's too good and too successful that anyone would ever let it fall by the wayside. I made provision, you see. If something untoward were to happen to me – and being arrested and having to flee the country definitely qualifies as that – I arranged things so that the company would immediately be put out to tender, lock, stock and barrel. That way it wouldn't be broken down and sold off piecemeal but kept as a whole entity, a going concern. My people's jobs are safe. There may be some restructuring, a handful of compulsory redundancies perhaps, the odd boardroom resignation, but the vast majority of the workforce will still be clocking on as usual, for the same salaries and pensions as before. I'm not a complete idiot, inspector. I'd always assumed the Conquistador would get his comeuppance sooner or later. His lifespan was finite. It was a good run while it lasted. Only now..." His eyes took on that faraway, despairing look again. "Now I really don't know that it matters. That anything matters."

"What happened to you out there?" Mal waved to indicate the world beyond the cell's humidity-blotched walls – the land, the rainforest.

"I'm touched by the concern," Reston said, coming back to himself. "I didn't think I mattered to you so much."

"I'm curious, that's all. Necalli here says there's this phenomenon called bewilderness, a delirium people can lapse into in the forest, a kind of fugue state. Is that it? Is that why you've come over all weird and spacey?"

"No. I couldn't really explain it if I wanted to."

"Why not try?"

Reston deliberated. "I think," he said eventually, "that the world is a lot stranger and more complex than any of us suspects. I think there are truths we've forgotten or been forbidden from remembering. I think you and I, inspector, locked in our own little struggle, our own little battle of wits and wills, just have no conception of the bigger picture around us. We're fleas. No, ants. We're ants. Tiny, insignificant, anonymous, scurrying about on our missions and errands, oblivious to the fact that there are giants among us. They can control us, stamp on us, manipulate us, squash us without even trying. We're nothing to them except objects of curiosity and sometimes distant affection. Am I making any sense?"

"None whatsoever," said Mal.

"But keep going with the deep philosophical stuff," said Aaronson archly. "It's really enlightening. I can feel my brain expanding. Wow."

"I'm wasting my breath," Reston said. "You can't know unless you've experienced it for yourself. Seen *them* in action."

"Them?" said Mal. "Who's them? Your Xibalba chums?"

"Oh no, not them." Reston looked pained. "No, they learned the same lesson I've learned but, sadly, the hard way."

There was only one inference Mal could draw. "They're dead?"

"All of them. Wiped out, like crumbs off a tablecloth. It's not even like they had a chance. They might as well have not been there."

Necalli leapt in. "You're saying a whole band of separatists has been eliminated? Well, that's marvellous. I need details. Is there some kind of proof? Where are the bodies?"

"No bodies." Reston gave a hollow laugh. "Only dust. Proof? I suppose you could go looking for a dirty great hole that's been blasted somewhere in the forest. I couldn't begin to tell you where, but get an aircraft up there, go scouting around, you're sure to find it."

"And what was responsible for this 'dirty great hole'?"

"A disc. Blown to smithereens. I watched it go up. I was there, right in the middle of it. Right in the middle of the explosion, and I just stood, wasn't touched, safe as houses."

"Yeah, right," said Aaronson.

"Hmm," said Necalli, thinking. "Now that might account for it."

"For what?" said Mal.

"We got multiple reports yesterday – some sort of loud bang to the north of here, early in the morning. Like a single clap of thunder, only there were no storms in the region yesterday. People heard it in locations as much as fifty miles apart. We just assumed it was coincidence. Hunters in the forest, perhaps. A distant gunshot here, another one there, each fired at approximately the same time. Separate instances giving the false impression of being the same one. But if Reston's telling the truth, it seems it could have been a single major event after all. A disc, you say? Whose disc?"

"Theirs," said Reston. "Xibalba's."

"And why were they in possession of an aerodisc? What were they proposing to do with it?"

Before Reston could reply, there was a commotion in the corridor outside. Marching feet tramped briskly. Leather creaked and weaponry clattered. Then a brusque voice rang out.

"I'm looking for Stuart Reston. Which cell is he in?"

Next moment, a Serpent Warrior appeared in the doorway. He glanced in officiously. Two more Serpents came to a halt behind him.

"That him?" said the first, nodding at Reston. "Certainly looks like an Englishman to me."

"Who are you?" Necalli challenged.

"Who does it fucking look like I am?" came the sharp retort. "I'm a Serpent Warrior, I'm personally answerable to the Great Speaker, and whoever you are and whatever post you hold in this pissant little police station of yours, I outrank you by at least one thousand. So shut up and answer my question."

Mal could see Aaronson bracing himself to ask how someone was supposed to shut up *and* answer a question. A swift kick to the shin silenced him before he could speak. Now was not the moment for smart-arsery. There were few people who genuinely looked as if they shouldn't be messed with, and this Serpent was one.

"I meant," said Necalli, with tremendous self-restraint, "please identify yourself." He added, "Sir," almost having to cough the word out.

The Serpent Warrior entered the cell, ducking his snake-head helmet under the door lintel. "Not that I'm under any obligation to tell you, but my name is Colonel Tlanextic. The salient part of that sentence is 'Colonel.' As in, 'Fuck you, I'm a fucking colonel.'"

He thrust his face close to Necalli's, who, to his credit, didn't bat an eyelid and didn't back away.

"You need to justify why you've come barging in like this, Colonel Tlanextic," Necalli said. "What are you after?"

"Again, it's not your place to ask."

"It is. This is my station and I'm the duty officer."

"No," said Tlanextic, "what you are is a nobody in a nowhere town who's talking to someone to whom you're about as important as a smear of dog shit on the sole of his boot. Your lips are moving, but all I can hear coming out is a sound like a fart, and not even a loud one, just one of those hissy, squeaky ones that you sneak out between your arse cheeks on the bus and the passenger sitting beside you doesn't even notice because it's one of those farts that doesn't even have the decency to stink, it's not a manly fart, it's an effeminate fart, a five-year-old girl's fart. I can stand here and you can tell me whatever the hell you like about yourself and I won't pay a blind bit of attention because, have I mentioned this already? I. Am. A. Fucking. Serpent. Warrior. Colonel."

"All right," Necalli said, "you've made your point."

Tlanextic turned to his two colleagues. "Lieutenants? Either of you hear anything?" They shrugged, their faces deadpan but their eyes smirking. "Because I know I didn't. Nope, definitely didn't hear a thing. Perhaps a cockroach just scuttled past, I'm not sure."

Necalli sighed. "Just tell me what you want."

Tlanextic feigned a look of apology. "No, sorry, still getting nothing. Could be I'm going deaf. However, in the event that someone of the lowly stature of an earthworm's sphincter *is* talking to me, what I want is that Englishman over there, and I'm taking him. Where, why, or what fucking for, is none of your business. All you have to do is hand him over, say, 'You're welcome,' and then say, 'Is there anything else I can do for you, Colonel Tlanextic?' At which point I'll say, 'No,' and then I'll say, 'Oh wait. There is one thing. You can shove your head right up your own rectum.' And you'll reply, 'Of course, sir, and how far up would you like it to go? Colon? Ileum? Duodenum?' And I'll say, 'I honestly don't mind, as long as you're wearing that stupid pointy-eared pussycat helmet while you're doing it.'"

Necalli seemed to be visibly swelling up, as though outrage was a physical force inside him, an increase in air pressure. Mal watched him struggle to contain it. Necalli understood, as she did, that men like Tlanextic could not be argued with or resisted. They could only be endured.

"Have him, then," he said, with a pathetic, hapless gesture in Reston's direction.

"Yes, your permission wasn't required," said Tlanextic. "It wasn't even being sought. Boys?"

The two Serpent lieutenants elbowed their way into the cell, forcing Mal, Aaronson and Necalli to huddle up against the far wall. One of them unclipped a stun gun from his belt. He flipped a switch, the stun gun whined, and before Reston could move or resist he placed it against his neck and depressed the trigger. There was a sharp crackle of electricity, and Reston's entire body went slack. The two lieutenants hoisted his limp form between them and dragged him out into the corridor by the armpits.

"You're too kind," Tlanextic said to Necalli, then saluted him with sneering condescension and followed his men out.

IT WAS SEEING Reston actually being removed from her sight that spurred Mal to action. Up until then she'd understood what was going on, but been unable to process it. All at once she grasped that her quarry was being taken from her. Once again. For a third fucking time.

That was an insult that could not be borne. An affront too far. Nobody deserved to have Stuart Reston except her. Not even a high-and-mighty Serpent. Reston belonged to her by every moral right there was. Her future, her career, her self-respect, everything hinged on her carting the Conquistador back to London and depositing him at the commissioner's feet. Colonel Tlanextic, overbearing megabastard though he was, was *not* depriving her of what was probably her one and only shot at redemption.

She propelled herself out of the cell, barging Necalli and Aaronson aside. In the corridor she grabbed hold of Tlanextic just below the armlet that bore the five-circles symbol denoting his rank. He stopped in his tracks but didn't deign to turn.

"Whoever's hand that is, they'd better remove it by the count of three," he said, "or be prepared to lose it. One. Two."

"Give him back."

"Three."

He swung round. Mal let go. "Colonel, please. I've come five and a half thousand miles for that man. I know this isn't my jurisdiction, but he's a British citizen, a British criminal, and I'm a British Jaguar. He's mine."

Slowly, patiently, Tlanextic said, "Listen, dear. That was a very brave thing you just did, grabbing me. Well done. You should be proud of yourself. Not many would have had the nerve. But let's leave it there, eh? You do not want to take this any further. Quit while you're ahead."

"No," Mal said, terrified by her own boldness. "Give him back. He's not yours to take."

A flicker of amusement passed across Tlanextic's face. Then his eyes hardened, his mouth twisted, and next thing Mal knew, something struck her with sledgehammer force and she was down on the floor, her ears ringing, pain lancing down her jaw and up through her skull.

Tlanextic shook out his fist. "By all the Four, that girl's got a hard head." He peered down at Mal as she squirmed and groaned. Then he about-turned and motioned to his lieutenants to carry on. They resumed dragging Reston towards the staircase.

"Wait," said a thick, unsteady voice behind them.

Tlanextic looked back to see Mal rising to her feet. She was using the wall for support. Her legs seemed barely able to function.

"What?" he said, exasperated. "You want me to deck you again?"

"By the power vested in me by His Very Holiness the High Priest of Great Britain," she said, "I demand that you hand Stuart Reston over."

"Hold on, men," Tlanextic said to his lieutenants. "This won't take a second. Listen, Miss British Jaguar." He crossed back over to Mal. "Maybe your Nahuatl isn't what it ought to be, so I'll keep this as simple as I can. Me Serpent Warrior, you not. Get it? Me very big man round these parts, you silly little white policewoman with funny accent. Me told what to do by Great Speaker himself. In pecking order, me up here." He raised a hand level with his eyes. "You down here." He lowered the hand to his crotch. "In more ways than one."

"With all due respect, colonel," said Mal, "go screw yourself."

There was a gasp from behind her – Aaronson. At the same moment, Tlanextic punched her again, this time in the solar plexus. It was a mighty wallop, carrying all his weight behind it, and Mal collapsed to her knees, winded and in agony. She fought for breath. The world wavered darkly around her. As if from a great distance, his voice booming and echoing, she heard Tlanextic say, "All right. You've made your point. Enough's enough. Next time, it'll be my *macuahitl* rather than my fist. This is over."

She fought the tide of blackness that was threatening to engulf her. *Do not pass out, do not pass out.* She clutched the wall, hauling herself upright inch by trembling inch. Bile burned in the back of her throat and she felt close to throwing up. Aaronson was desperately urging her, "No, boss, don't. It's not worth it. Stay down." Even Necalli, who hardly knew her, was offering the same advice.

"Is that..." she said hoarsely to Tlanextic. "Is that... all you've got... you big pussy?"

Aaronson clawed his face in anguish.

Tlanextic's expression turned to one of pure spite and fury. He snatched the stun gun off the belt of his junior officer and sprang at Mal with the device humming in his hand. He touched it to her chest – her left breast, to be exact – and pain like she'd never known before coursed through her. Her whole body seemed all of a sudden not to belong to her. It was a convulsing, juddering bag of meat that she just happened to be connected with. She felt her bladder let go and warm wetness spreading between her legs. She heard sounds coming out of her throat that she didn't think any human being could make. Tlanextic kept the stun gun pressed to her, his thumb hard on the trigger. His eyes were alive with sadistic pleasure.

Eventually the stun gun's charge ran out. The pain subsided, but Mal's body still kept twitching spastically. Had she not been leaning against the wall, she would be sprawled in a heap on the floor by now. She tasted blood from where her teeth had clamped down involuntarily on her tongue. She could smell singed cotton and skin, and her own urine.

The effort it took to lift her head was almost superhuman. Harder still was finding the muscular control necessary to peel back her lips in a grin.

"I've used... vibrators... with more power... than that," she gasped.

Colonel Tlanextic stared at her in open disbelief. *What does it take to put this woman down? How can anyone be so obstinate, so insanely stubborn?*

"Please, colonel," Aaronson implored. "Don't do anything more. She's had enough. She didn't mean to be disrespectful. She's passionate about her job, that's all. Takes it very seriously indeed. That's no crime, eh? I mean, we're all basically on the same side, aren't we?"

Tlanextic raised a hand: *shut up.* He peered closely and quizzically at Mal – her wan face, her strivingto-focus eyes – as though she were some kind of zoo animal he'd never seen before. He was trying with all his might to fathom her. Both Aaronson and Necalli fully expected that within the next few seconds he would draw his *macuahitl* and run her through.

Instead, he laughed. It was a laugh that was utterly devoid of warmth, but it came from the belly and it went on and on.

Tlanextic found her amusing.

More than that, he grudgingly admired her. The laughter was congratulation.

"Fuck me rigid," he said. "You've got a serious hard-on for this man, haven't you? What's your name anyway?"

"Vaughn," Mal said feebly. "Chief Inspector Malinalli Vaughn of Scotland Yard."

"Well, Chief Inspector Malinalli Vaughn of Scotland Yard, I'll tell you what. I like you, and you might even come in useful as a translator if Reston gets uncooperative and insists on using your own gibberish language again. You've just earned yourself the right to accompany us to Tenochtitlan. How about that?"

Accompany them to Tenochtitlan? It wasn't what Mal wanted. Not at all. But it was the best she was going to get, she knew, and it would keep Reston within her sight. The alternative? She didn't think she had one.

"Sounds... fine," she said.

"Good," said Tlanextic. "You know, I could do with a dozen like you under my command. Men?

Take note. You think you're tough?" He wagged a finger at Mal. "This bitch – *this* is tough."

"My sergeant comes too," Mal added, gesturing vaguely in Aaronson's direction.

"Whatever. No skin off my nose. Long as you both keep up. Time's wasting." Tlanextic set off along the corridor at a firm and forthright pace.

Mal, with Aaronson propping her up, followed.

TWENTY-THREE

Same Day

THEY FLEW OUT over Lake Texcoco, skimming above the wavelets that turned the expanse of freshwater into a vast sheet of crepe paper. The Serpent disc was a small, short-range craft with a spartanly furnished interior, and Mal and Aaronson perched at the rear of the cabin on a narrow bench adjacent to the armoury and uniform lockers. With Colonel Tlanextic's permission, Mal had helped herself to a spare pair of Serpent Warrior trousers which just about fit, changing out of her own soiled trousers and underwear while Aaronson acted as a human curtain, shielding her from sight of everyone else on board. Tlanextic hadn't even been tempted to laugh when she'd made her request. To him it had seemed simply a practical solution to an unfortunate sartorial mishap.

"Why are we doing this, boss?" Aaronson whispered. He nodded over at Reston, who was slumped inside the disc's prisoner transport cage, wrists and ankles chained together. The one-time Conquistador looked despondent, utterly defeated. Cage and restraints seemed superfluous. Reston was going nowhere. "We're never getting him back. Even if the Serpents let him live, there'll be nothing left once they've finished with him. Nothing worth anything."

"If they kill him, at least we'll get to see justice done," Mal replied. "But as long as there's a chance I can still bring him home, however slim it is and whatever condition he's in, I'm going to keep hanging on for it."

"I swear, if you didn't hate the bloke so much, anyone would think you were in love with him."

"Don't be a twat."

"I'm just saying. It's a thin line. You've been hounding him so hard. Cops and villains sometimes get this attachment for one another, don't they? It's a, whatchemacall... Symbiotic relationship. Mutual thing. Can't live with each other, can't live without."

"When you're quite done with the cheap psychoanalysis..."

"Myself, some of the young roughs I've arrested – they're quite beautiful, in that scrawny, surly way of theirs. A few of them know it and they've made offers. You know, 'Let me go free. I'll do *anything* you ask.' Can't say I haven't been tempted."

"I trust you haven't given in."

"No, never. But I'm not blind. He's a looker, that

Reston. If you like 'em posh and well-spoken, that is. And he flirts with you."

"He does not."

"Hello? Back of the paddy wagon? What was that if it wasn't flirting?"

"Sergeant, please shut the fuck up."

"The more you deny it..."

"...the likelier I am to plant my fist in your face," Mal said. "Listen. Right now I'm feeling like refried shit. I know you're only taking the piss and that's just how you are, but I really can't be arsed with it. Enough."

"Okay, boss. If you say so."

"Believe me, I do."

Soon the bulwarked bulk of Tenochtitlan filled the windshield. The aerodisc rose and banked left, smartly circumnavigating the island city, and made its approach from the far side. It decelerated to a hover above a landing pad painted distinctively with a snake's head motif. As it touched down an honour guard of six Serpents appeared, forming lines either side of the gangplank. They had lightning guns slung across their backs and *macuahitl*s at their waists as well as the traditional ceremonial Serpent halberds, which were tipped with outcurving obsidian blades. They snapped to attention and saluted as Colonel Tlanextic exited the disc. His two lieutenants followed, with Reston shuffling between them as best his foot manacles would allow. Mal and Aaronson took the rear. The Serpent guards eyed them with curiosity but, since they were obviously with Tlanextic, nobody made a move to challenge them.

"What now?" Aaronson said out of the side of his mouth.

"Unless or until Tlanextic tells us to bugger off, we stick with him."

"I can't believe I'm here." Aaronson gazed with wonder at the buildings around them, the towers and close-clustering ziggurats, their angled planes gilded by the mid-morning sun. "I mean, actual Tenochtitlan. Can't wait to tell my mum. She'll be so envious."

"We'll buy postcards later. Keep walking."

Tlanextic led his party to a lift and they descended to ground level, where transportation was waiting for them in the form of an open-topped train. Tenochtitlan boasted a neg-mass passenger monorail for the use of Serpents and the numerous bureaucrats, functionaries and servants who tended to the Great Speaker's needs. It criss-crossed the city in an intricate narrow-gauge system that was raised up, straddle-beam style, on squat pylons a couple of metres above the ground. Single-carriage trains glided along looping, intersecting routes with stops at the foot of every building on the island.

A driver ushered them on board, bowing so low to Tlanextic that his forehead nearly scraped the floor of the platform. Like the guards, he was puzzled by the presence of Mal and Aaronson but, also like the guards, he knew it wasn't his place to query. When everyone had taken a seat, he grasped the train's controls and guided it away from the platform.

A short while later they pulled in at the foot of the largest ziggurat on the island. Mal's breath caught. If she didn't miss her guess, this was none other than the Great Speaker's palace. Surely they weren't about to...

They were. Tlanextic disembarked, beckoning the others to follow. "Word of warning." This was directed at Mal and Aaronson. "If His Imperial Holiness consents to allow you to enter his presence – and it's a huge *if* – you do not look directly at him, you do not meet his eye, and above all else you do not speak to him unless he speaks to you first. Should you fail to abide by any of these stipulations, you die, simple as that. I'll make sure of it myself. Are we clear?"

Mal and Aaronson nodded. As soon as Tlanextic looked the other way, Aaronson turned to Mal, eyes agog, and mouthed the word "*Fuuuuck!*" She nodded to him in return, no less incredulous than he, but able to mask it better.

A funicular lift took them up the ziggurat's slanted flank. With every storey it rose Mal felt a mounting sense of unreality. She'd never in her life expected she would even set eyes on the Great Speaker, let alone be in the same room as him. Now, that possibility loomed. Within minutes she could be standing before the emperor of an entire planet, the most powerful man who had ever existed. An immortal, no less, gifted with prolonged life by the gods themselves. Moctezuma II, in the half-a-millennium-old flesh.

Mal Vaughn was not a vain woman, but at that moment she found herself wishing she looked better than she currently did, with her borrowed trousers and her practical travelling clothes. Not forgetting the bruise she could feel growing on the side of her face, courtesy of Tlanextic's roundhouse right. She fingered the puffy, stretched patch of skin delicately.

"Don't worry, boss," Aaronson confided. "You still look fine. Every inch the plainclothes Jaguar. So what if you're a bit ragged round the edges? It's good for the image. Adds a touch of authenticity."

"Thanks," said Mal. "I think. How's the acrophobia?"

Aaronson was standing with his back turned to the lift's three outer sides, which were all glass. "Long as I don't think about it, I'm fine."

The lift deposited them a couple of floors shy of the ziggurat's summit. Tlanextic went ahead while the rest of them cooled their heels in a reception area. In order to distract herself from the nerves fizzing in her stomach, Mal tried to engage one of the Serpent lieutenants in conversation. He was having none of it.

Eventually Tlanextic reappeared. "The Great Speaker will see us now."

"All of us?" said Mal.

"Yes, that does fucking include you. Get over it. Let's go."

A short trapezoid passageway led to an antechamber dominated by a massive circular door. The entire surface of the door was covered by a mosaic of jewels taking the form of the four-quadrants symbol that represented the interrelatedness and universality of the Four Who Rule Supreme. It was an outlandishly lavish and opulent thing. The north quadrant, the cardinal direction associated with Huitzilopochtli, consisted of slivers of white opal across which rainbow glints of iridescence chased one another. The south, which belonged to Tezcatlipoca, was a jigsaw of flakes of purest midnight jet. The east, Xipe Totec's province, was a scintillating mass of deep yellow citrine, while the west quadrant, Quetzalcoatl's, was nothing but rubies.

There was scant opportunity for Mal to marvel, however. No sooner had they arrived at the door than it began to slide open. The quadrants parted, each withdrawing separately into the frame, and X-shaped gap expanding to reveal a round aperture. Tlanextic went through, inviting everyone with him to do the same.

The room on the other side was large and richly furnished but not as much as Mal had been anticipating. She'd expected a throne room, gold everywhere, more precious metal on show than the mind could take in, and a ceiling so high you could hardly see it. Instead, it was a single-storey space whose floors and walls were an expanse of plain black marble, buffed to a mirror shine. There were oblong onyx columns carved with sacred emblems. There were suites of sofas and armchairs upholstered in dark leather. It was more like a very swanky open-plan living room than anything else, Aztec-themed but ultramodern.

A row of windows occupied the far wall, and beyond them lay a terrace the size of a *tlachtli* court, dotted with parasols and outdoor furniture. At the parapet, a very tall robed figure stood with his hands clasped behind his back, admiring the view. He didn't look round as Tlanextic ushered everyone out onto the terrace, but a slight shift in the position of his shoulders indicated that he was aware of their presence.

For a long time, nobody moved or spoke. Tlanextic, Mal, Aaronson, Reston and the Serpent lieutenants waited. The tall figure continued to enjoy the prospect over Tenochtitlan, across the wave-wrinkled lake, all the way to the skein of shoreline. The sun beat down but a cooling breeze mitigated its heat. The parasols fluttered.

At last the Great Speaker turned. His enveloping golden mask flashed dazzlingly, so bright it hurt to look at. It was a smooth, almost featureless blister of polished metal, with two tiny eyeholes and a grille-like slit for a mouth. It was beautiful and inhuman, like the face of a sculpture or an automaton, something manmade and empty of emotion. Yet there was a gracefulness about it too, and likewise about the Great Speaker himself as he raised a hand in greeting, the fingers fanned like a dancer's.

Mal was mesmerised. Enthralled. Nothing she had read about the Great Speaker, none of the clips she had watched on TV, had prepared her for the experience of seeing him in the actual living flesh. He had a stillness and physicality that seemed to radiate outwards and fill the air around him. It was almost as if he was touching her – touching all of them – even at a distance of several yards. This, she realised, was the aura of true power. This was a man who rightfully inspired awe.

Tlanextic fell to one knee and dropped his head, and Mal and the others took their cue and followed suit, all apart from Reston, who remained standing with a bland, indifferent expression on his face.

The Great Speaker acknowledged the show of obeisance with the slightest of nods. When he spoke, his voice resonated deep and clear like a gong. The mask did not muffle it at all.

"You may rise," he said, adding, "Those of you who had the good manners to bend the knee."

"Your Imperial Holiness," said Tlanextic, "I bring you Stuart Reston, as instructed."

"Yes," said the Great Speaker, studying Tlanextic's prisoner. "Yes, indeed. The man who donned Conquistador armour and thumbed his nose at the Empire for many months. Quite the nuisance you were, Mr Reston, at least to your own countrymen and your High Priest. But the Empire is huge and thick-skinned, like a rhinoceros, and your little provocations were like the bites of a gnat. You scarcely penetrated its hide."

Reston mumbled something.

"What was that?" The Great Speaker cupped a hand to his ear in a dumbshow of deafness. "Didn't quite catch it."

"I said, 'But I'm here, aren't I?'"

"The implication being...?"

"Well, despite your protestations, the Empire must have felt *something*, mustn't it? I must have stung. Otherwise why the volcanic eruptions? And why has my sorry arse been hauled all the way over to your palace? Stands to reason. Oh, and by the way, while I have you, and because I'm never going to get an opportunity like this again... You're a big fat phoney. Immortal? Ptah!" He spat at the Great Speaker's feet. "Just the latest in a long line of anonymous dictators. Tell me, does it get stuffy in that mask? Does it stink of the sweat from all the others who've worn it before you?"

Mal couldn't control herself. She delivered a knuckle strike to Reston's waist, just where his left kidney was, so that he doubled over, grimacing in pain. "Don't you behave like that before the Great Speaker. Don't you dare."

The Great Speaker cocked his head, as if amused. "Ah yes, the British policewoman. Vaughn. Am I right in thinking, Miss Vaughn, that you're the one who headed up the Conquistador investigation?"

"I did, Your Imperial Holiness. It was my job to end his terror campaign. And I suppose you could say I achieved that."

The Great Speaker inclined his head to examine Mal. Through the mask's eyeholes she glimpsed a pair of irises so dark brown they were almost black. There seemed to be a vast depth of intelligence in those eyes, and a cold aloofness too. These, surely, were the eyes of someone who had lived for over five hundred solar years.

"How fascinating," he said. "Such fire and tenacity, yet such insecurity too, buried away inside. I think you sometimes feel you're doing the right things for the wrong reason, Inspector Vaughn, or else the wrong things for the right reason. You punish yourself, and yet to live with such inner turmoil must, I would have thought, be sufficient punishment in itself."

Mal was dumbfounded. He had read her – comprehended her – at a glance.

"As for you..." The Great Speaker returned his attention to Reston, who was still smarting from Mal's blow. "Your insolence doesn't perturb me in the least. You are nothing to me. Once, for a very brief while, you seemed a cause for concern. But that time is gone. I have you before me, and you are a small and pathetic individual indeed. Your opinion of me is of no consequence, and neither are you, in and of yourself."

"Then how about letting me go," said Reston, "if I'm so insignificant?"

"Because you might still have your uses. Colonel?"

Tlanextic straightened. "Sir."

"First of all, you can dismiss your subordinates. We shan't be needing them."

"You heard him, men." Tlanextic jerked a thumb. "Take a hike." As the lieutenants departed, he gestured at Mal and Aaronson. "And these two, Your Imperial Holiness?"

"They may stay. It would seem churlish to dismiss them, in light of how far they've travelled to be here. I wouldn't like them to go home thinking the Great Speaker ungracious or niggardly with his hospitality." He said this with a sly lilt to his voice, the tone of someone who enjoyed his whims and his freedom to indulge them. "Besides, who knows? Inspector Vaughn may yet be leaving with her prize."

Yes! thought Mal.

"It all depends on how helpful he is. Oh, and these things, colonel." The Great Speaker waved at Reston's bonds. "Not called for. Take them off."

"If you insist, sir."

"I do. I'm not frightened of Mr Reston. While he's shackled, it implies that he is a danger to me. Untying him will dispel *that* illusion. Losing the chains will weaken his position, not strengthen it."

Producing a key, Tlanextic unlocked and removed the manacles. "One step out of line," he hissed at Reston, "and you're dead meat. You so much as sneeze suspiciously, you'll find a sword through your heart before you've even wiped your nose."

"Now then, Mr Reston," said the Great Speaker. "Let's all relax and talk in a civilised fashion. I want information. I'm curious to know about events that occurred in the rainforest. I have reason to believe you've recently been in contact with certain parties who may bear a certain animosity towards me."

"Xibalba?"

"Come now, don't be facetious. You know I don't mean them. Poorly equipped separatist guerrillas with their foolish dreams of a Mayan state? I couldn't care less about them. If the Conquistador is a gnat, they are smaller still. Microbes, perhaps. No, I'm talking about beings of considerable power. You've met them. I know you have."

"I have no idea what you're –"

Quicker than the eye could follow, quicker than seemed humanly possible, the Great Speaker shot out a hand and seized Reston by the neck. Then, exerting no apparent effort, he raised him off the floor, using only the one arm. Reston clawed at the hand with both of his, trying to unpick the gloved fingers, straining and gurgling. His face reddened. His eyes bulged. His legs kicked violently but uselessly. He hung there, suspended, choking, for nearly a minute before the Great Speaker relented and set him back down.

"There, now," he said as Reston, bent over, wheezed for breath. "I was hoping I wouldn't have to resort to those sorts of cheap bullyboy tactics. I'm not barbaric by nature, not in my day-to-day affairs. When it comes to getting results, I far prefer words to the fist. So let's try again. Three days ago, out in the rainforest, certain energies were released."

"The aerodisc blowing up," said Reston hoarsely, gulping out each word.

"No. Other energies. Of a kind the world has not known in many a year. I detected them. I am, you might say, a spider, and the world is my web. I sit at the centre of it, feeling the hum and quiver of every strand. When there is an anomaly – anything that might upset the precise, orderly running of my domain – I am aware of it. There is a presence out there in the forest, just a few miles away. I sense that you have met it. The moment you stepped out onto this terrace, I knew. It has left its mark on you. You are redolent of it. I can see it on you. *Smell* it on you. Smell *him*."

"Him," Reston echoed.

"Yes. And where he goes, can the others be far behind?"

"You're referring to –"

"Who do you think I'm referring to?" the Great Speaker snapped. Then he composed himself, his voice resuming its serene purr. "So tell me. How is he? What sort of a mood is he in? What does he want? What are his plans?"

Very quietly, almost in a whisper, Reston said, "Quetzalcoatl."

"Yes. Quetzalcoatl. Of course, Quetzalcoatl. Who else?"

Mal scowled. What the hell were these two talking about? Quetzalcoatl? What did *he* have to do with anything? She saw similar perplexity on Aaronson's face. Tlanextic, by contrast, looked only mildly fascinated, as though the mention of the god's name came as no surprise. It was evident that she and Aaronson were the odd ones out here, ignorant of some vital facts known to everyone else present.

"He..." Reston paused. "He told me nothing. Nothing about any plans. Just demonstrated what he and the rest of them can do. It wasn't even a fraction of what they're capable of, I don't think. They barely broke a sweat."

"And what was it? What did they do?"

"They killed – they *swatted* – Xibalba."

"How interesting. Why the Mayans? What did they do to deserve it?"

"Nothing, just failed to listen."

"You don't suppose this indicates Quetzalcoatl is on my side?"

"You'd have to ask him. Like I said, he told me nothing."

"Come on," the Great Speaker pressed him, "he must have given some hint of his goals. What game is he playing? Why has he returned? Why now?"

"I don't know. I really don't."

"But it seems as though he confided in you to some extent. Favoured you. After all, he killed those others but let you live. Why?"

"Beats me. I think he had a soft spot for me. Or felt sorry for me. One or the other."

The answer seemed to jibe with the Great Speaker's own view. "Yes, that sounds about right. He does like his pets, does old Quetzalcoatl. Fond of the lesser beings and the afflicted. Like Xolotl. And that disgusting syphilitic old cripple Nanahuatzin. So he didn't mention me at all?"

Reston searched his memory. "Maybe. Sort of. Indirectly. In passing. He talked about not doing what Xibalba was hoping to do, not resorting to drastic measures. A nonviolent resolution. And there was something about 'unfinished business.' I suppose that might apply to you, the Empire, all of that."

"Nonviolent," said the Great Speaker, musing. "That would be just like him. Always thinking he's above such things, always trying to plant his flag on the moral high ground, when really he's no better than anyone else."

"But he isn't the actual, genuine..." Reston began. Then his voice dropped, taking on a note of numb resignation. "He is, isn't he? There's no point trying to fight it any more."

"Yes."

"But then that would mean..."

"I, Mr Reston, am what I appear to be, and so much more."

By now Mal was beyond confused. It seemed the two of them had lapsed into talking in riddles. She was seized by the urge to butt in and demand they speak straight, stop being so damn cryptic...

All at once, the Great Speaker tensed. His whole body went rigid, right to the fingertips, every inch of him alert.

"Your Imperial Holiness?" said Tlanextic, partway unsheathing his *macuahitl*. "What is it?"

"Quiet!" The Great Speaker turned his head, fixing his attention on the eastern horizon. "Oh yes," he said slowly. "There you are. Peekaboo. I see you."

Mal followed the line of his gaze but could see nothing out of the ordinary, nothing that hadn't been there a moment earlier. It was the exact same view as before: the lake, the far-off shore, the folds of hill beyond.

"Come on, then," the Great Speaker said. "It's time we had this reunion. Long overdue, I'd say."

"Sir," said Tlanextic, "is there trouble? Perhaps we should get you inside, down to one of the command bunkers. You'll be safe there."

"No, it's not trouble, colonel. At least, nothing I can't handle. I think what's coming could be called an official delegation."

Reston was looking eastward too, and Mal could tell he was anxious, even though there was no obvious threat.

Then she spotted them – a trio of tiny dots in midair, dark against the shimmering hazy blue of the sky.

Some kind of aircraft?

They came closer, growing in size. They were moving fast, quicker even than an aerodisc could travel.

They were...

People?

Three of them.

Winged.

Flying.

The hairs on the back of Mal's neck stood on end.

"Colonel Tlanextic?" said the Great Speaker. "I'd recommend you don't do anything rash or precipitous. You'll regret it. Just stay where you are. That applies to all of you. Be calm. Show due deference."

He spread out his arms.

"Gods are coming."

TWENTY-FOUR

Same Day

THEY DESCENDED, LANDED.

All three were unusually tall, like the Great Speaker, and were kitted out in sleek versions of traditional Aztec dress. The pairs of wings, attached to them by ornate harnesses, were rigid arcs of metal which swivelled on pivots, for steering and braking. The shoulder-mounted units from which they sprouted were clearly what lent the wearers the power of flight. They gave off a familiar faint hum; portable neg-mass generators.

The wings stowed themselves automatically as the three men landed, retracting and folding neatly away behind their wearers' spines. The neg-mass units fell silent. The three looked around at the group assembled on the terrace. One of them, the tallest and by some margin the handsomest, bestowed a look of recognition on Reston – a slightly frowning one, as if surprised or puzzled to see him. Hesitantly, warily, Reston returned it. It was obvious to Mal that they knew each other, and some of Reston's recent conversation with the Great Speaker began to make sense. These were the people they were talking about, the ones Reston had had a run-in with in the rainforest.

But who were they?

And how come they had personal antigrav capability? That wasn't possible, as far as Mal was aware. The Japanese had expended huge amounts of time, money and resources on trying to scale down the size of neg-mass technology from its original specifications. They hadn't managed to by much, and if they couldn't, no one could. The dream of individual flight had yet to become a reality. Except, here it was.

The Great Speaker turned his head, looking at each of the three arrivals in turn. Finally he said, "Well, well, well. It was inevitable, I suppose. You left me alone for long enough. I was beginning to think you'd forgotten about me."

"I wish," said the tallest.

"Oh, so that's how it's to be, is it?"

"No, I apologise. It was a cheap shot."

"So you've come to kiss and make up. Or am I to view this visitation in a more sinister light? As a prelude to something worse?"

"It all depends."

"On?"

"How you choose to play things."

"It's been a long time. Can't we simply let bygones be bygones?"

"I'd be glad to. But some deeds are hard to overlook, or forgive."

"Such as?"

"What you've been up to in our absence, for starters," growled another of the three. This one was superbly muscled and completely hairless, with a belligerent jut to his jaw.

"You don't like what I've done with the place?" The Great Speaker put a hand to his chest in the manner of someone mortally offended. "And here was I thinking I'd been an exemplary caretaker. Preserving the legacy. Making the most of what we'd started. Maximising on the potential."

"This was never what we envisioned," said the third of the flying men. "A worldwide dictatorship based on conquest and terror – that was never the plan. Quite the opposite."

"Then perhaps you should have thought about that before you all flounced off and left me to it. If you'd been really committed to the project, you'd have stayed on and helped see it through. Instead, you abandoned me here on my own. That gave me *carte blanche* to continue as I saw fit. You can't hold me solely accountable for how everything's turned out. You're to blame, too, by walking away."

"You've interfered with the climate," said the first, sidestepping the Great Speaker's accusation.

"Wouldn't you have?" the Great Speaker said affably. "The planet needed warming up. Who in their right mind would want to live in the Arctic Circle, or even a temperate zone, if there didn't have to be one? Thanks to me, hundreds of thousands of square miles of permafrost and tundra is now fertile land, freed up for agricultural use. I've helped feed the world. Besides, these are the kind of temperatures I'm used to. Call me sentimental, but I wanted to make earth more like good old Tamoanchan – more like home."

"You've not shared all the knowledge, as we agreed. You were meant to introduce further technology in stages, as and when mankind was ready."

"So I've held a few items back? So what? There's plenty to keep the humans going as it is, and they have fun reverse-engineering and customising what they've already got. If you ask me, they're not to be trusted with the full repertoire of what's available. They're such little tinkerers. They might misuse it."

"Use it against you, you mean?" said the hairless, hostile one. "To overthrow you?"

"That's one possibility. Or against each another. They're their own worst enemies, humans are. They need an eye kept on them at all times, to stop them recklessly abusing and harming their own kind. That's one of the many beneficial functions this Empire of mine performs. It brings peace and stability."

"Stability?" said the handsome one. "They murder one another and call it sacrifice."

"A necessary evil. Our original scheme, as it stood, was a recipe for anarchy. You realise that, don't you, Quetzalcoatl? You were going to hand the humans everything we have, with few limitations in place.

They're an innately irresponsible lot. They'd have ended up destroying themselves in no time. Without me, without the curbs and vetoes I've imposed, it's a safe bet that there wouldn't now be an Earth for you to come back to. You'd be standing on a charred, devastated ball of rock, another lifeless satellite of the sun. You should be thanking me for making the best of the hand you dealt me, which was, if I may say, an unenviable one. Instead, you come swanning back after an inordinately lengthy absence and you have the nerve to act all superior and judgemental."

"I've been no such thing," said the one the Great Speaker had called Quetzalcoatl. "I've been quite reasonable, I feel. So far."

"Typical. That 'so far.' That's just like you. Can't help yourself, can you? Such self-righteousness. Such forbearance. The great and mighty Plumed Serpent, who thinks he's so much better than the rest of us, so pure and untainted. Yet beneath that 'I'm so perfect' exterior, you're just as venal, just as calculating, just as fallible."

"You can't provoke me."

"Oh, but I can," said the Great Speaker. "I know how. I know precisely which buttons to push. As I once proved, didn't I, brother?"

Brother? thought Mal. She looked from the Great Speaker to Quetzalcoatl and back again. She could see Reston doing the same, and he was as taken aback as she was. If the Great Speaker was Quetzalcoatl's brother...

"All of you," he went on, addressing the three.

"I know how to irk you, how to goad you, how to mislead and dupe you. That's always been my way. My role. Every family has to have its black sheep, and I'm sorry, Xipe Totec, but it's not you, however much you'd like to think it is."

The hairless man gave a careless shrug.

"But it isn't. You're a dark horse, maybe, but never a black sheep. You're violent and cruel, but you toe the line. When push comes to shove, you always side with the majority. You do as you're told. As do you, Huitzilopochtli."

The third of the three glowered at him.

"The Hummingbird. Bright as the sun. But none too bright in other ways. A good footsoldier but hardly an independent thinker."

"Ignore him, Huitz," said Quetzalcoatl. "You too, Xipe. He's trying to get a rise out of us. Let's not give him the satisfaction."

"Don't you *want* to be antagonised, Kay?" said the Great Speaker. "Isn't that secretly, deep down, the very thing you've come for? An excuse to lash out at me? I'm sure it is. That business with Quetzalpetlatl, it's got to be eating you up inside, even now. Our beautiful sister. So fresh. So innocent. So voluptuously fertile. How long had you been quietly lusting after her, unable to admit it even to yourself? How long had you been watching her, yearning to have her? How long, and then I gave you the opportunity to? I never forced you to sleep with Quetzalpetlatl, or her with you. You desired her, she reciprocated, and all I did was pave the way, arranging it so that the feelings you'd both kept locked inside could come out. And did I get any recognition for that? Any gratitude? No. Just an explosion of temper, the hissy fit to end all hissy fits, and then this exile, like a ship's captain being marooned on a desert island by mutineers. 'It's all yours. You look after it. No telling when we'll be back, if ever.' You think you've got a bone to pick with me, Kay? I have a whole skeleton's worth to pick with you."

The Great Speaker's voice didn't rise once during this tirade, but a distinct note of petulance entered it. All at once he came across as less than the supreme, all-powerful emperor he was supposed to be.

At the same time, Mal was halfway to becoming convinced that he was more. Much, much more.

"Take it off," said Quetzalcoatl, biting back anger. "The mask. I want to see your face. I don't want to talk to the Great Speaker any more. It's the person beneath the mask I'm interested in."

"This? Off?" The Great Speaker rapped the mask with his knuckles. It rang like a bell. "Why not? Gets so stuffy in here anyway."

He placed a hand either side of the golden head-covering and hoisted it off, setting it down on a nearby table.

"There. That's better. Fresh air."

The face that stood revealed was a handsome one like Quetzalcoatl's. There was a clear resemblance between the two of them, from the high domed forehead to the prominent cleft chin. They could easily, as the Great Speaker was claiming, be brothers. Twins, even. The Great Speaker, however, had a less attractive cast to his features. He looked haughty, where Quetzalcoatl looked noble. His eyes were that little bit closer together and deeper set, that little bit less frank and open. His complexion was several shades darker, too, black coffee as opposed to Quetzalcoatl's café-au-lait. As the two of them faced each other, it was as if one was the distorted image of the other, a reflection seen in a mirror that somehow removed sincerity and replaced it with cunning.

"There you are," said Quetzalcoatl. "Just as I remember. You haven't changed a bit, Tezcatlipoca."

MAL HAD PASSED beyond astonishment and entered a state of being where nothing felt solid or certain and where everything that had once made sense no longer did. A kind of wild hilarity kept bubbling up inside her, threatening to break out as a mad cackle. Had Aaronson not been next to her and looking not one iota less stunned, she'd have wondered if she was losing her grip on sanity. Was she dreaming? Was she in the throes of a drug trip which she couldn't remember embarking on?

Had the Great Speaker really just removed his mask before her very eyes?

Had Quetzalcoatl really just addressed him by the name Tezcatlipoca?

Were these four beings on the terrace – these four who were sharing the same space as her, breathing the same air – really none other than the Four Who Rule Supreme?

It was inconceivable.

Impossible.

Absurd.

And yet Mal knew it was true. It must be. She felt it at a level inside her that had nothing to do with rationality and everything to do with intuition. Her brain was screaming at her that this was all some extraordinary, elaborate stunt. Someone was having her on. Any moment now, the four of them would turn round and wink and say, "Gotcha!" Meanwhile, her heart, her gut, her *soul*, was insisting that yes, it was exactly as it appeared. There could be no mistake. She was witnessing a meeting of the full complement of the Four, the first in five hundred solar years. Gods had returned to the earth. Or, in Tezcatlipoca's case, had never been away.

"Look at them," said the Great Speaker, alias Tezcatlipoca. "What a staggering revelation this is to them." He meant Mal, Aaronson and Reston, of course; Colonel Tlanextic gave every indication that he had known his master's true identity all along. He was coolly enjoying the startlement on the others' faces. "They've been led to believe the Great Speaker is Moctezuma the Second, but that was just a cover story, a convenient fabrication. It came down to a choice. Which would be the easier to swallow, that a man could be granted extraordinary longevity, or that Tezcatlipoca now ruled them?

"People might wonder, why Tezcatlipoca? Why not one of the other divine visitors? Why not Quetzalcoatl himself? I was aware I wasn't the most popular of the Four. So I concocted the role of Great Speaker, usurping the identity of an emperor already beloved of his people. Moctezuma himself was none too pleased when he learned that he was about to be forcibly supplanted as ruler. Ironic, really; here was a man who had presided over so many human sacrifices, who had chalked up countless deaths in the name of his own glory, yet he was profoundly reluctant to give up his own life. He struggled quite a bit. Screamed and bit like a howler monkey under my hands."

"You... killed him?" said Mal.

"Someone had to," Tezcatlipoca replied airily. "Seemed simplest to do the job myself. It happened in his private quarters, not far from this spot. There were no witnesses. It was just Moctezuma and myself in a room, the last true Aztec emperor and the last god left on earth. He perished, I disposed of the body so as not to leave a trace behind, and next day this entity called the Great Speaker emerged, claiming to be a Moctezuma energised by godly power, a Moctezuma who would live and rule forever by divine decree.

"I wasn't entirely sure at first that people would fall for it. The priesthood, especially, I thought would see through the imposture and demand proof that I was the emperor in new clothes. In the event, everyone was duped. Some perhaps had their doubts, but went along with it anyway because up until then Moctezuma, with the gods' aid, had overseen expansion of Aztec territory on an unprecedented scale, and as the Great Speaker I quickly established that the future would hold more of the same, even though the gods were now gone. I promised them the world, as a matter of fact. It was what the Aztecs wanted to hear, so they were willing to set aside any misgivings they might have had and take me at face value. I told them that the gods had raised me up, elevated me to a higher order of being. I planted the seeds of a story which grew into a legend and from there to a simple fact of truth, a cornerstone of the Empire. People will believe anything if it's in their interest to do so."

"A grotesque hoax," said Quetzalcoatl.

"But it worked, and it's what I do best – sleight of hand. Am I not the Smoking Mirror? Do I not distort and obscure? We can't help our natures. Might as well criticise Xipe for being a feral beast or Huitz for being worthy but dull. Or yourself, Kay, for being a stuck-up prig."

"Be very careful what you say," Xipe Totec growled.

"Oh, I do. All the time. Am I not great at speaking?"

"I mean it."

"Or what? You'll kill me? You're welcome to try, Flayed One. But you know as well as I do that we're evenly matched. It would take a lot more than you've got to finish *me* off. I reckon, in truth, that I'm the equal of the three of you put together, and that's barehanded, without armour or any other form of defence or weaponry. Shall we put that to the test?"

Huitzilopochtli and Xipe Totec looked at Quetzalcoatl, who offered a tiny shake of the head. *Not here; not now.*

"Thought so," said Tezcatlipoca. "What do you want from me, then? Am I to relinquish my Empire to you? Is that it? Step down and let you take from me something I've spent five centuries building?"

"I'd like you to reconsider your position, at the very least," said Quetzalcoatl. "We can dismantle what you've created and raise something better in its stead, something more in line with our original aims. We won't throw out everything you've done. We'll keep what works and discard the rest."

"The Empire is the glue that binds this world together. Get rid of it, and I assure you, the human race will tear itself to pieces in pretty short order. There'll be chaos like you couldn't imagine. Nation pitted against nation. Ancient, long-buried antagonisms rising up again like reanimated corpses. I know what these people are like. I've been living among them for far longer than you ever did. Colonel Tlanextic? Am I not right? You tell them. Without the Empire, how long do you think this planet would last?"

"Couple of years," said Tlanextic, "if not months. Not long. Everyone scrambling for advantage, trampling on everyone else in the stampede to get to the top. Powder keg, and billions of sparks shooting in all directions. Next stop, extinction."

"I never said it would be easy," said Quetzalcoatl. "Rectifying the situation will require time, great care and trouble. But it can be done, I'm sure of it. I'm prepared to put in the effort. We all are. We co-ordinate, administrate, make the transition from dictatorship by personality cult to multi-state democracy as smooth as possible. I've drawn up plans. A timetable. I could show you, Tez. It'll take a decade, no more.

A decade, by which time humans will have learned how to manage without the Empire and be living in relative harmony and prosperity. What we do first of all is set up a global governing body, a talking shop where individual countries can air their grievances and settle disputes without recourse to conflict. It could even be here on this very island, manned by elected representatives from all of –"

Tezcatlipoca interrupted him with a noisy, elaborate yawn, fanning his mouth with one hand. "Sorry. Drifted off there for a moment. What were you saying? Some guff about a global government. Well, I can tell you right now, it'll never work. Humans can't agree on anything, unless they're forced to. You conjure a lovely utopian idyll, Kay, but take it from me, it's unrealisable; not here, not on this planet. A pipe dream."

"I have faith in people."

"And I have knowledge of them," Tezcatlipoca shot back. "And my practical, hands-on experience trumps your ignorant optimism. Let's face it, this whole enterprise of ours was doomed from the very start. We set out to nurture and enhance an entire species, make it as civilised and united as it could be, evolve it to a higher level of sophistication, but the only way we were ever realistically going to do that is the way I've done it, through fear and intimidation. Humans just don't have it in them to behave themselves, to act responsibly. They need to be bullied. That's how they treat each other all the time. It's the only language they understand."

"I refute that. You have an appallingly low opinion of this race, Tez."

"And you, Kay, have an appallingly high one. It's one of your bad habits. Like incest."

"Do not mock me!" Quetzalcoatl yelled, making a lunge for his tormentor.

"Ah – ah – ah!" said Tezcatlipoca, standing his ground and wagging a finger. "Unwise."

"Heed your own advice, Plumed Serpent," said Huitzilopochtli. "Don't rise to the bait."

Quetzalcoatl glared at Tezcatlipoca, but did not make a further move.

"There they are," said Tezcatlipoca, triumphantly. "Those true colours of yours. The real Quetzalcoatl behind the façade of compassion. The man behind the mask. Your own duality in evidence – though some might call it two-facedness. You came to ask me to surrender my Empire. Here's my answer: No. You can't have it. I'm proud of what I've accomplished here. I like being the Great Speaker. It suits me. I enjoy having several billion sentient creatures under my command. I relish the thought that the inhabitants and resources of an entire planet are at my beck and call. I have power. I have status. I have respect. This is *mine*. You obliged me to become what I've become. You can't now just turn up and expect me to un-become it. I am Tezcatlipoca, the Smoking Mirror, the Great Speaker, and to put it bluntly, you, Quetzalcoatl, brother of mine, and all the rest of you, can go fuck yourselves."

He paused for breath, his last phrase lingering sourly in the air.

Mal looked at the two brothers, who were bent towards each other like the sides of an arch. Enmity crackled electrically between them, a long-held, deep-seated loathing that was all the more intense because of their shared blood. No one could hate quite as hard as close kin could, as she well knew.

"Fair enough," said Quetzalcoatl at last, stiffly, straightening. "Our positions are clear. I gave you every chance, Tez, remember that. Now get ready. What you won't give up willingly will have to be taken from you by force of arms."

"Get ready?" replied Tezcatlipoca with a look of sheer delight. "I've been preparing for years! I knew this moment might come. Provision has been made. Contingency measures are in place. Come at me as hard as you like, Kay. Do your worst. I can handle it. Whatever you dish out, you're getting back fourfold. That's a promise."

"War," said Quetzalcoatl. He sounded weary, resigned, but somehow not surprised.

"If you want to glorify it with that name. Me, I'd call it a takeover bid. A coup d'état. And like any attempted coup, it will be ruthlessly repelled and quashed."

Quetzalcoatl thumbed a button on a controller strapped to the palm of his hand. The wings on his back extended gracefully and he took off from the terrace. Xipe Totec and Huitzilopochtli did the same.

"I truly regret this," Quetzalcoatl said as he rose into the air. "I wish we could have settled things peacefully."

"Don't talk rot," Tezcatlipoca replied. "You couldn't be happier. Right now I can almost hear your conscience rubbing its hands with glee."

Quetzalcoatl heaved a sigh and soared, Xipe Totec and Huitzilopochtli trailing in his wake. Within moments, the three were above the horizon, and then lost from sight.

"So," said Tezcatlipoca, turning to Colonel Tlanextic. "I think that went as well as could be expected. Nice to see the old bastards again and get everything out in the open. There's nothing like a family feud, is there? Gets the blood pumping, the heart racing. Makes one feel alive again."

"What do you want from me, Your Imperial Holiness?"

"Well, of course we must break out the battle gear and set up our defences. This is what generations of Serpent Warriors have been training for. The drills, the dry runs, the endless manoeuvres – this is where it all finally comes good."

"Yes, sir. Understood. I'll get on it straight away."

"With any luck we can have it all wrapped up and done within a day or so, I can still attend the Beijing conference as planned, and nobody will be much the wiser. Institute a media blackout throughout Anahuac, would you, colonel? Get the Jaguars to contact all journalists within the country, foreign and local. Embargo on all photography and filming within a twenty-mile radius of Tenochtitlan, not to mention interviewing. Standard penalties will be enforced for infringement. No reason need be given."

"I'll get on it right away, sir."

"But before that, there is one other thing."

"Sir?"

"Those three." Mal, Aaronson, Reston. "They've gone from being an interesting diversion to loose ends, and I do so despise loose ends. They've seen too much. Now that they know who – what – I am, they're only going to get in the way and be a bother. Two of them resent being deceived, I can tell, and the third despises me anyway. I can't think of anything more imaginative to do with them, so kill them for me, would you? There's a good fellow."

Tezcatlipoca retrieved his mask and headed indoors.

TWENTY-FIVE

Same Day

COLONEL TLANEXTIC UNSHOULDERED, primed and levelled his lightning gun, all in one swift, practised movement.

"You heard him," he said. "Let's not make it difficult, eh? Just stand there in a row, all nice and tidy, like three erect pricks. It'll be quick. You won't feel a thing."

"Colonel..." said Mal.

With a pained expression: "What?"

"Don't. You don't have to do this."

"If the Great Speaker decrees that you're to be killed, then you're to be killed."

"Why? We're not going to be any sort of trouble. We're on the same team as you. Me and Aaronson are, at any rate."

"I know, and it's a shame because I like you, Vaughn. You're my kind of woman. And your swishy friend there seems all right too, for one of his sort. Under other circumstances I could see us sitting down together and getting blind roaring drunk and having a fucking good laugh. But orders are orders. You understand that. Especially when they come from a god, no less. So chin up, take your medicine, be a good servant of the Empire. And you..."

He swung towards Reston.

"Where d'you think you're going? I saw. Sidling over towards those chairs. Don't think I don't know what you're up to. Crafty little shit. You I'm saving until last. Those two are a chore. You, you bastard, are going to be a pleasure."

"Colonel, I'm begging you," said Mal.

"It's no use, boss," said Aaronson. "He's not listening. It's all that fat between his ears. Stops the sound getting in."

"Ooh, meow," sneered Tlanextic. "If I had feelings, they'd be hurt."

"Is there a Mrs Tlanextic?" Aaronson asked.

"None of your business."

"I'll take that as a no. Doesn't surprise me. You don't strike me as the marrying kind. I'll bet when anyone asks, you say you're wedded to the job. Say being a Serpent doesn't leave room in your life for anything else, wife included. But the truth is, you don't actually like women. Pretend to, but deep down, though you'd never admit it, your tendencies go the other way. I can tell. I've met your sort before."

"Oh do shut up."

"The gruffer they are, the more macho they act, the more they're kidding themselves. Then there's all your talk about pricks and arseholes..."

"I have an l-gun here, remember? Pointing right at you."

"And you do so love your big gun, don't you? Compensating much?"

"Right, that does it. I was going to shoot her first, out of respect. Order of seniority and all that. But you, faggot, just lost the few extra seconds of life you were going to have."

"Bring it on, closet case."

Tlanextic took careful aim at Aaronson. But while Aaronson had been taunting the Serpent Warrior and providing a distraction, Reston had made the most of it and begun inching sideways again. Now he sprang, hurling himself towards the nearest cluster of chairs. He snatched one up. It was a well-made wooden thing, solid but not too heavy.

He spun towards Tlanextic. Tlanextic turned to face him, a fraction too late. Reston flung the chair. It sailed straight at Tlanextic, hitting him and the gun. Tlanextic staggered backwards, colliding with a parasol and toppling it; the parasol collapsed as it fell, closing like an anemone around Tlanextic, and he fell too, engulfed in billows of canvas.

"Hurry!" Reston yelled. "Let's go!"

He sprinted for the edge of the terrace. Mal was rooted to the spot, unsure what to do. Her understanding was that you should stand and take your punishment, not flee from it. That was the Jaguar way. Though she had pleaded with Tlanextic and tried to talk him round, she had done so in the knowledge that it was futile. All she had in fact been trying to do was buy time for herself, a few precious moments in which to make sense of the gross, arbitrary injustice about to befall her. It was galling to think that, for once, she had done nothing wrong, just happened to have been witness to something she wasn't supposed to see. How did that warrant her death?

"Boss," said Aaronson. He gripped her arm, and the physical contact broke the spell she was under. "We have to get out of here."

Tlanextic was fighting his way out of the fallen parasol, struggling to emerge like a chick from an egg. He was swearing his head off.

"Do you want to die for no good reason?" Aaronson urged.

No, Mal decided. No she did not.

She set off with Aaronson towards the parapet. Reston had already clambered up onto it and was surveying the drop to the next tier of the palace.

"Great thing about ziggurats," he said. "Makes for a handy escape route, if you haven't got an abseiling rope on you."

He propelled himself off. Mal glanced over the edge. It wasn't more than twelve feet to the terrace. She stepped up onto the parapet, as did Aaronson.

"Stay put, English fuckers!" roared Tlanextic. He had finally extricated himself from the parasol and was rising to his feet.

Together, Mal and Aaronson flung themselves off. In the nick of time, too, as a lightning gun discharge struck the exact spot where they'd been perched.

Mal landed on all fours. Aaronson came down more heavily next to her, cracking one knee on the terrace's flagstones, but he was up again in a trice and limping for the next parapet. Mal ran after him.

Reston, ahead, was preparing to make the jump. He glanced round, just in time to see Tlanextic appear at the edge of the upper terrace.

"Move!" Reston yelled out to the two Jaguars.

Tlanextic drew a bead on Mal.

"Quick!" Reston grabbed her hand.

Mal was about to bark at him to let her go. How dare he touch her! But next thing she knew, Reston had plunged over the side, dragging her helplessly with him. They crashed in a heap together on the next terrace down, Reston taking most of the impact with his own body. Aaronson followed, hurdling the parapet. He landed even more badly than last time, his ankle twisting under him with an audible crunch.

"Oww! Fucking shit!"

He rolled onto his back, clutching his leg, grimacing.

Reston and Mal, meanwhile, quickly disentangled themselves from each other. Mal scurried over to her sergeant's side.

"Is it broken?"

"Don't think so," Aaronson gasped. "Hurts like a bitch, but I think I only sprained it."

"Then you can walk on it. Get up."

Aaronson staggered to a standing position. "I'm

sorry, I'm crap with heights, you know that. It's throwing me off. I'm not thinking straight."

"Let's just keep going."

Mal helped Aaronson to the next parapet, taking his weight while he hobble-hopped alongside her.

"One more jump and we should be out of range," Reston said. "Tlanextic's already got a poor shooting angle, and it'll only get worse. Unless he follows us down, that is."

As if in response, an l-gun bolt struck the terrace a few feet from where they stood. The impact left a smeary blue afterimage in their vision and a black sunburst of charring on the flagstones.

"See? What did I say? His accuracy's compromised."

"You ever get tired of being a smartarse, Reston?" Mal said.

"Sometimes. But then things get interesting again and I remember who I am."

Aaronson made an even bigger hash of his third jump than he had the previous two. Hoping to take the impact solely on his good leg in order to protect his injured one, he ended up sprawling awkwardly onto his side. He gamely got up again and made for the next parapet, but it was clear he was in no state to carry on descending the terraces in leaps and bounds like this.

"Fuck it, boss. You go on ahead. I'll find another way out of here."

"Don't be a dickhead, sergeant. We can do this. Just don't think about it too hard."

"How many more levels are there? Another

twenty at least. I'm never going to manage it. I'm only holding you up."

"What're you going to do instead? Fly?"

"Go indoors and through the building. Find that lift."

"Not a good idea," said Reston. "There'll be Serpents all over the place."

"So? I act all innocent. They don't know yet that we've got a kill order hanging over us."

"Hey!" came a cry from above. "Forget about me?"

Tlanextic had sprung down from the topmost terrace to the one below, and now the three of them were squarely in his sights once more. The only reason he hadn't fired yet was because the lightning gun was still powering up for its next shot.

"Listen, you two," Reston said to Mal and Aaronson. "There isn't time for this. If we don't put distance between him and us, we're dead, don't you get it?"

"I can't," Aaronson said.

"You can," Mal insisted.

"No, *you* can, boss. And you will."

"What?"

"Go." He said it softly, but in a way that brooked no argument.

"No," Mal said, equally adamant.

"Yes. I can look after myself. Your best chance is Reston. You want to live? Go with him."

"He's got a point, Vaughn," Reston said.

"Shut the fuck up. This has nothing to do with you."

The l-gun's whine reached its highest pitch, a constant shrill note signalling readiness. Tlanextic aimed carefully, determined not to miss a third time.

Reston straddled the parapet. Over Mal's shoulder, Aaronson gave him the nod, and Reston wrapped his arms around her waist and kicked off backwards.

"No!" Mal screamed as they plunged together.

A table broke their fall, shattering to pieces under them. A servant who had been busy laying out lunchtime cutlery, yelped in fright and scuttled away.

Mal rose, groaning, from the splintered debris of the table, looking up just in time to see Tlanextic open fire at Aaronson. Aaronson darted to one side. It was a valiant but vain effort. The bolt of plasma found its target. A glancing blow, but a hit all the same, thumping into Aaronson's shoulder and spinning him sideways. He fetched up against the parapet, sprawled half over it. A hole had been burned through his shirt, through which Mal could see blackened skin, fat white blisters, and raw red weeping patches. Worst of all was the smell that reached her, the stench of grilled meat, human meat, her friend and colleague's.

Aaronson's eyes rolled. Mal could scarcely imagine the pain he was in. She called to him, but he didn't respond. His jaw was slack. Shock was setting in. If the parapet hadn't been propping him up, he would have sunk to the floor.

And now Tlanextic came down a level, nimbly, l-gun singing in his hands. He strode to a vantage point directly overlooking Aaronson, moving with complete assurance, the air of a hunter who knew his prey was injured and helpless and going nowhere. His eyes were narrowed but deadly calm, not unlike the eyes of the moulded golden snake crowning his helmet.

Mal snatched up a leg of the table, the only throwing weapon she could find. She launched it at Tlanextic, but gravity and the angle of elevation were against her and she missed. He pretended not even to notice.

"I'm not what you said I am," he told Aaronson. "Not at all."

Aaronson, to his credit, managed to splutter out a reply. "Denial."

Tlanextic pulled the trigger.

Aaronson's body rocked as tremendous, searing heat pulsed through it. A hand convulsed into a claw, clutching the parapet, skin fusing to stone. Eyeballs erupted from their sockets like two boiled eggs bursting. Legs kicked.

Then it was over. Aaronson shuddered and lay still, a smoking, twisted wreckage of himself.

What Mal said next came from her gut, a howl of pure rage. "Tlanextic, you cocksucking, motherfucking cunt bastard!" She used her mother tongue. Nahuatl didn't have as many swear words as English, and none of them was as truly satisfying.

In return, the Serpent colonel offered her a gloating grin. "I have no idea what you just said, Inspector Vaughn, but that's your pal sorted. And guess what? You're next."

"I'll fucking kill you." She part drew her *macuahitl*. "Come down here. I'll fucking have you, I will."

"I've a better idea. I stay here, you stay there. Soon as my gun's recharged, I'll put you out of your misery."

"Coward. Come down and fight." Hot, angry tears were flooding down Mal's cheeks, and she wasn't ashamed of them. She didn't care.

"I'd rather just stick where I am, if you don't mind. High ground. Tactical advantage. Be patient. Couple of seconds from now, this'll all be over."

Reston tugged her arm. "Not like this," he said. "We can't win against him like this. He's right, he's holding all the aces. Let's run. We can still get away."

"Leave me the fuck alone, Reston."

"We run now, we can get him later. It's the only course of action that makes any sense. Otherwise you're just going to die, and there'll be no chance of payback for what he did to your sergeant."

"Ah, here we go," said Tlanextic. Yet again, the gun was ready. "Why don't you two stay standing next to each other like that? Nice and convenient. I can probably get you both with the one shot."

"Vaughn," Reston hissed. "Think logically. Don't just throw everything away."

Mal wasn't conscious of making the choice. All she knew was that, suddenly, she was making a dash for the parapet. An l-gun bolt exploded somewhere just behind her, close enough that she could feel the blast impact in her heels.

FOR THE NEXT five minutes, she jumped and ran, jumped and ran, keeping pace with Reston. Her knees began to throb from the repeated jarring of twelve-foot drop after twelve-foot drop. Tier by tier they descended the ziggurat palace, with Tlanextic still tenaciously giving chase. Now and then a lightning gun bolt came their way, but the shots were always wild, Tlanextic taking them on the hoof, hoping for rather than expecting a hit. The benefit from this was that, however briefly he paused to fire, each time it put that little bit more distance between them and him. When they finally made the last jump down to ground level, he was a full five tiers behind.

They were on an open plaza, with nothing to take cover behind other than a couple of ornamental fig trees in cubic urns. Tlanextic would have a clear line of fire once he had reached the plaza himself, which would be in mere moments.

Reston didn't hesitate. He had spied something across the plaza. Without a word he shepherded Mal towards it. She went uncomplainingly, her own survival instincts telling her she was best off deferring to *his* survival instincts.

One of the monorail trains had just pulled in at the plaza. Its passengers were a janitorial crew toting mops, buckets and brooms. Reston barged past them up the platform steps, scattering them and their cleaning implements, and leapt into the carriage behind the driver.

"Tell me how this thing works," he ordered the startled man. "Now!"

"Who the hell are —"

"Oh, sod it." Reston yanked the man out of

his seat by his tunic and tossed him out onto the platform. "How hard can it be? Vaughn. Get in."

Mal stepped aboard while Reston slipped into the newly vacated driving seat.

"Hey," the driver said hotly, springing to his feet. "You can't do that. That's my train."

He tried to climb back in. Mal decked him with a single punch, knocking him cold.

At the same time, Tlanextic's voice rang out across the plaza. "Halt! You fucking stop right there!"

Reston was still studying the control console.

"Reston..." Mal said.

"Give me a moment."

"We don't have a moment. Tlanextic's coming."

"I know. I'm just trying to figure out which lever's the brake and which is the throttle."

"Oh for – !" Mal leaned over and thrust forwards the lever that was marked in increments from 1 to 8. The train gave a jerk and began to move.

"How did you know that was the right one?"

"It couldn't be more obvious. And I was paying attention on the way over here. I watched what the driver did."

Reston made a face. "Ah. At that point I wasn't really bothered about much." He pushed the throttle lever further forwards as the train drew away from the platform. There was a clear, straight stretch of track ahead and the train eagerly gathered speed.

Tlanextic charged to the very tip of the platform and launched yet another plasma bolt at them. It fell well short of its target, and his subsequent loud grunt of exasperation told them that the shot had finally drained the battery pack. The l-gun was now dead. Enraged, he hurled it impotently after them. It bounced and clattered along the track and fell off, fetching up at the foot of the support pylon below.

Mal allowed herself a smile. They had escaped the bastard. He stood no chance of catching up with them now.

She said as much to Reston.

He glanced over his shoulder, past her. "Don't speak too soon," he said.

A second train was arriving at the plaza, transporting a quartet of Serpent Warriors. Tlanextic commandeered it, flagging the driver down and telling him not to stop. Taking up position beside the driver, he instructed him to pour on speed. "Those two in front are criminals – enemies of the state. The Great Speaker wants them dead. Get us as near to them as you can."

The driver gunned the engine. Meanwhile, Tlanextic ordered all four Serpent Warriors to draw and prime their l-guns. Not antipersonnel; full charge, kinetic component. They were to blow that train to hell.

"Well, this just got a whole lot fucking better," Mal muttered.

Reston pushed the throttle all the way to 8. The train thrummed hard, accelerating.

"There's six of them and only two of us," Mal said, eyeing their pursuers. "Our train's lighter so we can go faster, right?"

"Negative mass is negative mass," Reston replied. "The greater the weight, the more charge you need to counteract it, but once that's achieved, the amount of energy required to generate impetus is much the same. We may have a slight edge over them in terms of power drain, but you can measure the difference in micro-wattage."

"But they can't actually gain ground on us."

"Not as long as we keep going flat out. The question is, are we out of firing range?"

A bolt zapped the track a few metres to the rear of the train.

"And there's the answer," Reston said. "Only just."

"Only just is good enough."

"Yes. Problem is, at some point we'll come to a corner and have to slow down. We'll decelerate before they do, and there's our lead gone. They'll have a window of opportunity."

"Then we don't slow down."

"I don't know much about trains but I'm pretty sure that wouldn't be wise."

"Let's put it to the test, shall we?" said Mal, pointing ahead.

Roughly two hundred metres from where they were, the track began describing a long, gentle curve to the right, winding between the bases of two buildings. Reston clamped his lips grimly together, clearly having to resist the urge to pull the throttle lever back from 8. The train was travelling at a fair lick, perhaps fifty miles per hour, levitating effortlessly along the broad silvery rail. As it hit the start of the turn it began to shimmy, and as the curve deepened the motion became a seasickly sway. The train's apron scraped against the rail's outer edge. There were stuttering, burping squeals of metal on metal. Sparks flew. The centrifugal force was tremendous and Mal bent hard to the side to counteract it. Looking back, she saw the Serpent train falling behind. The driver had automatically curbed speed when approaching the bend. Tlanextic berated him, cuffing him round the head and telling him not to be such a fucking wimp.

Their own train was shaking wildly from side to side now and seemed keen to part company with the track. Then the curve straightened out and the noise and disturbance gradually subsided.

"Yeah!" Mal shouted to their pursuers. "How's about that, arseholes? You're never going to get us. Might as well fuck off back home and polish your helmets."

"What did I tell you about speaking too soon?"

Mal looked back round and saw to her dismay that there was another bend coming up. This one was a full ninety-degree turn, snaking to the left.

"I'll have to rein it in," Reston said. "Otherwise we'll fly clean off." He drew the throttle down a notch to 7, then for good measure to 6. "We'll still be going too fast, though. And..."

"And what?"

"Simple geometry. As we hit the apex of the turn, the angle will bring us closer to them."

"Fuck my luck."

"Succinctly put. Hang on. This is going to get bumpy."

It did indeed get bumpy, so much so that Mal had to cling onto the headrest of the driving seat in order to keep her balance. The screeching was deafening. Several times it seemed as though the train was going to tear free of the track. She could feel it twisting against itself, inner torque juddering mightily through it.

And then, halfway through the turn, as Reston had predicted, the Serpents opened fire. Their train was just hitting the bend. They had a chance and they didn't squander it.

Bolts arced across from their train to the one Mal and Reston were in. The Serpents had time to loose off only one shot apiece, four shots in all.

All four came close, strafing, blitzing, simultaneously, blindingly.

One made contact.

Fortunately, the bolt struck the end of the train, nowhere near the drive mechanism – the power cells and neg-mass exciter – which was located in the middle, beneath the passengers' feet. Damage was done, but not instantaneously catastrophic damage. The train's tail end exploded outwards, shards of metal caroming and ricocheting back along the track. Mal was thrown to the floor. She got up to find the train didn't have a back any more, just a jagged gap that looked as though a shark had chewed a whole section of bodywork off. The rearmost bank of seats was bent up at a crazy angle. Smoke trailed behind them.

But they were still going. The train was making terrible noises, a ragged-edged keen of protest, but it was still moving forwards and didn't appear to have lost much in the way of momentum. Coming out of the curve, Reston nudged the throttle back up to 7, and the train jerkily responded. He tried 8, and the noises worsened but there was a further hike in speed nonetheless.

They entered another straight section.

"Do you have any idea where we're going?" Mal said, shouting to make herself heard above the train's caterwauling.

"Does it matter, as long as it's away from Tlanextic?"

"I mean, do you have a plan? Or are we just going to tour round Tenochtitlan for the rest of the day until we get bored?"

"South," said Reston. "We head south. The harbour end of the island. Steal a boat there and make for shore."

"That's it?"

"I'm open to other suggestions, inspector."

She had none.

They hurtled on, the ruined, screeching train drawing curious looks from everyone it passed by. A junction loomed, and a light on the control console flashed and a buzzer beeped.

"It's asking if we want to switch direction," Mal said.

"The points are set for straight ahead, but left looks southbound to me. Let's take it." Reston jabbed the button beside the light. A segment of the track slid ponderously leftward, and the train, complaining, transferred onto the new course. "Hope that was right decision."

Tlanextic's train also made the interchange, much more smoothly, and Mal could see that it was gaining on theirs, incrementally but remorselessly. She could see on the Serpent Warriors' faces – Tlanextic's in particular – a growing sense of triumph. They were holding fire with their l-guns, but only because they were waiting for the moment when her and Reston's train became an unmissable, point-blank target. It wouldn't be long now.

She had to slow the Serpents down somehow, if possible stop them altogether.

The displaced bank of seats gave her an idea. She made her way along the train to them.

"What are you doing?" Reston wanted to know.

"Trying to help. Just keep driving."

The seats had been wrenched almost completely free from their mounting. Only a couple of screws still moored them in place. One of the screws was sheared nearly all the way through and Mal was able to snap it with a good, hard kick. The other, however, was more or less intact. She didn't have a screwdriver on her but she did have her trusty *macuahitl*. She inserted the edge of the blade under the screw's head and began levering. She squatted down and gave it all she'd got, heaving on the sword handle, using every ounce of strength in her shoulders and thighs. It seemed that the screw would never budge. Her muscles would give, or her *macuahitl* would, before it did.

Then there was an abrupt sharp *creak* of progress. The screw squeezed up a few millimetres from its socket, and the seats jiggled that little bit more freely. Encouraged, Mal redoubled her efforts.

"Get a move on, Vaughn," Reston said. He could see what she was up to but also how close the Serpents were getting. "Put your back into it."

"Could you..." Mal gasped through clenched teeth, "kindly... just do your thing... and leave me... the fuck alone... to do mine?"

At last, with a sudden grinding surrender, the screw came out. The bank of seats stood rattling loose on the floor of the train.

Mal had been intending to pick up the seats and lob them at the train behind with as much accuracy as she could manage. At the very least the sight of a bank of seats hurtling towards him would cause the driver to apply the brakes, and if she got lucky the thing might get jammed between train and rail, forcing the Serpents to halt, maybe even causing a crash.

Just then, however, one of the Serpents chose to fire an exploratory shot, to see if the fugitives' train was near enough yet. It wasn't. The bolt fell short. But only by a foot or so. A few more seconds and even that slender margin of safety would be eroded.

There wasn't time for anything elegant. Mal settled for booting the seats off the back of the train.

They cartwheeled down the track towards the oncoming Serpents. Tlanextic yelled out a warning and everybody ducked. The seats failed to become wedged beneath the train; instead, they collided with the windshield, which shattered in a sparkling shower of glass shards that sprayed over the five Serpents and the driver. The seats then spun on past the train, landing behind and careering off, a mangle of tubular steel and plastic padding, through the windows of an adjacent tower.

"Nice try," Reston commented.

"Worth a shot," Mal said, as the driver of the other train popped his head up again and so did the Serpent Warriors, all of them shaking glass fragments out of their clothes.

"Uh-oh," Reston then said.

"Oh, what now?"

"Look."

"Bugger."

Dead ahead, there was a third train. It was trundling along at a leisurely pace, empty apart from a driver who seemed in no hurry to get anywhere and was blissfully unaware of the two trains barrelling up from behind. He was just idling along from platform to platform like a cabbie cruising for his next fare.

"Does this thing have a horn?" Reston said.

"Racket we're making, it's a wonder he hasn't heard us already," said Mal. "Oi!" she shouted at the top of her lungs. "Dickhead! Shift yourself! Unless you want to get rammed."

The driver in front turned and his eyes went saucer wide. He scrabbled to push the throttle forward, and his train started to speed up.

Their train was still zeroing in on his, though, and fast. Reston didn't dare ease off, not with the Serpents breathing down their necks. A shunt was unavoidable.

"Brace yourself," he told Mal.

Their train rear-ended the one in front. At that point, Newtonian physics took over. The front train, boosted from behind, jetted forward at even greater speed. The driver let out a squawk of terror, clinging to his control console for dear life.

Mal and Reston's train, meanwhile, its nose now a crumpled mess, was brought almost to a standstill by the impact. The Serpent train continued rocketing towards it as rapidly as ever. The driver of the latter hit the brakes, but there wasn't enough time.

"Jump for it," said Reston.

Mal was already jumping for it.

Both she and Reston threw themselves clear of the train a heartbeat before the Serpent train ploughed into it. The Serpent train rose off the track and mounted theirs, with a godawful cacophony of metal crunching and men screaming in panic. The two vehicles, conjoined, went scraping on down the track, parts flying off, sparks shooting everywhere like a firework display. One of the Serpent Warriors was jettisoned from his seat and flung like a ragdoll headfirst to the track bed, breaking his neck. The others, and the driver, just hung on helplessly as the violent, slewing ride ran its course. Friction and inertia eventually brought the locked-together trains to a halt some five hundred yards further down the line. They settled at an ungainly angle on the rail, silent and spent, like a pair of old drunkards after an uproarious bender. Everyone still aboard was too shaken up to do much but groan and give thanks that they were alive. The antigrav-particle exciters on these trains were well-reinforced, but even so it was a small miracle that neither one of them had been breached.

By the time Colonel Tlanextic got himself together to clamber out and head back along the track to look for the two English fugitives, they were long gone.

His wrath was terrible to behold. And exceptionally loud. Proceeding on the assumption that Mal and Reston were still within earshot, which they were, he informed them that this was *his* island, *his* domain. It was swarming with Serpent Warriors. They could run but they wouldn't get far.

"You're mine," he roared. "I'll find you. I'll find you and fucking slaughter you. It's only a matter of time."

TWENTY-SIX

Same Day

STUART WAS FEELING more like his old self than he had in weeks. Since leaving England, in fact. He was in desperate trouble, he knew. He and Vaughn were on the run in Tenochtitlan. Tenochtitlan! They were fugitives marked for death in the Great Speaker's own redoubt, a city teeming with highly trained, dedicated and ruthless soldiers. Colonel Tlanextic's next move would surely be to put out an all-points bulletin with their descriptions. Every Serpent Warrior under his command would be on the lookout for a white male and white female, both in their early to mid-thirties, one armed with a *macuahitl*. As things stood, their chances of reaching the harbour without being spotted, challenged, shot at and captured were next to nil. And in the unlikely event that they did make it, it was far from guaranteed that they'd be able to get themselves a ride on a boat. All in all, their prospects were bleak.

But even as he and Vaughn raced to put distance between them and the monorail track, Stuart felt positive. Alive. Hopeful, even. The more so as Tlanextic's bellowed threats reached his ears.

This, it seemed, was who he was meant to be: a man facing insuperable odds, beset by enemies, with nothing to fall back on but his wits and skills. He was a born desperado, a natural underdog. The Stuart Reston he had been for most of his life – rich kid, socialite, plutocrat, top of the heap – was a guise he'd worn so long that he'd ceased to realise it wasn't really him. Only after he'd lost everything was he able to break free from the shell he'd built around himself and become something truer to himself.

It helped, too, that the indomitable Malinalli Vaughn was running with him now. It made a very pleasant change from having her running *after* him.

They crossed concourses and traversed raised walkways. Stuart kept the trend of their progress as southward as he could, but it wasn't easy. Tenochtitlan was a maze. There hadn't been any overarching design behind its layout. The ziggurats and towers had simply accumulated over time, one rising up in the space beside another until the entire island was covered. The train network made sense of the muddle and was obviously the most practical and straightforward way of getting around, but the monorail was no longer safe for him and Vaughn to use. On foot, sticking close to walls, skulking, steering clear of passersby, they could maintain a lower profile and, hopefully, evade detection.

He explained his choice of tactic to Vaughn.

"If you say so," was her reply. "You've done more fleeing from the authorities than I have."

"Yes, and I'm alive to tell the tale. So I must know a thing or two about it."

"That or you've been phenomenally lucky."

"Comes down to the same thing, doesn't it? Who cares how I get there, as long as the end-result's in my favour?"

"I liked you more when you weren't so smug," Vaughn said.

"No, you didn't."

"No, you're right. I've never liked you."

They came to a blind alley, and Stuart proposed a pause to rest and take stock. Vaughn, short of breath, agreed it was a good idea.

In the alley, they hunkered downwind from a set of bins. Tenochtitlan, for all its majesty, had its grubby areas, as any city did. You couldn't have thousands of humans crammed together in a confined space, with their effluent and their detritus, and expect absolute cleanliness everywhere. Waste water trickled down the alley's central gutter. A rat poked its head out from a downpipe, didn't like the look of the two humans, and withdrew. The contents of the bins, as garbage was wont to in this climate, reeked.

"Aaronson," murmured Vaughn. She was staring broodingly at her palms, which were badly grazed from when she'd leapt clear of the train. "That poor bastard. Why? It's not fair. He didn't have to die."

"The Great Speaker thought he did. And Tlanextic."

"But Aaronson never did anything wrong. He was a cheeky sod, and sometimes his tongue was a bit too sharp for his own good, but..." Her eyes were red-rimmed. "Those fuckers. Those pieces of dogshit."

"These are the people you've been working for all this time, Vaughn."

"Don't you start."

"I'm just saying, you shouldn't be surprised how the powers-that-be have turned on you. They can do that. It doesn't bother them. We're all of us expendable, as far as they're concerned."

"I'm not in the mood for a lecture. Stop it or I'll use this fucking sword on you."

"Okay." Stuart relented. Right now Vaughn was his only ally, and it wouldn't do him any good to make her more upset than she already was.

A few moments later she said, "Were those really...?"

"The Four? Not so long ago I'd have said no, don't be so daft. Now? I'm pretty sure they are. I don't see what else they can be."

"Fuck. And the Speaker is Tezcatlipoca. I never saw that coming. If there'd been a choice of which of the gods, out of all of them, had to be left in sole charge of earth, he's the one I'd least want it to be. Even Xipe Totec would have been preferable. Even Mictlantecuhtli."

"Mictlantecuhtli? I wouldn't go that far. Xipe Totec, although he's not a pretty sight when his skin's transparent, you still sort of know where you are with. Mictlantecuhtli, on the other hand..." He mimed a shudder.

"How come you met them?" Vaughn asked. "Why did they reveal themselves to you, of all people?"

"Believe me, it wasn't my doing. I'd give anything not to have been the one. They may be gods, but they're far from benevolent. Even Quetzalcoatl's got a mean streak. Azcatl's pretty hardcore, too. You should see him in action."

"Azcatl? The Red Ant?" Vaughn almost laughed.

"I know. The myths don't make much of him. All I know is the one about Quetzalcoatl bullying him to reveal where his grain store is. In real life, though, Azcatl's not someone you want to mess with. All of them are like that. You just feel so *inferior* when they're around. Particularly when it's someone like Tzitzimitl, who couldn't disguise her scorn for me."

"You don't think that's just you? Your sparkling personality?"

"Could be," said Stuart. "And in answer to your earlier question, they revealed themselves to me because I happened to be there and it was convenient. No other reason. I wasn't specially selected or anything like that. Quetzalcoatl injured me and had a fit of guilt about that, and then saw a way I could be useful to him. I'm not useful to him any more, apparently, judging by the way he almost completely blanked me when we were up on the Great Speaker's palace."

"He had other things on his mind."

"Maybe. I think..." Stuart hesitated. "I think, to them, humans are playthings, not much more. 'As flies to wanton boys,' et cetera."

"Don't recognise the quotation, but then I didn't have a posh education like you."

"Shakespeare. And we didn't study him at 'posh' school, either. Too Christian. I sought out his work for myself when I was older. Complete, unexpurgated editions of the plays are hard to track down. I found one of the last ever Victorian ones, got it from a black-market dealer in Hull. Set me back a pretty penny, I can tell you."

"We're the gods' pets, then, is that what you're saying?"

"At best. We intrigue them, the way a strange species of animal – I don't know, the duck-billed platypus for instance – intrigues zoologists. All said and done, it turns out we're nothing more than a worthy project to them, a charity case. That's how this whole Empire nonsense got started. The gods saw us, thought we were cute, adopted us and tried to make us better, more like them. And then it all went belly up, and this is the mess we're left with, the aftermath of Quetzalcoatl and Tezcatlipoca's big spat."

"I don't understand. So are the myths true or aren't they?"

"I think they are, sort of, and also not. I think they're versions of the truth which explain the gods' behaviour, and the Great Speaker – Tezcatlipoca – has allowed them to become religious currency because it suits his ends. The creation story, for instance. It's a way of telling us, reinforcing to us, that the gods made everything. They're the ones responsible for the world and we owe them an unrepayable debt of gratitude for that. Of course, what they actually did was take a race at a pre-existing level of civilisation and develop it, mould it in their own image. They didn't make the world, they remade it. And us with it."

"It's..." Vaughn moved her hands as though she were literally groping for words. "It's hard to take in."

"Tell me about it. Why do you think I was so spaced out when you first saw me in that cell? And I wasn't even a believer in the first place, so I can't begin to imagine the sort of effect this must be having on one of the faithful."

"I've never completely been one of the faithful," Vaughn protested. "I've had my doubts, now and then. The Empire just seemed... logical, and belief in the gods was an integral part of it. But now that I know what the gods are actually like, I'm not so sure about them."

"Proof of faith has destroyed your faith."

"Yeah, hilarious irony, right? It's like that thing about how you should never meet your heroes. You'll only be disappointed."

"Idols with feet of clay," said Stuart.

"So," said Vaughn, after a pause, "next, I suppose, there's going to be an attack on this place. The good gods versus the bad one."

"'Good' is relative in this context, but yes, that sounds about right. They won't do it by halves, either. Whatever Tezcatlipoca has up his sleeve by way of a defence, it had better be a decent one, for his sake."

"Any idea how long before it all kicks off?"

"How would I know?"

"You're the god expert."

"Am not. But if pushed I'd say it won't be long. Quetzalcoatl's not one to hang about. Sometime today, for certain."

"All the more reason for us to get out of here, and sharpish."

"Quite. Getting caught up in the middle of a war between gods is not something any sane person would want."

Something caught Vaughn's eye – something passing by the alley's mouth. She got to her feet and padded stealthily to peer out. Then she beckoned to Stuart and pointed.

He saw what she had seen, understood her meaning, and gave her a grinning thumbs-up.

THEY SHADOWED THE priest and the acolyte for a couple of hundred yards until the perfect spot for an ambush presented itself. It was a garden of contemplation, a small oasis of tropical greenery amid the urban labyrinth, where a fountain tinkled and a colony of chattering capuchin monkeys fed on berries in the treetops. Moments after the priest and the acolyte entered the garden's lush verdant haze, Stuart and Vaughn followed them in.

It was over quickly, with scarcely a sound. The acolyte put up more of a struggle than the priest, but then he was younger and fitter. Stuart had to subdue him with a chokehold. Vaughn made short work of the priest, coshing him with the pommel of her *macuahitl*.

They dragged the two unconscious bodies into the shrubbery and stripped them of their ceremonial garb. Then they changed out of their own clothes, Vaughn ordering Stuart not to peek at her in her underwear, on pain of death.

"Long as you promise not to do the same to me."

"Like I give a shit."

"You realise we're committing hieratic fraud? A capital offence?"

"Again, like I give a shit."

"Vaughn, you're a changed woman."

"Maybe. Now turn your back."

When they had finished donning the priest's and acolyte's vestments, Stuart tore his shirt into strips, which they used to truss and gag the near-naked holy men. He reckoned, what with everything else that was going on, no one would miss these two for several hours.

"Still wish you'd agreed to killing them, though."

"My plan, my rules," said Vaughn. "I don't hate the priesthood like you do. Besides, however careful we were, we might have got blood on the vestments. This way's neater."

Stuart adjusted the priestly headdress until it sat straight on his head. "Now, remember. Three paces behind me at all times. Mustn't arouse suspicion, must we?"

"I'm a female acolyte. Of course I'm going to arouse suspicion."

"Then try and walk more like a man."

"I will if you do."

"Oh, ha ha."

They strode out from the garden, one behind the other, robes swishing behind them, and for a time it seemed as though it would be plain sailing. Nobody they came across ventured them a second glance. Priests and acolytes were a common sight in Tenochtitlan, even Caucasian ones, and besides, the city was now in a state of alert and had become a hive of frenetic activity. People were rushing to and fro on errands and urgent missions. Serpent Warriors were on the march, quickstepping in phalanxes towards various destinations. Some were making for the airfield, where a fleet of aerodisc gunships awaited. Others were on their way to man strategic positions on the outer walls, carrying with them lightning guns of a kind Stuart had never seen before, large-barrelled and bulkier than the average l-gun, closer in size to a conventional bazooka. Still others disappeared down stairwells that led to entrances to what must be underground bunkers. All of them were too intent on their business to spare a thought for much else.

Nevertheless, Stuart and Vaughn made sure to stay as inconspicuous as possible. They walked at a sedate priestly pace, even though they would rather have been hurrying. Their lack of ritual tattooing was another giveaway, so they kept their faces hidden by bending their heads low, in attitudes of pure piety.

When the huge trapezoid gateway came into view, Stuart dared to think they were going to make it after all. The gate was shut, of course, and guarded, but surely no Serpent Warrior would refuse a demand from a priest to open it. Freedom was just moments away.

"My good man," Stuart said, gesturing loftily at the leader of the team of Serpents overseeing incomings and outgoings at the city's sole public access point. "Captain...?"

"Ueman."

"Captain Ueman. My associate and I wish to go outside. Kindly let us through."

"Through to what, if you don't mind my asking?"

"The harbour."

"Again if you don't mind my asking, why?"

"I'll thank you to use my proper title when addressing me," Stuart said with all the hieratic haughtiness he could muster.

"Your Holiness," said Captain Ueman, "I mean no disrespect, but it's an, ahem, unusual request. There's nothing out there but boats and water. If you want to leave the city, surely a disc would be more convenient."

"Such impertinence!" Stuart snapped. He was beginning to wonder whether he could pull this off. A couple of the other Serpents were looking with intense curiosity at Vaughn, who lowered her head even further and kept her robe gathered tight around her to disguise her figure. Her short choppy hair was at least vaguely masculine, even if the rest of her was distinctly not.

"How dare you presume to question me?" Stuart continued. Cowing the captain was perhaps his only hope. "I'll have you know I'm here at the behest of the Great Speaker himself. You're aware that we're facing imminent enemy assault? I've been assigned the task of inspecting the harbour and seeing to it that all civilian personnel who've come by boat evacuate the area immediately."

"That order's already gone out. They're all starting to head for the shore."

"And I'm responsible for ensuring they all get well out of harm's way. Now, which is worse, would you say? That I fail to do so and commit a dereliction of duty, or that I return to the Great Speaker and tell him that a certain Captain Ueman hindered me from performing my appointed task? Which do you think would make his Imperial Holiness angrier, and with whom?"

Ueman flinched. His cheeks paled a little. "It may not be safe out there. The attack could come at any minute. I'm only concerned about your welfare, Your Holiness."

"I'll take the risk. I can do no less, when the Great Speaker commands."

Ueman was, against his better judgement, persuaded. He turned to his men and gave the order for the gate to be opened. One of the Serpent Warriors pressed a lever that triggered the release mechanism. Arm-thick bolts withdrew, a motor churned, a drive chain clanked and, with monumental slowness, the gate began to roll aside.

Stuart glimpsed lake. Seconds from now, he and Vaughn would be haring down to the harbour to bag a place aboard one of the handful of boats that had yet to unmoor and slip away from the quayside.

Then one of the Serpents who was squinting at Vaughn said, "Sir? This may sound strange but I'm pretty sure this acolyte's a girl."

There was no time to hesitate. Stuart grabbed Ueman and kicked his legs out from under him. As the Serpent captain collapsed, Stuart took possession of his *macuahitl*, yanking it from its scabbard. He slashed the shoulder strap of Ueman's lightning gun and deprived him of that as well.

Vaughn, for her part, seized hold of the arm of the Serpent who had rumbled her. She twisted it round back against itself almost to dislocation point, so that the man was forced to double over. Then she kneed him three times in the face, relieved him of his l-gun, and let him fall.

The other Serpents were too startled to respond instantly. Members of the hieratic caste just weren't prone to using violence, and especially not with such brisk, brutal efficiency. By the time they had their l-guns out, Stuart and Vaughn had the drop on them. *Their* guns were charged up and ready; the Serpents' weren't even primed.

"Choice," Stuart told them. "Try to stop us leaving, and die. Let us go, and live."

To emphasise the point, he pressed the barrel of his l-gun to the nape of Captain Ueman's neck, between his helmet and his tunic collar. Vaughn, meanwhile, covered the other Serpents with her gun.

"Rush them, men," Ueman said. "Your lives don't matter and neither does mine. These are the fugitives we were told to look out for. You outnumber them. They can kill two of you at most before you reach them. *One* of you, if they shoot me first."

There was logic in this, to a Serpent Warrior. Ueman's men primed their guns and trained them on Stuart and Vaughn. Vaughn swung her gun this way and that. "Who wants it? None of you, not really. So back the fuck off." But the Serpents weren't deterred. They began to move in, and Stuart began to beat a retreat towards the still opening gate. Vaughn went with him, continuing to warn the Serpents off.

They were at the threshold of the gate, inches from making good their getaway, when a half-dozen armoured figures dropped from the sky.

Stuart's first thought was that it had begun. Quetzalcoatl and the rest of the gods were had launched their invasion.

Then he realised that these suits of armour, although similar to the ones the gods had worn, were squarer, sharper, sleeker in many respects. They lacked wings like the ones he had seen on Itzpapalotl and Huitzilopochtli. Instead, they had sets of fins along the forearms and calves to lend them control and stability in flight. They were emblazoned with a snake emblem on the torso, and the helmets were also snakelike, the faceplates protruding to a pointed, reptilian tip and featuring bulging, yellow-tinted eyes. All of the suits were uniformly bright green, the green of a mamba's skin, except for one which bore additional flashes of gold along the arms and around the collar.

The armoured Serpent Warriors – it was the only thing they could be – landed in a semicircle. The new arrivals' l-guns were throbbing with charge and, moreover, bigger than the ones the two fugitives were carrying.

One of them – the gold flashes marked him out as the senior officer – put a hand to his helmet. The faceplate vanished, exactly as Stuart had seen the doors at the gods' underground lair do. Beneath lay the less than amiable features of Colonel Tlanextic.

"That's as far as you go," he said.

"Shit," said Vaughn.

"Thought you might try and pull a stunt like this," Tlanextic said. "Impersonating priests – that's a bit of a low trick. But going for the gate, the most obvious exit route... Sensible, I suppose, but still so predictable."

"I had my suspicions about them, sir," said Captain Ueman. "Honestly I did. Something didn't seem quite right. No tattoos, for one thing, but I thought maybe some of these foreign priests don't go in for them."

"No excuses, captain. You screwed this one like I screwed your mother last night. I'd discipline you on the spot, but under the circumstances we're going to need every warm body we've got. So if you survive the shitstorm that's coming, you'll be executed afterwards. Understand?"

"Yes, sir. Absolutely, sir."

"Up off your knees then, you useless little fuckstain. Take your unit and go to the bunkers and get armoured up like us. You" – to one of the Serpent guards – "shut that gate. And you" – to Stuart and Vaughn – "you come back this way, the pair of you, so we can get a clear shot. And, naturally, you'll be putting down those l-guns. I can tell you for free, they won't do you a gnat's fart of good. Not against this stuff we're wearing."

Stuart decided to put that to the test and unleashed the charge from his l-gun. The bolt struck Tlanextic full on. He didn't even stagger. The plasma slithered around the armour in a network of crackling ripples which dissipated to nothingness. Tlanextic guffawed. Stuart might as well have chucked a bucket of lukewarm water over him, for all the effect he'd had.

"Impact-dispersant outer layer," the colonel said. "It can withstand just about anything that's thrown at it. Don't ask me how the fuck it works. Redistributes the force along microscopic substructures or some such, I'm told. It *does* work, that's the main thing. Resists heat, kinetic momentum, everything. As you've seen. Again. The l-guns. Down."

There was no alternative. Stuart laid his lightning gun on the ground. Vaughn reluctantly relinquished hers too.

"Good. Now, over there. Against the wall." Tlanextic jerked his gun, and Stuart and Vaughn shuffled in the direction indicated.

The armoured Serpents lined up, firing-squad-fashion.

"Any last requests?" Tlanextic asked.

"Yeah. Go fuck yourself," said Stuart.

Tlanextic shrugged, in as much as the restrictions of the armour allowed him to. "Who wouldn't, if they could? What about you, missy?"

Vaughn stared daggers at him. "I'm going to kill you for what you did to Aaronson. I swear it. With my bare hands, if need be."

"Maybe. In another world, another life. Is that it? All done now? Big-dick shows of bravado over? Men. Take aim."

The l-guns came up to shoulder height. Stuart stared down a half-dozen barrels, each with a bore the diameter of a drainpipe.

"This is top fucking gear we've got here," Tlanextic said. "The very best. Aztechnology the Great Speaker has been sitting on for centuries, keeping back for this moment. Finally we get to use it, and I'm the commanding officer!"

"Bully for you," said Stuart.

"Just letting you know, you should feel honoured. I mean, these l-guns – you're going to be their first official victims. One of them alone'll reduce you to a skidmark. So many at once? You won't even be cinders. You'll be floating atoms."

"Are you going to do this or what?" said Vaughn.

"Patience. Allow me to enjoy the anticipation."

"Or is the idea to bore us to death first with your jabbering? Because if so, it's working. I'm already halfway into a coma."

"Oh, so brave, Inspector Vaughn."

"*Chief* Inspector, if you don't mind."

"Sorry, yes, of course. I forgot. So this is the

famous British pluck that kept the Empire at bay for all those years, isn't it? The never-say-die spirit. Standing tall even when it's futile."

"Seriously. I'm close to passing out. The world's going grey."

Stuart, in spite of everything, had to laugh. "Vaughn, if you only knew how sexy I'm finding you right now."

"And you can put a sock in it and all," she said.

"I mean it. I'm so turned on. If there weren't all these men in tin-can suits pointing guns at us, I'd be moving in for a snog."

"And you don't think you'd be getting a knee in the nads in return?"

"Honestly? No."

"Dream on, loser. Just because we're about to die together, doesn't mean we were destined to live together."

"Who's talking about living together? I value my independence. A grand affair, on the other hand..."

Vaughn made a disgusted face. "I'm feeling a little ill."

"So am I," said Tlanextic. "And puking in one of these suits is not advisable. Let's put everyone the fuck out of their misery. On my mark. Three."

Stuart braced himself. Oblivion. Obliteration. He was terrified, but resigned. At least there would be peace. He'd no longer be tortured by memories of the wife he had lost, the son he would never see again.

"Two."

Sofia. Jake.

He felt a hand creep into his. It was damp and trembling. He grasped it firmly.

Vaughn wanting comfort in her last moments. Physical contact with someone, anyone, even a man she professed to hate.

"One."

In excruciating slow motion, as if the cogs of the world were winding down, Stuart saw Tlanextic's mouth begin to shape itself for the next word it had to say: *Quitlequiquizhuizque!* Open fire!

Then there was a tremendous pressure at his back. He felt himself being shoved forwards onto his face, as though by an immense hand. Something boomed, incoherently loud. Objects fell from the sky, a rainstorm of rock. He was engulfed in roaring darkness.

So this is what it feels like, was his thought. His, he supposed, final thought. *This is death*.

It was strangely comforting. Strangely like sleep.

TWENTY-SEVEN

Same Day

"RESTON. RESTON!"

Vaughn's voice, coming to him as though from miles away, at the other end of a long tunnel.

"Reston, you fuckwit, wake up!"

"Ladylike as ever, Vaughn," he said, or rather tried to say, but his mouth and throat were clogged with dust and all he managed was a choking fit.

"Reston, get up. Arse in gear. It's started. It's happening."

The dust was in his eyes too. He blinked hard to part his eyelids. It was like cracking eggshells.

Vaughn's face was coated with grey. Her hair was bedraggled and hoary.

"You look a sight," he croaked.

"So do you. There's blood all down the side of

your face. Gash in your head, but I don't think it's too deep. Here we go. Up you come."

Stuart clambered shakily to his feet, Vaughn helping.

"You said..."

He didn't need to finish the sentence. It was abundantly clear *what* had started.

There were figures in the air. Glittering armoured creatures. They flashed to and fro like dragonflies.

Battle stations. Tenochtitlan was under siege.

As he watched, a familiar iridescent shape soared overhead, brandishing an equally familiar spear-launcher. Braking to a hover, Huitzilopochtli targeted the apex of a nearby ziggurat. A spear streaked down. The building's top storey erupted in flames. Stuart felt the rumble of the blast through his soles.

Armour-clad Serpent Warriors swarmed up to engage with the god, but he was already jetting off at speed, disappearing over the rooftops.

In his wake came a dark figure, almost a silhouette. Itzpapalotl, the Obsidian Butterfly. The Serpents turned their attention on her. Plasma bolts came her way thick and fast, but Itzpapalotl evaded them with ease, jinking and barrel-rolling. She flew right into the midst of the Serpents, where they were clustered together the most tightly. She shot through them like a black dart, emerging the other side unscathed.

Serpents fell from the sky, parts of them missing. Severed arms, legs, heads tumbled with them.

"Can't stay here gawping," Vaughn said. "Look, we've got a way out."

Stuart turned. The section of outer wall they'd been put up against for execution was no more. A hole had been blown in the upper part of it, and the landslide of rubble made a kind of steep ramp leading to the gap.

"What about Tlanextic? Where –?"

"He's fucked off to repel the attack. Must've assumed we were dead but didn't have time to check. More pressing matters to attend to."

"Dead?"

"There was a whole bunch of debris on top of us. We were buried, you more than me. I've been digging you out from under it for the past ten minutes while all hell's been breaking loose."

"You saved me? When you could have got away on your own?"

"Don't make a big thing out of it. Call me sentimental, but I reckon I owe you one."

"Actually I think you owe me two at least."

"And the Reston arrogance ruins the moment yet again. Come on."

Vaughn set off up the escarpment of rubble. It was loose and treacherous, and she was obliged to scramble on all fours like a lizard to reach the summit. Stuart made even heavier weather of it. Pain was setting in. He felt bruised all over, his body battered as it had never been before. Nothing worked quite the way it should. His head throbbed. Nevertheless he made it to the top, where Vaughn was flapping a hand frantically at him.

"Almost all the boats have gone. There's only one left. I think they're having engine trouble or something. Crew are running around like blue-arsed flies trying to fix the problem."

She slithered down the other side of the wall onto the narrow strip of cliff edge below. Stuart could see the boat bobbing in the harbour. It was a garbage scow; bags of refuse that its crew had decided not to load sat heaped on the quay alongside it. He could faintly hear a sailor on deck yelling down through a hatch to someone in the hold. A moment later a head popped up from the hatchway and a hand holding an adjustable wrench gesticulated to the wheelhouse. The sailor relayed a message to whoever was in the scow's wheelhouse – the captain, presumably – and then there was a mechanical coughing and a blurt of diesel smoke. A cheer went up from the other crewmembers.

"Hurry the fuck up!" Vaughn shouted at Stuart. "They've got it started."

Stuart lowered himself stiffly to the clifftop while Vaughn sprinted for the zigzagging leading down to the harbour. She yelled and waved as she ran, hoping to catch the scow's attention.

Meanwhile, the siege continued. Huitzilopochtli and Itzpapalotl were, as far as Stuart could tell, the sole attackers, but the two of them were causing enough devastation and destruction for a strike force a hundred times as large. They operated according to a pattern. Huitzilopochtli inflicted property damage while Itzpapalotl ran interference for him, keeping the Serpent Warriors off his back. He was the heavyweight bomber, she the smaller, nippier fighter craft giving him clear passage to his targets.

Softening up, Stuart thought. A first phase of attack to weaken defences and sow disarray. A teaser for the main event.

Vaughn tackled the harbour road vertically. Rather than follow its back-and-forth course she vaulted the guardrails and slid down the embankments between one incline and the next. All the way she kept calling to the scow, begging it to wait. Just half a minute! Civilians wanting safe passage off the island!

Perhaps none of the crew heard her above the noise of the scow's engine and the booming detonations rolling across the city. Perhaps some of them did, but refused to listen, too concerned for their own lives. Perhaps the sight of a female acolyte was just too bizarre to make sense of. Whatever the reason, the boat didn't stop. It chugged out onto the lake at flank speed and was a hundred metres from its berth at the quay by the time Vaughn got there. She jumped up and down on the spot and implored the crew to turn back, to no avail. Stuart saw one of the men on deck give her what seemed like a shrug of apology. The others pretended not to notice her.

A volley of foul language echoed across the water from Vaughn, and then she slumped to the quay with a grunt of frustration.

Stuart put a hand on her shoulder. "Don't worry."

She rounded on him. "Don't worry? *Don't worry!?* We're trapped on this fucking island, there's a major-league conflict starting up around us, and we just lost our only way off."

"Who says? What about the Serpent aerodiscs?"

"Do you know how you fly one?

"Well, no, but maybe we can find someone who does and coerce them into being our pilot."

"Sounds pretty thin to me."

"Me too," Stuart admitted. "It's not our only option."

"Go on. I'm all ears."

He looked up. A squadron of armoured Serpents were flying above in echelon formation, on course to intercept yet another raid by Huitzilopochtli. Itzpapalotl came at them like a bowling ball hitting the pins, scattering them in all directions.

"If we could get our hands on a couple of those suits..."

"You're not serious."

"Oh, but I am. We wouldn't need anyone else to fly us out of here. We could do it ourselves."

TWENTY-EIGHT

Same Day

THE LAST THING Mal wanted to do was head back into the beleaguered city. It was counterintuitive. Worse than that – it was downright crazy.

But Reston, damn him, was right. The Serpents' suits of armour were their one real shot at escaping. She didn't know how difficult the suits were to fly. Probably quite difficult. But simpler, surely, than a disc.

As she and Reston made their way back up the harbour road, they met a crowd of people heading in the other direction. It seemed the idea of hitching a lift on a boat had occurred to several of Tenochtitlan's ancillary and domestic staff. They'd crawled out through the shattered part of the wall, only to discover that the harbour was now empty, but they were continuing anyway, because conditions had to be less hazardous to health outside the city precincts than within. Mal and Reston butted past them, against the tide of exodus, and climbed the wall and over the breach. A look back showed Mal that several of the workers were so desperate to leave that they had dived into the lake and begun to swim. It was a good five or six miles to shore, a distance even a strong swimmer would struggle to cover. She wished them luck.

Just as she and Reston re-entered the city, there was a lull in the onslaught from above. Huitzilopochtli and Itzpapalotl had fulfilled their mission remit and returned to base. Serpent Warriors patrolled the skies, scanning the horizon. Gunships were now airborne, too. They soared out to form a defensive perimeter a mile around the island, their double-barrelled weapons nacelles swivelling.

On the ground, non-armoured Serpents were regrouping and entrenching. Blockades were set up at strategic points throughout the city: on plazas where there were clear lines of sight and enfilading crossfire was possible, and at street chokepoints where any invaders coming in on foot could be pinned down and pincered. Heaps of rubble from ruined buildings were put to use as shooting cover. Holes in façades became sniper nests. Places of refuge were established too, for the injured and for noncombatants who'd been caught out in the open.

All of this impacted Mal and Reston, hampering their progress through the city. Their aim was to infiltrate one of the underground bunkers. That was where the suits were stashed, Reston reckoned, recalling Colonel Tlanextic's instruction to Ueman and his men to "go to the bunkers and get armoured up." But the bunker entrances were now the city's most heavily fortified spots, which seemed to confirm his theory but at the same time made it almost impossible to take practical advantage of. It was tricky even getting near them, and they had several too-close-for-comfort encounters with Serpents. They couldn't risk being spotted by the soldiers; Tenochtitlan might be on a war footing, but the two of them were still officially wanted. Colonel Tlanextic was under the impression they were dead, but that false report couldn't yet have filtered out among the main body of his troops. All in all, although they had a clear objective, the obstacles to attaining it were well nigh insurmountable.

Reston remained upbeat.

"What we have to do," he said, after they had once again been stymied by the concentrated Serpent presence at a bunker entrance, "is lie low and wait. As Quetzalcoatl's lot step up their attack, order will break down. Chaos will be our best ally. Maybe by nightfall we'll be looking at a whole different set of circumstances. And then, of course, we'll have the cover of darkness on our side as well."

"You just don't give in, do you?"

"You say that like it's a bad thing. Would you rather I turned into a quivering jelly?"

"No, it's simply, I find it really annoying, and I shouldn't. Not now. Not any longer."

"Not when it might work in your favour."

"Yeah. Exactly."

They found themselves a bolthole on the third floor of a ziggurat that turned out to be the administrative hub of Tenochtitlan, a warren of offices where smartly dressed workers cowered under their desks or congregated in frightened huddles, unsure what to do with themselves. The borrowed hieratic vestments, though tattered and torn now, were still in good enough condition and still carried enough inbuilt authority to allow Mal and Reston to walk the corridors unopposed and unquestioned, especially since everyone else was so preoccupied with other matters. They searched for a room that was unoccupied and would provide a good vantage point. One door they tried opened onto a supply closet where a pair of respectable-looking middle-aged bureaucrats were in the throes of strenuous upright sex, she braced against the shelves with her skirt hitched up, he taking her weight and pumping hard with his pants round his ankles. Both were so engrossed in their business that they didn't notice the intrusion.

"Get it while you can," Mal observed, quietly closing the door.

"An office romance blossoms under adversity," said Reston.

"Now or never."

"Could be dead within the hour."

The room they ended up taking over as their own was a corner office whose two converging walls of plate-glass window afforded a clear, uninterrupted view outside. There was a crossroads below, a cocourse with a monorail platform and a bunker entrance. Diagonally opposite the office building lay a block which Mal quickly deduced must be a Serpent Warrior barracks – rows of small rooms, each with a single narrow bed and little in the way of interior decor. Adjacent stood a water tower and, behind that, the functional concrete bulk of a fusion plant, the city's source of power.

She used the desk to barricade the door, and for the next few hours she and Reston crouched by the windows and watched.

It was a hell of a show, and they had the best seats in the house.

ABOUT AN HOUR after Huitzilopochtli and Itzpapalotl called off their initial assault, they returned for more. This time they brought along Quetzalcoatl himself.

Quetzalcoatl was as adept at aerial combat as the other two gods. He was also invulnerable, thanks to the spherical forcefield which enclosed him like an oily bubble and absorbed direct hits from the Serpents' l-guns.

The Serpents, however, had upped their game since the previous attack. Not only were gunships in play now, but the sentinels on the outer walls were contributing intense surface-to-air barrages. The gods found making their approach runs to the city much harder. Beeline flying was impossible: Huitzilopochtli and Itzpapalotl had to dodge and swerve, and even Quetzalcoatl was knocked off-course by the pulses of heavy plasma fire. His forcefield repeatedly took a pounding and he was batted this way and that like a *tlachtli* ball.

Tenochtitlan did suffer during the second wave, but not as badly as before. When the three gods relented and pulled back, it seemed more like a retreat than a tactical withdrawal.

In the hiatus that followed, many of the armoured Serpents returned to the ground and trooped off down into the bunkers.

"Bingo," said Reston. "Bet you anything they're going to recharge their suits' power packs."

"Probably to have a pee, too. I would if I'd been stuck inside one of those things for so long."

"Only you would think of a practicality like that."

"Hello? Woman."

"Yes, and therefore incapable of bladder control."

She punched him on the arm, hard enough to leave a mark. "I bet you'd just piss inside it if you had to."

"Actually, I would."

"You're even fouler than I thought."

"You're talking to a man who lay in a pile of fresh corpses for two hours, pretending to be one of them. I know foulness."

"Yeah," Mal said. "D'you know, when I realised that's how the Conquistador must have got away from the City of London ziggurat, all I could think was how fucking batshit crazy this guy must be, whoever he was."

"And now?"

"I still think you're batshit crazy, but I sort of understand why. The Empire took everything from you."

"It took something from you too."

"My brother, you mean? Yeah, maybe, but the difference is, I gave Ix up. I'm the one who threw him to the wolves when I could have saved him. Because he compromised me. He was like a stain. Being related to a petty crim could have nobbled my career. So I scrubbed him off me, publicly, thoroughly." She gave a bitter chuckle. "I told myself it was for his own good but really it was for mine. All said and done, he was still my big bro, wasn't he? And I should have protected him."

"You did what you felt was right at the time. You can't condemn yourself for it."

"Oh, yes I bloody can."

"Well then, you mustn't. Or else you'll end up like me."

"Perish the thought."

"I mean it. There isn't a day goes by that I don't wish I could have helped Sofia, done more for her."

"What, though? It wasn't your fault at all, as I understand it."

"Wasn't it? I married her."

"You didn't make her how she was. You didn't drive her to do what she did."

"I knew, going in, that she was a bit flaky. But she seemed so right for me. For the man I used to be," he amended. "Want to know why I first asked her out?"

"Because she was a catch, the trophy wife every bloke with a fat wallet was trying to bag?"

"No. Well, yes. But it was also because... I already knew about her, but when I actually laid eyes on her for the first time, at some drinks party or other, she was picking a piece of hors d'oeuvre out of her teeth."

"Really?" Mal said. "That was it, the big attraction? She was picking her teeth?"

"She thought nobody was looking and she was digging at something stuck between two molars. Levering it out with one manicured, lacquered fingernail. This great swanlike society beauty. This ethereal, worshipped creature. Doing something so mundane and ordinary, her mouth wide open, hand rummaging away. That was when I knew I was in with a chance. That was also when I knew I could love her. She was human, after all."

He looked wistfully out of the window.

"You like a bit of grit in the works, don't you?" Mal said.

"If life's too easy, what's the point?"

"And yet the rest of us – the 'other half' – we're all trying to fight our way up out of the muck, into the so-called good life, a life like you had."

"Who's content with their lot?" Reston said. "No one. Except maybe the Great Speaker."

"Not even him, judging by how he whinged to Quetzalcoatl."

"True. Then again, he seemed enthused by the prospect of this war. Like it was something he was looking forward to, after so long. Speaking of which..."

There was the distant sound of l-guns discharging on the outer walls.

"Looks like things are hotting up again."

THE GODS' THIRD strike was broad-based and comprehensive. They didn't confine themselves solely to the air. Ground forces were also deployed.

The first sign was a terrific commotion originating from over in the direction of the main gate. There was shouting and a mass of concentrated gunfire. Shortly afterwards, non-armoured Serpent Warriors came hurrying into the concourse below the administrative ziggurat. They were on the run, pulling back, harried by an enemy.

"Xipe Totec," said Reston. "And Mictlantecuhtli."

The Flayed One was in full shock-mode, his skin transparent, all his viscera on display. Mal looked on with fascinated disgust as he cut a swath through the routed Serpents, wielding a pair of hook-shaped knives with finesse and almost surgical precision. He darted about, dodging his enemy's shots; he seemed to have a sixth sense as to where the next plasma bolt was coming from. And his blades flickered and slashed, and here a Serpent fell with his torso opened wide from shoulder to waist, and here another Serpent staggered in circles with blood fountaining from a severed jugular, and here a third screamed and tried to stem the flow of life jetting from the stump of his arm.

"It's like, he's showing you his insides before he shows you your own," Mal breathed.

Reston nodded. "Sort of a visual promise, isn't it? 'Look, here's what's coming your way.'"

Alarming as Xipe Totec was, however, he was nothing compared with Mictlantecuhtli. If the former was a scalpel, the latter was blunt force trauma. The Dark One strode like a juggernaut, implacably, as though nothing could daunt or deter him. His hands were encased in massive black gauntlets, and with these he did two things: deflected incoming l-gun shots and killed human beings. Often he would be performing the one action with one hand and the other with the other simultaneously. The gauntlets were large enough that a Serpent's head could fit inside their grip, comfortably, at least until Mictlantecuhtli squeezed and the head was crushed, helmet and all, like a pistachio nut. A punch from one of those huge metal fists was capable of removing an entire arm at the shoulder. A swat easily disembowelled.

It was a hopelessly one-sided battle, right up until the moment armoured Serpents began buzzing out of the bunker like angry wasps and joined the fray. They pressed Xipe Totec and Mictlantecuhtli hard, pinning them down with ferocious salvoes of gunfire, forcing them to spend all their effort defending.

One Serpent was at the forefront of the fightback: Colonel Tlanextic. Mal felt herself tense up at the sight of that gold-zigzagged armour. She willed Xipe Totec to get the better of him, or Mictlantecuhtli. Either of the gods was welcome to kill Aaronson's murderer. If she was unable to do it herself, she would settle for that.

No such luck, however. Tlanextic and the other armoured Serpents succeeded in repulsing Xipe Totec and Mictlantecuhtli and driving them off the concourse. The battle raged on down the streets of Tenochtitlan, out of view.

The few Serpents remaining at the bunker entrance had a brief respite. They reinforced their positions and tallied their living and their dead. By now the sun was setting. For a time, the air thickened and turned smoky gold. The sky was blood-red, then amethyst, then purple-grey. Stars winked. Streetlights came on automatically. Everything was still and quiet.

Then, amid the shadows on the concourse, shapes started to move.

At first Mal thought it must just be tired eyes, a trick of vision. That or wisps of dust being whisked up by breezes.

"Did you see that?" she murmured to Reston. "Down in that doorway just now. And over there by the monorail track. I could have sworn..."

"There's something there, all right. Animals of some kind."

"What?"

"Not sure."

The Serpents themselves had noticed they weren't alone on the concourse. They swung their l-guns in different directions, trying to train them on the creatures flitting and scurrying between pools of darkness. To Mal, from the fragmentary glimpses she was catching, the animals looked like large rats or perhaps small dogs. But they were furless, leathery-skinned, and their movements weren't right. There was something of the reptile about them, not least the long tapering tails, and also something disturbingly humanoid, especially the paws, which bore a marked similarity to hands and feet.

All at once a Serpent screamed. One of the creatures had latched onto his back. He reached behind him, clawing desperately, and the animal squirmed out of his grasp and wrapped itself round his neck. It had a shovel-shaped muzzle, and twin rows of serrated teeth glittered like diamonds in the lamplight. It sank its jaws into the man's throat and, with one wrenching twist of its head, tore out his trachea, Adam's apple and a great deal of gristle and muscle. Blood gushed over it, and the creature became frenzied, burrowing deeper into the Serpent's neck, hind feet scrabbling for purchase on his uniform, tail lashing the air.

This first drawing of blood was the cue for a concerted wave of attacks. More of the repugnant monsters sprang from the shadows onto the Serpents. Some threw themselves down off ledges and cornices and bit their faces, while others writhed up their legs and went for the soft parts at the crotch. Plasma bolts crisscrossed as the Serpents tried to fend off the creatures, but the vast majority of the shots were wild, fired by panicked or pain-wracked fingers. Martial discipline went to pieces in the face of an enemy that was so obscenely swift and that didn't play by the standard rules of engagement.

"Just what the hell *are* those things?" Mal said.

Rhetorical question. She wasn't expecting Reston to have the answer.

It turned out he did. "Over there." He pointed to one of the streets that fed onto the concourse. At the corner, lurking, was an old woman with wild white hair and an eager, gloating posture. "That's Tzitzimitl."

"So those animals would be..."

"The Tzitzimime."

The Demons of Darkness. The mindless, rapacious servants of the mother goddess. According to the myths, they were destined one day to overrun the earth and devour all humankind.

Mal felt an old familiar chill creep through her. As a child, she had had nightmares about the Tzitzimime. There'd been one particular textbook at school, a religious primer, which had carried pictures of them, an artist's pen-and-ink impression of how the demons might look. Those black, leering homunculi had plagued Mal's sleep for years.

The flesh-and-blood reality was worse still. Uglier and more vicious than even that textbook draughtsman could have imagined.

Most of the Serpent Warriors were on the ground now, shrieking in horror and agony as the Tzitzimime ate them alive. Their suffering filled the old crone with delight. Tzitzimitl clasped her hands and shivered, and now and then did a little stiff-kneed jig on the spot.

"What did I tell you?" Reston said. "She really doesn't like us."

It wasn't long before there were just three Serpents left, and they were attempting to get to the bunker and find sanctuary there, but the Tzitzimime kept cutting them off from the entrance. Every way they turned, there was a pack of the creatures spitting and snarling. They tried feinting at them, but the Tzitzimime simply feinted back. Eventually the Serpents were surrounded, encircled. Their lightning gun batteries were drained and for metres around they could see nothing but squat, quivering bodies and rows of deadly sharp teeth.

They were done for and they knew it. One of them made a proposal to the other two. All three drew their *macuahitl*s.

"Those won't be any use," Reston commented.

"I don't think that's what they're up to," said Mal.

She was right. The three Serpents formed themselves into a triangle. Each held up his sword point-first at the chest of the man on his right. Then one gave the command and they drove the swords home. All three fell, as one, and the Tzitzimime scampered onto the fresh corpses and feasted.

A sharp, loud whistle from Tzitzimitl had the Tzitzimime pricking their ears and raising their gore-streaked muzzles. A second whistle, and they abandoned their meals and hurried towards her, a great flowing carpet of low-slung bony beast. They assembled at the goddess's ankles, clambering over one another and fawning for her attention. Tzitzimitl gave them all a gracious smile, patted a few heads, then set off with the Tzitzimime trotting behind her in a long obedient line, onwards to whatever atrocity she planned next.

"She bred them, didn't she?" Mal said. "Trained them. *Made* them."

"I'd guess so."

"They were little bits of this and that. A bunch of different animals put together."

"I think these gods can do things human scientists can only dream of. Manipulate genetics. Splice elements of one creature into another. You should see Xolotl. He's half dog, half man, but it's hard to tell where one ends and the other begins."

"So that's another gift they didn't give us: how to tamper with nature."

"Do you think it would have done us any good to have it? Or, no, put it this way – do you think we'd have done any good with it?"

"No."

"Exactly. On the plus side, Tzitzimitl has at least given you and me something."

Mal surveyed the concourse, now little more than an abattoir. "A clear run to that bunker."

"So what are we waiting for?" said Reston.

TWENTY-NINE

Same Day

THEY PICKED THEIR way across the concourse, around the heaps of slain Serpent Warriors. Here and there lay the charred body of a Tzitzimime. Mal found the creatures far harder to look at than the mutilated human remains; they were unnatural things, hideous and insidious. She steered clear of them as best she could. One, still just alive, snapped feebly at her ankle as she passed. She considered running it through with her *macuahitl*, but she liked the idea of the animal suffering a lingering death, and she didn't want its blood besmirching her blade.

The sky was alive with explosions. Again and again the darkness was lit up by a bright flash, followed by a long resonant *boom*. Tenochtitlan was taking a pounding, but it was also dishing one out in return. An aerodisc streaked overhead in pursuit of an armoured god, blazing away with its lightning guns. The sound of street skirmishes echoed between the buildings.

The bunker entrance was sealed by a pair of broad, heavy doors, secured by a chunky combination lock.

"Any guesses as to the code?" Reston said.

"Search me."

"Then we'll just have to use the universal lockpick – brute force." He went and fetched two of the Serpents' l-guns that still carried some juice. Handing one to Mal, he said, "Aim for the middle, the gap where the doors meet. Full charge."

Standing well back, they zapped the doors repeatedly until the guns ran dry. When the smoke and their vision cleared, they found that they had created a gap just large enough for a person to squeeze through. They waited a minute or so for the twisted edges of the hole to cool; when the metal was still hot to the touch but not burningly so, they slithered inside.

A trapezoidal tunnel stretched ahead, illuminated at intervals by caged lightbulbs and descending at a shallow gradient. They proceeded down it, alert for danger. Every so often the walls around them shook as yet another building above them took a hit.

The tunnel disgorged into a huge chamber. A dozen suits of Serpent armour stood in rows, mounted on purpose-built modules. There were scores of empty modules for all the suits currently in deployment in the field. Weaponry hung on racks. A small team of technicians were checking the equipment, running battery tests and diagnostic workups. They were obviously doing their best to ignore the noises coming from above, busying themselves with tasks so as not to have to think about the devastation being wrought on their city. Anxiety was etched on every face; shoulders were hunched, voices were strained.

She and Reston were not spotted coming in. They ducked behind a workbench strewn with random pieces of armour. There, in whispers, they debated their next move. Reston proposed taking one of the technicians hostage and using him as a bargaining tool to force the rest of them to get two suits ready. "They can tell us how to activate them, how to fly them, everything."

"You think they'll go for that?"

"Look at them. They're scared out of their wits. These are civilians, not soldiers. They don't want to die."

"Okay. But this had better work."

Mal drew her *macuahitl* and stole across the floor to the nearest technician, a thin, bespectacled and extremely gawky young specimen. Coming up behind him, she put the blade to his neck and said quietly in his ear, "Do not scream. Do not panic. Just do as I say and I promise you won't get hurt. Nod if you understand."

He did.

"There are two of us," she went on, "and we want two of those suits of armour. You and the other boffins set them up for us, get us into them, and instruct us on what to do with them. Help us out, and this can all be over with in no time. Yes?"

Another nod, accompanied by a small, terrified whimper.

"Great. Call everyone over, then, quick as you can. Any false moves, any funny business, and the last sound you'll ever hear will be the hiss of your breath escaping through the hole in your windpipe."

"Ahem," said the technician, trying to clear a very dry throat. "People? Little problem here. Can I have your attention?"

IT WENT SURPRISINGLY smoothly. The technicians were a biddable lot, as Reston had predicted. One of their own being held at swordpoint was a convincing argument for co-operation. Being smart men and women, they grasped that they were in the presence of two individuals who were not only capable of killing them all, but quite prepared to if the situation demanded it. They knuckled down, and within minutes two of the suits had been trundled out from the racks and Mal and Reston were being given a crash course in flying technique.

"These things are actually beautifully straightforward," said one of the technicians, the seniormost and by all appearances the man in charge. "A complex system with an uncomplicated interface. The flight dynamics – roll, pitch and yaw – are all conditional on your own movements. Basically, lean or bend in the direction you want to go and the armour will comply. The antigrav excitation selector is incorporated into the helmet, so as to keep both hands free. You lower your head to descend, raise it to ascend. That's the only part that takes some mastering. The rest is no trouble."

The suits had to be put on in sections. Mal kept her *macuahitl* and the hostage technician in close contact while the pieces of armour were clamped onto her and linked together. He trembled like a leaf throughout the process, casting imploring looks at his colleagues as if to say, *Please don't do anything rash*. They obliged, and Mal and Reston were soon fully suited.

It felt weird being contained head to toe inside this hard, jointed casing. Mal experienced a stifling surge of claustrophobia. She wanted to rip the armour off, get out of it any way she could. *Be calm*, she told herself. It was only a few pieces of light metal. She moved a leg experimentally, then an arm. It barely felt any different from normal – a little more resistance, that was all. She flexed one gauntleted hand. The segmented fingers rippled like caterpillars.

"Faceplate appears and disappears at the touch of this sensor," said the head technician. He pressed a spot on the side of Mal's helmet, and all at once everything went yellow and she realised she was staring out through the snakelike lenses. "The tinting on the eye screens filters out glare from l-gun bolts. That's crucial after dark, so as not to compromise your night vision."

Reston tried his faceplate too. "Nice."

His voice came directly to Mal via her right ear.

"All the suits are in constant comms-link contact," the head technician explained. "There are two channels, proximity and general. Proximity, the default setting, works up to a range of three hundred metres. General is a wide-spectrum band that picks up all Serpent Warrior chatter at all times. Is there anything else you want to know?"

"Is there anything else we *need* to know?" Reston replied.

"I don't think so. Now, will you kindly let poor Yolyamanitzin there go? The boy looks like he's about to faint."

"Give us a couple of l-guns and we're done," said Mal.

The guns were lodged into her and Reston's hands. Mal laid her *macuahitl* aside and gave Yolyamanitzin a gentle shove. "Off you go." The young technician almost collapsed to the floor in relief.

"I would wish you godspeed, but I can't bring myself to," said the head technician, finding some courage now that none of his people was in direct danger any more. "Whoever you are, coming in here dressed in holy garb, you don't deserve to get away with this. The Great Speaker knows all, sees all. Vengeance will be his."

"What you mean is you're going to blab to him about us as soon as we're gone," said Reston.

"That's right." The man blinked defiantly. "And to Colonel Tlanextic."

"How?"

"Through the hotline link."

"What hotline link? That one over there?" Reston was looking at a console with a number of telephone receivers attached to it, each a different colour.

"That very one."

Reston charged up his l-gun and blasted the console to pieces.

"Not any more you're not," he said.

MAL LIFTED HER head... and flew.

It was strangely exhilarating and exhilaratingly strange. Her feet were off the floor. She was floating. She had to resist the urge to waft her arms and legs as though treading water in a swimming pool.

She lifted her head again and rose a little higher. She wobbled uncertainly in the air. She felt on the verge of overbalancing and inclined herself forwards ever so slightly to compensate. All at once she was in motion. The further over she leaned, the faster she went. Wishing to decelerate, she instinctively straightened up. The suit of armour halted, returning to hover mode.

"This is..." She couldn't think of a word for it.

"I know!" Reston beamed, executing a tentative midair pirouette. "Where has this been all my life?"

Mal tried for speed again, bending forward until she was near horizontal. The armour flung her towards the tunnel, far faster than she was expecting. She collided with the edge of the entrance and rebounded off. Picking herself up off the floor, she marvelled that she hadn't felt a thing. It had been like sprinting headlong into a wall of cotton wool.

What was it Tlanextic had called it? "Impact-dispersant."

Phenomenal.

She resumed her progress through the tunnel, warier than before but only marginally. Reston caught up and flew alongside her. They exchanged looks through the snake-eye lenses. His eyes were boyishly wide. He was having fun. And so, she had to admit, was she.

The bunker doors could be opened manually from the inside; Reston turned the wheel, and the doors ground grudgingly apart a few inches, then stopped, refusing to go any further. They'd warped them when they'd blasted their way in, and they no longer neatly followed their tracks.

"Let's see if we can get them to budge the old-fashioned way," he said, and grabbed one and began to tug sideways.

What happened next surprised them both. The door started to bend as Reston pulled on it. The more pressure he applied, the more it curved inwards. Solid metal buckled in his hands as though it were cardboard. Finally, with a cracking screech, both the top and bottom edges of the door jumped out of their tracks and the whole thing hung askew.

"Well, either I don't know my own strength," Reston said, "or this suit enhances the wearer's muscle power by a factor of ten. The head technician didn't mention *that*."

"Maybe he just wanted us out of there as soon as possible," Mal said.

"Imagine if I'd had one of these instead of my Conquistador armour. Imagine what I'd have been able to accomplish then."

"Don't even think about it."

"Too late. I already have."

"Let's focus on the now. We still have to get off the island, and armour or not, I have a feeling it isn't going to be easy."

"Why not? The only people who'd have any interest in stopping us are Serpents, and to them we look like, well, them. They won't bother us."

"Yeah," said Mal, "but to Quetzalcoatl and pals we look like Serpents too. And on recent evidence, gods don't show their enemies much mercy."

Reston was sobered. "Ah. Good point. We'd better go carefully, bettern't we?"

"No shit, sunshine."

OUTSIDE, THE CONCOURSE was as before, a field of corpses. Wounds and spilled blood glistened blackly in the lamplight.

The worst of the fighting seemed to be taking place over on the west side of the city, so they elected to head east. As she took off into the open air, Mal was filled with a giddying sense of possibility. The exhilaration she'd felt down in the confines of the bunker was magnified a hundredfold. This suit of armour could transport her *anywhere*.

She reminded herself not to get cocky. Just because they'd got themselves some paddles didn't mean they weren't still up shit creek.

They rose into the night sky, Tenochtitlan dropping away beneath them. In mere moments they were level with the summits of the ziggurats, the tops of the towers. Shoreline lights twinkled in the distance – so far and yet, now, so near. Below her, Mal could see fires raging in at least three areas of the city. The eye screens on her faceplate reduced the brilliance of the fires to the muted throb of embers in a grate, but these were still clearly, from their size alone, serious infernos. One whole ziggurat was ablaze from lowest tier to highest, sending up dense clouds of smoke. An tanker aerodisc was scooping up water from the lake and dumping it onto the flames, but in vain. Elsewhere there were intermittent strobe flickers of l-gun fire. It was a garish, hellish scene. Mictlan itself surely had nothing that could compare.

If there is a Mictlan, Mal thought. The gods were real, but somehow that made the myths attached to them seem less plausible, rather than more. It was like the first time she'd realised, around the age of thirteen or fourteen, that her parents weren't the infallible, matchless beings she had believed them to be. They were just humans after all, with as many faults and failings as she had. It was that kind of loss of innocence. Nothing was safe any more, nothing sacred. Every measure she knew had had to be recalibrated.

When she and Reston had gained sufficient altitude, they set a course for the shore.

They had gone a mile – less – when trouble reared its head.

"Airborne troopers, please identify yourselves."

Mal and Reston looked around. Looked at each other. Was someone talking to *them*?

"I repeat, airborne troopers, currently eastbound out of Tenochtitlan. Who are you and where do you think you're going?"

The challenge had come over the comms link, but neither of them could see where it originated from.

"You two," said the voice testily. "The ones heading away from the combat zone. I'm talking to you. Please respond. Over."

"Er, yes," said Reston. "We're, er... This is us. Where are you?"

"Right up your backside."

And there, behind them, out of nowhere, loomed a Serpent gunship. Mal and Reston slowed to a hover, and the aerodisc braked accordingly. A trio of pilots were visible in its cockpit. One of them spoke into a microphone handset, and the suspicion-filled voice resumed in Mal's and Reston's ears.

"Sound off," it said. "Name, rank, platoon."

"Uhmmm..." Mal was stumped. They hadn't banked on something like this. "I'm Lieutenant..." She groped for a Nahuatl surname. "Yolyamanitzin." It was the last one she'd heard, the first one that came to mind.

Unfortunately, Reston had had the exact same idea, and just as Mal was dubbing herself Yolyamanitzin, so was he. He even awarded himself the same rank as her.

"Let me get this straight," said the pilot. "You're both lieutenants and you're both called Yolyamanitzin?"

"Yes," said Reston. "Funny thing, eh? And we're not even related."

The pilot wasn't buying it. "And your platoons? Which? Viper? Boa? Cobra?"

"Viper," said Reston decisively. "Both of us. Another coincidence."

"Nice try, dickhead. Serpent platoons are known by numbers, not the names of snakes."

"Yeah, nice try, dickhead," Mal muttered.

"So, really, who the hell are you two? And give me one good reason why I shouldn't blow you out of the air."

"We're on a special mission," Reston said, stalling for time. Surreptitiously he flicked a switch and his l-gun started to power up. "Top secret. For the colonel."

"Yeah, pull the other one. What accent is that anyway?"

"British," said Reston, and in English he added, "Vaughn. Brace for evasive action."

"What was that?" said the pilot. "Didn't catch that last bit."

"I said..."

And Reston opened fire.

Someone on board must have been anticipating this very move, because just as Reston unleashed the bolt the gunship flipped up onto its starboard side. His shot grazed the hull, leaving only a scorch. Then, still canted almost perpendicular, the aerodisc lunged forwards, its front-facing l-gun nacelles belching plasma.

But Mal and Reston were already racing away, flat out, in reverse. The gunship gave chase. More plasma bolts blistered around them, and they both twisted and sidewinded. There was no skill to their manoeuvring, only desperation, but the suits of armour were superbly responsive, almost as if they wanted what their wearers wanted. One bolt struck Mal a glancing blow. She was barely aware of it. She felt like laughing. But the next instant another caught her full on, and although the armour took the brunt, it seemed there were limits to the levels of energy discharge it could absorb. Mal was sent spiralling through space. Flecks of brightness whirled against a dark background. She couldn't tell what was up or down, what was firmament or lake surface. She struggled against the spin, and finally managed to correct it and right herself. Her head took a few seconds to catch up with the rest of her.

As the dizziness cleared, she got her bearings. The gunship was hounding Reston hard, and only by some miracle was he eluding its fire. He managed to loose off the occasional shot of his own, but the disc outclassed him in terms of both gunpower and airspeed. He was fighting a rearguard action and it wasn't doing him any good; it was only a matter of time before the Serpent pilots got in the two or three hits in quick succession that would polish him off.

"Reston! Keep that thing busy. I'm coming to help."

"Whenever you like, Vaughn. No hurry. What are you going to do?"

"I have an idea, although I'm not too fond of it."

They were using English. The pilots would be aware they were hatching something but wouldn't know what.

"Well, like I said, no hurry. Whatever works for you. Any time in the next three seconds would be fine."

Mal took a deep breath – *I can't believe I'm doing this, I can't believe I'm doing this, I can't believe I'm doing this* – and soared towards the gunship. It opened up at her with its rear nacelles, but she made herself the zippiest, most elusive target imaginable, corkscrewing and loop-the-looping unpredictably, like a fly avoiding the swatter. Soon she was above the disc, out of the line of fire from any of its guns. She dived down and crash-landed on it, belly-flopping. Momentum carried her slithering across its roof to the front, where the cockpit windshield was.

Clinging on with one hand to the ridge of the windshield fairing, she started hammering the glass with the other. The pilots yelped in alarm. Over the comms link, the one who'd spoken earlier shouted at her that she was a madwoman. What was she trying to do?

"What does it look like?" she replied in Nahuatl.

The gunship went into a series of crazy bucking-bronco manoeuvres, the pilots doing everything they could to throw Mal off, but she hung on, still doggedly punching the windshield. The glass was tough but the suit of armour, or perhaps the woman inside it, was tougher. Spiderweb cracks appeared. Then a hole. Finally, with a sudden sucking crash, the entire curved sheet of glass caved in. Wind pressure drove the fragments into the cockpit at bullet speed. Mal heard screams. She detached herself from the disc and shot upwards.

The gunship slowed to a complete halt. Reston did a hairpin turn and aimed his l-gun at the hollowed-out windshield frame, and pumped a full-charge bolt into the cockpit. The disc rocked and shuddered. A tongue of flame erupted from the front like a dragon's breath.

The gunship began a leisurely, seesawing descent, like an autumn leaf falling. It hit the lake surface quite gently, with a discreet splash. Its neg-mass drive was still functioning but was cycling down, so the disc remained buoyant on the water for nearly a minute before it began to sink. Still afire, it slipped into the darkness below with a surge of boiling bubbles and a hiss of steam.

Reston flew to Mal's side. "We are definitely even now. That was magnificent stuff."

"It was, wasn't it?"

"I thought I was a goner for certain."

"To be honest, I thought so too."

"And now, surely, we have an uninterrupted journey to shore. Nothing else could possibly go –"

He broke off.

"Me and my big mouth."

Mal saw what he saw.

Flying gods. Three of them.

Huitzilopochtli. Itzpapalotl. And Quetzalcoatl.

The Hummingbird God's flame spear launcher was on his shoulder, its missile pointed directly and unarguably at Mal and Reston. Or, as Huitzilopochtli saw it, at two enemy soldiers.

"Yes," Mal said to Reston, "you and your big fucking mouth."

THIRTY

Same Day

"DON'T SHOOT!" STUART flung his arms up into the air.
"Hold your fire. We're not what you think we are."

Hutizilopochtli's stance did not shift.

"Look. I'm going to move my hand now. Easy does
it. I'm going to tap the side of my helmet here, like so."

Stuart didn't know if any of the gods could hear
him through the faceplate. He hoped they could,
for his and Vaughn's sake. At the same time, he
was trying to send out all the right signals through
posture and attitude alone. *We're no threat. Don't
attack*.

"And hey presto," he said, as his faceplate
vanished. "It's me."

The three gods looked at one another. Quetzalcoatl's
and Huitzilopochtli's expressions were flat – hard to

interpret. As for Itzpapalotl, her all-covering helmet gave away nothing whatsoever.

"I'm Reston. Stuart Reston. Remember? I know I'm just a human, but surely you remember me, Quetzalcoatl."

He had no idea how good a god's memory was when it came to lesser beings. Perhaps mortals were as hard for a deity to distinguish from one another as, say, laboratory mice were for a scientist. Quetzalcoatl had recognised him on the terrace of the Great Speaker's palace but, it seemed, just barely. He'd offered a passing nod, but that was all. Bigger fish to fry, maybe. Or maybe Stuart's face had been familiar but one he couldn't place. He had forgotten the man whom he'd briefly taken under his wing only a few days earlier. Stuart had reverted to being just another anonymous human, one among the billions of such creatures who infested the earth.

"We're not Serpents," he said. "We've just borrowed these suits to get out of Tenochtitlan. Vaughn? Show them your face too."

Vaughn's faceplate winked out of existence.

"See? When you came to visit Tezcatlipoca earlier today, the two of us were there. But we've nothing to do with him. Not allies, not anything. The moment you left, as a matter of fact, he tried to have us killed."

Quetzalcoatl cocked his head. A thin-lipped smile appeared.

"Yes, I know you," he said. "The Serpent armour threw me off. Huitz? Lower your weapon. These are friends."

"Fucking phew," Vaughn said, with feeling, as Huitzilopochtli did as told.

"But you should count yourselves lucky," Quetzalcoatl said. "We were this close to attacking. The only thing that prevented us was seeing you take down that aerodisc. It made us curious about you. Serpent Warrior versus Serpent Warrior? If not for that..."

"If not for that," said Huitzilopochtli, "your bodies would be lying beside the gunship on the lakebed even as we speak."

Itzpapalotl nodded in agreement.

"So it was actually a good thing we got waylaid," Stuart said to Vaughn.

"Every cloud..." she replied.

He turned back to the three gods. "Well, I must say, Quetzalcoatl, it's a pleasure to make your acquaintance again. But now, if you don't mind, Vaughn and I will be on our way. The more distance we put between us and Tenochtitlan, the better. That place is a deathtrap."

"Of course," said the Plumed Serpent. "As you wish."

As Stuart started to float past, however, Quetzalcoatl held up a hand. "Although, perhaps..."

Stuart's heart sank. What now? What did this god want with him?

"Perhaps I ought to accompany you, at least part of the way. Huitz? Itzpapalotl? Carry out the next raid without me. Be careful."

"Really," Stuart said, "you don't have to."

"If I don't escort you, someone else in the pantheon may mistake you for genuine Serpent Warriors, and this time there might not be anything to give them pause for thought."

"Ah. Fair point. Wouldn't want that to happen."

"I daresay not."

So, WHILE HUITZILOPOCHTLI and Itzpapalotl carried on towards Tenochtitlan to bombard the city yet again, Quetzalcoatl flew in the opposite direction with Stuart and Vaughn. They kept to a moderate pace, so were able to talk without yelling.

"You're winning, right?" Vaughn asked. "Looks that way to me. Tezcatlipoca's men are putting up a fight, but really it's a foregone conclusion."

"Things are going in our favour, so far," Quetzalcoatl replied. "But by no means has it been an easy ride. We've taken casualties. Mixcoatl, the Hunter God? Serpent Warriors cornered him and overwhelmed him through sheer numbers. I saw it myself but was too late to save him. And Coyolxauhqui —"

"The Moon Goddess."

"I sent her in before anyone else, to infiltrate the city and scout out the lie of the land. Her stealth capability should have protected her. Not even Itzpapalotl is her rival when it comes to blending in with her surroundings. However, we haven't heard back from her, and I fear the worst. She may even have fallen foul of Tezcatlipoca himself. He's the only one who could have detected her presence. Then again, it's unclear whether the Smoking Mirror has taken a direct, personal role in proceedings as yet. I'm minded to think that he hasn't, that he's still orchestrating from the sidelines, simply because our side still appears to have the upper hand. When he does become fully involved, it could alter everything."

"He's that powerful?" said Stuart.

"Oh, yes." Quetzalcoatl looked grave. "That and more. Tezcatlipoca could singlehandedly turn the tide of this battle."

"So why hasn't he tried to yet?"

"Why should he bother, when he has a whole army to fight on his behalf? If I know my brother, he's using his Serpent Warriors as a shield. We throw ourselves against them and break them, but break ourselves in the process too. They're there to wear us down. When they're at their lowest ebb, then and only then will Tezcatlipoca emerge, because then we, his foes, will be at our lowest ebb as well. His reputation for cunning is not undeserved."

"It sounds to me," said Vaughn, "like you're scared of him."

"I am. I don't mind admitting it. Any sane being would be."

"Is that one of the reasons why you left him here on his own? The real reason?"

"It did have some bearing on the decision, yes," said Quetzalcoatl. His hair flowed in a long dark mane behind him with the passage of flight. "Angry as I was with Tezcatlipoca, I was unwilling to antagonise him too greatly. His rage, when roused to its fullest, is immense. Earth-shattering. It seemed wiser simply to back off and leave him where he was. Giving him dominion over your planet was a way of appeasing him, I suppose. Had we not done that, had he and I continued at loggerheads, there's no telling how things might have turned out."

"But you're happy to run the risk of antagonising him now."

"I couldn't, in all conscience, permit his reign to continue. I had to do something."

"So you might say this is kill or cure."

"That, unfortunately, is a fair summation of the situation, Miss Vaughn. The game is being played for the very highest of stakes. Should we lose, Tezcatlipoca will not only wipe out all of us, his peers and aggressors, but he may well unleash further calamity on the people of earth. It would not be out of character for him to commit another genocide, as he did in America, purely out of pique. He might go even further than that."

"You could try negotiating with him again, couldn't you?"

"You saw how well that went last time."

"But you've had a bit of a barney and now the air's been cleared. You could both say enough's enough and call a truce, and everyone will still have their dignity. That's how it is with boys and their willy-waving, isn't it? You make your point, then tuck them away again."

Quetzalcoatl smiled at her turn of phrase. "There is so much ill will between my brother and me.

Too much. Our meeting earlier was a formality as much as anything. This – this conflict – it was the inevitable, the only outcome. It had to be. You must appreciate, surely, that I'm not fighting just for myself? This isn't purely for my own satisfaction, not at all. I'm fighting in order to make amends to you, and all humans, for my intemperate, badly-thought-through decision half a millennium ago. I'm trying to reverse the consequences of a great failure."

"Better late than never, I suppose," Vaughn said.

"I like you," Quetzalcoatl said with a chuckle. "Reston, I like your mate."

"She's not my –"

"I'm not his –"

"She speaks her mind," the god went on. "She doesn't kowtow. She's precisely the reason the human race appeals to me. You have drive, vigour, a zest to be more than you are. When I first came here, I saw such potential in you all and I knew it was my duty to coax it out of you. I promise you now, if Tezcatlipoca is defeated – *when* he is – I shall resume exactly where I left off. I'll help guide you forward to become the very best you can be. Decades from now, you'll be so transformed, you'll scarce be able to recognise yourselves. You'll possess every last scrap of our technology and have the wisdom to use it well, you'll live longer than you could ever imagine, and, oh, the places you'll go and the things you'll see...! Here, right now, is when it could all begin anew for you."

All at once, Ah Balam Chel's words returned to Stuart: *It's a period of transition as one world age pivots around and becomes the next. Creation begins anew. Life is transformed.*

"Seems you might have been right after all, you wily old bastard," he murmured.

"Didn't catch that," said Vaughn. They were approaching the lakeshore – one of its dark, forested, uninhabited reaches, a ragged littoral of swampland and stream inlets.

"I was just remembering Chel. The leader of Xibalba."

"And he...?"

"...told me not so long ago about the Mayan calendar and how it predicted that the world is about to come to a pivotal moment. A crossroads, I suppose you could say. And here, it seems, we actually are."

"The end of the fourth world age, the beginning of the fifth," said Quetzalcoatl. "Yes, I know of this. Why do you think we came back now, of all times?"

"Even you believe there's something to it?"

"Everything goes in cycles, Stuart. The seasons, the planets. Why not time itself? The Mayan astronomers were clever people. They kept immaculate records, observed the patterns, made the calculations. They knew about wheels within wheels. The earth rotates on its axis but also orbits the sun. A whirlpool turns, and within it are independent eddies. As in nature, so in time, for time is integral to nature."

"Hold on, what is all this bollocks?" Vaughn demanded. "Can one of you kindly explain what you're rabbiting on about?"

Stuart paraphrased as best he could what Chel had told him about the *Popul Vuh*, *b'ak'tun*s and world ages. "It's all coming to a head," he said. "The big day's arriving. Soon. Very soon. In fact, anyone know today's date? What with one thing and another, I've lost track."

Vaughn frowned. "Three Rain One Movement One House. But I had to think about it. That's the kind of day it's been."

"Then that means tomorrow's Four Flower. Tomorrow's it. When the counter zeroes and resets."

Quetzalcoatl gave a confirming nod. "No coincidence. I'm not one to ignore the immense pull of time's tides. The world has reached a crux. Tezcatlipoca knows it too. That's another reason why he's holding himself in reserve. He senses that, come tomorrow, he will be in line for either total victory or total catastrophe, and so shall we. All is poised in delicate balance. The fifth age will begin either with the Smoking Mirror more secure than ever on his throne or else cast down and destroyed, and whatever state the earth is in when the new age commences, so will it remain until the age after that. The status quo at tomorrow's end will be the status quo for the next five thousand solar years. And that is why we *must* beat him. We are humankind's one and only chance of being rid of Tezcatlipoca, its one and only chance of a bright new dawn, and so we are acting at the most auspicious time there is for us to act."

He led Stuart and Vaughn in a decelerating descent towards a patch of rainforest. They threaded through the canopy and between the trees, down to an area Stuart thought he recognised, even in the darkness. The gods' inverted ziggurat lay belowground here.

"This is where we part company," Quetzalcoatl announced as they touched down. "You two may carry on to wherever you wish."

Stuart detected a hidden current in the Plumed Serpent's voice, a note of invitation.

"Or," Stuart said, "we can come in with you. Maybe as allies?"

"Yes," said Quetzalcoatl, casually, as if it hadn't occurred to him. "If that's what you'd like."

"Why?" said Vaughn.

"Why?" The god mused. "Good question. Let me see. Could it be that, as humans, you might have a vested interest in the future of earth? It is, after all, your planet. Your home. And could it be that I would value having the two of you fighting at my side? I saw how well the two of you fared against that gunship, how you prevailed in the teeth of overwhelming odds, the teamwork you showed..."

"Teamwork?" Stuart and Vaughn exclaimed in unison.

"Not to mention your evident resourcefulness – purloining those suits of armour and adapting to their use so swiftly."

"Let me get this straight," said Vaughn. "You're recruiting us?"

"Asking if you'd care to help out, yes," Quetzalcoatl replied. "The struggle is as much yours as ours."

"But you don't need us, surely."

"Two more assets in the theatre of conflict? Two more arrows in my quiver? Why ever not?"

"We're not gods."

"No, but you're humans and therefore ought to be as keen to fight for your destiny as we are, if not far more so. But if the idea doesn't appeal..."

At a gesture from Quetzalcoatl, the opening in the undergrowth appeared, just as Stuart remembered it. A pillar of light shone up from below, and through the rectangular hatch the tiers of the upside-down ziggurat could be glimpsed, shelving away deep into the ground.

"Bloody hell," was Vaughn's only comment.

Quetzalcoatl made to go down the steps. "I'm glad to have made your acquaintance, both of you. I know now for certain that humankind is worth fighting for and preserving, and indeed worth dying for. Perhaps, if nothing else, you could wish me luck?"

"No," said Stuart. "Wait."

Quetzalcoatl halted at the lip of the staircase. Didn't look round.

"What the hell, I'm in."

"Reston..." said Vaughn.

"He's right, Vaughn. This is about us. Our future. It would be wrong not to get involved."

"Are you nuts?"

"So you keep assuring me. But listen. This is the fight I began as the Conquistador, against the Empire. The same campaign, only taken to the highest level. It'd be a shame to have come so far and not go all the way. Might as well see it through to the end." He added, "It's not as if I've got much else to do with my life."

"Don't," she said as he moved towards the hole. "Don't go down in there with him."

"Why the sudden show of concern?"

"It's not concern. It's just... If you do, I'm going to have to go too, you bastard."

"No, you aren't."

"Yes I fucking am, because A, there's no way I'm going to let you hog all the glory, and B, I'm still itching to have a crack at that wanker Tlanextic."

"Both of which are sound justifications," said Stuart. "And is there by any chance a C?"

"Yeah. You're an idiot, and idiots need other idiots to watch their backs."

THIRTY-ONE

Same Day

THEY SAT IN the refectory. Mal was famished. She hadn't eaten since – when was it? Last night? Must be, judging by how her stomach was growling. There was food on the tables, and more kept arriving, courtesy of two goddesses, Coatlicue and Quetzalpetatl, who waltzed out from the kitchen to deposit dish after steaming dish on the tables. Both of them were beautiful in different but equally bountiful ways, the matriarch goddess statuesque and imperious, Quetzalcoatl's sister voluptuous and long-legged. Mal couldn't help envying their figures and their height, and supposed that that was what you were meant to do with goddesses of a certain kind. They had to be what a woman aspired to be and a man desired to have, otherwise what was the point of them?

Mostly, however, she concentrated on the grub, because it was superb and her belly badly needed filling.

More than once she caught Reston eyeing up Quetzalpetatl's rear view as the younger goddess sashayed out of the room. She found this unreasonably annoying.

"Out of your league, mate," she commented. "Way out."

"That wasn't why I was looking at her."

"Oh, I know exactly why you were looking at her and exactly which part of her you were looking at and all."

"Well, maybe a little. But the question I was actually asking myself was, if she was *my* sister, would I sleep with her?"

"That's terrible."

"Just idle speculation."

"No, what I mean is, you're trying to shift the blame for everything onto *her*, aren't you? It was all Quetzalpetatl's fault because she's so sexy. That's such a man thing to do. Like blaming a rape victim for dressing provocatively. 'She was asking for it.'"

"As I understand it, Quetzalpetatl and Quetzalcoatl were equal partners in crime – if incest is a crime."

"A moral one, if not a legal one."

"Anyway, the real culprit's Tezcatlipoca, surely. He's at the root of this whole sorry saga."

"Does it matter?" Mal said impatiently. "We're having dinner served to us by gods. I for one am just going to soak that fact up for the time being. The rest's immaterial." She tore off a sliver of cornmeal pancake and used it to scoop up a generous blob of chocolate-infused guacamole. It was delicious. The one word she didn't want to use to describe the taste – but she couldn't think of a better – was *divine*.

Reston looked down at himself. He was in borrowed clothing, as was she. The outfits hung baggily off both of them, several sizes too large. God garb, furnished by Quetzalcoatl.

"It's weird," he said. "I didn't have that Serpent armour on for long, but now I feel almost naked without it."

Mal nodded. "Who has it, again?"

"Quetzalcoatl said he was taking it to Toci. She's their resident science queen."

"To soup it up."

"And make it look less like Serpent hardware so as we don't take friendly fire by mistake."

"Why not just give us new kit instead? They must have spare suits of armour lying around."

"Nothing that would fit us, or haven't you noticed? I'm six foot and I'm a shrimp compared to them. Which makes you –"

"Steady."

"I was going to say perfectly proportioned, for a human."

"No, you were going to say even shrimpier."

"Hello! Hello!"

This fruity cry accompanied the arrival in the refectory of a woman, or was it a man? He or she strode straight up to the table and enfolded Mal and Reston in a double embrace, drawing them in towards a chest that was both muscular and soft. "You again," he or she said to Reston. "And this time you've brought your other half. Well done, you."

"I'm not his –" Mal began wearily.

"Dear," said the androgyne, all seriousness, "I'm Ometeotl. I know opposites, I know what complements what, and I know other halves. You're his. I can tell at a glance."

"No, really."

"You're everything he is not. He is everything you're not. You define each other as sea defines land, and between you is the beautiful friction that can only come when equal and opposing forces meet, like the crash and tumble of surf on a shore. I'm so glad you've both volunteered to join the fight. It's a sign – an encouraging one. Two humans who are oneness in duality. Couldn't be more apt."

Ometeotl let go of them and bustled onward to another table, where food awaited to be pounced on and devoured.

Mal couldn't look Reston in the eye, and vice versa.

More of the gods entered, but these ones, unlike Ometeotl, were footsore and battle-weary. They filed past, giving Mal and Reston looks that ranged from curious to hostile. None spoke to them save Mictlantecuhtli, who leaned in close and intoned, "Quetzalcoatl has extended his protection to cover you both. That is the thing that is keeping you alive for this heartbeat, and this one, and this one" – he snapped his fingers in time – "and it is the only thing.

Do not make me regret my consent to abide by the Plumed Serpent's wishes and my suppression of the urge to slay you where you sit. By which I mean, do not let us down in the field of combat tomorrow and be the weak link that breaks the chain. Or then, truly, you will know the Dark One's ire."

From anyone else, threats of this order would have brought a sharp retort to Mal's lips and possibly an invitation to step outside. But she had seen Mictlantecuhtli in action, and there was nothing in his face but hard, implacable menace. It radiated off him in invisible waves. He was an abyss, everything that was hopeless and pitiless in the world, everything that was despairing and brutal. She had seen eyes like his on stone-cold killers and also on their victims, but in neither case as chilling or as dead.

"Told you," Reston said after Mictlantecuhtli had moved on. "Next to him, Xipe Totec's a teddy bear."

"I heard that!" the Flayed One called out through a mouthful of chilli pepper gruel. "Watch your tongue, human."

Mal was feeling deeply uncomfortable and eager to leave. She'd never been in a room where she was so obviously unwelcome, not even as a Jaguar when raiding a suspect's home or rousting a cell of heretics. Just as she was about to get up to go, however, in came Quetzalcoatl himself. A hunched, dwarfish little creature lolloped along at his side. Xolotl, she presumed.

With little preamble Quetzalcoatl launched into a speech.

He gave an assessment of how the siege had gone so far. "According to plan – but plans have a nasty habit of falling apart, with little warning."

He congratulated his fellow gods on their martial prowess and on the vast differential in the casualty totals on either side. "Two of us have fallen, and that is two too many, and I mourn the sacrifice that Mixcoatl and Coyolxauhqui have made. But their loss is all the more reason to persist and prevail."

He advised everyone to take advantage of this pause in their assault. "Rest, recuperate, and prepare yourselves for a resumption of hostilities at first light."

Finally he drew attention to the two new additions to their ranks. "They represent the determination and forthrightness of this race that we have come to cherish. In siding with us, they prove their own worth and the worth of our cause. They are the best of their kind."

"Which isn't saying much," griped Xipe Totec.

"And that makes them the equal of any of us," Quetzalcoatl continued, staring hard at his heckler. "Their comparative physical shortcomings aside, they have heart, and heart is what counts."

Ometeotl cheered and clapped loudly. No one else did.

"'Til tomorrow, then," Quetzalcoatl concluded. "'Til the end."

MAL AND RESTON were assigned separate but adjacent rooms for the night, featureless, bare-necessities spaces like belowdecks cabins on an oceangoing freighter. Mal settled down on the narrow bed and closed her eyes. She was beyond exhausted. It had been an extraordinary day as well as a long and arduous one. Was it only this morning that she had been woken by the phone call from Mixquiahuala Jaguar HQ? A few hours and a lifetime ago. Now Aaronson was dead and Reston was, against all odds, an ally and not an enemy any more. Her whole world had been turned upside down and inside out. Everything was wrong and yet somehow right. She felt as though she was a riddle she'd always believed she knew the solution to, only to discover that the true solution was something else altogether.

To cap it all, tomorrow she was going to be part of a brigade of gods – gods! – attacking the home of another god with a view to ending him and his Empire. The same Empire she'd served loyally and indefatigably for nigh on a decade.

Little wonder that, for all her numbing fatigue, she couldn't sleep.

Eventually she got up.

She touched the door to her room and it vanished.

Keyed to my own bio-data. And it just pops out of existence. There's another thing to keep the old brain awake and racing.

She padded barefoot down the corridor to the next room.

Hesitated a hundred times about knocking, then knocked.

Then that door vanished too, and there stood

Reston, in just his underpants. A well muscled torso, with just the right amount of chest hair nestled between his pectorals.

Dammit.

"Can't sleep," she said.

"Me either. Should. Can't."

"Can I come in?"

"Shouldn't. Can."

She did.

They stood apart but facing, within reach of each other.

She put a hand on his forearm.

He moved the arm so that her hand fell into his.

"Ought we?" she said.

He nodded. "Ought. Will."

She took a step towards him. "You're still a smug dickhead, Reston. Know that."

"Stuart," he said.

"Mal."

THIRTY-TWO

4 Flower 1 Movement 1 House
(Friday 21st December 2012)

STUART LAY STROKING the hair of the maddening, mesmerising woman who lay snuggled against him. Her cheek was against his chest and she was snoring ever so slightly.

He cast his mind back to the previous night and smiled. Vaughn – Mal – had proved to be an energetic, enthusiastic lover. No surprises there. What had taken him aback was her overwhelming *need*, like the hunger of the starving. He had responded in kind, and there had been that sort of tough tenderness, that gentle greed, which typified the best lovemaking. The two of them had slotted together, fitted together, in a way Stuart had never experienced before. Not even with Sofia had he known the same mutual rightness or the same instinctive synchronisation. Barely speaking, communicating almost entirely through their bodies, he and Mal had brought each other to a climax that was gloriously gratifying. Mind-blowing, in fact. A moment of ecstasy that had erased all thought and ego, leaving no room inside him for anything other than itself. After that, sleep had come crashing over them both like a tidal wave.

If last night was a one-off, if it never happened again, Stuart could live with that. And if it wasn't, if it was the start of something more substantial, he could live with that too.

He was, he realised, content. For the first time since Sofia and Jake died, he was at peace.

Mal's serene sleeping face told him she was too.

Pity that today was scheduled to be –

A tremor shook the room.

Not just the room.

Stuart could feel it – the entire underground edifice shuddering around him.

"Huh, whuzzat?" said Mal foggily.

"Don't know." He leapt out of bed. "But I'm pretty sure it's not good."

The tremor subsided.

Then came another, fiercer, more violent.

"Earthquake?" said Mal, swinging off the bed and pulling a sheet around her.

"I don't think we're in a seismic activity zone." Stuart danced into a pair of underpants. "And even if we are, earthquakes feel like waves on a rough sea. This is more like –"

A third tremor overwrote the second. Everything in the room vibrated and shook.

Stuart disappeared the door. Distant shouts of alarm echoed along the corridor. He dashed out, Mal following. The first of the pantheon they encountered was Azcatl, who was scurrying along like one of his beloved arthropods.

Stuart grabbed him. "What's going on? What is this?"

"Unhand me!" snapped the Red Ant. "We're under attack is what's going on. Tezcatlipoca's forces. They've found us somehow. I must marshal my best shocktroops."

He hurried onward. Stuart looked at Mal. "Armour time."

"Where is it?"

"Toci's lab. Which is... this way, I think."

In truth, he had no idea. But as they ran, he hoped they would bump into another of the gods who would give them directions.

In the event, they bumped into Itzpapalotl. Stuart didn't know it was her, having never seen her sans armour. All he saw was a tall and impossibly athletic female, almost as dark-skinned as Mictlantecuhtli, moving with obvious urgency but not in a blind panic. He made a deduction and called out her name.

"We need our armour, too," he said. "Where do we find it?"

Without breaking stride, the Obsidian Butterfly made a gesture: *follow me.*

Two levels down, near the bottom of the inverted

ziggurat, lay a chamber that was part armoury, part laboratory. The equipment that filled it was mostly unrecognisable to Stuart and Mal, a plethora of sleek machines and subtle instruments whose nature and purpose they could only guess at. What was familiar was the jumble of it all. Offcuts and oddments littered workbenches. There were disorganised shelf-loads of tools and spare parts. Everywhere, a sprawl of unfinished projects and experiments-in-progress. Scientific chaos was scientific chaos, no matter if the scientist who generated it was also a goddess.

Itzpapalotl went straight to her suit of midnight-black armour and began clamping it on. Huitzilopochtli was already here, doing the same. A woman with a thatch of blonde hair and keen, beady eyes – Toci, it must be – was busy loading flame spears into the rack the Hummingbird God toted on his back.

"Toci, please, our armour...?" said Stuart.

Toci wagged a finger distractedly towards a corner of the room. The Serpent Warrior suits were set out on armatures, no longer as snake-featured as before. The helmets had been reshaped, their fronts flattened and the eye lenses joined up into a single bulbous visor. All of the sections had been recoloured, not mamba green now but a silvery blue that would afford some camouflage in the daytime sky. There were other modifications, such as l-gun attachments on both arms and the tips of blades projecting from the wrists.

"Been busy on those all night," Toci said. "You'll find them very much improved, although there's a limit to what I could do, given the crudeness of what I had to work with. Tezcatlipoca was never much of an engineer, and I discern human touches everywhere – shortcuts, quick fixes, general bodging, no finesse. The lightning guns are activated by studs on the palms of the gauntlets. They recharge more rapidly than you'll be used to, and last longer too. The blades extend to full length with a flick of either arm and retract the same way. Both of you, I understand, are proficient with swords. Of necessity, these ones are short, but they'll cut through anything short of a forcefield."

"Forcefields," said Stuart. "Any chance we have those?"

"Exclusive to Quetzalcoatl. Mictlantecuhtli has his gauntlets, Xipe Totec his knives, Huitzilopochtli his flame spears... Each a particular suite of capabilities, to fit each's individual style and temperament. There is no sharing or crossover. That is not our way. Be grateful for what you've got."

Another tremor rocked the gods' lair. It felt less potent than previous ones, but Stuart assumed that that was because they were deeper underground.

"Hurry," said Itzpapalotl. It was the first word Stuart had heard her utter, and he wasn't sure if the remark was directed at him and Mal or not.

The two humans helped each other into the customised Serpent suits, fast as they could manage. When only the helmets remained to be put on, Mal said, "Here we go. Can't say I'm not dreading this."

"You'd be crazy if you weren't."

"So much at stake."

"We'll just do what we can, leave the heavy lifting to the big boys like Huitzilopochtli."

"Stuart..."

He shook his head. "Last night was last night. I get that."

"No, what it is, is, I don't understand how I can have spent so many weeks wanting to see your heart cooking on a brazier, and now, suddenly, all that's gone. Now I'm actually worried about you."

"Maybe Ometeotl was right. We're meant to be together but until now the circumstances were against us. I mean *radically* against us."

"It's almost like some kind of joke, isn't it? Like the world was doing its very hardest to keep us apart."

"If 'apart' is another way of saying 'at each other's throats,' then yes, I'd agree."

"If I don't make it through this..." Mal began.

"In that case," Stuart said, securing his helmet on, "it's unlikely either of us will make it. The point is moot."

Mal had her helmet on too, so they were now talking via the strange intimacy of the comms link. "You don't want to hear what I have to say?"

"I do," Stuart replied. "And I will. But afterwards, all right?"

Itzpapalotl and Huitzilopochtli were leaving.

"Right now," he went on, "we've business to attend to. The world's not just going to save itself, you know. It's time for the new, improved Conquistador to go out there and shine. Oh, and his sidekick Jaguar Girl too."

"Call me your sidekick again, and I'll kick you in the side," Mal growled. "Fucker."

"That's the spirit."

"Fucker, fucker, fucker."

"Eloquent as always. Let's go."

TAKING FLIGHT, THEY followed in the wake of Itzpapalotl and Huitzilopochtli, up through the centre of the ziggurat to the hatch. When they emerged onto the surface, it was like entering some fiery, howling maelstrom. There were Serpent Warriors *everywhere*, swooping, swarming, shooting. The rainforest around the hatch was ablaze. Flames crackled. Smoke churned. The air was thick with falling ash and embers. L-gun fire streaked between the burning tree trunks, and now and then huge, not-so-far-off explosions erupted, seeming to shake whole acres of landscape.

Itzpapalotl and Huitzilopochtli wasted no time in engaging the enemy. Within seconds, Serpents were being blasted out of the air or sliced to ribbons.

It took Stuart and Mal slightly longer to gather their wits. A pair of Serpents came zooming at them on an attack run. Stuart targeted one, Mal the other. Plasma bolts zigzagged from their forearms and struck the Serpents with staggering force. One hurtled backwards into a cedar, crashing against the trunk and flopping down to its base, broken inside his armour. The other was sent sailing sideways and collided with a third airborne Serpent. They fell together in a tangle, and Mal was on them before they could extricate themselves from each other. She flicked her arm as Toci had instructed and the blade in her gauntlet snicked out to its full extension. One of the Serpents raised his l-gun and Mal slashed at it unthinkingly, slicing the barrel in two. The Serpent was almost as startled as she was, and his eyes widened further as she plunged the blade through his breastplate, deep into him.

The other Serpent made a bid to retrieve his own l-gun, which had been knocked from his grasp and landed a few yards away. He scrambled desperately on all fours, but was beaten to it by Stuart, who flew over him and alighted in his path, sword out. The next instant, a Serpent Warrior helmet went bouncing across the forest floor, with a Serpent Warrior's severed head inside.

Itzpapalotl and Huitzilopochtli had disappeared somewhere into the smoke haze, but more gods were emerging from below. Tzitzimitl and Azcatl took up positions on either side of the hatch, each accompanied by a retinue of monsters. Tzitzimitl had her leaping, yowling pack of Tzitzimime, while Azcatl was haloed by a dense, buzzing cloud of insects the likes of which neither Stuart nor Mal had ever seen. They were large, the size of a clenched fist, and appeared to be a hybrid of wasp, scorpion and stag beetle, with a stinger-tipped tail at the back, pincer-like horns at the front, and a yellow-striped abdomen.

Joining Tzitzimitl and Azcatl was a third god: the disfigured, hunchbacked entity whom Stuart remembered from his first ever visit to the refectory down below. Nanhuatzin, the Deformed One, limped up out from the hatch and stood, swaying somewhat. His arthritically clawed hands were outstretched, and a look of grim delight was discernible on his twisted face.

"Go!" Azcatl ordered Stuart and Mal. "Get out there. The main battle is that way" – he waved in a westward direction – "and that is where you can be the most help, if you can be any help at all."

"We can defend this spot," Tzitzimitl added. "No one will get past us."

"Are you sure?" Stuart said.

The crone's eyes flashed. "Watch."

A squadron of Serpents came gliding in through the pall of smoke. Tzitzimitl, with a loud whistle, despatched her Tzitzimime at them. The dark demon dogs sprang up and brought down one of the Serpents in midair. They dragged him to the ground and set about him in a snarling, slavering pack, going for the joints, the vulnerable chinks between sections of his armour. His screams, relayed by the comms, were shrill in Stuart's and Mal's ears. As the Tzitzimime tore him apart and ate him alive, he was begging for his mother to save him.

Meanwhile Azcatl unleashed his scorpion-wasp monstrosities, which whizzed towards the Serpents like rocks from a catapult. They butted through faceplates and set about stinging straight away, clinging on with their pincer horns while their sinuous tails jabbed and jabbed repeatedly into cheek and nose and eyeball. The venom worked almost instantaneously; their Serpent victims went rigid with paralysis and became floating corpses, hovering stiff and lifeless in the air, supported only by their suits.

As for Nanahuatzin, he waited until one of the Serpents strayed close to the hatch, and then he simply reached out and brushed the man with his fingertips. Something glistened briefly between him and the Serpent. Something was *transferred*. The Serpent turned and trained his l-gun on Nanahuatzin, but all at once his limbs went weak and wouldn't function properly. Over the comms link Stuart heard him say something about being unable to breathe. The man dropped the weapon and fumbled to get his helmet off. His face had gone a vivid, liverish puce. Sores were breaking out all over his skin, all manner of blisters, buboes and pustules. The whites of his eyes went scarlet. He opened his mouth to scream but no sound came out, only a vomitous gush of blood. He fell, wracked with agony, as what seemed to be every communicable disease that had ever existed infested his body, proliferating at an obscene rate. By the time he stopped writhing and lay still, fluids were seeping out through all the seals in his armour and his face was so distended by swellings and lesions that it no longer resembled anything human.

"Fair enough," Stuart said to the three gods. "Mal? This way."

They flew through the burning forest. They drew their heading by the rising number of Serpent corpses that littered the ground, a trail of the dead left by the other gods. The comms chatter they were picking up over their helmet radios grew as they approached. It wasn't long before they arrived at the epicentre of the battle.

There were several hundred Serpents in flight, orbiting an enormous humanoid machine, which advanced slowly, step by thunderous step. It was near enough the size of a house, with arms that ended in multiple lightning gun arrays and legs that balanced on jointed, talon-like feet. The l-guns cleaved trees in two and the feet crushed their toppled trunks to splinters as the giant thing waded purposefully through the forest.

Five of the gods were attempting to get near this mechanical behemoth, but the Serpents kept thwarting them, attacking in such numbers that the gods were too busy coping with them to achieve anything else.

On the ground, Xipe Totec and Mictlantecuhtli were close to being overwhelmed by the sheer number of opponents they faced. The Flayed One's knives flashed relentlessly, the Dark One's gauntlets crushed and bludgeoned, and still the Serpents kept on coming, crowding in on them from all quarters.

In the air, Itzpapalotl was unable to dart through the droves of Serpents. Whichever way she turned, she was intercepted and driven back by l-gun fire. Likewise Huitzilopochtli. His flame spears took out a half-dozen Serpents at a time, but every time he created a gap it was plugged by a half-dozen more.

Only Quetzalcoatl was making any headway, and then not much. He was barely visible through the crackling storm of plasma bolts that pounded against his forcefield. He flew like someone swimming against a powerful current, fighting for every inch of progress.

And still the massive manlike machine moved inexorably forwards.

"Tezcatlipoca," Mal said.

The Smoking Mirror could be seen through a screen of glass set in the thing's torso. He was enclosed in a kind of cat's cradle of light beams which synched his movements to those of the machine. He raised an arm, so did the giant. He shifted his legs, the giant strode.

"It's... a bigger suit of armour," Stuart said. "The biggest ever." He sounded, in spite of himself, impressed.

"Size isn't everything," Mal said curtly.

"Now you tell me. So what should we do?"

"Take him down if we can. He clearly wants to get to the gods' headquarters and destroy it, and all their backup and resources with it. Destroy them, too. We do our bit to stop him. Or rather, *you* do."

"Huh?" Stuart was startled by the sudden change in her tone of voice. It had dropped to an icy hush. She was staring hard at the forwardmost grouping of Serpent Warriors, the vanguard of the attack force. One of them stood out from the rest, distinguished by the gold patterning on his armour.

"There you are, you bastard," Mal said. She was aloft before Stuart could stop her.

"Mal!" he remonstrated. "No. He's a sideshow. He's not important."

"Maybe to you he's not," came the reply. "Colonel

Tlanextic!" She had switched to Nahuatl. "Can you hear me? I'm here. Over here. Come and get what's coming to you."

"The Vaughn bitch." Tlanextic's caustic voice cut through the babel of comms chatter, loud and clear. "How interesting. That's you in that silver suit?"

Stuart saw the gold-patterned figure break away from the main pack and head for Mal.

"I could have sworn you were dead," Tlanextic said.

"Should have checked more thoroughly, shouldn't you?"

"An oversight I shall remedy now."

"Remedy *this*, motherfucker," said Mal, and she let him have it with both her l-guns.

Tlanextic returned fire, and there ensued a dogfight which Stuart would have followed more closely if he himself hadn't come under assault from several quarters at once. The Serpents had finally latched on to him as an enemy combatant.

For minutes on end Stuart fended off a co-ordinated barrage of plasma bolts and delivered rapid-fire ripostes. Now and then he caught glimpses of Mal and Tlanextic weaving around and blasting away at each other above the tree canopy. He was also aware of Tezcatlipoca stalking ever onward in his ogre of a suit, forging a path through the rainforest.

At one point, amid all the bedlam, it seemed as though the gods had made a breakthrough. Xipe Totec had dispatched enough Serpents to give himself some breathing space and a clear run at Tezcatlipoca. Mictlantecuhtli urged him forward, promising to handle any interference that might come his way.

Huitzilopochtli had an opening too. He had at last punched a hole through the endless flocks of Serpents. Tezcatlipoca was in range and in his sights.

Xipe Totec sprinted towards the left leg of Tezcatlipoca's suit, while Huitzilopochtli levelled his spear launcher at Tezcatlipoca's head.

Stuart sensed that this was when everything could change, the fulcrum moment that would set the battle seesawing in the gods' favour.

Then Xipe Totec stumbled. That was when Stuart realised the Flayed One had been injured. With his skin transparent, wounds were not immediately obvious. Spilled blood did not show up against the wet muscle tissue on display. Several Serpents must have got in lucky shots before Xipe Totec slew them. He was weak, failing. His charge towards Tezcatlipoca was a last-ditch suicide run.

And Tezcatlipoca knew it. As Xipe Totec lost his footing, the Smoking Mirror turned his ponderous armoured bulk towards him. One of the legs rose. Xipe Totec scrambled upright and continued his bid to reach Tezcatlipoca. But the vast foot overshadowed him. It descended like a five-ton piston. The Flayed One's knives shot up. In defence? In defiance? It was hard to say.

Tezcatlipoca crushed Xipe Totec underfoot as a child might crush a snail on a garden path. The Flayed One became the Flattened One. He *burst*, and now all of his viscera were exposed. He was a lump of gristle and offal attached to the underside of Tezcatlipoca's foot. The Smoking Mirror stamped down again and again, smashing and mashing Xipe Totec until there was even less of him left, just a gory smear.

Huitzilopochtli overcame his shock at seeing a fellow god annihilated and loosed off a flame spear at Tezcatlipoca. But the Smoking Mirror lashed out with one of his vast arms, batting the projectile aside so that it spun end over end and detonated amidst the foliage of a tree. As the Hummingbird God hurried to reload his launcher, Tezcatlipoca calmly lined up a shot with the same arm.

Huitzilopochtli looked up, flame spear in hand.

Looked down the hollowness of that l-gun barrel.

Knew he was out of time.

He hung in the air, resigned, and was enveloped in a tremendous torrent of plasma.

Little remained of Huitzilopochtli as he fell to earth, just a charred, spindly effigy, like a scarecrow that had been pulled off a bonfire.

Tezcatlipoca's guffaws of joy came loud and clear over Stuart's comms. His giant metal shell seemed to laugh too, rocking up and down in grotesque emulation of its driver.

Mictlantecuhtli lunged for Tezcatlipoca, emitting a roar, a primal wordless bellow of rage. He ploughed through the massed ranks of Serpents, scattering them to either side. Stuart followed in his slipstream. The Dark One took an l-gun salvo from Tezcatlipoca full-on, crossing his gauntlets above his head to shield himself, and plasma broke over him like rain on an umbrella. He lumbered on, skin smouldering, and began pounding away at Tezcatlipoca's leg, the same leg that had squashed Xipe Totec. He managed to put a few dents in it before the Smoking Mirror used his other leg to kick him like a *tlachtli* ball. Mictlantecuhtli was propelled high into the air, disappearing into the depths of the forest.

Stuart stood alone and horribly exposed. Tezcatlipoca towered over him. He fired off a shot at the glass screen in the armour's chest. The bolt didn't leave so much as a scratch.

"Ah, the erstwhile Conquistador." Tezcatlipoca was plugged into the Serpent Warrior radio frequency. "Still around to plague us. Well, not for much longer."

Tezcatlipoca's arm came down. A half-dozen lightning-gun barrels were pointed Stuart's way.

"Incoming!"

That was Mal, and she streaked down from on high, locked in a frantic embrace with Tlanextic. Twisting and turning, the two of them rammed sideways into Tezcatlipoca's arm. The plasma bolt meant for Stuart gouged a furrow in the ground inches to his right.

Stuart didn't hesitate. He sprang at Tezcatlipoca's foot, flicking out his swords. Toci had said they would cut through anything.

Let's see, shall we?

He cross-cut into the metal of the foot with a simultaneous outward swing of both blades. Unbelievably, there was almost no resistance. Stuart found himself looking at a deep X-shaped slash in the armour's skin. Hydraulics and cables were laid bare. Sparks spat.

He darted behind Tezcatlipoca and cut again. Surely he could stop the mechanical beast by hobbling it.

Next thing he knew, he was flat on his back. Tlanextic was on top of him. The Serpent colonel pummelled him hard, landing armour-augmented blows which Stuart could feel even through his own armour.

"You don't get it, do you, Englishman?" Tlanextic said. "The Empire is eternal. The Empire is unstoppable. *Gods* cannot stand in its way. Do you honestly think a turd-eating little maggot like *you* can?"

"Mal..." It was partly a question, partly a plea. Where was she? If Tlanextic was free of her, then what had become of her?

"I shook the bitch off. Our landing took more out of her than me. I'll deal with her after you. Now, just fucking lie there while I beat you to death, eh?"

Stuart couldn't bring the swords to bear. He was nailed to the earth by Tlanextic's remorseless thumping.

"I know this armour's limitations," Tlanextic crowed. "I know what it can handle. I'll open you up like a sardine can. I'll shatter you. Pulverise you."

The impacts were intensifying. Stuart could feel the armour losing integrity. Tlanextic's blows were starting to hurt.

How much more could he withstand?

How much could the armour?

He put everything he had into an attempt to shove himself upwards, against the force of Tlanextic's onslaught. He lodged an elbow in the soil, so that one sword was pointing upwards. Tlanextic grabbed his wrist and levered the arm away. Stuart fought to raise it again. Tlanextic continued to hammer him with his other hand.

The sword wavered between them, now vertical, now at an angle. The pain in Stuart's chest was mounting. There was a sudden sharp spike of agony, accompanied by a *crack* that he felt as much as heard. A rib. He cried out involuntarily.

Tlanextic's eyes held nothing but the grim resolution of a loyal solider keen to see his mission through.

Then, all at once, his gaze became vacant and the punching stopped. There was no longer any resistance against Stuart's arm.

Without pausing to question what had happened, Stuart rammed the sword up into Tlanextic's belly.

"Too late, slowcoach," said Mal. "I got there first."

Tlanextic was doubly impaled. Mal had skewered him from behind, Stuart from the front.

The Serpent colonel was still alive, but paralysed, helpless. Mal reared back, Stuart rose, both of them heaving Tlanextic upright. They held him fast between them like some sort of human spit roast. Tlanextic's hands moved feebly, groping for the blades as if he genuinely hoped to pull them out of himself. It would have been a pitiable sight, had it been anyone else.

"I promised you, didn't I, colonel?" Mal said. "Not quite with my bare hands, but close enough. You should never have turned your back on me."

She gave the sword a vicious twist. Tlanextic let out a wet, sucking gasp.

"The Empire..." he choked.

"Fuck the fucking Empire," Mal said, and twisted the sword even further.

Tlanextic shuddered. His eyes rolled to white.

On an unspoken cue, Stuart and Mal withdrew their swords. Tlanextic's body crumpled to the ground.

They took a moment to survey each other.

"Your armour's knackered," Mal observed.

"Yours isn't looking too clever either."

Both suits were covered in dents and scored with scorch marks. Mal's visor was cracked. Stuart's breastplate had been beaten concave, like a steel drum. His torso throbbed. Every heartbeat brought a spasm of pain in his ribs.

"Where's Tezcatlipoca?"

Mal turned. The battle had moved on, but it wasn't difficult to figure out which way it had gone. "Just follow the big damn tunnel in the trees."

THEY CAUGHT UP with Tezcatlipoca in no time, and what was immediately clear was that Stuart's assault on the giant suit of armour's heel hadn't crippled it but had slowed it. The thing was limping now, teetering a little each time it put its left foot down.

It had almost reached the hatch.

Quetzalcoatl was still valiantly trying to force his way through to Tezcatlipoca, and Itzpapalotl the same, but enough Serpent Warriors remained to hinder them. Tzitzimitl, Azcatl and Nanahuatzin continued to protect the entrance to their base from raids by advance parties of Serpents. Xolotl was there too now, harrying and savaging the enemy.

"One more try," Stuart sighed.

"With our suits in the state they're in?"

"No one said life was easy."

"No one ever does. I wish one day someone would."

As they started forwards, a figure charged out from the trees, head down like a maddened bull.

Mictlantecuhtli used a fallen trunk as a springboard to propel himself up onto Tezcatlipoca's back. He collided fists-first with the giant suit of armour and rebounded. Tezcatlipoca was staggered by the blow. Mictlantecuhtli picked himself up and went on the offensive again, this time striking behind the knee. The giant went down onto its other knee. The Dark One leapt straight onto its head, his sheer momentum toppling the machine flat onto its face. It crashed to earth, limbs flailing cumbersomely. The impact of its toppling nearly knocked Stuart and Mal off their own feet.

Mictlantecuhtli's gauntlets clanged down onto the giant's back. Sparks flew, and fragments of metal. At that moment Itzpapalotl shook off the cluster of Serpents around her and swooped to assist the Dark One. Wrenching, tearing, battering, they prised their way into the behemoth like treasure seekers digging for gold.

Stuart was convinced Tezcatlipoca had had it; Mal was, too. The Smoking Mirror's remaining life could be measured in seconds.

Then the back of the giant erupted outwards, and

Mictlantecuhtli and Itzpapalotl were sent flying amid a welter of shards and debris.

From out of the hole in his immense machine, like a parasite worming its way out of its host body, crawled Tezcatlipoca. He looked unhurt. Worse, he looked unruffled. He was clad in a form-fitting metallic bodysuit whose mercury-like surface offered a dim, warped reflection of everything around him. This was, Stuart assumed, another form of armour. Tezcatlipoca had been wearing a suit of armour inside a suit of armour.

"Well, that was fun," the Smoking Mirror said. The armour's mask was a perfect, gleaming replica of the face beneath it. "I was dying to take my walking tank out for a test drive. I'm just amazed I got this far with it. Do you hear me, Quetzalcoatl? Almost at your doorstep before you managed to take me down. Sloppy. I expected more from you."

Tzitzimitl gave one of her shrill whistles. Her pack of Tzitzimime, as one, broke off from attacking Serpent Warriors and loped towards Tezcatlipoca.

The Smoking Mirror allowed them to get close, then raised an imperious hand and engulfed almost the entire pack in a sizzling, coruscating blast of energy that came straight from his palm. Most of the demon dogs were cremated on the spot, to Tzitzimitl's howling dismay, but a few dodged the attack and raced on. They jumped up onto the sprawled machine and pounced on Tezcatlipoca. He swiped several aside, then grabbed one by the hindleg and swung the creature like a club, using it to bludgeon the others. Savage snarls turned to yelps of pain and terror. Tzitzimitl sobbed and tore at her hair as her beloved monsters were methodically beaten to a pulp. Soon none was left alive, and a blood-spattered Tezcatlipoca stood with a mangled Tzitzimime in his hand and a dozen more shattered corpses at his feet.

Now it was Azcatl's turn, but his scorpion-wasps didn't fare any better. They couldn't penetrate Tezcatlipoca's armour, or even gain purchase on its smooth contours. Azcatl guided them to attack again and again, moving his hands like an orchestra conductor, manipulating the swarm remotely, shaping their actions. Tezcatlipoca just stood there and laughed.

"Is that the best you can do, Red Ant?" he sneered. "Your trouble is, you think too small-scale. I, on the other hand – I imagine bigger. Always have. And that is why I rule a planet, while you rule *insects*."

A sphere of brilliance exploded outward around him. It came and went in a dazzling instant, and when it was gone, none of the scorpion-wasps remained. They had all been obliterated, literally in a flash.

"No!" Azcatl cried.

At that moment, Quetzalcoatl took radical action. A score of Serpent Warriors surrounded him on all sides, subjecting his forcefield to a 360° point-blank assault with their l-guns. Quetzalcoatl switched off the forcefield, and shot upwards at the same time.

The Serpents blasted one another, while Quetzalcoatl soared free...

...and plummeted straight down onto Tezcatlipoca like a living missile, hitting him feet-first.

The two brothers slammed together into the giant armour beneath them. They rose as one, grappling hand to hand. Quetzalcoatl's features showed nothing but implacable determination. "This ends now, Tez," he said through clenched teeth.

Tezcatlipoca's mask reflected Quetzalcoatl's face back at him, dark and distorted. "Long past time," he replied.

"How did you even find us?"

"It was easier than you think. Coyolxauhqui. She gave me the co-ordinates of your little hidey-hole."

"Not willingly, I'll bet."

"Not at all. She took some persuading. It was the promise of an end to her pain that finally broke her. And an end did come."

"Bastard!" Quetzalcoatl roared.

They took off, still locked in a mutual death grip. Smoke swirled in vortices as they ascended. Xolotl ran in circles, howling in distress as his master rose out of sight.

Stuart didn't know if his armour was still fully functioning. He raised his head and lifted off unsteadily. The armour felt sluggish, but it was working.

"Stuart!"

"I have to follow them, Mal. This is the endgame. I have to see how it plays out."

"But all these Serpents still left..."

"The gods can handle them."

It was true. Tzitzimitl and Azcatl had no

more mutant creatures on hand to deploy, and Nanahuatzin's disease-giving abilities were of limited use, but Mictlantecuhtli and Itzpapalotl were both back on their feet. The two of them could mop up the Serpents, no trouble.

Mal went after Stuart. She couldn't deny it: she too had to find out how this was all going to end. She told herself she and Stuart might be of help to the Plumed Serpent, but knew it was unlikely. She was motivated by sheer curiosity, nothing more.

Above the canopy, they spotted Quetzalcoatl and Tezcatlipoca racing westward. The Smoking Mirror had broken free from his brother's clutches and was streaking away at astounding speed. The Plumed Serpent was in hot pursuit. It wasn't hard to guess where Tezcatlipoca was headed. Only one thing lay in that direction: Tenochtitlan.

EVEN IN PRIME condition, Serpent armour was no match for the gods'. Stuart and Mal lost sight of Quetzalcoatl and Tezcatlipoca before reaching Lake Texcoco, and arrived at the island city several minutes after did. They searched all over, scanning the ruined towers and fire-gutted ziggurats. Eventually Mal spied a group of people – engineers in overalls – fleeing across a plaza in a panic. It wasn't hard to guess what they running from, and where.

The city's fusion plant sported a fresh, gaping hole in its roof. The building resounded to tumultuous bangs and crashes, as though boulders were being tossed about within. Stuart and Mal made a careful descent into its interior.

The plant's main chamber was strewn with rubble. Walls, floors and support columns all bore man-size craters. Steam hissed from fissures in the massive ducts leading from the turbines.

Quetzalcoatl and Tezcatlipoca rampaged to and fro. Every now and then they strayed close to the confinement unit, a huge, electromagnet-studded steel torus which contained the fusion plasma and kept it at the density necessary for a chain reaction to be effective. The two gods had eyes for nothing but each other. They battled with the passionate hatred that only close kin could feel. Every blow that landed was struck from the heart. Weapons had been set aside for the time being: this needed to be physical, the direct, personal infliction of pain. Centuries of estrangement and pent-up resentment were spewing out in a flood of rage. Neither of them would stop – or be content – until the other was dead by his hand.

Who was winning? It was hard to tell. They seemed evenly matched. Tezcatlipoca was the stronger, to judge by how he threw his brother around, hoisting him off the floor as though he was a foam-stuffed dummy and hurling him with ease. Quetzalcoatl, however, had speed on his side. Repeatedly he got inside Tezcatlipoca's defences to deliver a punishing series of jabs and hooks, until Tezcatlipoca was able to push him off with a powerful counterattack.

Mal, as she hovered beside Stuart, looking down

on the conflict, was conscious of being a witness to something unique and epochal. The air around the two gods seemed alive with energy, as though their rivalry was charging the atmosphere like a thunderstorm. They were superhumans trying to tear each other apart, in a world where, to them, everything was made of tinfoil and paper. Effortlessly, Tezcatlipoca sent Quetzalcoatl sailing through a plate glass partition. Equally effortlessly, Quetzalcoatl wrenched a control console off the floor and brought it crashing down on Tezcatlipoca's head.

"We're helpless," she said.

"Even if we weren't, we can't get involved," Stuart said. "This is their fight. They have to settle it their way."

"I hate feeling so useless."

"I'd suggest prayer... only it's them we're supposed to pray to."

Tezcatlipoca locked his fingers around Quetzalcoatl's neck. The Plumed Serpent broke the grip, slamming Tezcatlipoca's arms outwards, and sent his brother reeling with a headbutt so hard that it partially shattered the silvery mask. He pressed home the advantage by shoving him hard against the confinement unit.

A ragged sliver of Tezcatlipoca's face was now exposed. He glared up at Quetzalcoatl, hatred blazing in his visible eye. Quetzalcoatl punched him repeatedly, relentlessly. Blood spurted from Tezcatlipoca's nose. The mask crumbled away in fragments until there was none of it left, just a jagged hole in the front of

Tezcatlipoca's helmet. The Smoking Mirror flailed at his brother, trying to ward him off, but Quetzalcoatl kept up the attack, seeming to sense that this was it, the decisive moment.

"Please..." Tezcatlipoca mumbled.

Quetzalcoatl halted.

"P-please, brother. Enough."

"You submit?"

Tezcatlipoca nodded weakly.

Quetzalcoatl backed off.

Tezcatlipoca grinned. "Gullible as ever, Kay."

Light burst out of him. Quetzalcoatl staggered backwards, stunned.

"You had me on the ropes," Tezcatlipoca said, straightening. "Yet you couldn't bring yourself to do what had to be done – finish me off. A conscience like yours hamstrings you."

With a roar, Quetzalcoatl threw himself at him. Again, Tezcatlipoca collided with the confinement unit, this time with such force that its outer shell ruptured.

An alarm sounded. A recorded voice announced, "Torus breached. Torus breached. Plant will go into automatic shutdown."

Mal turned to Stuart. "I don't know about you, but I'm getting the hell out of here."

"What for?" he replied. "There's no danger to us. The fusion reaction dies down as soon as the power to the magnets is turned off. There may be a plasma escape, but while we're hovering up here, we're not near enough for that to matter. The only people liable to get burned are those two."

Quetzalcoatl bore down on Tezcatlipoca, one forearm to his windpipe. "I *can* kill you," he growled, "and I will. You're nothing but scum. Our mother should have strangled you at birth."

"You keep blaming me for your own failings, Kay," Tezcatlipoca said, choking the words out. "Accept some responsibility for once in your life."

"I blame you for everything. I'm innocent."

"Kill me then, if it'll make you feel better about yourself. But know this. If I die, so does this world and everyone on it."

"What?"

"Yes. All these humans you're so fond of. All gone."

"You're lying."

"Am I? Don't you think I didn't anticipate that a moment like this might come? I've installed a failsafe system in this armour. If it stops detecting any life signs, it initiates a countdown. A signal is sent out worldwide to every fusion plant on every active volcano."

"This is nonsense."

"The fusion plants go into overdrive, forcing massive eruptions. Earth's volcanoes, all fifteen hundred of them, explode simultaneously. Fault lines shatter. Tectonic plates are split asunder. An entire planet rips itself to pieces."

"You wouldn't."

"The infrastructure is in place. If I can't have this world, then neither can you."

"I don't believe you," said Quetzalcoatl. "When has anything that's come out of your mouth ever been true?"

"I'm telling the truth now. I know how precious this world is to you, the high hopes you have for its inhabitants. You wouldn't risk their lives just to take mine, would you?"

"Try me."

"Then go ahead. Do it."

The confinement unit juddered beneath Tezcatlipoca's back. Tongues of translucent orange flame licked out from the fissure near his head.

"You can't win, Kay," said the Smoking Mirror hoarsely. "Kill me, you lose. Don't kill me, you also lose. I've outwitted you again, brother. You may be the noble one, but I'm the smart one. Brains beat good intentions every time."

Quetzalcoatl bent further over his brother, pinning him down harder.

Stuart swooped down to his side. "Don't," he said. "Can't you see it's what he wants? He's goading you. Don't play into his hands."

The Plumed Serpent didn't look round. "Stay out of this, Reston."

"I can't. I believe him, even if you don't. As the Great Speaker, he had control over volcanoes. He must have known all along that he might need a backup plan, something that would be sure to deter you. This is it."

"Heed your human mascot, Kay," said Tezcatlipoca. "He's wise."

"Leave him be, Quetzalcoatl," Stuart urged. "There must be some other way of resolving this."

"This is not your concern!" Quetzalcoatl bellowed,

and with an almost casual flick of his arm, he swatted Stuart aside. Stuart struck a wall, and his chest filled with fire. It felt as though more than one rib was broken now. It hurt simply to breathe.

Mal came down and squatted beside him.

"We have to stop him," Stuart told her.

"Great idea. How?"

There wasn't a *how*. The fate of the world now hung on a god's whim. It was all down to Quetzalcoatl.

"These are my terms," said Tezcatlipoca. "Let me go free. Return to Tamoanchan, you and the others. Never return here again. Accede this world fully to me. It's no longer your project. It hasn't been for half a millennium. It's mine."

"No."

"I understand humans far better than you do. They're not worth your time. They don't deserve to be exalted, only ruled and managed. Look at those two over there. A killer and a slave. And they're about the best of the lot."

"Humans are admirable. As a race. As a whole."

"Stop deluding yourself."

"Stop trying to delude me."

"I'm being honest. Perhaps it's time you started being honest with yourself."

"I'm not listening to you. I listened to you before, and..."

"Yes, that turned out well, didn't it?"

"Be quiet!" Quetzalcoatl snapped.

"You and Quetzalpetatl..."

"I said be quiet!"

"Sisterfucker," Tezcatlipoca spat.

Quetzalcoatl hauled Tezcatlipoca sideways, so that his head was over the breach in the confinement unit.

Fire lashed out in flickering lambent arcs, touching Tezcatlipoca's face.

Tezcatlipoca screamed.

So did Mal, in protest. So did Stuart.

Quetzalcoatl held his brother's face to the scorching curls of plasma. He closed his eyes tight. Tezcatlipoca shook and shuddered, bucked and squirmed. Skin blackened and peeled. Flesh melted. Smoke coiled upwards. Soon bone showed through.

Quetzalcoatl let go only when his brother's body fell still. He dropped Tezcatlipoca to the floor and heaved a deep, trembling sigh. He stood staring at the faceless corpse for several moments.

"It had to be this way, Tez," he said. "Don't you see? It had to be."

MAL ROSE. "WHAT have you done?" she said, in cold fury.

"Freed you. Liberated you." Quetzalcoatl's tone was matter-of-fact. *What could be more obvious?*

"But the failsafe... The fusion plants..."

"Tezcatlipoca had your race so brainwashed, so cowed, you'd fall for anything he said. Luckily I was able to see through his deceit."

"How can you be so sure?"

"I know my brother. This was a desperate, last-ditch gamble. Of course it was. He was preying on my one real weakness – you humans. He would never –"

Faintly, through their feet, they felt a vibration. It swelled then faded, like the hum of a tuning fork.

"He would never..." Quetzalcoatl repeated, faltering.

The vibration came again, stirring up dust.

Quetzalcoatl took off, zooming up through the hole in the roof.

Mal knelt by Stuart again. "Think you can move?"

"Everything hurts, but yes."

Their suits of armour carried them unsteadily skyward. Outside, above Tenochtitlan, Quetzalcoatl was scanning the horizon in all directions. His movements were agitated.

"This can't be," he muttered. "He wouldn't. He didn't."

"You fool," said Mal. "You big fucking arrogant twat."

"How dare you talk to me like that?" But it lacked conviction.

"It's happening, isn't it? Just like Tezcatlipoca said."

"I..."

"You didn't listen. You were too bound up in your petty vengeance. And now look what you've done."

"I can fix it." This, too, lacked conviction.

"Oh yeah? Fucking *how*?"

"I can..." Quetzalcoatl broke off. He bowed his head. "I don't know how."

"You've screwed us all. Do you realise that?"

Faintly: "Yes." Then, with a little more strength: "But I can save you. You two, at least. Come with me."

"Where to?"

"Tamoanchan."

"Tamoanchan exists?" said Stuart.

"It's a world," said Quetzalcoatl. "And such a world, too. A world where there are many like us. Where you can be like us."

"You aren't gods, are you?" Somehow, Stuart had known this all along. Ever since his first visit to the underground ziggurat. "You call yourselves that, and by comparison with us you are. But you aren't. Not really. You're scientists, that's all. Scientists and warriors."

Quetzalcoatl's silence confirmed it.

"From somewhere like earth."

Another silence.

"You live longer than us, you've discovered more than us, and you enjoy being hailed as gods by us. But you aren't and never have been."

"It seemed as good a description as any," Quetzalcoatl said. "A useful shorthand. And what is 'god,' after all, but the name a lesser being gives to a superior one? A dog's owner is god to that dog."

"Superior?" said Mal scornfully. "That's a laugh. You're so superior, how come you just signed our planet's death warrant?"

"I'll say it again: come with me. We'll join the others. There's still time. We can leave. Tamoanchan lies just a sidestep away. Our underground ziggurat isn't just our beachhead, it's our transportation – a gateway through the interstices between worlds."

"Go with you," said Stuart, "and be treated like talking monkeys for the rest of our lives?"

"It won't be like that."

"Oh, no?"

"I can look after you. I'll – I'll hold you up as ideal specimens of your kind."

"Specimens," snorted Mal.

"Look at the two of you. Oneness in duality. Duality in oneness. My people will respect you. Revere you, even. I guarantee it."

The sky had begun to shimmer – waves of gossamer iridescence rippling across the blueness. The surface of Lake Texcoco pulsed and heaved. The walls of Tenochtitlan quivered. Birds took to the air, squawking in fright.

"It's that or perish," Quetzalcoatl insisted. "I'm offering you survival. Just you two, alone out of billions. You should be flattered. Honoured."

Stuart and Mal looked at each other.

"Choose," said the Plumed Serpent, holding out a hand to them. "Now or never."

THIRTY-THREE

Same Day

THEY ALIGHTED ATOP a high, undamaged tower. They removed their helmets, smoothed out their hair, raised their sweat-drenched faces to the breeze.

You could feel it. Hear it. The earth groaning. The world turning on itself, harming itself. Hot, unnatural gusts of wind blew, constantly shifting direction. Whitecaps criss-crossed on the lake in overlapping layers. The sun seemed to dance in the sky.

"So," said Mal to Stuart.

"Be fair to him, it was a generous offer."

"Motivated by pure guilt. The bastard never really meant it."

"I think he did. But we'd never have lasted there. Tamoanchan. We'd have been curiosities at best. Zoo creatures."

"We've done the right thing."

"We've done the right thing. We should feel proud."

"The only thing I feel is scared."

He slipped an arm round her and hugged her close, even though it was exquisite agony for him.

"Gods are lies," he said. "And liars. They leave nothing but pain and disaster in their wake. We're better off without them."

"Yeah, better off." Mal gave an acerbic laugh. "Volcanoes are blowing their lids all across the globe. Seas are going to boil. Earthquakes are going to crack continents in two. But hoo-fucking-ray for us, we don't have gods any more."

"It'll be quick."

"You think?"

"I hope."

"And no chance of...?"

"Civilisation pulling through somehow? Doubt it. The skies will be clouded with ash for years to come. Maybe some people won't be killed instantly, a few, but there'll be no sunlight, no crops, nothing for them to eat."

"Shit."

"Precisely."

They were silent for a while, listening to the far-off, elemental rumbling that seemed to come from everywhere and nowhere.

"I don't love you, Stuart Reston," Mal said, "but I could have."

"I'm very loveable, once you get to know me."

"You stuck-up arsehole."

"True. True."

And so they sat side by side on the high tower, at the heart of a decapitated Empire, and waited for the world to end.

Acknowledgements

Let's just name names. In no particular order: Jes Bickham, Gary Main, Andy Remic, Jonathan Oliver, David Moore, Ben Smith, Michael Molcher, Nick Sharps, Andrew Miller, Jonathan Morgantini, Kirsty Reid, Eric Brown, Adam Roberts, Roger Levy, Nick Archdale, Hugo Degenhardt, Andy Neal, Ian Whates, Keith Brooke, Kit Reed, Philip Palmer, and Paul and Kelly Wilson. Writing's a solitary, sometimes lonely business. It's nice to have people around who make it less so.

And, as ever, I couldn't have done it without Lou. True 100%.

JAMES LOVEGROVE'S *PANTHEON* SERIES

THE AGE OF RA

UK ISBN: 978 1 844167 46 3 • US ISBN: 978 1 844167 47 0 • £7.99/$7.99

The Ancient Egyptian gods have defeated all the other pantheons and divided the Earth into warring factions. Lt. David Westwynter, a British soldier, stumbles into Freegypt, the only place to have remained independent of the gods, and encounters the followers of a humanist freedom-fighter known as the Lightbringer. As the world heads towards an apocalyptic battle, there is far more to this leader than it seems...

THE AGE OF ZEUS

UK ISBN: 978 1 906735 68 5 • US ISBN: 978 1 906735 69 2 • £7.99/$7.99

The Olympians appeared a decade ago, living incarnations of the Ancient Greek gods, offering order and stability at the cost of placing humanity under the jackboot of divine oppression. Until former London police officer Sam Akehurst receives an invitation to join the Titans, the small band of battlesuited high-tech guerillas squaring off against the Olympians and their mythological monsters in a war they cannot all survive...

THE AGE OF ODIN

UK ISBN: 978 1 907519 40 6 • US ISBN: 978 1 907519 41 3 • £7.99/$7.99

Gideon Coxall was a good soldier but bad at everything else, until a roadside explosive device leaves him with one deaf ear and a British Army half-pension. The Valhalla Project, recruiting useless soldiers like himself, no questions asked, seems like a dream, but the last thing Gid expects is to find himself fighting alongside ancient Viking gods. It seems *Ragnarök* – the fabled final conflict of the Sagas – is looming.

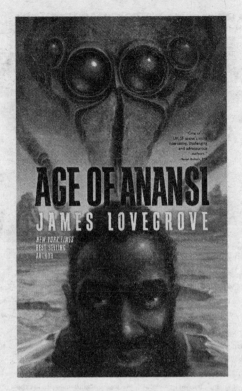

EPUB ISBN: 978 1 84997 341 0 • MOBI ISBN: 978 1 84997 342 7 • £2.99/$3.99

Dion Yeboah leads an orderly, disciplined life... until the day the spider appears. What looks like an ordinary arachnid turns out to be Anansi, the trickster god of African legend, and its arrival throws Dion's existence into chaos.

Lawyer Dion's already impressive legal brain is sharpened. He becomes nimbler-witted and more ruthless, able to manipulate and deceive like never before, both in and out of court.

Then he discovers the price he has to pay for his newfound skills. He must travel to America and take part in a contest between the avatars of all the trickster gods. It's a life-or-death battle of wits, and at the end, only one person will be left standing.

AN ALL-NEW EBOOK NOVELLA

'difficult to put down... a thoroughly entertaining novel that I would recommend to those looking for a summer blockbuster'
Sacramento Book Review
on *Age of Odin*

New York Times Best Selling Author
JAMES LOVEGROVE

UK ISBN: 978 1 907992 04 9 • US ISBN: 978 1 907992 05 6 • £7.99/$7.99

POLICING THE DAMNED

They live among us, abhorred, marginalised, despised. They are vampires, known politely as the Sunless. The job of policing their community falls to the men and women of SHADE: the Sunless Housing and Disclosure Executive. Captain John Redlaw is London's most feared and respected SHADE officer, a living legend.

But when the vampires start rioting in their ghettos, and angry humans respond with violence of their own, even Redlaw may not be able to keep the peace. Especially when political forces are aligning to introduce a radical answer to the Sunless problem, one that will resolve the situation once and for all...

 WWW.SOLARISBOOKS.COM

Follow us on Twitter! www.twitter.com/solarisbooks

Cover TBC

UK ISBN: 978 1 78108 049 8 • US ISBN: 978 1 78108 050 4 • £7.99/$8.99

BLOOD ON THE EASTERN SEABOARD

The east coast of the USA is experiencing the worst winter weather in living memory, and John Redlaw is in the cold white thick of it. He's come to America to investigate a series of vicious attacks on vampire immigrants – targeted kills that can't simply be the work of amateur vigilantes. Dogging his footsteps is Tina "Tick" Checkley, a wannabe TV journalist with an eye on the big time.

The conspiracy Redlaw uncovers could give Tina the career break she's been looking for. It could also spell death for Redlaw.

OCTOBER 2012

 WWW.SOLARISBOOKS.COM

Follow us on Twitter! www.twitter.com/solarisbooks